Reunion

Karen
KINGSBURY
with Gary Smalley

TYNDALE HOUSE PUBLISHERS, INC. ~ CAROL STREAM, ILLINOIS

Visit Tyndale's exciting Web site at www.tyndale.com

Visit Karen Kingsbury's Web site and learn more about her Life-Changing Fiction at
www.KarenKingsbury.com

TYNDALE and Tyndale's quill logo are registered trademarks of Tyndale House Publishers, Inc.

Baxter Family Drama is a trademark of Tyndale House Publishers, Inc.

Reunion

Published in association with the literary agency of Alive Communications, Inc.,
7680 Goddard Street, Suite 200, Colorado Springs, CO 80920, www.alivecommunications.com.

Library of Congress Cataloging-in-Publication Data

Kingsbury, Karen.
Reunion / Karen Kingsbury with Gary Smalley.
  p. cm.
  ISBN 978-0-8423-8688-3 (sc)
  1. Adoption—Fiction. I. Smalley, Gary. II. Title.
PS3561.I4873R485 2004
813'.54—dc22   2004006001

New repackage first published in 2009 under ISBN 978-1-4143-3304-5.

Printed in the United States of America

15 14 13 12 11 10
7   6   5   4   3

To our families, who—

together with us and all who believe—

will one day be part of the greatest reunion ever.

And to God Almighty,

who has, for now,

blessed us with these.

ACKNOWLEDGMENTS

In addition to our families and our wonderful support teams, we'd like to thank our friends at Tyndale House Publishers for sharing our dream and vision and helping make the Redemption series a reality. A special thanks to Ron Beers, Becky Nesbitt, Anne Goldsmith, Andrea Martin, Jill Swanson, Travis Thrasher, and Linda Gooch for their determination to make this series everything it could possibly be.

Also, thanks to our agent, Rick Christian, at Alive Communications. You were handed the reins of this project halfway into it and have seen it through to completion. Thank you for advocating excellence in every area involved with finishing this series.

A special thanks to Beka Hardt and Bethany Larson, director and coordinator of Christian Youth Theater in Vancouver, Washington, for inspiring a story line in *Reunion* that will lead to my next set of books—the Firstborn series. And thanks to Pastor Matt Hannan for inspiring me—through his sermons—to continue to let God's truth shine through the stories I bring you.

Finally thanks to Almighty God for giving us a series of books that illustrate the truth that no matter what happens—there is redemption in Jesus Christ.

CHAPTER ONE

ELIZABETH BAXTER found the lump on March 7.

She was in the shower, and at first she brushed past it, figured it to be nothing more than a bit of fatty tissue or a knotted muscle or maybe even a figment of her imagination. But then she went over it with her fingertips again and again. And once more, until she knew.

No question—it was a lump.

And a lump of any kind meant getting an immediate check. This was a road she'd traveled before. If a breast-cancer survivor knew one thing it was the importance of self-checks. She stopped the water, dried off, and called her doctor while still wrapped in a towel.

The mammogram came three days later, and a biopsy was performed the day after that. Now, on a brilliantly sunny morning in mid-March, in the private office of Dr. Marc Steinman, Elizabeth sat stiff and straight next to John as they waited for the doctor to bring the results.

"It's bad; I know it is." Elizabeth leaned a few inches to the side and whispered, "He wouldn't have called us in if it wasn't bad."

John did a soft sigh and met her eyes. "You don't know that. It's probably nothing." But his tone lacked the usual confidence, and something wild and fearful flashed in his eyes. He tightened his grip on her hand. "It's nothing."

Elizabeth stared straight ahead. The wall held an oversized, framed and matted print of a pair of mallard ducks cutting a path across a glassy lake. *No, God, please . . . not more cancer. Please.* She closed her eyes and the ducks disappeared.

A parade of recent memories marched across her heart. Ashley and Luke sitting side by side at Luke and Reagan's wedding reception, reconnected after so many years apart; Kari and Ryan exchanging vows at a wedding in the Baxter backyard; little Jessie taking her first steps; Maddie and Hayley holding hands for the first time after Hayley's drowning accident.

They need me, God . . . they still need me. I still need them. Please, God . . . no more cancer.

Footsteps sounded in the hall outside, and Elizabeth's eyes flew open. "Help me, John." Her voice was pinched, panicked.

"It's okay." John leaned closer, letting her rest on him. "It'll be okay."

The doctor entered the room, a file clutched beneath his arm. He stopped, nodded, and sat at the desk opposite them. "Thanks for coming." He opened the folder and pulled out the top sheet of paper. His eyes met first John's, then Elizabeth's. "I have the results of your biopsy."

A pause followed, and John cleared his throat. "She's fine, right?" John's tone sounded forced, unnatural.

The doctor opened his mouth, but Elizabeth already knew. She knew the news would be bad, and in that instant she couldn't think about surgery or radiation or how sick she was bound to get. Neither could she think the unthinkable—about regrets or do-overs or things she wished she hadn't done. Instead only one question consumed her soul.

How in the world would her family live without her?

The idea of meeting with the birth mother gave Erin Hogan a bad feeling from the beginning.

Their adoption attorney had warned them against it, but with four weeks until their baby daughter's birth, Erin couldn't tell the woman no. Sam agreed. Whatever the outcome, they would meet the birth mother, hear what she had to say, and pray that nothing—absolutely nothing—would damage the dream of bringing home their daughter.

The meeting was set to take place in thirty minutes at a small park not far from Erin and Sam's Austin home, where they would spend an hour with the birth mother, Candy Santana, and her two children.

On the way out the door that day Erin's stomach hurt. "Sam?" She paused near the nursery door and gazed in.

"I know." He stopped at her side and ran his fingers over her arms. "You're worried."

"Yes." The nursery was entirely pink and white: pink walls and a white crib with pink bedding, and dresser topped with pink teddy bears. It smelled faintly of fresh paint and baby powder. Erin folded her arms and pressed her fist into her middle. "Everything's been going so well." Her eyes found Sam's. "Why now?"

"I don't know." He kissed the top of her head and studied the nursery. "Maybe she wants to see how excited we are."

The possibility seemed like a stretch. Despite the warm March Texas morning, Erin shivered and turned toward the front door. "Let's get it over with."

The short ride to the park was silent, mostly because Erin was afraid to talk, afraid to speculate about what might happen or why in the world the birth mother would want to meet them now. Without the social worker or attorney or anyone official. They parked the car and headed toward a picnic table.

Ten minutes later a young woman and two small girls headed

toward them. Next to her was a thin man with long hair and mean, dark eyes.

"Who's he?" Erin whispered. They were sitting on top of the table, their feet on the bench as they waited.

Sam frowned. "Trouble."

The approaching couple held hands. As they drew closer Erin felt the knot in her stomach grow. Candy was very pregnant, dressed in worn-out, dirty clothes and broken flip-flops. The man's arms were splattered with tattoos. On one was a rooster with a full plume of feathers and the word *cock* in cursive beneath it. The other arm had the full naked figure of a woman framed on top by the name *Bonnie*.

Erin swallowed to keep from shuddering. She lowered her gaze to the girls, who were running a few feet in front of the adults. Candy's youngest daughter was maybe two years old and wore only a droopy diaper. The other girl, not much older, had a runny nose. Both children had blonde matted hair, lifeless eyes, and vacant expressions. The look of neglect and emotional disconnect.

The same way Candy's unborn child would look one day if something happened to the adoption process, or if Candy changed her—

No, God . . . don't let me think like that. The couple was a few feet away now, and Erin could feel the color draining from her face. *Please . . . get us through this meeting.*

"Hi." Candy gave them a look that fell short of a smile. The right side of her upper lip twitched, and she rubbed her thumb against it. "This is Dave. The baby's dad."

The baby's dad? A thin wire of terror wrapped itself around Erin's neck. "Uh . . ." She forced herself to smile. "Hello. I'm Erin."

Next to her, Sam held out his hand to the tattooed man. "Hi."

Dave shook Sam's hand, but refused to look either Sam or Erin in the eyes. Instead he shifted his gaze from Candy to the girls, to the ground, and back to Candy again. He grunted something that might've been a greeting. Erin wasn't sure.

For a moment no one said anything. Then Candy cleared her throat and glanced at her daughters. The youngest had picked a dandelion and was chewing on the stem. "Hey!" Candy pointed at the girl and let loose a string of expletives. "I told you a hundred times don't be stupid, Clarisse, and I mean it. You ain't a goat; take the flower outta your mouth."

The girl lifted her eyes in Candy's direction. "No!" She put the flower stem between her lips.

Candy mumbled something as she stomped over to the child and grabbed her arm. "Let it go!"

Fear filled the girl's eyes. She dropped the flower and tried to back away from Candy. The woman released Clarisse's arm and snarled at her. As she returned to the table she seemed to realize what she'd done, the way she'd behaved toward her daughter. A nervous look flashed in her eyes, and the lip twitched again. Candy managed a frustrated smile. "Crazy kids."

Erin didn't know what to say. She looked at her hands, at her wedding ring. *God . . . what's this about?* She lifted her eyes and looked from Candy to Dave.

The tattooed man cleared his throat and gave Candy a pointed look.

Candy nodded and turned to Erin. "We, uh . . . we have something to talk to ya about."

The knot in Erin's stomach doubled. She felt Sam take her hand and give it a firm squeeze. "Okay." Erin massaged her throat for a few seconds. "We're . . . we're very excited about the adoption. Nothing's changed."

"Has something changed for you, Candy?" Sam's voice was even, but his words made Erin's heart miss a beat.

Candy and Dave exchanged a look, and the twitching in Candy's lip grew worse. "No, it's just . . ." She looked at the ground for a moment. "We kinda ran into some money troubles, you know? Tough to get a job when you're, you know, pregnant and everything."

The instant Erin heard the word *money*, she relaxed. Was that all this was about? Candy was short on rent and needed a few hundred dollars? Their attorney had warned them against giving Candy additional money. Her financial needs during the pregnancy had already been taken care of, and Candy had signed a paper agreeing not to ask for anything extra.

But if she needed more money, then so be it. A few hundred dollars and they could all move on like before. Erin's heart rate slowed some. Her baby's face came to mind, the smooth skin and fine features, the way she'd always pictured her. Amy Elizabeth, their first child. Everything would be okay after all. Everything.

Sam was nodding, looking at Candy. "That happens." A fine line of moisture gathered along his upper lip. "Money gets tight for everyone."

Dave shifted his weight to the opposite foot. He gripped the tattoo on his left arm. "What she's saying—" he cocked his head—"is we need more money."

There it was. Erin swallowed. In case they'd had any doubts, now the request—a request all of them knew was against the rules—was out in the open. She caught Sam's look and gave him a silent go-ahead.

He stared at Candy. "Have you talked to the lawyer? I believe we agreed on what you needed."

"It wasn't enough." Candy glared at Sam. "You try raising kids and being pregnant on that kind of money."

Raising kids? Erin gritted her teeth. Candy wasn't raising the girls; their pastor had confirmed that on several occasions. Candy's mother was taking care of them. The fact that they were here now was purely show.

"Here's the deal." Dave pressed the toe of his worn boot into the ground and dug his hands in his pockets. He grinned, and Erin could see a gold stud in the center of his tongue. "We need more."

For a while no one said anything. The girls were quiet, still playing a distance away. Finally Erin found her voice and directed her attention to Candy. "How much?"

Above them, a warm wind played in the trees that lined the park. Candy pursed her lips. "Five thousand."

Erin had to grip Sam's arm to keep from falling off the bench. *Five thousand?* The adoption had already cost them their entire savings; they could never come up with that much money before the baby was born.

Candy was saying something, trying to explain, but Erin couldn't concentrate, couldn't hear anything but the number.

Five thousand dollars?

The figure tore at the picture of the unborn baby, the picture Erin had created in her mind of a little girl cradled in her arms. She gasped for breath and turned toward her husband. "Sam . . ."

He covered her hand with his, his teeth clenched. The figure was still finding its way to the recesses of Erin's mind when Dave delivered the final blow.

"Five thousand in twenty-four hours." He flashed a smile that fell far short of his eyes. "Or the deal's off."

※

The blood test had been the doctor's idea.

Not because he doubted whether she was HIV-positive. In fact, since he'd taken over Ashley's case, the doctor had called the original lab and discovered that they had done two tests with the original blood sample. Both were positive. Rather, he wanted a complete panel on her, a breakdown of her enzymes and mineral levels and every other test that might determine how healthy she was, how compromised her immune system. And most of all, what method of treatment to take.

Ashley expected the results to come by phone, the way they had the last time, but this warm Friday morning stuck in the middle of a stack of mail was a thick envelope from the lab. Ashley studied it as she made her way back into the house.

Cole was inside, writing his alphabet on a piece of paper. He grinned at her from the dining-room table as she walked in. "Hi,

Mom." His feet didn't quite reach the floor, and he swung them under his seat. "I'm on T already."

"Really?" Ashley's eyes were back on the envelope. "That's great, buddy. Tell me when you're done so I can check it."

She went into the kitchen and set the rest of the mail on a desk by the telephone. She stared at the thick envelope, slipped her thumb beneath the flap, and pulled out the stapled document.

Next to her name, the top sheet read "Lab Results."

Ashley had no reason to feel nervous or strange about the results. She already knew she was HIV-positive; it was only a matter of how her blood was holding up under the compromise of HIV, and whether any sort of progression toward full-blown AIDS could be seen.

Her eyes darted over the page, anxious for the summary lines, the places where any untrained person could make sense of the numbers and calculations. Then, at the bottom of the first sheet she saw it. A simple few lines with only a few words that made Ashley's heart skitter into a strange and unrecognizable beat.

She sucked in a quick breath and blinked hard.

It was impossible; she couldn't believe it, wouldn't believe it. Someone had to have made a mistake.

Her head began to spin, and she gripped the counter to keep from falling to the floor. She had to find Landon, had to tell him.

"Mommy . . . I'm all done!" Cole's singsong voice called out to her from the adjacent room. "Come check."

"Okay." Ashley's face was hot and tingling, the way she felt when she got too close to a campfire. "Just a minute." She pressed her hands against her cheeks and jerked back. Her fingers were freezing. She found the results line again. They couldn't be right, could they?

A chill made its way from the back of her head, down her spine, and into her feet. *God, is it true? Is it really true?* Then one last time she studied the lab results and began to imagine that maybe—just maybe—they were right. It wasn't possible, but still . . . what if? What if she'd come this far, given up so much, only to find out this? She wasn't sure whether to scream or shout or break down on the floor and cry.

But she was sure of one thing.

If the results were accurate, from this moment on, her life would never be the same again.

CHAPTER TWO

DR. STEINMAN WAS STILL TALKING, still explaining her results, but Elizabeth hadn't heard a single word. She could only think of what this meeting would mean to her family.

The doctor stopped talking and looked at her, waiting. "Do you understand what I'm telling you, Elizabeth?"

She glanced at John, still sitting beside her. He had a tight grip on her hand, but his face was cast down, his eyes closed. She wanted to shake him, make him look up and smile and tell her everything was going to be okay. The way he'd been telling her that before the doctor told them the results.

But the doctor was waiting. She turned to him and gave a slight shake of her head. "I . . . I guess I don't understand."

A tired breath came from Dr. Steinman. He was a friend of John's. This couldn't be easy for him, either. "What I'm saying is yes, Elizabeth, the cancer is back. The mammogram showed a shadow on your other breast, and the biopsy tells me that whatever we're dealing with, it's stronger, more aggressive than before." The doctor bit his lower lip and looked from Elizabeth to John. "I'm sorry; there's no other way to say it. I'm recommending a double mastectomy. I'd like to do it Monday."

This time every word hit its mark. Elizabeth couldn't remember how to exhale, couldn't react or speak or do anything but sit there, frozen. Double mastectomy? Monday? It was impossible, utterly ridiculous. She'd been cancer-free for more than ten years, well past the five-year mark that deemed a person winner of the battle.

The doctor was waiting for her response, but she couldn't talk, couldn't move or even blink her eyes. If she said anything at all, then the doctor's diagnosis would be real. She would be sitting across from him in his office, John at her side, receiving the worst news of her life. And so she said nothing, only leaned hard into John's arm.

That's when she saw his eyes. For the first time in those awful minutes, Elizabeth caught a look at her husband's face and saw how grim the situation truly was. John's eyes were filled with fear. On occasion, she had seen John cry, seen him weep when Luke returned to the family or tear up when he walked Kari down the aisle. But this was the first time she'd ever seen raw, terrifying fear in her husband's eyes.

Dr. Steinman put Elizabeth's file back together and looked at both of them. "If Monday won't work for you, I'd like to do the surgery as soon as possible." He stood up, hesitated, and moved toward the door. "I'll leave you alone so you can talk about it." Another awkward pause. "I'm sorry, Elizabeth, John . . . I'm sorry."

When he was gone, John stood and helped Elizabeth to her feet. She gathered her purse and like wound-up robots, they left the office hand in hand, silent. John drove and all the way home they said nothing, the shock of the news still detonating in Elizabeth's heart and soul and mind, the way she was sure it was detonating in John's.

It was a school day, and Cole—in his last year before kindergarten—was at home with Ashley because of her appointment. Just a checkup, they'd told the kids when she went in for her mammogram. They didn't say a word about the biopsy or the reason for today's appointment. The last thing Elizabeth wanted was a rash of phone calls the moment they heard the news.

Better to let them believe—for a little while longer—that their worlds were finally running smoothly, that the woman they loved and counted on wasn't about to undergo the battle of her life. She opened the car door, got out, and began to walk. Only when she heard John's voice did she turn around.

"Elizabeth . . . wait." He climbed out and leaned against the car. "We need to talk."

"Fine." She closed her eyes and breathed in, long and slow. The air smelled sweet, of early spring and damp earth giving way to life. Her knees trembled, and the ground beneath her felt suddenly liquid. The façade could only hold up for so long. She blinked her eyes open.

"Where are you going?"

Only one place would do for this conversation. "Follow me." Each word was an effort, an exercise in control. "Please, John."

She waited until he was at her side, until his hand was in hers. As they set out, he had a sense of purpose, a way of taking the lead, and something about that touched Elizabeth's heart. Because he knew where she wanted to go. He was reading her mind, even now. Especially now. When she was reeling from the worst news of her life.

They walked across the gentle slope of their backyard to the footbridge that crossed the stream behind the house. There, not far from the bridge and framed by a hedge of brush and budding trees, was a bench still covered in leaves from the previous fall.

"Here?" He looked at her, his expression blank, frozen.

Words wouldn't come so she simply nodded.

Years had passed since they'd come here. Long ago—when the kids were still in school—the bench was their private place, the spot where they talked about Kari's schoolgirl crush on Ryan Taylor, where they prayed that Brooke would develop social skills to go with her bright mind and determination. It was the spot where they shared talks about Ashley and her teenage rebellion, where they came when Elizabeth wondered if Erin's meal skipping indicated the early stages of an eating disorder. Finally, it was the place where they prayed for Luke, that he'd find the compassion he sometimes seemed to lack.

The bench had heard it all.

Elizabeth and John would slip out for an evening walk, taking in the boundaries of their property, talking about their day, and always they would wind up at the old bench. From the bench Elizabeth could see the back of the house, and her children busy inside it. The bench was quiet, removed from the chaos and constant disarray that their house had been back then. Their conversations could take place uninterrupted, graced only by the background music of flowing creek waters, rustling leaves, and the cry of an occasional lone hawk.

Several years back—when the kids moved away and privacy was no longer an issue—their evening talks moved to their bedroom and the overstuffed chairs in front of their small fireplace. But that place would never do now. Not when her entire house would be screaming with memories, each room and corner shouting about all she had to lose.

No, the bench was as close as she wanted to be.

John turned to her and said nothing, just studied her, his face masked in shock. Then, without another word, he drew her close. "Elizabeth . . ."

She slipped her arms around his waist and they came together, their bodies finding that familiar fit Elizabeth loved. The fit that would change when the surgeon was finished with her. A million thoughts welled up, demanding expression. But when she opened her mouth, the sound that came out was a gut-wrenching, broken cry, desperate and mournful and so powerful it made her weak at the knees.

"John . . ." His name was more wail than word. She held her breath, grasping for even a modicum of strength. "Why?"

He held her up, the way he had always held her up whenever

life was hard. They stayed that way a long time, Elizabeth allowing just the surface of her sorrow to spill onto John's shoulder. As she wept she could feel him shaking, feel his shoulders trembling against hers, because this—this was bigger than anything they'd faced yet.

But even now it wasn't bigger than the God they'd spent a lifetime serving.

She steadied her knees and placed her hands on his chest. Prayer. They needed to pray before she could even begin to consider the future. She searched his tearstained eyes. The sun beat down on them, but it did nothing to ward off the chill in her bones. "Pray, John . . ." She sniffed twice and stared at the brilliant blue sky overhead. When her eyes found his again, she looked to the depths of his soul. "Pray before we lose another minute. Please."

He hesitated, but only for a heartbeat. "God . . ." He closed his eyes and his voice broke. He worked his hands around her waist, chin trembling. "God, you know why we're here."

Elizabeth kept her eyes open, watching him, hating how their lives had been turned upside down by a single diagnosis. They weren't really doing this, were they? How could the cancer be back?

John stood straighter, clinging to his composure. "You are not limited by medical reports or statistics or cancer. We trust you, God. Please—" a shaky breath slipped through his lips—"please give Elizabeth a miracle." His voice was strained as he finished. "In Jesus' name . . . we beg you, God."

They stayed that way until both their tears were dry, holding on to each other so neither of them would fall. Then John brushed the bench clean, and they sat down.

Elizabeth had never felt this way in all her life. A strange mix of adrenaline and sorrow and anger and panic welled within her and coursed through her veins, so that part of her wanted to weep, and another part of her wanted to run for her life.

John wove his fingers between hers. "Will you do it?" He turned to her. "The surgery?"

Her throat grew thick as she watched him, the only man she'd ever loved. She kept her eyes locked on his. "Of course I'll do it. I'll do it Monday, like he asked. I'd let them cut my arms off if it meant more time with you and the kids."

"How—" he sighed in a way that made him sound far older than his nearly sixty years—"how do you feel?"

"About the surgery?" Her body was still cold, still shivering. She snuggled closer to John. "Or the cancer?"

"All of it."

"Scared." Elizabeth leaned her head on his shoulder. "Mad. Desperate. Determined." A sad sound came from her throat. "It changes every few seconds."

"The surgery is better than it used to be, more accurate." John turned toward her. "But still . . ."

"Still I lose my breasts."

"Yes." Defeat and frustration and helplessness jumbled his expression.

"I guess I'm not thinking about that yet." Elizabeth lifted her head and studied the old house a hundred yards away. "I'm thinking what if it doesn't work?" She looked at him. "What if it's already spread?"

"It hasn't." John gritted his teeth and she watched the muscles in his jaw flex twice. "You can't think that way."

"It's possible, John. You know it." She looked at the house again. "I was thinking on the way home, you know how we talk at church about heaven and being ready to die? about how heaven will be better, and eternity is where life really begins?" She sat up straighter. "I can't remember how many times I've told myself I wasn't afraid to die." Her shoulders lifted in two small shrugs. "I know all the right verses. 'What is our life but a mist that appears for a little while then disappears'. . . or 'To live is Christ; to die is gain.' I've spoken them dozens of times and always felt at peace with the idea of death."

A breeze sifted through the trees above them. John ran his thumb over the top of her hand. "And now?"

"Now—" her eyes narrowed, seeing into the distant future— "now I only want to live long enough to see Ashley and Landon set a date for their wedding, to see Cole finally have a father, to know that Hayley's going to be okay, and to meet Erin and Sam's new little daughter. To be there for Kari when she and Ryan have their first baby and to help Ashley when she . . . if she comes down with AIDS."

Tears filled her eyes again, and once more she turned to John. "I don't want to be a mist that appears for a little while, John. I don't want to go to heaven, not yet. I want to see my kids and my grandkids grow up. Not being there scares me to death."

John squeezed her hand. "So fight it." His voice held determination for the first time since they'd gotten the news. He framed her face with his free hand. "Fight it with everything you have. And when you don't feel like fighting, lean on me and I'll fight for you."

"I will." She sniffed. "I'll fight it with every breath." She searched his face, his eyes. The love coming from him was so strong it felt as if that alone might heal her. "Know what I want?"

"What?" He lowered his hand to her knee.

"I want a reunion with all the kids." She looked up again, seeing beyond the blue sky. "We could go somewhere warm with a beach—Sanibel Island, Florida, maybe. We could go in July or August, when everyone could get away."

"Hmmm." John cocked his head. "Our thirty-fifth anniversary is August twenty-second. Maybe that week."

"Yes!" It was the first time she'd felt even a little excited all day. "If we tell them now, everyone would have time to make it work."

"Elizabeth . . ." John's tone changed. "This reunion . . . is it because you're sick? Because you can't be thinking like that, like you need a last time together. Not now."

Fear took another stab at her. "I've been thinking about this long before my tests. I want this, John. No matter what happens."

"Okay." His eyebrows relaxed some. "It has been a while since we've all been together."

Something happened in her soul at the sound of his words. *All together.* It had been a while since she'd thought of him, but now her heart demanded she take stock of her life. Even the parts she'd spent a lifetime trying to forget. "Of course—" she searched his eyes—"we'll never really be *all* together. Not all of us."

John's face went blank. He opened his mouth as if he might argue with her, because they'd all been together hundreds of times over the years. But then he stopped. Ever so slowly the real meaning of her statement struck him. A gradual dawning, an understanding, and then the pain hit. Hard and relentless, she watched it take its toll on his expression. He released her hand, stood slowly, and took a few steps toward the house.

Instantly Elizabeth regretted saying anything. They'd promised, after all, agreed all those years ago that they could never look back. But if time was running out, Elizabeth had to at least think about it. She couldn't change the past, but she could acknowledge it.

Minutes passed before he spoke. When he did, his shoulders were broad and stiff, his voice laced with a new kind of pain. "I knew it."

She stood and went to him, looping her arm around his neck and leaning against him once more. "Knew what?"

He looked at her. "You couldn't forget."

"This isn't the first time."

"I know, but we always promise." Control eased into his features and he pursed his lips.

"Sometimes we last a year or two years. It's been more than three this time." Elizabeth held on to him, her knees weak again. "But it never quite goes away."

"Well, now it has to." John's voice was firm, but kind. "We

have enough to think about." He took in a sharp breath through his nose and shook his head. "That door's been closed for thirty-five years."

"I know." Elizabeth kissed him on the cheek. "I'm sorry. I guess . . ." She looked at the creek, the way the waters never stopped running no matter the season. "I guess the diagnosis makes me want to take stock."

A long breath left him. "I understand." He brushed his lips against her forehead. "Let's focus on what's in front of us, okay? That's all we can do."

Elizabeth changed the subject, and they talked about the next few days. They'd have the kids over for dinner Sunday night and tell them the truth—that their mother's cancer was back and she would most likely have surgery that Monday.

"Brooke isn't going to take it well." Elizabeth felt the thickness in her throat again. "Not after what happened with Hayley."

"I think you'll be surprised." John took her hand again and led her toward the footbridge. "Brooke's stronger than before. She might handle it better than the others."

"Maybe." Elizabeth followed him over the bridge and across their backyard. "Let's not tell them about the reunion just yet."

Once they were inside, John led her into their bedroom, closed the door, and took her in his arms. "There's something I didn't say out there."

"What?" The way he held her made her breathless, the embrace of a man who still wanted her despite time and all it had stolen from them.

"The way I see you—" he looked beyond her heart to the center of her soul—"the way I desire you, Elizabeth, will not change, not ever. You will still be the only woman who has ever turned my head, the most beautiful woman I've ever seen."

Of all the things he might've said to her right then, nothing could've touched her spirit the way those words did. "John . . ." She placed her hands along the sides of his face. "I love you."

Desire shone in his eyes. Not the passionate sparks of youth, but a longing born of years of intimacy. He kissed her, and a slow tender urgency began to fill the moment. "I've loved you all my life, Elizabeth. Always."

Their kisses continued and his hands moved along her sides, touching her in a way he wouldn't be able to in only a few short days. Then, for the next hour—ignoring work or time or her cancer diagnosis—John showed her the kind of love she'd spent a lifetime knowing, a love that wouldn't change ever.

Not even when her body did.

John waited until Elizabeth was asleep before making his way downstairs to his chair, the one where he did most of his late-night thinking and praying.

That he'd gotten through the day was a miracle, a testimony to God's strength at the center of his life. Because he understood his wife's test results better than he'd let on, better than she understood them.

Dr. Steinman had no choice but to schedule the surgery. Elizabeth's biopsy showed her cancer at a stage that went beyond mere mastectomy. It was very advanced. Almost every time, women with a biopsy like Elizabeth's would have surgery only to find the cancer had spread to their lymph nodes.

So Elizabeth was right to be thinking about dying.

Not that he would ever tell her that. They could do the surgery and find more cancer and even give her a death sentence and never—not once—would he stop believing that God could turn the whole thing around. Not after Hayley's miracle.

He eased himself into the old chair and stared at the five framed photographs lining the fireplace mantel. The senior portraits for each of the kids.

His eyes closed and he thought about the battle ahead. *God . . . give us a miracle. I can't make it without her.*

A stirring brushed across his soul, and he remembered something Pastor Mark Atteberry had said the previous Sunday. He'd been doing a sermon series on Easter, and all it meant. There in the garden the night before he was crucified, Jesus wanted to pass on what lay ahead of him. But he prayed a simple prayer, one that echoed across John's heart now.

"Not my will, but yours be done."

John let the words play in his mind a few more times. They seemed right for Jesus, but for him? John Baxter? He was merely a man, and since this morning, not a very strong man, at that. He couldn't possibly pray the way Jesus had in the garden.

God, I'd be lying if I prayed for your will now. Instead I'm begging you, God, make her well. Take me if you want, but make her well. She . . . she means so much to all of us, God.

He opened his eyes and saw the pictures again, their five children. Why had Elizabeth brought it up today, after three years of forgetting? They hadn't ever really been *all* together? Was that how she saw it? She found the strangest times to remember, and whenever she did, it sent him reeling for the better part of a week.

What had they told each other back then? That they'd do what they had to do and never look back, right? Wasn't that it? Today was a time to talk about Elizabeth and the kids and whatever time they still had left together. A time to pray that cancer would be defeated in this battle, the way it had the first go-around. This wasn't any time to remember the hardest part of their lives, a part they were supposed to have buried long ago.

If only every few years she wouldn't bring it up.

John blinked and stared at the faces of his kids once more. Maybe he was being too hard on his wife. He was no better than she, really. How many times had he sat in this chair and stared at that mantel, at the spot to the left of Brooke's picture, and wondered what the boy would've looked like at seventeen? What he looked like now? How often in the moments before falling asleep had he let himself go back to everything he and Elizabeth had been through.

He liked to think he never looked back, that he could live with their decision to keep the past hidden. Hidden from their children and from each other, and most of the time even hidden from themselves.

They'd done what they had to do. Period.

No options, no second thoughts, no regrets.

But in reality, he was no better at forgetting the past than Elizabeth was.

In fact, he'd be lying if he didn't admit to thinking about it at least every now and then. Maybe more often than that.

Not because he'd known what she was talking about almost as soon as she'd mentioned the fact that they'd never really all been together. But because he'd known instantly how long it had been since that awful time in their lives.

He looked at the calendar on his wristwatch. Thirty-five years, seven months, two days.

Exactly.

CHAPTER THREE

BY FRIDAY NIGHT, Erin had figured out a way to get the money, and an hour later Sam was convinced, too.

They'd sell his little Ford Contour, and until they could afford a second car again, Sam would drop Erin off at school each morning on the way to his computer job. He'd skip lunch so he could leave an hour early and swing by to pick up Erin sometime around five o'clock.

By the time they had the For Sale signs made, Erin had talked herself into believing the arrangement was actually a good thing. They'd save on insurance and gas, and she'd have a reason to stay and correct papers until Sam picked her up each day.

"You really think this'll work?" Sam raised an eyebrow. "We oughta call the attorney and tell him what Candy and Dave are up to. They'd never get away with it."

"And we'd never get the baby." Erin took hold of Sam's arm, her tone full of quiet desperation. "Please, Sam. Just pray someone buys the car."

He looked at the sign. "Five thousand dollars for a car that's not even two years old?" A sad chuckle slipped from his mouth. "It's worth more than twice that. Someone better buy it."

The next morning Erin followed Sam to the busiest supermarket in Austin, especially on a Saturday. He parked the car at the front of the lot—in an area set apart by the market for individual car sellers. Erin noticed her hands were shaking as she stepped out of the van and headed toward Sam's car.

God . . . let this work, please. That baby is ours, not hers.

My grace is sufficient for you, daughter.

The response came so quick, so certain that Erin froze in place, right in the middle of the supermarket parking lot.

"Erin, look out!" Sam shouted at her from where he'd parked the Contour.

She jumped and ran lightly to Sam, her head spinning. "I . . . I'm sorry. I couldn't think for a minute."

"Okay." Sam put his hand on her shoulder and stared at her. "Listen." His expression told her he was more scared than angry, but his tone was sharp. "Don't panic on me, Erin. God's in control, remember? Wasn't that what you kept telling me when we started this idea?"

Erin's heart was racing, her forehead damp with sweat. What had happened back there? The words had come to her as certainly as if someone had shouted them at her from across the parking lot. But they didn't come at her through her ears, the way it usually worked. Rather they came straight into her heart, through her heart, maybe.

What was it she'd heard?

My grace is sufficient for you. Wasn't that it?

She clenched her fists and dug her fingernails into the palms of her hands. *Breathe out,* she told herself. *Breathe out and say something.* She looked at Sam and forced a weak smile. "You're right. I—" she shook her head—"I'm sorry. I guess I'm worried it won't sell."

"It'll sell."

"But what if it doesn't sell this weekend?" They had convinced the baby's birth parents to give them two days—the entire weekend—to come up with the money. But the tattooed man had

KINGSBURY / SMALLEY

been adamant about having the money by Sunday night. "You heard what he said."

"It'll sell, Erin."

"But if it doesn't, how can—"

Sam put his finger to her lips. His expression softened and he pulled her into his arms. They stayed that way while passersby and car shoppers milled around them, as other prospective car sellers moved their vehicles into the parking area and left.

Finally, Sam spoke. "It's hard on me, too." He pressed his cheek against her hair. "I keep asking God what's going on, what he's doing, letting that woman work us over like this. Why does having a baby have to be so hard?"

Erin's anxiety faded and she drew back, studying the man she loved. This was new for Sam, this allowing her to see a glimpse of his true feelings. No matter what he said or how stoic his composure, he was every bit as scared as she. He was looking at her, and she searched his eyes until she could feel a connection deeper than ever before. "Thank you."

"Thank you?"

"Yes." She motioned to their little car. "Thank you for coming here, for loving me enough to sell the car and tell me the truth about how you feel. It means a lot."

"Well . . ." His chin quivered but he coughed twice and shook his head, the way Erin had seen him steady himself a few other times in their marriage. "I want that little girl, Erin. I want her as badly as you do." He sucked in a hard breath and dug his hands into his pockets. "Let's pray God feels the same way."

They left the car and drove home together in her van. Two hours later they were having lunch when the phone rang. Sam took it and moved into the next room. After only a few minutes he hung up and found her again.

"So?" Erin tried to read his face, but she couldn't.

"It sold." His smile didn't quite reach his eyes. "The man has cash; he'll meet us at the car in an hour."

Erin raised her fists in the air, stared at the ceiling, and shouted out loud. "Yes!" She looked at Sam again. "Everything's going to be okay—I can feel it."

He nodded, but what remained of his smile faded.

"Sam?" Her excitement dissolved like sand in an ocean wave. "What's wrong?"

Air filled his cheeks and he pursed his lips, releasing his breath slowly the way he did when he was frustrated. "I'm not sure this is the right thing."

Her world tilted and she stared at him. "Which part? Selling the car?"

With slow steps he crossed the kitchen and sat down at the table. "All of it." He reached across and took her hands. His were ice-cold. "We just lost our car, Erin. So we give Candy and Dave the money and then what? The next day they ask for another five thousand and where does that leave us?" He lowered his brow. "Haven't you thought of that?"

Fear danced in circles around her, laughing, mocking her.

Of course she'd thought of it, but only for the briefest partial seconds. This was the possibility she hadn't allowed herself to consider: that somehow the scary-looking man Candy claimed was the baby's father might be playing games, taking them for a ride without ever intending to give the baby up.

She bit her lower lip. Her voice was pinched, racked with an unimaginable fear. "What choice do we have?"

"That's just it." He paused. "There is no choice."

His answer told her that regardless of where the journey took them, he was as committed as she to the outcome.

An hour later they sold the car, collected the money, and left the parking lot with a sense of doom. Erin used Sam's cell phone to call Candy. "We have the money."

The woman's voice was instantly cheerful. "Really? Five thousand dollars?"

"Yes. Like you asked."

"Okay—" Candy hesitated—"meet at the park again."

Erin's body ached. The conversation was making her feel tired. "When?"

"In an hour."

Erin and Sam parked their van not far from the grassy border of the park and waited. Even with the engine off, Sam held tight to the steering wheel and stared straight out the windshield. Beside him on the console was a manila envelope with five thousand dollars cash inside.

He tapped his fingers on his knee and looked at Erin. "Why doesn't this feel right?"

A sigh slipped from Erin's lips, and she folded her hands on her lap. "I know." She looked out the window and shook her head. "Sitting here like criminals waiting to make some under-the-table deal."

"I keep asking myself why I feel guilty, like maybe we're supposed to call the social worker or the attorney."

A beat-up car pulled into the parking lot, different from what Candy had driven the last time. As it came closer, Erin squinted. Candy was in the backseat. Dave—the man who claimed to be the baby's father—was in the passenger seat, and behind the wheel was an older, bearded man with dark drifter eyes.

Erin leaned toward Sam. "Great."

"Right." Sam rolled down the van window, his eyes on the people in the car, his voice barely a whisper. "Now I feel much better."

Dave climbed out, gave a shady glance over one shoulder then the other, and looped around the front of the car to Sam's window. "Candy says you got the cash."

"I have it." Contempt filled his voice. Sam's expression was frozen, his lips a thin angry line.

Erin watched her husband take the envelope, hesitate a second or two, and then hand it to Dave through the window. Sam was an even-tempered man, but one time when Erin had seen him really angry, he'd put his fist through a wall. Now he looked about ready to do the same thing to Dave's mouth. She held her breath. *God . . . help Sam. Don't let him say anything that'll make this worse.*

At first Dave looked like he might turn around and leave as soon as the envelope was in his hands. Instead he opened it, pulled out the bundle of hundred-dollar bills, tucked the envelope under his arm, and began counting. The man was shaking so badly, the envelope made a loud rustling sound.

Drugs, Erin thought. *He'll use every dime for drugs.* She looked past Dave at the car and saw the driver pass what looked like a marijuana joint back to Candy. The two laughed about something and Candy passed it back to the driver.

An aching started in Erin's stomach. Everything felt crazy and out of control. Adoption wasn't supposed to be like this, was it? Hadn't they only been following their pastor's advice, adopting a child who wasn't wanted? So how had everything become sordid? *This is so dirty, God, so wrong. What're we supposed to do? Please . . . please show us.*

Dave must've been satisfied with his count because he stuffed the cash back into the envelope and said something that drove a knife through what was left of Erin's sanity.

"You still want the baby, right?"

"Listen." Sam clenched his teeth and made a sharp inhale through his nose. "Don't mess with us."

"Ooooh." Dave chuckled and looked over his shoulder at his friends, as if they might understand something funny had just happened. With his mouth open it was easier to see just how many teeth he was missing. He looked back at Sam, held out his hand, palm down, and gave it a series of dramatic shakes. "You scare me, man."

"I'm serious." Sam sat a little straighter. "We did what you asked. Now get Candy home and take care of her." He started the engine. "We'll see you at the hospital."

Dave cocked his head, the smile suddenly gone. "I asked you a question, man. You still want the baby or not?"

Erin couldn't make out her husband's expression, but she

could see by the tension in his posture how close he was to losing control. *Please, God . . .*

Sam turned slightly so he was facing the man. "If we didn't want the baby, we wouldn't be here."

"Okay." Dave's expression eased and he chuckled again. "Stay by the phone." He winked as he took a few steps backward. "I'll be calling."

And in that instant, Erin felt her hopes crash against the rocks of reality and splinter into a million pieces. The bribes were not over, and they were quite simply out of money.

When Dave was gone, Sam turned to her. The knowing in his face told her that he, too, was aware of the situation they were in. If Dave asked for more money, they would have just one choice.

Call the attorney and tell him the truth, even if they lost the baby daughter in the process.

❧

Most of the time, Candy could care less what people thought of her.

She had a roof over her head and a loaf of bread in the refrigerator. Couldn't ask for more than that. The kids stayed with her mother most of the time, and when it was her turn, so what if they didn't eat much? Big deal. A lot of kids had it worse.

Besides, she was never cut out to be a mother.

She was a druggie, a floozy, the sort of trash that never lived in one place more than a few months. But at least she wasn't uppity like the couple in the van. At least she knew her place in life, and this late in the game she wasn't looking to change, didn't waste time on what-ifs and might-haves or a batch of regrets the way some of her friends did. If people didn't like her then bully for them.

But as the car she was riding in sped out of the parking lot, she felt a nudge of remorse. Second thoughts, maybe, or a gasp of air from a conscience long dead. The plan was pretty nasty, could probably land them in jail if they weren't careful.

Actually it wasn't her plan; it was Dave's. And it was a good one. Kids were nothing but brats and hard work. She'd learned that after she popped the first one out. The plan didn't come about until she told Dave how much loot she'd raked in from the rich couple. All for having a kid and giving it away.

Dave's eyes had grown narrow, and a thin smile had worked its way into his cheeks. "I think we just hit the jackpot, Candy."

"The jackpot?" Candy wasn't doing hard drugs, not since she found out about the kid. Just some bourbon and weed here and there. She took a drag from a joint and frowned at him. "What jackpot?"

"They want the kid, right?" He'd sat forward, his face registering the kind of excited look he usually got when they scored a dime bag.

"'Course they want the kid." She'd exhaled a blue ribbon of smoke that curled toward the ceiling of their studio apartment. "They paid for it, didn't they?"

"Not yet, they didn't." He'd chuckled and folded his hands on the table. Then he told her about the plan. Candy would meet with the couple, tell them she was a little low on cash. "Hint around, you know. Like if you don't get the money you can't think about giving up the kid."

"Okay." Candy rubbed her arms and gave a few slow nods of her head. "I think I'm seeing it."

"Yeah, and then . . ." Dave had taken a drag from her joint and held the smoke several beats. He raised one eyebrow, slow and sarcastic-like. "If they cough up a few thousand, we wait a few days and tell 'em we need more."

Candy had worried about that. Not because of her conscience but because it sounded almost illegal. "You don't think the cops could get involved, do ya?"

"Nah, the cops got better things to do. Welfare's just glad we're getting rid of a kid this time."

Candy had liked the way he said *we,* because as far as she knew Dave was the baby's father. But she couldn't be sure. Lots of crazy nights back before she got pregnant. But this ownership thing was new to Candy. A man happy to lay claim to one of her kids. Unless . . .

She twisted her expression. "You ain't thinkin' of keeping half the money, are you?"

Dave had cast her a look that defined disgust. "Of course!" He rattled off a few choice words. "I'm working for it, right?" He waved his hands at himself. "This is me sitting here, right?"

Candy had thought about that and figured it was okay. The idea was his, after all, and if he helped collect the money the least she could do was split it with him. "Okay." She'd slapped her hand on the table. "I'm in."

The memory died there as Candy stared out the windshield from the backseat of the speeding car. "Hey, Scary, slow down, will ya? I'm knocked up, remember?"

"Ah, shut up." Scary was Larry Brown—Dave's buddy from the penitentiary. He turned to Dave and laughed out loud. Funny stuff, telling a woman to shut up.

"Listen, Scary, I'm havin' second thoughts."

Dave glared at her over his shoulder. "Second thoughts? Look, Candy, we're in this thing. You and me and Scary. No turning back now."

When the money moved from a few thousand to maybe ten thousand or more, they'd brought Scary Larry in. Scary was a forger from the old days—documents, birth certificates, driver's licenses. You name it; he could forge it. Scary had a plan that took the baby's price tag to a place Candy hadn't dreamed.

Get the couple to pay everything they could pay. Then turn at the last minute and sell the baby to someone else. Forge a paper that made it look like the couple had changed their minds about the baby. Move a few towns down the road, hook up with another lawyer, another rich couple, and make a flat-out killing when it was all said and done.

Twenty, maybe twenty-five thousand dollars total. Twice the money for a few easy meetings in the gravel lot of the local park. Scary only wanted five for his part, so that still left maybe ten thousand each for her and Dave.

Still . . .

Dave turned back toward the front and huffed. "Second thoughts! You're crazy, woman, you know that? This is the best thing we've come across in a long time."

Candy stared at her big belly and she could hear the lady. What was her name? Erin something? The lady had tears in her eyes when she talked about having a little girl, like having babies was some hard thing for her. That's what the social worker had said, that being rich didn't mean you could automatically have babies.

The lady in the van still deserved the kid, even if they could make a killing switching couples.

They were almost back to the apartment. Scary had the papers in the back of his car, the ones he'd forge so they could move to another town and find another couple. Dave and Scary acted like it was their baby, but it was hers. She could give it to whoever she wanted. The plan had sounded good at first, but now, well, what was the rush? She could always do the whole thing again. Have another baby, sell it, make five or ten thousand extra before the delivery.

By the time they got inside and sat down at the card table in the kitchen, Candy had her mind made up. As soon as the guys were sitting down she crossed her arms and gave a few shakes of her head. "I'm not doing it."

Dave and Scary were talking, but when they heard what she said, they stopped at the same time and stared at her. Candy wasn't afraid of Dave, even though he did have a temper. She'd been at the receiving end of it a time or two, but she always bounced back. Dave was just a little high-strung.

He shoved his chair back, jumped up, and came so close the

toes of his shoes were touching hers. "What're you mumbling over here?"

"I said . . ." She lifted her chin, looking him straight in the eyes. Dave hated when she did that; he liked it better when she showed a little "proper fear," as he called it. Candy didn't care. This was her baby. "I said, I'm not doing it."

"Not doing what?" Dave straightened himself up and puffed out his chest. His tone told her he was serious.

"Get as much money as you can from that couple in the van—that's fine." She glanced at Scary. His eyes were as cold as a kitchen knife. "But that couple gets the kid. I told 'em they could have her, and I wanna keep my wo—"

His hand hit her before she could finish.

The blow knocked her to the floor, dizzy and angry and more sure of herself than ever. He'd done this before, but never so hard. This time, the windup had come from nowhere.

"That's what you get for changing your mind." He snarled at her and gave her shin a quick kick for good measure.

"Oh, yeah . . ." If he wanted to be a jerk she could play, too. She struggled to her feet and steadied herself. Her face stung, and a dull headache worked its way up from the back of her neck. She heaved herself at him, shoving her hands into his shoulders.

The jolt moved him back a step or two, but he was at her again as soon as he had his balance. This time he cocked back, and before she had a chance to turn around, he hit her square in the face, just above her left eye. The blow knocked the wind from her and left her sprawled across the floor, furious.

"Dave, what're you doing?"

Candy heard Scary's voice, felt the floor move as Scary took heavy steps toward them, but she couldn't see anything. Her hands were over her eye, and the area above her eyebrow was warm and wet.

"It isn't up to her!" Dave yelled the words.

Candy shuddered. He was breathless, still raging from the

fight inside him, no doubt. Suddenly a new thought occurred to her. If Scary wasn't here, how far would Dave go? Would he hit her again, even lying there on the ground? And something else . . .

What about the baby?

She pulled herself to the corner of the room and caught a glimpse of her white sweatshirt. It was covered with blood. From the corner of her good eye she saw Dave and Scary fighting, wrestling to the floor. They were shouting at each other, throwing punches, but the room was swaying. Worse than when she smoked dope all afternoon.

"Help me . . ." Her voice didn't sound very loud, so she tried again. "Help!"

A sick feeling came over her. She grabbed at a breath, but it wouldn't come. Not all the way, and she suddenly remembered what to do. Press on the cut; that would stop the bleeding. She'd done that one other time when Dave got in a fight at the bar and some guy lay gushing blood all over the floor. Someone shouted something about pressure on the cut, and Candy had gotten on all fours to help the guy.

She shoved her fist against her eye, but the pain made the sick feeling worse. "I said . . ." Her head hung down until her chin touched her chest. "Help . . ."

Someone started moving toward her, and she lifted her face just enough to see it was Dave. His expression was frightening, madder than ever before. He was coming closer . . . closer . . . closer. . . .

And then there was nothing but darkness.

❧

There was only one place Erin wanted to be.

The moment they got home, she set her purse down in the kitchen and turned to Sam. "I think I'll go rest for a while." She angled her head and said nothing about the nursery. But she didn't need to. His eyes told her he knew exactly where she was going, and something else, too.

He was okay with it.

"Whatever happens, Erin, I love you." He crossed the kitchen, kissed her lightly on the lips, and picked up a stack of papers. "I'll be in the office."

The nursery was the first bedroom on the left. Erin slipped inside and shut the door. She scanned the room, the pink-and-white wallpaper, the crib overflowing with pink bedding and quilted pillows, the delicate lamp and pretty furniture. Her favorite was the oak rocker—a piece her mother had given her before they moved.

"I figured you'd give it to Kari or Brooke." Erin had been surprised, almost overwhelmed, at the idea that the family rocker might be hers.

Her mother had run her fingers lightly over the top edge of the chair. "I rocked every one of you kids in this chair." She lifted her eyes to Erin. "Kari and Brooke have recliners, and Ashley doesn't have room. Besides, I want you to have it, Erin. You'll need it one day; I believe that with all my heart."

The memory faded. They'd tried so long to have a baby. There were times she wondered whether her mother was right, whether she'd ever use the rocking chair for her own baby. But since learning about Candy, since making the decision to adopt and finding out that the baby was a girl, Erin had been sure that everything was going to work out. She'd have a baby after all, and the chair where each of the Baxter kids had been rocked would now be used to rock her own precious little one.

She crossed the room and eased herself into the old chair.

Always the nursery could bring Erin comfort. When she worried about the adoption process or whether Candy was taking care of herself, she had only to step into the nursery to feel God's peace and serenity surround her. Everything would be all right. The baby would be fine and Candy wouldn't change her mind.

In the nursery she was sure about it all.

But now the setting sun cast strange shadows across the carpet, and anxiety wouldn't leave the room. How could it, when the facts stood like a block wall between her and the baby she so desperately wanted? She blinked and tried to convince herself it was all a nightmare, that they hadn't really just sold their new car for half of what it was worth and handed every dime over to a man who clearly had a drug problem.

How did they know he was really the birth father, anyway? And what about his flip comment, something about contacting them next week?

Erin closed her eyes and set the rocker in motion. Her arms came together around her middle, and for the first time in a long time she actually felt it. An aching in her arms, an emptiness that only a baby could fill.

God . . . I've already connected with that child. She's mine even though I've never held her, never loved her. Tears stung her eyes and she sniffed. She wouldn't cry now, wouldn't believe it was all really falling apart. But still . . .

Another ache came over Erin. She closed her eyes and rocked a little more, back and forth, back and forth. And she realized what it was. She missed her mom. Every time they'd talked recently Erin hadn't been honest, hadn't told her exactly how strange things had gotten.

If only her mom were here, she'd say something positive, help find a light in what was becoming a dark, dismal tunnel. At the very least her mom would hold her. Erin sniffed again. That way she could break down the way she wanted to. Her mom understood how important this baby was, how special all babies were, however they came into the world.

Funny, too. Early in the process Erin had wondered whether she and her mother would connect over the adoption experience. Her social worker had suggested a mentor, a woman who had adopted children before, someone she could bond with through the process.

But no mentor had materialized.

Her mother knew nothing about giving up a child, nothing about what Candy was going through, or the frightening thoughts Erin battled when she worried Candy might change her mind.

But her mother understood love.

And a child was about love, whether she grew beneath a mother's heart or in it. Over the months Erin and her mom had shared dozens of conversations about the baby Candy was carrying, and always Erin was grateful for her mother, wishing their houses were blocks apart the way they'd been back in Bloomington.

Erin opened her eyes and stared at the empty crib.

She and her mother had sometimes dreamed for hours on the phone about names and ballet lessons and the joy of raising a little girl. Other times Elizabeth had convinced Erin not to fear the future—even if Candy seemed unstable. Over the months, her mom had become a best friend, the ultimate sounding board and encourager. Because she was the perfect mentor.

Even if she knew nothing about adoption at all.

CHAPTER FOUR

ASHLEY'S HANDS WERE shaking and she was only halfway to the doctor's office.

She'd called him as soon as she opened the test results envelope Friday morning, but he was booked for the day. He had Saturday calls at the hospital so he'd suggested the afternoon meeting time. Ashley would've met him on the moon if she had to. Whatever it took to have him explain the results face-to-face. So she understood them completely. Otherwise she couldn't possibly take the news to her family, not after all they'd been through.

She turned left on Main Street and focused on the road ahead of her. "God . . . go with me when I get there. Please . . ." She said the words out loud, the way she often prayed. It helped her remember that no matter how alone she felt, the Lord was with her, sitting beside her.

So much was riding on this day, on the meeting she was about to have with the doctor. Her mouth was dry, and she ran her tongue along her lower lip. Without taking her eyes off the road, she found a piece of gum in the front pocket of her purse, slipped off the wrapper, and popped it between her lips.

She hadn't been this nervous since the day a month ago when she and Landon gathered her family together and announced their engagement. The moment came alive again, and Ashley smiled. They had called her parents from the cemetery, where Landon had met her just after her friend Irvel's graveside service.

"Mom, it's me." Ashley sat beside Landon on a bench in the park adjacent to the cemetery. "Is Cole taking a nap?"

"He's awake." She hesitated, her voice lower than before. "We've been talking about death. He still has questions about Irvel's dying."

"Okay, well . . . hey, guess what?" She didn't wait for an answer. "Landon met me here."

"Landon came?" Her mother's tone brightened. "How wonderful, honey. Why don't you bring him over?"

"Actually—" she looked at Landon and grinned—"Landon and I have something to tell you. Something important. An announcement, I guess." She giggled. "We're going to drop my car off at my house and be right over, okay?"

By the time they had arrived at the Baxter house, her parents and Cole were gathered around the table with Kari, Ryan, Brooke, Peter, and the kids. It wasn't mealtime, so the moment Ashley and Landon walked into the house and across the dining room, all faces turned their way. Ashley found her mother and saw a knowing bit of emotion in her eyes.

"Wow." Ashley stopped, her eyes wide. "You're all here." Her throat grew too thick to speak, and she gave a few quick shakes of her head, her eyes downcast. She didn't want to cry, but her heart couldn't take more emotion than she'd already felt that day. Irvel dying, then this. In all her life she had never thought she'd have this moment, the chance to stand before her family and tell them the greatest news of her life. At first because of her own determination to avoid Landon, and later because of her affliction with HIV. But now . . .

Landon had taken her hand. He looked from Ashley's dad to her mom and at the other faces at the table. "Cole . . ."

Her son—not quite six years old—gave Landon a little wave. "Grandma says you have a 'nouncement."

"That's right." He held out his arms. "Come here, Cole. I want to tell you something."

Cole slid his chair back and ran to Landon, jumping into his arms and letting Landon lift him up high the way he'd done when Cole was little. "So what's your 'nouncement?"

"We, uh . . ." He'd smiled at Ashley, a smile that told her even though they were venturing into uncharted waters, he would never change his mind, never wish he'd walked away to find someone who wasn't sick. He turned back to Cole, aware that the rest of the family seated at the table was watching. "Cole, I've asked your mommy to marry me, and she's said yes."

A gasp came from Cole. "Really?" The only thing wider than his eyes was his smile.

"Really." Ashley leaned in and kissed him on the cheek. Cole had loved Landon almost as long as she had.

No one stayed seated at the table.

They let out soft gasps and quiet exclamations as they left the table and surrounded Ashley and Landon and Cole.

Cole looped his arms around Landon's neck. "Does that mean you'll live with us and be my daddy?"

Landon pulled Ashley tighter, and she saw his chin quiver. "Yes, Cole. I'll be your daddy forever."

Ashley's heart had overflowed with emotions she'd never felt before. How long had Landon wanted this moment, to claim Cole as his own? She bit her lip, a stab of guilt having its way with her for the flash of a second. If she hadn't been so stubborn they would've shared this moment a long time ago.

Her mother had made it through the circle, and Ashley saw she had tears in her eyes. For a while they only looked at each other, sharing a hundred unspoken memories: Ashley's rebellious teenage years, her shame after returning home from Paris, her efforts at keeping Landon away, her sorrow when he left for New York City, her heartache over losing Irvel. All of it played

out in her mother's eyes. Then their foreheads came together
and they hugged. When her mother spoke, Ashley alone could
hear her words. "It's about time."

Ashley turned into the hospital parking lot, still lost in her
memories. Their announcement that day felt different, more
emotional than when Kari had announced her engagement to
Ryan or when any other bit of good news had been shared with
all the Baxters. This time the news was bittersweet. Ashley and
Landon would finally be together, the way they always should've
been together.

But everything about their tomorrows was uncertain. Yes, Cole
would have a father, and for now the two of them would have
Ashley. But somewhere down the road heartache was bound to
have the last word. Because of that, the emotions that day in the
Baxter dining room were a mix of incomparable joy and borrowed sadness.

When the group had drifted back to the table, Landon stayed
close to Ashley. He explained that he'd quit his job with the
New York Fire Department, and that he'd be starting back at the
Bloomington station the following week.

"Do we have a wedding date?" Ashley's father raised his eyebrows, his tone hopeful.

"Not yet." Landon paused and Ashley heard the pain in his
voice. He would've married her that afternoon, but Ashley
wanted to wait. He looked from Ashley to the others. "We're
waiting to see what Ashley's new doctor says, what kind of treatment she should have." His smile was marked by determination
and unshakable faith. "Sometime this summer, we hope."

Several weeks had passed since then, and Landon had asked
several times about her test results. They weren't being rushed
this time, and the doctor had said it could take longer because
the blood panel was more detailed.

In the meantime, she and Landon and Cole had been insepa-
rable. She was still working at Sunset Hills Adult Care Home,
and Landon had started back with the Bloomington Fire Depart-

ment. Cole was in preschool four days a week and took his afternoon naps with his grandma at the old Baxter house.

But every day Ashley would get off work well before dinner, pick up Cole, and stop by the station to see Landon. If he wasn't working, they'd head for the park or down to the lake or back to Ashley's house. Landon would wrestle with Cole, push him on the backyard swings, or chase him around the yard wearing a football helmet five sizes too small.

At night, they'd read books with Cole and tuck him in. Sometimes Cole asked a question about the wedding—when it would happen, where it would be, whether Landon would move in with them that day or not. Landon usually pulled him into a hug and rocked him for a while, instead of answering right away. Then he'd say something like, "As soon as we have a plan, you'll be the first to know, okay bucko?"

Cole would be satisfied with that. The three of them would share another round of hugs and say good night.

The most challenging times had been after Cole was asleep.

Ashley had figured that with no sad good-byes looming over them, they'd have an easier time sticking to a reasonable curfew and avoiding temptation. But the passion and desire that had marked their visits those past few years had only intensified. They'd start watching a movie or playing a card game and that would lead to talking—deep conversations about how lonely he'd felt in New York or how he'd wanted to stick it out because that's what his buddy Jalen would've done if he'd lived. As they talked, they'd move next to each other on the couch, holding hands, leaning against each other. And then the conversations would get more intimate, about the way he thought of her constantly after she left New York or about Ashley's inability to let Landon go no matter how often she'd tried to.

They also talked about the wedding, how Ashley wanted to be married at her family's church and have a big reception, somewhere with a dance floor large enough for all the guests.

But no matter what they talked about, eventually their eyes

would find each other and the conversation would stall. It had been that way yesterday, hours after she'd gotten the strange test results. Cole had been in bed, and they were sitting side by side talking about something at the fire station.

"So I went into the supply room and—" Landon stopped midsentence.

Ashley turned so she could see him better. "Into the supply room and . . . and what?"

A chuckle sounded in his throat. "I can't do this, Ashley."

She pressed her shoulder into the sofa back and grinned, amused at the pained look on his face. "Can't do what?"

"Supply rooms?" He moaned and let his head fall against hers. "How can I be telling a story about supply rooms when all I want to do is kiss you?"

She laughed and even as she was still catching her breath, he placed his hands on her face, eased her closer to him, and kissed her. It lasted a long time, and was colored by a longing that was greater than either of them.

Of course, in the end it had been easy for Ashley to pull away, to stop before anything serious happened. Like every other time they'd wound up in this situation, a single thought of her health, of being HIV-positive, and she would take a deep breath, stand, and help Landon to his feet. In an instant, disgust with her situation would replace the desire. "I'm tired, Landon." She would smile to hide her real feelings. "Let's call it a night."

No matter how badly she wanted to lie in his arms and give way to the feelings he stirred inside her, she wouldn't put him at risk. Maybe her doctor would give her safe ways to be intimate with him. If so, she'd explore those after they were married. For now, she loved him too much to let their kissing get out of hand.

She was out of her car now, and a cool breeze lifted her pants legs and played around her ankles. Spring in Bloomington was always like this—summer one day, winter the next, almost as if the seasons were battling to see which would win out.

Her hands trembled, and her heart beat faster than before. But she wasn't afraid. In the next hour she'd know more about her future than she had in all her years combined.

She made her way inside and smiled at a woman behind the information desk. "I'm looking for Dr. Dillon's office. He said he'd be here today."

The woman directed her to the third floor, and five minutes later Ashley found the door with his name on it. Holding her breath, she knocked. Every heartbeat seemed to shout the same thing over and over at her: *Soon, Ashley . . . soon, Ashley . . . soon, Ashley.*

She'd have all the answers soon.

The door opened and Dr. Dillon smiled at her. "Come in." He ushered her to a chair in front of a big desk, and he took the one behind it. "You said you wanted to talk about your results?"

Ashley pulled a folded piece of paper from her purse, opened it, and read the results one more time. Then she pointed to the line near the bottom that read "HIV." "Right here, Doctor. Could you . . . could you explain this to me?"

A grin spread the width of the man's face. "It says negative, Ashley. You know what that means, don't you?"

Heat filled her cheeks, and she gave a quick shake of her head. "I'm HIV-positive, Dr. Dillon. You know that. I showed you my last test and you told me—" she grabbed a quick bit of air—"you told me the other lab had done the test twice. Just to be sure, and so we did these tests at your office to see how close I was to getting AIDS, and now I get this—"

"Ashley . . ." The doctor held up his hand, his eyes dancing with joy, his smile gentle and sympathetic. "You don't have HIV. The test I had them do takes longer because it's much more detailed. I trust it completely." He leaned back and tossed his hands in the air. "You're fine, Ashley. Perfectly fine. I contacted the lab yesterday after you called, and they verified the information you have in your hand. The test was negative."

Ashley's mouth hung open, and the room began to spin. All the emotions she had held at bay since opening the test results

surrounded her, filled her so she could do nothing but cover her
face with her hands and let the reality sink in.

She was HIV-negative? She didn't have a disease lurking in her
bloodstream that would make her sick and put Landon at risk
and rob her of every beautiful thing she and Landon and Cole
wanted for their future? She didn't have it?

Since taking the first HIV test, she had simply owned the
truth. She'd been intimate with a promiscuous man, and now
she would pay the price with her life. Her prayers, in the
meantime, had been directed toward staying healthy as long
as possible, and wanting someone to take care of Cole once
she contracted AIDS and died. She had even asked God to give
her the courage to see a doctor, to accept whatever treatments
that would bring.

But never had she prayed that the results might be wrong.

HIV had been a life sentence, her body a prison from which
she could never escape. But now . . . now the test results were
the key to that prison, and the sense of freedom made her forget
for a moment that Dr. Dillon was even in the room.

God . . . did you heal me or was it negative all along? And if it
was negative all along, how awful that she'd wasted a year of her
life worried that she had the beginnings of a deadly disease.

The thought blew across the canvas of her mind, and she
blinked her eyes open. She could hardly be angry. It didn't matter, really, how God had done this. He was giving her a second
chance at life and there was only one thing she wanted to do.

Sprint from the doctor's office and find Landon.

Instead she looked at the doctor. He was still grinning, his
eyes damp. "How . . . how does something like that happen?"
she asked.

"A false positive?" The doctor leaned forward and sifted
through a pile of papers on his desk. "I figured you'd ask that.
I pulled together some information on false positives so you'd
understand better."

"You mean you've heard of it happening before?"

"Oh yes." His smile faded. "The Centers for Disease Control keeps statistics on this sort of thing. Out of every ten thousand people tested for HIV, ten will show up positive. Eight of those will be false positives, and only two in ten thousand will actually have HIV."

The statistics hit Ashley like a brick. "What?"

"Yes." Dr. Dillon frowned. "It's discouraging. Roughly 83 percent of HIV-positive tests are false."

"How come the public doesn't know that?" Ashley could hear the frustration in her voice. *Calm*, she told herself. *You're one of the 83 percent, remember?* She exhaled and folded her hands on her lap. "I had no idea."

"It's tough. HIV is a very real risk; people around the world are still contracting it every day, still dying of AIDS every day. Lots of people are working to find a cure for it." Dr. Dillon tapped the paper in front of him. "If the statistics about false positives get out, the Centers for Disease Control could lose momentum for funding. So they downplay the truth. That's just my opinion."

Ashley couldn't draw a breath. Eighty-three percent of positive HIV tests were false positives? She forced herself to concentrate. "Can't they come up with a better test?"

"The standard test is less expensive and takes less time. The problem is that countless conditions in a person's body can throw the test off, cause it to show positive when in fact it's negative. That's why both your first tests came back positive." He shrugged. "You might've had a different virus at the time, a higher level of one type of protein or mineral, or any number of other conditions that could've caused the false positive."

"So everyone who gets a false positive has to be retested—is that it?"

"Exactly. That way the more detailed test can be performed right away, and a false positive can be ruled out." The doctor handed her the paper with the information. "Didn't the other hospital lab technician tell you to see your doctor right away?"

A fresh wave of guilt smacked Ashley in the face. "Yes." The single word felt like it weighed a thousand pounds. Of course they told her that: Get a retest, see your doctor, figure out a plan. She'd known for months now what she was supposed to do. Both her father and Brooke were doctors, after all, and both of them had demanded she get in to see a specialist.

But she hadn't wanted to do it, hadn't wanted to look a doctor in the face and hear him chart out what little remained of her life. Getting treatment, going in for monthly blood tests, expensive medication, all of it was more than she could think about. So she'd put off making the appointment.

The full weight of her procrastination hit her. If she'd done as she was supposed to, she and Landon would've been married by now. She thought about the deadly warehouse fire he had fought in Manhattan before he made the decision to return to Bloomington. He never would've been there if she'd said yes to him, if she'd not been so afraid of seeing a doctor.

A shudder worked its way through her, and she closed her eyes again. *God . . . thank you for bringing him back to me. Thank you.*

I know the plans I have for you, daughter . . . plans to give you a hope and a future, and not to harm you.

The verse was her favorite, and it came softly to her now, brushing over the rough edges of her heart and bringing peace to her anxious soul.

"Ashley? Do you need a minute alone?"

The doctor's voice brought her back and she looked at him. She felt like crying, but at the same time she was so happy she laughed out loud. Never mind the mistakes she'd made in the past. God was bigger than all of them, and suddenly she was filled with a kind of joy she'd never known before.

A sense of freedom and knowing and abundant life all wrapped into one big flame that lit her up and made her feel like shouting. God had given her a second chance! She had Cole and Landon and love and life and now . . .

She gathered her purse and the paper and shook Dr. Dillon's hand. "If there's nothing else, Doctor, I have to meet someone."

"I'd like you to come twice a year for checkups, just to keep an eye on your other blood levels. Sometimes after a false-positive HIV test we find something out of whack that needs an adjustment, but nothing serious."

Ashley was already halfway to the door. She nodded, thanked the doctor, and darted into the hall. When she was outside she flipped open her cell phone and called Landon. She glanced at her watch. Five to four. Perfect. He would be off in five minutes.

On the second ring, she heard him pick up. He knew she was seeing the doctor today, but he had no idea about the test results. "Hey, Ash." His tone was soft, intimate. As if not a minute's time had passed since their kiss on the couch last night. "How was the doctor?"

Tears flooded her eyes as she leaned against the outside wall of the hospital. "Landon . . ." Saying his name released more of the emotions building within her. She waited until the lump in her throat eased some. "Meet me at Lake Monroe. At our table, okay?"

"Now?" Alarm sounded in his voice. "Ash, what is it? Stay there, honey. I can meet you. If this is something bad, don't worry about—"

"Landon." A nervous giggle slipped out. She cleared her throat. "It's nothing bad. I just need to see you face-to-face. I want to talk at the lake, okay?"

He hesitated. "You're sure you're okay?"

"Yes." She had more control now. "Lake Monroe in fifteen minutes, all right?"

"Okay. I'm on my way."

CHAPTER FIVE

THE RIDE TO Lake Monroe was the longest in Landon's life.

Of all the situations he'd faced and survived in the past three years, something told him this would be the most memorable. Finding his friend Jalen in the rubble of the collapse of the twin towers was of course unforgettable. Working in New York City had been a rush, with countless dangers and sorrows, but still it was only a job.

Ashley was his future, his fiancée, the only woman he'd ever loved. This afternoon she'd seen the doctor, and whatever he'd told her was big enough that she wanted somewhere special to tell him the news.

He turned left out of the fire-station parking lot and heard her voice again in his mind. *It's nothing bad . . . nothing bad . . . nothing bad. . . .*

But what if it was? What news could the doctor possibly give her that would be dramatic enough to make her start crying the way she had when he answered the phone? He tightened his grip on the steering wheel and flexed the muscles in his jaw. *God . . . nothing more, please. Not now. I want to marry her and love her and be a family with Cole. Please, God . . .*

He arrived at the lake before her, parked, and sauntered down the hilly path to their table. It was the spot where the Baxters had their family picnic every August, the place where he and Ashley had stayed late one night talking about her time in Paris, the details she'd never shared with anyone else.

Damp leaves lay across the table's surface. Landon brushed them off, climbed up, and sat on the tabletop facing the shore, his feet on the bench. The lake was choppy, a cool breeze playing across the top of the water. Rain was forecast for the middle of the week, but the afternoon sky was crystal clear, a brilliant blue that splashed light through the still-bare trees and made the whitecaps on the lake shine like so many diamonds.

Would life always be like this with Ashley? Each doctor's appointment a stoplight of sorts, flashing red until another test or an experimental drug might give them a green light and allow them to journey on together until the next stop?

Landon stared at the sky and tried to see beyond it. This was what Ashley had tried to protect him from, the uncertainty that came with her diagnosis. He gritted his teeth and dug his elbows into his knees. All the more reason why he'd be strong for her today, whatever the news. So what if their lives were dotted with a dozen doctor's appointments every year? At least they had today.

Hearing a car in the lot behind him, he turned around. After a minute, Ashley appeared. Dressed in thin cotton sweatpants and a bulky sweater, she spotted him and stopped. Then a smile appeared, first in her eyes and then across her face. "Landon!" She ran lightly down the path until she was standing in front of him, breathless, her eyes dancing.

For the first time since her phone call Landon considered an outlandish idea. What if the news hadn't been bad or neutral? What if the news had been good? He gave a quiet laugh. "Whatever the doctor said, I didn't think you'd run down the hill laughing."

She gripped his shoulders and searched his eyes. "Landon, the test was negative."

He felt his face go blank. "What test?"

Her smile faded and she took a step closer. "I don't have HIV. The doctor explained the whole thing to me. They . . ." Tears filled her eyes and spilled onto her cheeks.

Landon's heart thudded hard against his ribs. What had she just said? She didn't have HIV? He brushed his fingertips beneath her eyes and pushed her tears up along her cheekbones into her hair. She didn't have HIV? Did that mean she had full-blown AIDS, or something different? It couldn't possibly mean she was . . . his thoughts jumbled and he couldn't make sense of them. "I . . . I don't understand."

"It's true, Landon." She sniffed and made a sound that was mostly laugh. "The other tests—both of them—were false positives. I'm not infected. The doctor explained everything. I guess it happens a lot—false positives." She eased her hands along his arms. "I'm not sick; I'm not going to get sick." A sob escaped and she moved closer, hugging him, holding on to him. "I'm free, Landon. We're both free!"

The truth worked its way through him, and he held her so he would somehow believe he wasn't dreaming. This was really happening, wasn't it? Ashley was standing in front of him telling him the entire situation with HIV was behind them, right? He drew back enough to see her eyes, to search them and know for sure she was being straight with him, that there wasn't some part of the story she was leaving out. "You mean it, Ash? That's what he told you?"

"Yes." She pulled away, threw her head back, tossed her arms straight up, and did a victory shout. "Yes . . . yes . . . yes! Thank you, God!" Then she rushed into his arms again.

"You know what this means?"

"Yes." She did a series of small jumps and clung tight to him again. "Everything's going to be okay!"

"Not that." Landon nuzzled his face against hers. "It means we have to set a date."

"A date! Of course." Ashley's voice grew softer, more seductive. "How 'bout tonight?"

"Mmmm." He kissed her until both of them were breathless. Then he gave her a gentle push. "Okay, come on. I can't remember my name when you kiss me that way."

She grinned. "That's the plan, Sam."

"Tell me about it." He chuckled under his breath and felt a shiver run down his spine. He couldn't wait to marry her, to love her the way he'd longed to love her. A slow breath filled his lungs. His desire would have to wait. "I'm serious, Ash. It takes time to plan a wedding."

"My mom will help me." Ashley angled herself sideways and leaned against him, taking in the view of the lake. "She's great at planning weddings."

"So what's the date?"

"How 'bout July?"

Landon had the Saturdays throughout summer memorized. "July 5, 12, 19, or 26?"

Ashley laughed. "You've been thinking about this, haven't you?"

"Of course." His tone grew serious and he searched her eyes. "I want it to be everything you ever dreamed of, Ashley."

She thought for a moment. "Let's have it July nineteenth; that way it won't be too close to the Fourth."

"When should we tell your family?"

"Let's tell them tomorrow night!" Ashley glowed with the realization. "I forgot until now. Dad called and invited us for dinner. Kari and Brooke and their families will be there. It'll be perfect."

"Cole's going to be so excited." Landon ran his fingers down the length of her arms, his cheek next to hers as they stared at the shimmering water. "I can't believe it's all really going to happen."

"Me either."

He savored the feel of her body against him, the way she leaned into him almost as if he alone could keep her safe, shelter

her, celebrate with her whatever the future held. A thought occurred to him, something that hadn't hit him yet. Because of
her HIV, they had agreed not to have more children, that Cole
would be enough. But now . . . "I wanna have a dozen babies,
okay, Ash?"

Her answer took a long time. "Okay."

She was quiet, and he wondered if maybe she didn't want
children after all. But then he saw her cheeks. She was crying,
soft tears that fell despite the partial smile that played on her
lips. "We can have children, Landon. Can you believe that? God
is so good. . . ."

"Yes. Now if only it were July eighteenth." He snuggled against
her again, the truth about the news finally feeling real. "It's going
to seem like forever."

"For both of us."

"And Cole, too."

Ashley laughed. "He'll ask us every day, 'How many months,
Mom? How many weeks and days and hours?' "

A jet passed overhead, and the honk of Canadian geese
sounded in the distance. "I love you, Ashley Baxter." He turned
so he could see her eyes again. "I didn't need this news to love
you. But now . . . now look at what tomorrow holds."

Ashley looked straight to the deepest part of his soul. "Landon
. . . in the painting that is our lives, all we've been through together
to this point is only the backdrop. Today—" she sucked in a deep
breath—"this moment . . . is the first stroke, the beginning of the
most beautiful picture. A picture even I can't imagine."

She kissed him once more. Landon savored it because this
time it wasn't the kiss of longing and passion but of a love both
tested and true. A love that would see them through a lifetime
of highs and lows, the way Hank's love had seen Irvel through,
even to her dying day.

CHAPTER SIX

ELIZABETH USUALLY TOOK quick showers. Just long enough to shampoo her hair, wash up, and shave her legs. The whole time, her mind would race in a dozen different directions. Whether Cole was coming for the afternoon, how late John had to work, which errands had to be run, and what she'd cook for dinner.

But this was late Sunday afternoon, and dinner was already simmering in a Crock-Pot downstairs. John was in his study, working on patient files, and in two hours her family would arrive. By the end of the evening, they would all know the truth about her diagnosis: that she would be having a double mastectomy on Monday morning.

The hot water ran down her frame. Elizabeth reached for a fresh washcloth, her favorite one, a thick, soft white cotton cloth she'd bought in New York City last December as part of a set.

She intended to enjoy her last shower before surgery.

The soap was new also. A fragrant lilac bar she'd gotten as a gift for Christmas. Funny how she had let it sit, unopened, beneath her sink all these weeks. Too busy to open it and use it, when the plain green soap did the job just fine.

She rubbed the soap into the washcloth, and the lather filled her senses. She set the bar down and slowly worked the sudsy cloth across her chest.

She brought her right elbow up over her head, and her breast lifted to where it had been before children and time had taken its toll. No, they weren't much by the world's standards, but they were hers, a part of her. The part that had so often been the source of passion between her and John, the part that had brought nourishment and comfort to each of her five kids. The part that had filled out a sweater or a dress or a bathing suit.

Even after her first bout with cancer, she had taken her breasts for granted. Every time she looked in the mirror they were there, giving her a feminine shape and softening her thin frame.

She shifted the soapy cloth to her right hand and raised her left elbow over her head. Tomorrow they'd be gone, the part of her that had made her feel like a woman. She studied them, willing it all to be a mistake somehow. They didn't look diseased, did they?

The surgery would be brutal, barbaric. A surgeon's scalpel would press to her sides, leaving grotesque scars and mutated shallow valleys where once lay the curves of her chest. Was that all the further they'd come in cancer research? It was the twenty-first century and still the best option for cancer was to cut it out?

Elizabeth ran the cloth over her chest and willed herself not to cry. Of course cancer treatment had progressed. They had new medications now, treatments that ten years ago wouldn't have been an option. It was those types of treatments, and medications like the one Elizabeth had been taking, that had probably kept the cancer away for so long.

She finished washing the rest of herself. She thought about how strange it would be not to have her breasts, to move about without the gentle weight of her chest as part of her being.

Again she looked at herself and wondered. How would John see her after the surgery? Of course he'd told her a number of times that it wouldn't matter; after all their years together his love went far deeper than her looks, her figure. But still . . . he'd loved that part of her, hadn't he? And now, even if she wore prosthetics, he would know they were gone, the same way she would know it.

If only she could stay here in the shower, hot water running over her body, her figure still whole and complete. She closed her eyes and lifted her face to the pounding stream. For a long while she let it wash over her face.

She wasn't sure, but she thought maybe she was crying. Maybe mixed in with the water flowing down around her still-curvy body were more of her tears. They certainly came without warning since the diagnosis.

Time was getting away from her. She shampooed her hair and wondered if she'd have any of it left after the chemotherapy. It was still thick, still dark and shiny the way it had been when she was a teenager. Some gray had worked its way into her temples and near her forehead, but for the most part it was still dark.

Elizabeth thought about God, the Lord and Savior she'd spent a lifetime worshiping. Being a believer meant there'd be times like this; wasn't that what she'd learned over the years? Times when nothing made sense and all she could do was dig her fingernails into her faith and hold on for dear life.

It was the way she'd felt all those years ago when she and John found themselves in trouble, the way she'd felt when Kari's husband was killed, and again when Ashley was diagnosed with HIV. It was the way she'd felt when Hayley fell into a backyard pool last summer and came out a changed little girl.

And it was the way she felt now.

God . . . heal me. Let them open me up and find that it's all a mistake, please, God . . . She hesitated, the whisper of a prayer still on her lips, the stream of water washing the shampoo down her back. *If not, God . . . then give me the strength. Please give me the strength.*

Ever since the diagnosis, she'd finished her prayers that way. Not only because she needed strength to face the surgery and the cancer and her family tonight as she told them the news. But because every time she prayed, God gave her the same overwhelming sense. A sense that the cancer was worse than any of them realized, that the double mastectomy would only be the beginning.

And that sometime in the not-too-far distance, she would be leaving the people she loved so much.

It was a thought that terrified her beyond words, beyond her ability to take even a single step toward tomorrow. So she prayed for strength now as much as she'd been doing, and she was sure the Lord was listening. Because somehow she was able to turn off the water, step out of the shower, and dry off.

Knowing that every step led her closer to Monday and whatever the future held.

※

Kari was practically bursting with the news.

She held Jessie's hand as the two of them walked toward the football field. Jessie jabbered about the grass and the flowers and the birds overhead. "Mommy, see that birdie?"

"I do. He's pretty, isn't he?"

"He's a robin, Mommy." Jessie sounded like a cartoon character, her singsong voice small and petite the way everything about her was. "See his red. He's a robin."

"You're right, honey. Very good."

"Robins come in spring, Mommy. Pretty red robins, right?"

"Yes, honey."

Kari chuckled to herself and kept them moving. Jessie was still a towhead, but her blonde hair was getting darker all the time. At two years old she looked like a miniature Kari, but she was every bit as intellectual as her father had been.

Kari gazed at the blue sky and wondered again. If Tim could see his daughter, he'd be so proud. But the truth was, his mark on her life was all but gone. She was far more Ryan's little girl, a child full of life and light and her daddy's precious faith.

"Daddy!" Jessie pointed at a tall figure on the sidelines of the football field. She pulled her hand from Kari's and ran toward him, her yellow sneakers lighting up with every step. "Daddy . . . here I am, Daddy!"

Ryan was holding a practice with a few of the quarterbacks. Spring passing leagues would begin in a few weeks, and the guys had asked him to come out and throw a few balls around. It was Sunday afternoon, but Kari didn't mind. She'd been more tired than usual, and after church she and Jessie had spent the morning cleaning Jessie's closet, while Ryan headed for the school.

It wasn't until they'd finished cleaning that Kari had the idea.

She needed supplies at the store, so why not pick up a pregnancy test? Her period had been due a week ago, and her body just didn't feel right. She and Jessie had done their shopping, and when she got home she took the test to the bathroom and stared at it. The last time she'd taken a pregnancy test, she'd dreaded the results. This time would be different.

She and Ryan had wanted another baby, but month after month her period would come. They'd talk about what they might be doing wrong, how maybe it wasn't the right time, or maybe she needed vitamins, or perhaps something was wrong with him, something left over from the football injury years ago.

Whatever it was, their concern was beginning to demand some sort of plan. They had agreed to see a doctor this summer if Kari didn't get pregnant by then, and they'd even discussed the worst-case scenario. What if Kari couldn't get pregnant? Since Ryan still had most of his NFL earnings in a savings account, money wasn't an issue. They would do whatever they could to have a baby. In vitro fertilization, embryo implantation, whatever techniques were available.

Kari picked up her pace so she could keep up with the fireball who was their little daughter. "Wait for Mommy, honey . . ."

Jessie didn't turn around. Her ponytail flopped as she ran. "Daddy, here I am!"

This time he heard her. Out of all the noises on the field—a dozen voices, and the sounds of whistles and footballs being thrown and caught—he heard her and turned around. Even from fifty yards away Kari saw his face light up.

He dropped his clipboard and ran to meet her, arms out. "Hey, what's my Jessie girl doing out here?"

"Pretty robins, Daddy!"

He winked at Kari and caught Jessie as she jumped into his arms. Twice he twirled her around as fast as the wind; then he hugged her close and rubbed his nose against hers. "You and Mommy decided to get out, huh?"

"We're going swinging."

"Perfect." Ryan kissed her on the forehead and set her down. As big as he was—the tall former NFL tight end—Ryan Taylor couldn't have been more gentle with her or with Jessie.

He took the extra few steps to Kari. "You're gonna stay for a while?"

"Yes, but—" Kari gave his arm a light tug—"come here for a minute. I have something to tell you."

A pained look flashed in his eyes. "Honey, I'd love to but—" he looked back at the field—"the guys can only stay another thirty minutes." His eyes found hers. "Can it wait?"

"Sure." She smiled, determined to be agreeable.

"Thanks, Kari." He gave her a quick kiss. "You're the best." He gave a light tug on Jessie's ponytail. "Go play with Mommy now, okay? I'll be done in a little while and we can all swing together."

Jessie clapped her hands. "Goody, Daddy. You can swing with me!"

Disappointment ripped at Kari as she and Jessie turned toward the swings, but she refused to let it change her mood. She could wait half an hour, couldn't she? "Ready to swing, Jessie?"

"Yes!" She skipped ahead, moving as fast as her little feet would carry her. "Catch me, Mommy. Come on!"

The high school sat adjacent to the grade school, and often Kari brought Jessie here so they could play together and visit with Ryan on his breaks. This was the first time since winter that they'd made it here, and now that Jessie was older, Kari was excited about the months of football that lay ahead.

This was how she'd always dreamed it might be—married to Ryan, raising children at home without a career to sidetrack her. She'd done only a handful of catalogue modeling shoots since fall, and even then she wondered at the wisdom of taking the jobs. They didn't need her to work, and if God might bless them with more children, modeling would have to wait. Years, maybe.

"Okay, Mommy, push me!" Jessie was agile for her age and afraid of nothing. She worked herself up into one of the smaller swings, gripped the chains, and held on. "Ready!"

Kari set her purse and keys down and gave her daughter two pushes. Then she moved in front of Jessie the way she'd seen Ryan do it. She positioned herself right where Jessie's shoes would be able to hit her backside, and she bent forward some. As Jessie came swinging toward her, Kari made a loud noise and an exaggerated fall forward. "Hey . . . what're you doing, silly head?"

Jessie squealed with delight. "Again, Mommy! Again!"

Kari pushed her again and then hurried around in front of the swing, pretending to get kicked by Jessie's yellow sneakers. Kari rubbed her backside and made a funny face. "Listen you, Miss Silly Shoes, how come you keep kicking me?"

They played the game a few more times, and then Kari swept Jessie off the swing and tumbled with her in the nearby grass, tickling her and chasing her until they both fell onto their backs, exhausted.

Just as they were standing up, Ryan came running over. "Looks like I'm missing all the fun!"

"Yep. We played kick the mommy, tickle the daughter, and

chase." Kari blew at a wisp of her hair. "Now we're both tuckered out."

He studied them, his eyes bright, a reflection, Kari knew, of the way his heart was so full these days. She got to her feet and headed toward him. "About that thing I wanted to tell you . . ."

"Oh, sorry." He pointed back at the field. "We're done practicing, but I want you to meet someone. One of my new assistants. He worked with the Cowboys back when I was a player, but his wife's mother moved here a few years ago. She's being treated for some health thing through the hospital." Ryan shrugged. "He took a break from the pros and they settled into their house a year ago. When he heard I was coaching, he followed us last season. This year he figured if I can coach a bunch of kids and enjoy it, maybe he could too."

"Okay, that's great, but first let me tell you what I—"

"Remember, we had a meeting at his house last week? I told you about him that night, about his family and how his home is the way I want ours to be one day."

Kari couldn't think straight. She didn't want to talk about one of the coaches; she wanted to tell Ryan the news. She forced herself to concentrate. "Ryan, can't I meet him later? I wanted to—"

"Come on, sweetheart; it'll just take a minute. Really." He gestured toward the field again. As he did, Jessie came up and wrapped her arms around his legs. "The guy's coming right now. Meet him and then we'll talk."

"All right." Kari managed another smile. Ryan wasn't trying to be difficult; he was only excited about having a new friend. But she could hardly wait for the moment to be over.

A good-looking man came into view, tall with dark blond hair and the familiar build Kari had seen on other football-player friends of Ryan's. Beside him was one of the players from the high school team. The boy looked like he'd been crying.

"Don't ask," Ryan whispered. "I'll tell you later."

The coach and player were closer now and Ryan put his arm around Kari. "Jim Flanigan, this is my wife, Kari, and—" he pried Jessie off his legs and turned her to face his assistant—"our daughter, Jessie."

Jim patted Jessie on the head and shook Kari's hand. They talked for nearly ten minutes about the pro-coaching circuit and how hard it was to never know if you'd have a job from one year to the next.

"I thought I'd miss it more." Jim smiled, and his eyes had a familiar glow. "But God's given me something new here." He shrugged. "I figured we'd stay here a year or two, until Jenny's mom could be moved to the East Coast somewhere. But a year out of the pros and I can't say I miss it."

"Bloomington's not a bad place." Ryan patted the player on the shoulder and glanced at Kari. "You remember Cody? Cody Coleman. He'll be a freshman next year. One of our top receivers."

"Hi, Cody." Kari smiled at him. She enjoyed this. Any other day she would've wanted the conversation to last another hour. But her news was practically bursting out of her. "You've been over to the house before, haven't you?"

Ryan had the guys over for a barbecue before two-a-day practices each summer. She was sure she'd seen Cody before.

"Yes, ma'am." He nodded and looked down at the grass.

Now Kari was sure he'd been crying. Clearly he didn't want to be dragged into the conversation. He hung back some and pushed his toe at a clump of dirt.

"Anyway, Ryan was saying you have a great church." Jim cocked his head, and his grin brought out dimples in both cheeks. "To be honest, we haven't found a church home yet. Maybe we can join you next Sunday."

"Sure." Kari smiled, first at Ryan and then at Jim.

Ryan kept the conversation going. "I was telling Jim we'd like to have his family over after the service some Sunday. He has six kids, three of them adopted from Haiti." Ryan smiled at her, but something deeper shone in his eyes. "I thought it might be nice to hear their adoption story."

"Yes. That would be nice." This was why she loved Ryan so much. He was always thinking of her, always looking out for her. He wanted to make this new friend Jim feel welcome, but he also wanted the four of them to get together so Jim and his wife could share their adoption story. In case Kari never got pregnant and adoption was a road they chose to travel.

"We're a big group." Jim raised an eyebrow. "I'll have my wife call to see what we can bring."

"That'd be nice." Kari smiled at the new man. "I'd like to meet her. Sounds like you have quite the family."

They said their good-byes and Jim shook both their hands. Then he nodded at Cody, who quickly did the same. When they walked off together, Jim put his arm around Cody's shoulders and they appeared to fall immediately into heavy conversation.

For a moment, Kari forgot about her news. "What's the story with Cody?"

"He lives down the street from Jim and Jenny. I guess they've been talking for a while now."

"Was he crying?"

Ryan nodded, and the smile left his eyes. "Cody came clean with us today. He's been drinking."

"Oh." Kari's heart sank. The young man was clean-cut, with a chiseled face and good looks. What made a kid like that decide to drink? "I'm sorry. How bad is it?"

"Bad." Ryan stooped down and lifted Jessie onto his hip. "The last few nights he's been drinking so much he blacks out. He told us he didn't know if he could live like that another week. Like maybe he'd drink so much he'd never wake up."

"Ryan, that's terrible. Where's he getting it?"

"His mom. She's a single parent. Works at a strip club on the other side of the university. I guess she's pretty abusive."

"She beats him?" Kari pictured the stocky football player and had trouble imagining anyone pushing him around.

"Not like that. More with her words, telling him he's a failure, that he's a loser like his father, berating him for the smallest offense." Ryan shook his head. "There's more, but it isn't pretty." He nodded to Jessie. "I'll tell you later."

Sorrow filled Kari's heart as she started walking toward the swings. "Sad."

Ryan fell in step beside her. "Something has to be done about it."

"More swings, Daddy!" Jessie raised her hands toward the swing. "Please!"

"Okay, sweetie." Ryan set their daughter down on the same swing where she had played before. He set the swing in motion with a flick of his hand. Then he turned to Kari. "Cody turned fifteen last week. He's talking about moving in with Jim and his wife."

"Really?" Kari crossed her arms. "I thought they already had six kids."

"They do." Ryan shook his head and made a chuckling sound. "The family's amazing, Kari. They have this big old house with an apartment over the garage. Their kids' friends are always in and out, and next fall some college girl is moving into the apartment. I guess she's coming to Bloomington to start a Christian theater group."

"Wow."

"Yeah." Ryan gave Jessie another push. "The guy has all the money he could want, but his house isn't a showroom. It's filled with photographs of kids and all this well-loved furniture. It's amazing, really. You can feel God's heart the minute you walk through the door."

"Huh." Kari angled her head. "And now they're taking Cody in."

"It looks that way. If his mom will agree." Ryan slipped in front of Jessie and pretended to get hit on his bottom. He rubbed it hard and made a funny face at her.

"Silly Daddy."

After a few times he returned to the other side of the swing and pushed her again. "Cody needs a safe place where there's no alcohol. That's the only way he's going to survive." Ryan bit his lip. "He's such a great kid, Kari. Until today, he'd been talking to Jim in the evenings, coming by their house. But neither of us had any idea things had gotten so bad."

The sun was setting, and suddenly Kari remembered her news. She was about to say something when Ryan lifted Jessie from the swing and held her high over his head. "We're going to Grandma and Papa's house for dinner tonight; did you know that, Jessie?"

"Yay! I like Grandma and Papa's house."

Suddenly Kari had an idea. She could wait and tell Ryan the news at dinner, with everyone around. That way they could all celebrate the moment together. She and Ryan would laugh about how she'd come to the football field to tell him, and how they'd ended up talking about a handful of other things instead.

Besides, a sadness still hung over the moment, the thought of one of Ryan's football players so caught up in drinking that he feared for his life. How wonderful that Jim and his wife were willing to take him in.

Ryan was right. That was the kind of home the two of them planned to have one day, a place where kids would feel welcome and safe, where their own children could see them demonstrate Christ's love through example. Ten years down the road maybe, when they'd had a few more children of their own and life was a bit more stable than it was now.

Kari thought about the announcement she'd make tonight at dinner. Yes, their family was still becoming, but that was a good thing. In fact, she could hardly wait until they were all together at the Baxter house. She and Ryan were going to have a baby!

And nothing in the world could dampen that sort of news.

CHAPTER SEVEN

JOHN STAYED IN the kitchen with Elizabeth, helping her get the meal ready. The news wasn't out yet, and already a dark cloud seemed to hang over the house, as if the walls and windows knew the truth.

Elizabeth was sick. Maybe she was very sick. And the reality sat so heavy on John's heart he could barely find the strength to stay standing. Next to him she worked on the salad, a mixture of light and dark greens, chopped tomatoes and mushrooms, grated cheese, and sesame seeds.

This had always been Elizabeth's way. No bagged salad and instant croutons for Elizabeth Baxter. She'd been a home economics major when he met her, and no matter how busy or big their family grew, she always took time to cook them healthy meals. He admired her from three feet away, how she held the mushroom just so, working her knife across it and tossing perfect slices into the salad bowl.

"You're beautiful; do you know that?" He stirred a heavy wooden spoon through the bubbling beef stew in the Crock-Pot.

"John—" she lifted her eyes to him, but only for a moment—

"I'm making salad, for goodness' sake. You can't say I'm beautiful when I'm working." She set the knife down and brushed her hair out of her eyes with the back of her hand. "I look like I'm working."

"You always look beautiful when you're working." He left the spoon in the stew and moved closer. "Your eyes shine with thoughts of our kids and their families. And each vegetable or bit of cheese is your way of telling them you love them."

She lowered her chin, and her eyes grew damp. "How come you know me so well, John Baxter?"

"Thirty-five years, Elizabeth. Can you believe that? Thirty-five years I've been watching you make dinner and salad and meals for this family, and not once have I stopped and watched you and not thought you look beautiful." He touched the side of her face. "Are you okay? About tonight, I mean?"

"I'm not sure." She reached up and wrapped her fingers around his hand. "It won't be easy."

"No." John sucked in a slow breath. It would be the hardest night of his life, if he was honest. "We'll get through it, though. This way everyone'll be praying; everyone'll be behind you when you go in tomorrow."

She nodded and picked up the knife again. Three more mushrooms were sliced and tossed into the salad bowl before she looked up. "Why . . . why does it feel like the beginning of the end?"

"Oh, honey, come here." He folded her into his arms, stroking the back of her head, her thick dark hair. His words were for her alone, spoken straight to her soul, more of a whispered cry than a confident statement. "We can beat this thing; I know we can. You've gotta believe that, okay?"

The bell rang, and they heard the front door open. Elizabeth straightened and sniffed twice. She reached for a tissue and held it beneath her nose. "Pray for me, John. I don't want them to know something's wrong. Not yet."

She turned and blew her nose. He saw her slip her hands beneath the kitchen faucet, and he knew what she'd do. She'd stay there at the sink until the kids entered the house and then, because she was genuinely glad to see them, she'd put on a happy face and all would be well.

At least for another hour.

Kari and Ryan and Jessie arrived first. Kari hugged John, and he couldn't help but feel something was different about her. They explained that they'd spent the afternoon outside at the football field.

Jessie chimed in. "We did swings, Papa." She tugged on his pant leg until he patted her head. "It was so fun."

"I'll bet it was."

Ryan launched into a story about his newest assistant coach, the man who'd coached in the NFL and had a big family in town. There were more details, but John stopped listening. His thoughts were limited to Elizabeth, and how she was handling her emotions in the next room. How this might be the last time for a long time that their house would be filled with the sounds of happy children and grandchildren.

He'd visited friends with cancer before. The feel of death hung in the air, and happiness had a hard time gaining ground. It was hard to imagine the Baxter house that way, hard to picture cancer coloring the place where they'd all shared so much love and laughter.

Ashley and Landon and Cole arrived next, and again John was taken aback by the joy in their eyes. Was it his imagination or were Ashley and Landon practically bursting about some sort of good news? John tried to imagine what it could be. Ashley had seen her doctor that week, but nothing he could've said would explain the way his daughter's eyes were dancing tonight.

Then again, maybe there was nothing new. Maybe this was simply the way the two of them looked now that Ashley wasn't running from love. John led them into the family room where Kari and Ryan and Jessie were waiting. At the same time, Brooke and Peter and the girls came through the front door.

"Hi, everyone!" Maddie skipped into the family room, a lop-sided grin plastered across her face. "Guess what? Hayley held her own cup today!"

Peter and Brooke came into view, pushing Hayley's wheel-chair. "Hi, Dad." Brooke looked back at Elizabeth in the kitchen. "Hi, Mom. Another good day at our house."

"That's good." Elizabeth smiled from her place near the Crock-Pot. The transformation had taken place. Her sorrow was gone, and her eyes no longer brimmed with tears. Instead she glowed the way she always glowed when her family was around her.

"Maddie's right." Brooke looked at the others in the room. "Hayley held a cup today. For the first time!"

Hayley was strapped to her wheelchair, but her eyes lit up when she saw the room full of people. She lifted her hand in a weak gesture and looked at John. "Papa . . ."

John felt a lump in his throat. All of this was new. Her quick recognition, her ability to say a few words, and now holding her own cup. All of it was proof that God would always have the last word when it came to life-and-death situations. After Hayley's accident, no one thought she would live. He himself had prayed that God would take her home so she wouldn't have to spend her life tied to a bed in a special facility somewhere.

But God and Hayley had surprised them all. First they'd real-ized she could see, even after they thought she was blind. And in the months that followed, she recognized the people she loved, learned to sit up and swallow food. Her tubes and wires were removed and she was able to go home.

Yes, the ordeal had been a strain on Peter and Brooke, but they'd all survived. Even though Hayley wasn't the same child she'd been before the accident, she was precious and full of love and improving a little more each month. She could even pull herself around on all fours in a semi-crawling motion.

John went to her, patting her head and kissing her golden hair. "Hi, Hayley. Papa's glad you came over."

She made a slow laughing sound, and Brooke parked her chair

along the edge of the family room. "Her doctor still doesn't know what to make of it." Brooke smiled and took Peter's hand. When he said nothing, she continued. "No, she's not improving as quickly as before. That worries Peter."

He nodded. "It does."

"But she's still getting better. That's enough for me."

Peter managed a smile. "Me, too. Every day is a gift with Hayley."

"Daddy . . ." Hayley looked at him, and though her mouth hung open, the corners lifted in a smile.

"I love you too, baby." Peter stooped down and kissed Hayley's cheek. Then he looked at John and shrugged. "How can I be anything but grateful?"

"Coley . . . Coley . . . Coley . . ." Maddie jumped across the room like a kangaroo and took Cole's hands. "Guess what, Coley. I learned a new clapping game at school. Wanna learn it, too?"

"Hey, Maddie, you're a good jumper." Cole crossed his arms and studied his cousin. Then he began jumping in circles around her. "Let's see who can jump the bestest of all."

Jessie scampered across the room and did her best imitation of her big cousins. "I jump, too!"

"Good, Jessie." Maddie held hands with her little cousin and they jumped together, all the while laughing at Cole, who was still jumping in circles around them.

John breathed in the joy of it all. If only they could stay in this moment forever and ever, never sit down to dinner and eat the meal and come to the dreadful part at the end where they had to tell the kids the truth about Elizabeth. Sorrow welled within him, threatening to overtake him, but he pushed it back.

The sadness would come later.

⚘

Ashley could hardly wait to tell them her news.

She'd known the truth for more than twenty-four hours, and

the waiting had weighed on her every minute. Still, it made sense to wait and tell her family when they were all together. She and Landon had told Cole about the July wedding date, and that Mommy was very healthy. But they hadn't told anyone else.

The dinner was wonderful as usual. Not just the food, but the news that their mother shared about Luke and Reagan, and Erin and Sam. "Luke has an internship at an entertainment-law office in Manhattan." Elizabeth set her fork down and smiled at the others. "He thinks he might focus on that aspect of law when he's finished with school."

Ashley watched her mother and frowned. Something wasn't quite right about her—the enthusiasm in her voice, maybe, or a lack of expression in her eyes. She shifted her gaze to her father, but he was busy eating, keeping his eyes downcast.

She felt her face relax. It was only her imagination. Her mother was probably tired after making the dinner. Or maybe she was caught up in the storytelling. Ashley focused on the details again.

"Tommy's pulling himself up, trying to walk." Her mother took a sip of water. "And Reagan is taking an online course that'll go toward her degree."

The three of them still lived with Reagan's mother in her Manhattan apartment. But the arrangement was working out fine. Reagan's mother had plenty of room, and it allowed Luke and Reagan to focus on their future and not on living month-to-month trying to make ends meet in New York City.

"Erin and Sam are a little worried about the baby." Again Ashley thought her mother looked concerned, and now she understood why. Things weren't well with Erin. "The birth mother is grumbling about wanting more money. Erin promised me she'd call the social worker if the woman made any unusual demands."

The conversation wore on, and finally when they were almost finished eating, Landon leaned around Cole and elbowed Ashley lightly in the ribs. He grinned at her, and her heart swelled. He was practically bursting with the news. "Tell them."

Kari was sitting next to Ashley. She gave them both a curious smile. "Tell us what?"

"The good news!" Cole waved his napkin in the air. "Mommy and Landon are getting married in July!"

Before anyone had time to react, Ashley held up her hand. "That's not the news, actually."

The room was quiet, the faces of her family members puzzled, expectant. Her father put his fork down. "Is it something your doctor told you? Something about your treatment?"

"Yes." Ashley fought back a sudden wave of tears. "I'm not HIV-positive. The new tests—" she hesitated, gathering her emotions—"the new tests show I'm negative. I don't have anything wrong with me at all."

Tears appeared in her mother's eyes immediately. Elizabeth's fingers came to her lips and she stared, as shocked as the rest of them. "Are you . . . are you sure, Ashley?"

She nodded. "I'm sure."

"Oh, dear God," Her mom closed her eyes and brought her hands together in prayer. "Thank you, Lord . . . thank you."

Ashley blinked back the wetness in her own eyes. She looked at her father. His head was bent, and he rubbed his brow with his fingertips. Ashley could barely make out what he was saying.

"A false positive. I can't believe it. I should've insisted you be seen by a specialist sooner. I should've thought of a false positive." His eyes met hers, and the mix of joy and pain there was enough to move Ashley from her chair to the spot between her parents.

"It's okay." Ashley no longer felt tears in her eyes. "It doesn't matter anymore."

"All this time." Brooke sat back in her chair, her eyes wide. "We should've taken you to the doctor ourselves."

Kari made a fist and placed it near her lips the way she might if she was covering her mouth before a cough. For a while she only looked at Ashley, her eyes saying everything her words could not. Finally she swallowed hard, stood, and circled to where Ashley stood. "I'm so glad, Ashley. So glad."

The two sisters hugged, and after a minute Brooke joined them. "No wonder you set a date."

Ryan was sitting next to Elizabeth. He reached up and took Ashley's hand. His eyes sparkled, and Ashley squeezed his fingers. They had always shared a special friendship, and once, a lifetime ago, they'd even considered becoming more than friends. But only for an afternoon. Ryan could never have loved anyone but Kari. He slipped his other arm around Jessie, but kept his eyes on Ashley. "A day hasn't gone by when I haven't prayed this would happen, Ashley." He released her hand and leaned back in his seat. "God is so good."

Cole was clinging to Landon. His expression told Ashley he was confused about the show of emotions, the strange things being said about HIV. He looked at Landon, his eyes big. "What's HYV, huh, Landon? What's negative?"

"HIV." He kissed Cole on top of his head. "And negative means Mommy's very healthy, honey. We don't have to worry about her getting sick."

Relief flooded Cole's face. Ashley, Kari, and Brooke returned to their seats, each of them continuing their words of congratulations and gratitude and agreeing that only God could've given Ashley this second chance at life.

"Does Luke know?" Her mother looked up from her place at the table, relief spilling from her eyes.

The mention of Luke's name brought another wave of emotion for Ashley. Her little brother, the one she'd been so close to growing up, the one she'd told first when she learned that she was HIV-positive. "No . . . not Luke or Erin. Let's call them later, okay?"

"So when's the big day?" Peter was seated next to Hayley's wheelchair. He'd been feeding her throughout the conversation, and as such he'd been quieter than the others.

But Ashley had caught the emotion on his face. Just a few years earlier he and Brooke hadn't believed in God or the power of prayer or the fact that miracles still happened. But now . . . now faith shone in his eyes as surely as it shone in the eyes of everyone around the table.

"July nineteenth." Landon looked at Ryan and then at Peter. "We want to be married by Pastor Mark at the church and have a reception at the club down by the lake."

"I want a floor big enough for everyone to dance on." Ashley grinned at her mother. "Even you and Dad, okay?"

A flicker of something sad shot through her mother's eyes, but it was gone before Ashley could analyze it. "Sounds like a beautiful wedding, dear."

"Yes." Her father put an arm around Mom. "We'll be the first ones on the dance floor, right after you and Landon."

The conversation splintered as the group talked about yet another wedding, their third in as many years. But even before the conversation died down, Kari stood up and waited until she had their attention.

Ashley listened, enjoying the feel of Landon's arm on her shoulders, the closeness of him and Cole, and the reality of the news she'd just shared. She tried to focus on her older sister.

"Now it's my turn." Kari smiled at Ryan and Jessie, and then at the others. "I have something I'd like to share also." She lifted one shoulder and looked straight at Ryan. "I figured what better time than now, when we're all together."

Ashley leaned forward, suddenly interested. The blank look on Ryan's face told her that whatever the news, he hadn't heard it yet.

Kari's smile became a grin as she looked around the room. "I took a test today, and I'm pregnant." She made a soft squealing sound and looked at Ryan again. "We're going to have a baby!"

The color drained slowly from Ryan's face, and his mouth dropped open. He rose slowly to his feet and put his hands on Kari's shoulders. "Are you serious?"

"Yes." She gave a quick nod of her head. "I tried to tell you this afternoon."

Ryan winced. "But I kept putting you off."

"That's okay." She hugged him, and for a while the two of them rocked, lost in each other's embrace.

"We're having a baby? We really are?"

Kari stroked the back of Ryan's head. "Yes. A Thanksgiving baby, if my dates are right."

"Kari, I can't believe it." He kissed her, and then just as quickly he pulled back. They both looked around the room. "Sorry. I forgot where I was for a minute."

Ashley laughed first, and then the others joined in. Jessie tugged on Ryan's sleeve. "What, Daddy, huh, what?"

Ryan swung her into his arms and bounced her a few times. "Mommy's going to have a baby, Jessie! Isn't that great?"

Jessie didn't look quite as happy as the others. She stared at Kari's flat stomach. "Is the baby in your tummy, Mommy?"

"Yep." Kari tousled her daughter's hair. "The baby will stay there for a long time."

"Where is he, Mommy? He's not very big."

Giggles sounded from the group again, and Cole asked if he and Maddie could go upstairs to play. The children were excused, with Maddie and Cole promising to look after Jessie. Hayley, of course, stayed in her wheelchair next to Peter.

It was the time Ashley most enjoyed about a dinner at the Baxter house. The time when the meal was finished and they were past sharing details of their lives. The time when they often brought up memories of days gone by, of silly times and funny stories, a time when it felt wonderful to be part of a family like theirs.

The scene after a Baxter dinner was one Ashley had painted before, one that appeared on a canvas that hung in her own dining room, where it would always hang. The painting had come together in a way that surprised Ashley. In it, the faces and emotions and hearts of her family members all seemed perfectly captured in an array of colors. In the background, a cross hung on the wall and from it emanated a light that cast warmth over the entire scene. The painting was a gift from God, one Ashley couldn't have duplicated if she'd wanted to.

Ashley loved that piece because it reminded her of all that was important in life. Not too many years back, she would've considered herself an outcast at a dinner like this one. But now . . . now she knew the truth. No matter how far she had wandered, the Baxters' love for each other would never die. The painting exuded that very love, and Ashley wouldn't have sold it for a million dollars.

Usually their mother would put the kettle on for coffee and the conversation would drift in a dozen different directions. But this time Ashley saw her mother and father leave the room together. Something was wrong; Ashley was sure of it. But she couldn't imagine what. Not after the good news they'd already shared tonight.

Ashley joined her sisters and the men in clearing the table and doing the dishes. The whole time, she seemed to be the only one who noticed that her parents were no longer in the room. Maybe nothing was wrong, after all. Maybe they had only stepped outside to revel in the wonderful turn of events that had presented themselves today.

Or maybe they were figuring out how to call Luke and Erin at the same time and share the news with them.

Whatever it was, it couldn't be bad news.

Not on a day when all of heaven seemed to have come together and smiled down on the Baxter family.

⚜

John held on to Elizabeth in the next room while her tears came.

"I can't tell them, not now."

They'd excused themselves at Elizabeth's prompting. The conversation had been going in circles ever since. Elizabeth didn't want to ruin the evening, didn't want to cast a shadow over the news that Ashley was well and Kari was pregnant.

Especially a shadow as dark as cancer.

But John was adamant. "The surgery's tomorrow; we have to tell them."

"Let's tell them afterwards."

"We can't do that, Elizabeth; you know we can't." He wanted nothing more than to agree with her, to let the kids go home reveling in all the good news. But they would never accept the idea that their mother had undergone such major surgery without their even knowing about it. "It'll be okay."

"It won't." She sniffed and dragged the back of her hand beneath her eyes. "It's not fair."

"No—" John gritted his teeth—"it's not. But it would be worse to keep the truth from them."

For a long while neither of them said anything, and John knew he'd won. He was the leader of this family, and Elizabeth respected him as such. When her crying subsided, he spoke in soft tones near the side of her face. "I'll tell them; all you have to do is go out there and stand beside me."

She squeezed her eyes shut, and after a few seconds she nodded. No matter how badly they wanted to avoid the next ten minutes, there was no way around it. "We've always shared the good and the bad, Elizabeth. The kids wouldn't want anything less."

"I know." She straightened herself and looped her arm through his. "Let's do it."

As soon as they entered the dining room, Ashley spotted them. When she saw Elizabeth's tearstained face, her expression changed, and she tapped her sisters until they, too, saw that something was wrong.

John cleared his throat. No matter how strong he looked, he was dying inside. Only the grace of God kept him from buckling to his knees. "Your mother and I have something to tell you." He gave them a sad smile. "It's the real reason we asked you to come tonight."

One at a time, the adult kids made their way toward John and Elizabeth. He led them into the family room, grateful the grandchildren were upstairs playing. Peter wheeled Hayley into the room and positioned her near the chair Brooke had taken. When they were all seated, John led Elizabeth to the front of the room, where they remained standing.

"Dad, what is it?" Ashley couldn't wait. Her face looked stricken. "Tell us."

John tightened his hold on Elizabeth and felt her lean against him. "Your mother found a lump in her breast a couple weeks ago. She . . . uh . . . she had some tests done and we found out the news Friday." His voice broke. "I'm sorry." He sucked in a strong breath and looked at the faces around him. "The cancer's back. Your mother has to have surgery tomorrow morning."

Brooke, Peter, Kari, Ryan, Ashley, Landon—the news worked its way across each face, until finally Brooke found her voice. "Are you having a mastectomy, Mom?" The words were calm, but the terror in her eyes was an expression of how they were all feeling.

John could feel their fear like a physical assault.

Quiet tears were streaming down Elizabeth's face. She squeezed John's hand, her signal that she couldn't talk, couldn't even lift her eyes to look at them. Not yet.

"Yes." John tried to think like a doctor, tried to remember his medical training and the way he'd been forced to give bad news to hundreds of patients over the years. "A double mastectomy. Dr. Steinman is hopeful that he'll get it all if they operate quickly."

John had expected a dozen questions, but the shock was simply too great. They couldn't ask a single question that would change the facts. Their mother had cancer. Serious cancer. And tomorrow morning she would have a double mastectomy in a desperate attempt to save her life.

What could they say?

Their father's announcement had said it all.

One at a time they stood and found their way across the room. Some with tears, some with quiet whispers, they circled their arms around Elizabeth and John until they were one—one group of people who would stand together, stay by each other and see Elizabeth through, no matter what happened after tomorrow.

They would survive whatever came because they were Baxters, and that's what Baxters did. They stuck together—believing, praying, supporting each other whether the news was glorious enough to sing about.

Or the worst news of their entire lives.

CHAPTER EIGHT

BEFORE EVERYONE LEFT, Elizabeth found the strength to make a three-way call to Erin and Sam, and Luke and Reagan. With tones marked by forced happiness, Ashley and Kari shared their news first. The response was of course positive, Luke especially finding reason to shout out loud when he heard that Ashley didn't have HIV.

Then John finished the call by telling them about Elizabeth's cancer. Elizabeth closed her eyes for that part, certain she could hear Erin crying in the background. Sam had to finish the call for her, and both he and Luke promised to call the next day for a report.

Finally, when the kids and grandkids had gone home, Elizabeth got ready for bed and climbed in beside John. "You were right."

He rolled onto his side, and with his fingers he brushed her hair back from her eyes. "About telling them?"

"Yes." She sighed. "John, tell me this isn't the end." She looked at him, searching for a glimmer of hope.

"We've talked about this." He looked tired, the strength he'd shown earlier long gone. "We beg Jesus for a miracle and we be-lieve it'll happen. Look what God's doing with Hayley." John's voice gathered some of his earlier strength. "We have to believe, Elizabeth. Otherwise we're doomed from the beginning."

She nodded and sank deeper into the sheets. "I keep thinking about him, wondering where he is now."

John leaned up on his elbow. "Thinking about who?"

"You know who." Her eyes found his and a knowing was there, a knowing even John couldn't deny. "Come on, John. Don't tell me you don't think about him."

He breathed out in a way that revealed a lifetime of regret. "I try not to. Until you brought him up the other day, it'd been years, Elizabeth. Four years, maybe."

Quiet settled around them. "I thought about him the night before Luke's wedding." She blinked, staring at the ceiling, see-ing images from that winter night in New York City. "It was snowing outside, remember?"

"You stayed up and wrote a poem for Luke."

"I said something that triggered my thoughts. I said it was hard knowing my only son was getting married." Her voice grew pinched and she shook her head. "Only he isn't. He is my second son. Luke will always be my second son, even if you and I are the only two people in the world who know the truth."

John let his head fall back on the pillow, his eyes still on her. "We tried, remember? Back when you were sick the last time."

"Yes." Elizabeth pinched the bridge of her nose and squinted, as if somehow she could see back to that time in their lives. "The answer was what we'd expected."

"The adoption was closed, sweetheart." His voice was tired again. "It would take a miracle to find him, honey."

"He could find us."

"But why would he? It's been thirty-five years. He wouldn't know you were sick or thinking about him."

Elizabeth nodded and the conversation died. Before long, John kissed her on the cheek. This was the last time they'd kiss good night before her surgery. The last time they'd share a bed together while she was still whole, before she was cut apart, her breasts taken away forever.

"Kiss me again, John. Please." She moved onto her side and stared deep into his eyes. She knew that everything in her heart was already in his.

"Elizabeth . . . this isn't the last time; you can't tell yourself that."

She searched his face, the familiar shape of his cheekbones, his strong jawline. "But it is, John." Her voice was softer than the sound of the wind outside. "In some ways it's the very last."

He didn't argue. Instead he took her face in his hands and kissed her. Not a kiss of anticipation or sudden desire, but a kiss that told her he wasn't being quite honest in what he said. A kiss that put a coda on a lifetime of physical love, a love that would be changed forever when morning came.

When it was over, tears shone in both their eyes. John's forehead fell against hers, his cheeks wet against her own. "God . . . Almighty God, we know what we're supposed to say."

She could feel him trembling beside her, hear the emotion in his voice. Her arm came around his waist and she held him, not sure which of them needed the other more as John continued praying.

"We're supposed to ask for you to make sure everything goes well tomorrow. We're supposed to be grateful and hopeful, but to be honest, right now, God, we're confused and not sure how to feel."

"We're scared to death," Elizabeth whispered.

"Okay, we're scared to death." John exhaled hard. "I wanted to be honest, and now I'll say the rest. God, give us a miracle. I pray the doctors get into that operating room and find they don't need to operate at all. I pray the cancer is gone and Elizabeth can go home free of this awful disease. If not, I pray you heal her quickly, and that the cancer hasn't spread." He hesitated. "We're begging you for a miracle, Lord. One more miracle for the Baxter family. Please."

John kissed her once more. This time their eyes were dry, and John breathed a good night against her cheek. "Believe, Elizabeth. Don't stop believing."

"I won't."

He was asleep in ten minutes, the way he often fell asleep before she did. Even now, when he had more pain in his heart than ever before, he could sleep. It was his trademark.

But Elizabeth could only stare at the dark ceiling and let herself drift back—back to that time when she and John first met. Back when they were forced to do something they never wanted to do.

She wasn't sure if she fell asleep and dreamed it, or if it only felt that way. However it happened, the years melted away until she was back in 1967, her freshman year at the University of Michigan. Yes, she'd been a home economics major, but when they'd told the story to their kids over the years, it always jumped from their meeting to their marriage. Only Elizabeth and John knew the truth. That a lot of living and hard lessons had taken place between those two events.

John was a med student, and the two of them met at a mixer the summer before her freshman year. The event was intended for all new or returning students.

The ironic thing was how it had all come together. John never should've been there; he was too old. But he'd been living with a family, and their oldest son was also a freshman that year. John had taken him as a favor to the guy's parents. It should've been a slow evening, a time of chaperoning and making sure the young man got home at a decent hour.

Instead, five minutes after John arrived, he spotted Elizabeth across the room.

She was talking with a group of freshmen girls. Elizabeth's family lived down the street from the university, so she wouldn't stay in a dorm like the other girls. Rather she would attend only an occasional social event on her way to earning something no other woman in her family had earned: a bachelor's degree.

"Don't talk to boys tonight," her mother had warned her when she finally gave her permission to go. One of her neighbors, a junior home economics major, was taking her to the mixer, the school's way of getting freshmen involved before the school year started.

"Mama . . ." Elizabeth remembered feeling embarrassed. She was certainly old enough to talk to boys. "I'm almost in college. Don't you think I should be able to talk to boys?"

"Not boys you don't know." Her mother pinched her lips together. "What have we always taught you, Elizabeth? Boys only want one thing. Don't forget it."

Elizabeth's family had attended a strict denominational church back then, a faction that didn't believe in loud music, merriment, or dancing. Definitely not dancing. In fact, if her mother had known there'd be dancing at the party that night, she would never have allowed Elizabeth to attend.

But the school had done a good job of advertising, careful as they were back in those days to make the event sound tame, almost a mandatory function of having a successful freshman year.

Elizabeth knew the junior girl who was taking her. The girl's family attended church with her own, and that, too, made Elizabeth's mother feel better about the event. Still, she worried. And so she sent Elizabeth with the final admonition: "Don't talk to boys."

The moment Elizabeth had climbed into the junior girl's car, she knew the night was going to be nothing like her mother pictured it. The girl, Betsy, wore a skirt that fell just above her knees, and on her lips was a cherry red color Elizabeth had never seen on her before.

"You know how to dance, Elizabeth?"

Elizabeth chuckled and gave a final glance over her shoulder at her parents' house "Sure don't."

"Well—" Betsy turned up the music and something with a loud beat filled the car—"you will after tonight."

And so it was that Elizabeth was standing with a few other freshman girls near the punch table when John walked up, smiled at her, and said, "Hi."

"Hi." She felt her cheeks grow hot and she looked around. He must have been talking to someone else, she figured. Someone older or prettier. But he stayed, and his eyes never left hers. "I'm Elizabeth."

"I'm John. John Baxter." He shrugged. "I'm too old to be here, but I brought my little brother."

"Really?"

"Well, not exactly." John leaned against the wall and studied her. Later he would tell her that it was a classic case of love at first sight. He'd dated girls before, but no one had ever taken his breath away until he met Elizabeth.

He explained his situation. He had no parents—his father died in the war, and his mother, a few years later of a broken heart. "I live with these friends of my mother's, a family we've known for a long time." He gestured across the room at a gangly young man helping himself to a plate of food. "That's Bill. He's the oldest son of the people I live with. I told 'em I'd show Bill around and make sure he got home safely."

"I see." Elizabeth felt suddenly shy. "What year are you?"

"I graduated last year. I'm about to be a second-year med student." He smiled. "Other than coming here tonight, I haven't been anywhere but the library, school, and home again for the past year."

"So how old does that make you?"

John grinned at her, searching her eyes. "Twenty-three. Why?"

"Just wondering." Elizabeth felt a sudden sense of daring. She wasn't supposed to talk to boys, and here she was chatting with a young man five years her senior. What would her mother think of that?

"And you?"

"Eighteen. I'll be a freshman."

John poured two cups of punch and handed one to her. "You'll love it. They take good care of freshmen at U of M."

"I hope so."

"You dormin' it?"

"No." Her mother's warning sounded in her mind again. "I live at home. My parents' house is a few blocks from the university."

"Good." He nodded and a silence fell between them. Then, without warning, he set his punch down and took her hand. "Come on, Elizabeth. Dance with me."

She still had her cup in her hand, and a shot of terror coursed through her body. The dance floor was full of couples, all of them enjoying the music. But she couldn't, could she? Her mother would have a fit if she found out, make her go before the elder board and confess her sins one at a time.

But then, her mother wasn't here.

A smile came across her face and she lifted her cup to her lips. In a single swallow, she finished the contents and tossed the cup in a nearby trash can. "Okay, but I have to warn you."

"What?" John's eyes sparkled as they met hers. "What warning could a girl as pretty as you possibly have for an old guy like me?"

She lifted her shoulders a few times and gave him a half smile. "I can't dance."

"You can't?" He seemed genuinely surprised. Then he laughed and pulled her out onto the dance floor. "I guess I'll have to teach you."

He spent the rest of the night doing just that. When the mixer was over, Elizabeth knew how to do a modified version of the Charleston and the jitterbug, and she could swing dance in her sleep. Her legs ached from all the dancing, and before they said good-bye, John asked for her number.

Her mother's warning came back again: *"Don't talk to boys, Elizabeth. Whatever you do, don't talk to boys."*

"Well . . . uh . . ." She felt her face getting hot again. "How 'bout if you give me your number." She stared at her sore feet, afraid to meet his eyes. "My mother doesn't like me getting calls from boys."

"She'd rather have you calling them?" His tone was light, and they both laughed. But he did as she asked, finding a piece of paper and writing his number on it. "The school has events every weekend from now till fall; you know that, right?"

Elizabeth had heard something about it, but she had no plans to go. "I'm not sure."

John explained that the university administrators wanted students to get involved with each other and the school activities. "There's a trip to Lake Michigan next weekend, with a bonfire on the beach. Then the weekend after that they've put together a bowling trip and movie night." He took her hands and looked straight to a part of her heart no one had ever seen before. "I'll go to every event if you'll be there."

The idea sounded like it might work. She took his number and bid him good-bye. On the way home she asked Betsy about the social events set up for the rest of the summer. "Yeah, they're a blast. I'll probably go to all of them."

"Could you call and invite me? And make sure my mom knows the invitation is coming from you."

Betsy raised her eyebrow. "I saw you talking with that tall, dark, and handsome med student. Every girl in the room had her eye on him."

"They did?"

"Yes, but you wouldn't know—" Betsy gave Elizabeth a friendly poke—"because the two of you never took your eyes off each other."

By the time Betsy dropped her at home, the plan was in stone. Betsy called later that week and talked to her mother. Yes, the events were chaperoned; yes, she'd keep an eye on Elizabeth. No, she didn't think Elizabeth had talked to any boys at the mixer. Yes, she'd be sure to keep an eye on her at future events also.

"You understand, right?" Elizabeth heard her mother tell Betsy on the phone. "Elizabeth's a good girl, but she's very pretty. I'm not sure she knows how pretty she is, but the boys know. The last thing her father and I want is for Elizabeth to get mixed up with a boy. She needs to finish college first."

Elizabeth was mortified that her mother would speak that way about her to an older girl like Betsy. But in the end the plan worked beautifully. The next weekend students met at the west end of the university parking lot and caravanned to the beach. Elizabeth rode with Betsy to the meeting place. But she took the two-hour drive to the shore sitting beside John Baxter.

"This is the craziest thing I've ever done," she told him that day. The window was down and a warm breeze played in her hair. "I can't believe I'm riding in a car with you to Lake Michigan. My mother would die."

John told her later that he felt bad sneaking around the way they did those early weeks. But he was so taken by her that he'd lost his ability to think straight. That evening, after a day of playing in the surf and lying in the sun, she and John took a walk along the beach instead of attending the bonfire.

When the group was far enough in the distance, he stopped and turned to her. "Elizabeth, do you feel something?" His voice was smooth, gentle as the breeze off the lake.

Her heart pounded so loud she was sure he could hear it. "Feel what?"

"This." John took her hand and placed it on his heart.

Beneath her fingertips she felt a strong thudding, almost as if John had just finished a race or run up three flights of stairs. "Your heart, John? What is it?"

He lowered her hand but kept his fingers intertwined with hers. "It's you. It's how I feel when I'm with you. Like all the world could go away and I'd be the happiest man alive. Just standing here looking at you for the rest of my life."

"I . . . I don't know what to say."

"Feel yours." He nodded to her. "Go on, Elizabeth; feel it."

And she did. She reached up and placed her hand over her own heart. And sure enough, the hard, fast beating she'd felt when she touched his was the same in her heart now. Elizabeth studied John, the moonlight casting shadows on their faces. "What does it mean?"

Without saying another word, he closed the distance between them, took her gently in his arms, and careful not to press his body against hers, he kissed her.

She knew two things after that. First, she understood why her heart was beating so fast. It was because in less than a week she'd fallen in love with John Baxter. And second, she knew why her mother had warned her not to talk to boys. Because after kissing John, she didn't care about college or getting home on time or anything else her mother had ever told her.

All she wanted was to stand there forever, kissing John and getting lost in his eyes.

CHAPTER NINE

THE DREAM WAS only half over.

Elizabeth willed it to continue, willed herself to remember every part of their past—the height of their love for each other and the depth of their despair when their choices changed everything for both of them.

Her clandestine dates with John had continued. Always she would drive off with Betsy and get five minutes of lecture from the girl. "You're falling too hard for him, Elizabeth. He's too old for you. You need to spread yourself around a little, make some girlfriends . . ."

Elizabeth barely listened.

Once they arrived at each event's meeting place, she was with John every minute until it was time to go home. She was falling madly in love with John, experiencing feelings she'd never known existed. But she could share none of it with her mother or father, because they knew nothing of what was happening.

By the end of August, she found other ways to meet up with John. She'd claim to be going to the university to find her way around campus. "Mom, you know how hard it'll be to get to classes if I'm not familiar with the layout of campus."

Her mother had a perpetual worried look back then. She frowned. "Maybe I could take you around, help you find your way."

"No, Mom." Elizabeth tried to keep her tone light. "I'll ride my bike and explore on my own. That way I won't need your help on the first day of school." She patted her mother's hand. "I am in college, now, Mama."

Her mother agreed, even if it was reluctantly.

But Elizabeth never had any intention of making her way around campus. Instead she'd ride her bike to the corner store, where John would be waiting. They'd lock up her bike and take off in his car for some destination just off campus. They'd stroll arm in arm through the streets, visiting eclectic shops and sharing kisses in the parking lot before and after every outing.

"What are we going to do when school starts?" John was breathless after kissing her one afternoon. "I need to see you, Elizabeth."

Her feelings for him frightened her. "We have school, John. I guess we'll have to find time afterwards." And then she had an idea. "I could say I have to study at the library, and we could meet that way."

They agreed. One day they met at the store and drove to All-mendinger Park a few blocks off campus. They walked through a grove of stately oaks, holding hands, until they were hidden from the traffic on the nearby street.

John had seemed restless, more anxious than usual. When they stopped against a thick tree, he pulled her close and kissed her. As always he was careful to keep space between them. "Guess what?"

"What?" She didn't want to talk. She wanted to kiss him. Now, before they headed off for the afternoon and wouldn't have another chance like this one.

"The people I live with are gone this week. They went to Mackinac Island; they won't be back until Saturday."

"John?" Fear grabbed hold of her and shook her hard. She

trusted him, but there was something in his eyes she couldn't quite read. "What are you saying?"

"Nothing!" He chuckled and rubbed his palms on his jeans. "Don't get the wrong idea, Elizabeth. I was only thinking we could go there and watch a little TV, maybe play some cards. Have a little time alone before you had to go home."

In the years since then, whenever they talked about that summer, Elizabeth and John both knew they should've seen it coming. Two young people in love? Sneaking around behind her parents' back, and thinking that somehow they could spend the better part of a week in a house by themselves? without anything happening?

The plan was doomed from the start.

Still, on the first day nothing happened. They held hands and watched television, and John talked to her about his plans of becoming a doctor. All he'd ever wanted was to help people get well, to maybe discover some great new way of making people healthy.

Elizabeth shared her dreams also. She wanted to go to college but only so she could please her parents. Her real dream was to raise a big family. "A whole houseful of kids." She smiled at him. "I guess that's why I picked home economics as my major. At least my degree will make me a good wife and mother."

John admitted later that when she shared her heart with him that day, he knew there was no turning back. No matter what happened, he would marry Elizabeth, and whether her mother ever liked him or not didn't matter.

The second day alone in the house was worse than the first. They watched TV again, but they ran out of things to talk about. Not because they had nothing to say to each other but because they didn't want to talk. They wanted to kiss.

It was just before noon when they started kissing on the living-room sofa, and sometime after one before they looked at the clock again. They'd gone farther than they'd wanted to, farther than Elizabeth had dreamed of going. But they hadn't given in to their feelings entirely.

Elizabeth went home that night and stared at the mirror. She was so mad at herself she spat at her reflection. No wonder her mother had warned her about boys. Not because of what a boy would do if she ever got close to one. But because of what she herself was capable of.

She swore when she went to bed that she was finished lying to her parents, finished sneaking off to share an afternoon alone with John in an empty house. She even prayed about it, begging God to forgive her for the awful person she'd become and asking him to give her strength.

In later years Elizabeth had used the lessons she learned that week as a teaching tool for her own children. "God doesn't want you to be stronger than temptation," she'd told each of her five kids at one time or another. "He wants you to be smarter than it." She'd show them the verse in Scripture that advised people to flee temptation, not stick around and try to bargain with it.

But that summer Elizabeth had figured she could bargain just a bit longer. The next day she couldn't stop herself. She was rattling off another lie, getting on her bike, and riding off to meet John before she remembered even a single promise she'd made to herself the night before.

This time, John didn't turn on the television. He took her to his bedroom and showed her a stack of letters his father had written to his mother while he was fighting in World War II.

"He was a true hero, John," Elizabeth said after she'd read most of them. "His love for your mother was amazing."

"Yes." John stacked the letters back in a box and closed the lid. "That's the way I want to love my wife someday, with all my heart and mind and soul."

Elizabeth was suddenly nervous, sitting there on the edge of John's bed. She recalled the way she'd felt the day before, the contempt she had for herself after the compromises she'd made with John. "Let's go back to the TV room."

John agreed easily, and she relaxed some. He wasn't trying to seduce her, wasn't trying to put her in an uncomfortable situation. He only wanted to share something about his past with her.

They returned to the TV room, but nothing was on. For a while they played cards, but then he took her hand and told her how much he'd miss her once school started. "I'll be busy. Second year med school is tough. I'll be lucky if I can meet you at the library once a week."

"At least we'll have that time."

Before Elizabeth knew what was happening, their words fell away and they started kissing again. Only this time, they couldn't stop, couldn't bring themselves to find a voice of reason amidst the shouts of temptation.

Even now Elizabeth remembered the ways she convinced herself that afternoon. *I'm going to marry him one day, anyway . . . what's the difference if we have this time together? . . . We'll be apart soon enough, right? Besides . . . we'll stop before it's too late; I know we will.*

All of it, every word, was a lie.

They could no sooner stop themselves from giving in completely that afternoon than they could stop breathing. They had thought they could outwit temptation, but they were wrong.

That evening when she got home, she was sure the truth was written all over her face. She wasn't a virgin anymore, and she couldn't imagine ever showing her face to John Baxter again.

The next day she didn't meet him, couldn't let him see her the way she had become: cheap and easy and completely without virtue.

When she didn't show up at the store, John came to her house. He knocked on the door and when her father answered, he introduced himself as a friend of Elizabeth's.

She heard the conversation as she sat, terrified, at the end of her bed. Whatever John was doing, things would never be the same again with her parents. The strangest part of all was that

Elizabeth wasn't sure whether to run for her life or dart into the next room and throw her arms around John's neck.

John explained to her parents that he had met Elizabeth at a school function and fallen in love with her. Then he said the thing that stopped Elizabeth's heart in its place. "I'd like to ask your permission to marry her."

Her mother was the first person to speak. "My daughter has said nothing about you, Mr. Baxter. I'm sure this is all some kind of mistake. She's been told not to talk to boys, and especially not young men like you—"

"Wait a minute."

Elizabeth cringed. The voice belonged to her father, a man who made her mother look lenient.

Her father's voice filled the room. "Have you put my daughter in a compromising position?"

A compromising position? Elizabeth buried her head in her hands. *Don't say it, John . . . don't say it . . . don't tell them.*

He didn't. Instead he only insisted that he'd fallen in love with her and he wanted to marry her. In the end, her father threw him out of the house before Elizabeth could say hello or even see him.

That night her father told her she was never to spend time with John Baxter again. "You're a college girl, Elizabeth. You need to focus on your studies."

The next day Elizabeth left the house on her bike without asking. She planned to call John as soon as she got to the store, but she didn't have to. He was already there waiting for her. She fell into his arms, climbed into his car, and went with him back to the house where he lived. This time they both knew what they were doing, and they did it anyway.

John had told her several times in the decades since then that his actions were completely wrong, beyond reason. But without her parents' permission, he could hardly marry her. And without marriage, he had no idea how they'd ever love each other the way they were desperate to love each other.

Back then John hadn't been a believer. His father had talked about having a strong faith, a belief in Jesus Christ, but not his mother. Until the day she died, she blamed God for taking her husband, for leaving her son without a father.

John fell somewhere in the middle.

The faith of his father had intrigued him, but he couldn't remember ever attending a church service or reading a Bible. All of that changed the day early that semester when Elizabeth called with the news.

She was pregnant and terrified.

"Where are you?" John's voice shook with fear. "I'll come get you, Elizabeth. We'll run off and get married on our own."

"No! We can't do that, John. My parents would disown me. Besides, how would we live?"

"I could . . . I could quit school and get a job at the market. I could work two jobs, three jobs, if I had to."

"No, John." The tears had come then. "Listen to yourself! You want to be a doctor. That's your dream. I know we'll be together somehow; you know it, too. But we need my parents' help. They can let us get married and let you move in here with me. You can finish med school, and I'll stay in class until the baby comes. They'll have to understand."

"Elizabeth, no. You can't tell them."

She struggled to find the words. Ever since getting the test at the campus clinic, she'd walked around in a fog. She felt dead as she spoke. "That's exactly what I'm going to do. I'll tell them I'm pregnant and that we want to get married. Then I'll call you and tell you what they said."

Even now Elizabeth felt certain her parents had wanted to kill her that afternoon. They were horrified, disgusted, and embarrassed, and they said as much. "What will my church friends think, young lady?" Her mother kept her distance, as if maybe Elizabeth's promiscuity, even her pregnancy, might be contagious.

"Mom, this isn't about you. I fell in love, and I want to marry

John. He wants to marry me; he told you that when he came by that day."

Her father stood, then, and made a pronouncement. There would be no wedding, no son-in-law moving in with them to flaunt the fact that he'd gotten their virgin daughter pregnant.

"You will go away to a girls home in Indiana. I heard about it through a friend at work." Her father glared at her. "You will have the baby, then return to Ann Arbor and get on with your classes. At that point, all of us will carry on as if none of this foolery ever happened in the first place."

"Foolery?" Elizabeth shrieked at her father. "I love John Baxter, Daddy. I want to marry him, and I want to have his baby."

"Stop it!" Her father had never raised a hand to her, but in that moment he did. He stopped short of slapping her, but his face was red, and his voice shook with rage. "You'll go away, have the . . . the child." He spat the word *child,* as if it tasted poisonous on his tongue. "You'll give the baby up for adoption, come home, and forget the entire incident ever happened."

"It's my baby, Daddy. I don't want to give it up!"

"Then the two of you will be homeless together. I will not have you raising that man's child in this house."

By the end of the evening, Elizabeth had agreed to her father's plan. Not because she wanted to but because she had no strength left to fight him, and no option that seemed workable on its own.

That night she called John and told him their relationship was over. She had no choice but to do what her parents wanted, nowhere else to turn. John tried to discourage her, but he had no viable options either.

In the end, they both agreed the solution was a terrible one. But it was also their only one. She left the following week and spent nine months at the girls home. Though it was the worst season in her life, something wonderful came of it. She found a relationship with Jesus.

Prior to her time in Indiana, Elizabeth had only borrowed her beliefs from her parents. Theirs was a stuffy, legalistic faith and never one that Elizabeth owned deep in her heart. But those lonely months, missing John and knowing she'd made the wrong choice by leaving, she had no one but God to turn to.

She wasn't allowed phone calls out, and John wasn't allowed to call her. But he wrote, and once in a while one of the women who ran the place would sneak one of his letters to her instead of ripping it up, as her parents had instructed them to do with any letters from John Baxter.

In his letters, John expressed a similar revelation. "I've discovered a peace I never knew before," he told her. "Whatever we do when this is over, Elizabeth, we must always put God first. We were wrong for being together the way we were, but I was wrong most of all. Jesus wants me to know him before I can love you the way you deserve to be loved."

Elizabeth bore a healthy baby boy. He had blond hair and his father's muscular frame. Elizabeth was allowed to hold him for just one hour before he was taken away. She wanted desperately to call John, to let him hear his son's soft cries, to describe for him the way he looked with his beautiful skin and clear blue eyes.

But she wasn't allowed, so she memorized his face, his features, his newborn cry. Memorized all of it so she could tell John about him when they saw each other again. Then she prayed over the baby, begging God to give him a loving home with loving parents. "If it be your will, Lord, let me meet him one day. Please, God . . ."

When they took him from her arms, Elizabeth wept for the rest of the day. The ache of losing him was so strong she thought she might die from the pain. Two months later, when she was fully recovered—or at least physically recovered—she was sent home. Her parents tried to seem happy about her return, but Elizabeth didn't want anything else from them.

She had changed in the time she'd been gone, grown closer to God and farther from her parents. Somewhere out in the world was a little boy who belonged to her and John, a child she would never get to raise or hold or love. A child who would never know her. And all because her parents hadn't wanted their church friends to see their daughter pregnant.

The entire situation was a tragedy, and Elizabeth didn't wait one hour after returning home before calling John. They met at the library and found a quiet alcove where they could be alone, away from the curious glances of other students. Elizabeth had disappeared, after all. And now it was late July and she'd showed up again. Anyone who knew them could do the math and figure out what had happened.

Alone in the library that day, John held her and wiped away her tears and listened as she told him about the baby. John still had a lot of schooling to finish, but he'd gotten permission from the family he lived with so he could marry Elizabeth and have her live with him there, at least until he finished school.

And that's exactly what they did.

In a ceremony attended by very few people, and avoided by her parents, John and Elizabeth were married on August 22, 1968, a little over a year after they'd met. On their first night as husband and wife, they prayed that God would always be at the center of their marriage. And they asked him to help them never again think of the blond, blue-eyed boy they'd given up.

For most of the next four years they kept to their bargain. Then in 1972—after they'd found a small place of their own near the university—they had Brooke. In the hospital after delivering her, Elizabeth said just one thing, one thing that told both of them she never forgot the baby she gave away. "I'm glad it's a girl."

"Me too."

"Because a boy would remind me of everything I gave up."

Sometime after Brooke was born, Elizabeth's parents found them. They apologized for what they'd done, and the two families made peace. But Elizabeth knew they would never understand the price she'd paid for their lack of compassion.

The years passed, and girl after girl after girl came into the Baxter family. Elizabeth figured God wasn't going to give them a boy. He'd already done that, and she'd given him up. In the recesses of her heart, in a place she never shared with anyone, not even John, she wondered if maybe God was withholding a boy from them as his way of punishing her, reminding her that what she'd done was wrong.

But in 1980 she delivered Luke, their fifth and final child. A boy who looked exactly like the child she'd given birth to while living at the girls home in Indiana. In the hospital Elizabeth held him out for John to see. "Now you know, John."

He gave her a blank look. "Now I know what?"

"Now you know what we gave away. The baby I had all those years ago looked exactly like this one."

From the beginning, they felt Luke was a special blessing from God. Not that each of the girls wasn't special. They were. But Luke seemed to fill the aching places in both their hearts, the places that still longed for the son they'd given up, the places that still wondered where he was and how he was doing.

They settled in Bloomington when John took a job at the university hospital there. Only once did they ask themselves if maybe they'd taken a job in Indiana hoping that somehow they'd run across the son they gave up. It was strange, really. Of all the places they could live in the United States, only Indiana felt like home, so there had to be something to their thoughts.

After Luke's birth, they had an easier time keeping their promise, and only rarely did the subject of their firstborn son come up. They agreed that their children didn't need to know about the past—how rough a start their parents had as a couple, how they had a brother out there somewhere who knew nothing about them.

Not telling them had been a good choice—one Elizabeth and John never wavered from. The adoption had been closed. None of their children would have the right or the ability to find their older brother. Better to believe he hadn't existed at all, to convince themselves never to look back at that time in their lives. Nice to imagine that God had placed him in exactly the home he was supposed to be placed, to believe that he hadn't ever been theirs but the other couple's.

Still, there were times when Elizabeth was eighteen again, when she could feel that baby boy in her arms, see his expression, his eyes, and know that the longing in her heart would never go away completely. Times when she could feel that woman taking her baby from her arms, sense the immediate separation, see her turn her back and walk out of the room, and—

"Stop!" Elizabeth sat straight up in bed, her heart racing, chest heaving. "Bring him back here! He's mine, bring him back right now!"

John was awake instantly. He sat up and put his arm around her shoulders. "Honey . . . shhh. You're dreaming."

Her eyes darted around the room, searching for the door. "Get him, John, before it's too late."

John took hold of her arm and gave her a soft shake. "Elizabeth, wake up. You're dreaming, honey."

She blinked and slowly she felt herself ease back against the headboard. John was right. It had all been only a dream, a walk through time that led her back to the place where it all happened, to the moment when they took her baby from her.

And even now—hours before a cancer surgery that could signal her season of death—it felt like no time at all had passed. He was out there somewhere, wasn't he? The baby she'd given up. Closed adoption or not, there had to be a way to find him. Or a way for him to find her.

Elizabeth remembered all the work they'd done in the early nineties, back when she'd fought cancer the first time. They'd tracked down every loose thread, every connection, every person who might've known something about the adoption. Every door had led to a dead end, and they promised each other they'd never waste their time on such futility again.

"If we ever find him, it'll be because he finds us," John had said.

He was right back then, and he was still right now.

John was lying down again, already asleep. When she eased herself beneath the covers, a thought hit her. There was something she could do after all. She could pray. The same God who knew her and loved her and had a plan for her that went beyond the double mastectomy scheduled for the morning also knew and loved her firstborn son.

It was too late for building a mother-son relationship with the boy. He was thirty-five years old now. But it wasn't too late to make peace with him, to tell him how sorry she'd been to give him up, to see for herself that God had, indeed, taken care of him.

God alone knew where her boy was at that exact moment.

Suddenly, with an excitement that defied the situation, Elizabeth prayed a prayer she'd uttered thirty-five years ago: *If it be your will, Lord, let me meet him again someday. Please, God . . .*

She thought about the surgery she faced in a few hours.

And please, God, let it happen soon.

CHAPTER TEN

THEY HAD THIRTY MINUTES until the surgery—thirty minutes for John to ease his wife's fears, thirty minutes until life between them would change for a long, long while.

Maybe forever.

Elizabeth had been prepped, and now she was lying on a gurney, waiting for the moment when someone from the surgical team would come for her. So far, she hadn't wanted to talk about the surgery.

"Did you see the look in Ashley's eyes last night?" Elizabeth's hands were folded across her waist, her voice pleasant, as if they weren't in a fluorescent-lit hospital room waiting for her double mastectomy but rather enjoying a lazy Monday morning conversation.

John tried to focus. "She's loved Landon for a long time."

"Yes." Elizabeth's eyes shone. "But not as long as he's loved her." She pressed out the wrinkles in her sheet. "First the news about her health, then the wedding plans. As if God looked down on them and in a single day opened the way for all their dreams to come true."

The clock on the wall showed a steady march of time. Twenty-five minutes left. Just twenty-five. John squinted at her, trying to remember what she had said. The wedding, right? Yes, Ashley and Landon's wedding. He placed his hand on her arm. "The wedding will be beautiful."

"They're going to be happy. Don't you think, John?"

"Of course." John's heart beat harder than before. This wasn't the conversation he wanted to have with his wife, not now. Didn't she know how difficult the surgery would be? Hadn't she been listening when the doctor told her that, combined with her treatment, it could be months before she felt good again?

"Landon's right for her. Don't you think?"

"Yes, dear." John ran his fingers along her brow and gave her shoulder a gentle squeeze. The clock kept ticking. Twenty minutes until surgery. John gritted his teeth. There was still so much more he wanted to say. "Landon's perfect for her; he always has been."

"And Kari . . ." Elizabeth's eyes grew distant, her smile soft and warm. "I hope they have a boy. I think Ryan would do so well with a boy. Not that he isn't wonderful with little Jessie, because he is; in fact did you see him yesterday? Right after dinner Jessie—"

"Elizabeth." John stopped himself. He hated the frustration in his tone, hated the fact that he couldn't let her talk about the kids if she wanted to. But the minutes were disappearing and he still had so much to say. His eyes found hers, and he looked past the surface details, deep to where she was scared to death about whatever the next four hours held. His tone grew softer, kinder, and he gave a slight shake of his head. "I don't want to talk about the kids. The kids are fine; they're all fine."

Elizabeth hesitated for a minute and her eyes grew damp. Then she turned and faced the window. "We haven't talked about the reunion, John. I was looking online the other day, and I think Sanibel is a good choice. Maybe a few weeks before Ashley's wedding. We can fly into Fort Myers and take a shuttle to the island. I've always wanted an island vacation, John; you know that, right?"

He opened his mouth to speak, but she was still looking the other direction, and she didn't let him answer.

"Condominiums are reasonable along the shore, and the surf is gentle enough for the little ones." She barely paused to take a breath. "There's a dolphin cruise that leaves from the South Seas Resort on Captiva Island, about a half hour from Sanibel, so that would be something everyone could—"

"Stop." This time John stood and waited until she looked at him again. "If you want a reunion, we'll have one. Fine. But please, Elizabeth—" he took her hand in his and willed his eyes to stay dry—"please can we talk about it later?"

"Fine, John." Her tone was sharp, the way it never was with him. "What do you want to talk about? The surgery? Would you like to talk about the process of a double mastectomy and how I'll feel when I don't have my breasts anymore? Maybe I should tell you that every smell, every sound in this place reminds me of giving birth, of coming here because life was new. Not because it was ending."

The lines around her eyes and forehead relaxed, and the anger left her voice. "I'm sorry, John, but really, what point is there in that? I don't want to talk about how I'll look or feel after the surgery. I want to talk about last night's dinner and the kids and our summer reunion, because God alone knows whether I'll feel up to talking about it come tomorrow. I want this last hour to be normal, okay? Just me and you the way we've always been."

"But it's not normal." His eyes stung. "I want to know how you're feeling, and I want to tell you how wonderful you are, how brave. That you're the only woman I've ever loved and that our children are the adults they've become because of your unwavering faith and commitment. I want to hold your hand and listen to your fears and have you believe that whatever you go through after today, I'll be by your side."

"John . . ." Tears slipped out of the corners of her eyes and trickled down the sides of her face. "You were the first boy I ever talked to, and nothing could've kept me from you. Nothing. I've loved you with all my heart, all my being, for thirty-five years, the same way you've loved me." A sad smile played on her lips, and her eyes stayed connected with his. "Don't you think I know how much you love me? Or that you think the world of me? I don't need—" she gestured at the hospital bed and machinery around her—"I don't need a last-minute hospital scene to know what I've known all these years. Do you understand that?"

He bit his lip, holding the tears at bay. "Are you afraid?"

"Yes." The word was a tortured whisper. Her eyes searched his and for the first time today he saw a hint of the terror she was hiding. "Of course I'm afraid." She dabbed at her tears and looked at the ceiling. "I'm afraid I won't have the energy to take walks down by the stream with Cole or to play Barbies with Maddie. I'm afraid I'll spend my days throwing up and watching my hair fall out and that when nighttime comes, I'll be too tired and sick to make love to you." She covered her mouth with her fingers for a moment, struggling for control. "Yes, I'm afraid. Is that what you want to talk about?"

"Yes. Because it's real." John felt worse than before, but at least they were being honest. That had to be better than surface talk about the kids or some far-off summer reunion.

"Why?" She pointed at the clock, her tone frustrated again. "I have ten minutes until they come and get me. Why should we spend it borrowing pain from tomorrow?"

"Because." He pulled her fingers to his lips and kissed each of them, one at a time.

"Because why?"

"Because . . ." He drew back and studied her, the way she looked whole and alive and beautiful. "Because I'm scared, too. I want you to know. No matter how strong I act or seem or come across, I'm terrified of this, Elizabeth." He stared at her hands and slowly brought his eyes up past the curve of her chest to her eyes again. "I can't lose you."

As soon as his words were out, her expression softened. "John . . . my love." She reached up, framing his face with her hands, barely touching him. "Why didn't you say so?"

He gave her a lopsided grin. "I tried, but you know how it is, Elizabeth. I couldn't get a word in edgewise."

"John, I'm sorry." She held out her hands. "Come lie with me? Please."

With practiced ease he released the latch on her bed rail. When it was down, he stretched himself out next to her on the gurney and held her close. "Fight this thing, okay? I need you; we all need you."

"I will."

They held on to each other, saying nothing this time, nothing about their fears or the fact that this was the last time they'd be together before she began the fight for her life. Nothing about all they had to lose and all they'd enjoyed together up until this point.

They simply held on, as if minutes and doctors and surgeries might be put at bay if only they never let go. But the minutes dropped away one at a time, and John heard the door open. He didn't turn around, didn't acknowledge that anyone had entered the room.

He tightened his hold on Elizabeth. "Come back to me, okay?"

"Okay."

"I'll be here." He pressed his fingers to her heart. "No matter what happens, I'm with you."

She pressed her face against his. "Pray, John."

"I will. As long as it takes, I'll be praying."

Then with every bit of his remaining strength, John slid himself off the gurney, nodded to the members of the surgical team, and stepped aside. The two men took hold of the gurney and one of them nodded at John. "Dr. Baxter, we'll let you know as soon as we're finished."

"Call my pager; I'll be in my office."

The last thing John saw before they wheeled Elizabeth from the room was her eyes, deep and beautiful and frightened and accented with a glimmer of peace, a knowing that somehow, regardless of the outcome, God was in control. The way God had always been in control of their lives no matter what they faced.

And that glimmer of peace gave John the slightest sense of hope as he watched them take her around the corner toward the operating room. At Elizabeth's request, the kids were all waiting by their phones—not crowding the waiting room the way they wanted to. She told them not to worry; the surgery was routine. She'd talk to them afterwards. But the truth was something she'd told John the night before; she wanted to spend her waking hours today with him alone.

John walked, dazed, toward his office. It was a small, boxy room where he worked one day a week, overseeing hospital care and outlining release plans for his many patients.

The staff knew why he was here today, so only a few people did more than nod at him. Most looked the other way, giving him the space he needed to deal with the matter at hand. He entered his office, closed the door behind him, and did the only thing he knew to do.

He dropped to his knees, bowed his head, and let the sorrow come. Then he lifted Elizabeth to the God who had created her, the God who loved her and wanted his best for her. The God who was somewhere in this room, weeping right along with him.

❧

As they wheeled her into the operating room, Elizabeth folded her arms over her chest and cupped her hands along the sides of her breasts. It was still impossible to believe that in a few hours she'd wake up in a recovery room and they'd be gone. But sometime during the night, in the midst of her dreaming and remembering and praying about her firstborn, she'd found a peace about the surgery.

So she'd lose her breasts.

If she had to trade them for a life with John and her children, she would do it gladly. She would've given her arms and legs if it meant she'd have a ringside seat to see the story of their lives play out, year after year after year.

She wanted to see Ashley and Landon marry, and watch Cole thrive under the direction of a daddy. She wanted to hold Kari's new baby and cradle the child Erin and Sam were adopting. Certainly there would be more children in the season ahead. Luke would find a job and Reagan would finish school, and one day, if they chose to adopt, Tommy would have brothers and sisters. Same with Ashley and Landon, and Kari and Ryan.

Every Christmas there'd be more Baxter babies in the family photo, and Elizabeth didn't want to watch it happen from a window in heaven. She wanted to be here, to hold the babies and help her children get through the early years of parenting.

More than that, she wanted to see the next round of weddings. She wanted to sit beside John when Maddie and Cole and Hayley got married. Because Hayley would get married one day; Elizabeth was sure. Hayley would get better each year and eventually she'd be right there with her peers, walking and talking and learning as if she'd never spent twenty minutes underwater in a backyard pool.

Elizabeth wanted to see it all, feel it all, taste it all. Hold John's hand while it all played out before her. If losing her breasts was the price she had to pay to live that long, then so be it.

A team of people were working on her now, checking her intravenous line, measuring the dose of anesthetic.

"Elizabeth, we're going to give you something to put you to sleep, okay?"

"Okay." She pressed her hands against the sides of her chest again and closed her eyes. Memories flashed at her, the times when she'd cradled a crying baby against her breast or sat up in the wee hours nursing. A sigh came from the depths of her soul, and she blinked her eyes open. "I'm ready."

"All right, then." The young man tending to her was kind, his voice calm and reassuring. "I need you to lay your arms out straight, nice and relaxed."

She did as she was asked. *God . . . be with me. Take my breasts, but give me my life. Please, God . . . I'm not ready to die. Please . . .*

"Okay, you'll start to feel yourself getting warm and heavy." The young man slipped a dose of medication into her IV tubing. "Just relax, now. Try to count to ten for me, all right?"

"One . . ." *Please, God . . . be with me.* "Two . . ." *Let me live; let them get it all, please.* "Three . . ." *Be with John; he's so afraid that I'll . . .*

That was as far as she got.

Sleep claimed her. The last thought she had before going under was not about all she was losing this morning on the operating table. But it was about all she would get in return.

If only God might let her live.

CHAPTER ELEVEN

THE CALL CAME sometime after one o'clock. While her mother was in surgery, Erin hadn't eaten, hadn't done anything but clean the house and pray, begging God with every breath that the surgery would leave her mother free of cancer. Forever this time.

Her father had promised a phone call the moment he knew anything, and so far there'd been no word. So when the phone rang, she dropped the Windex and a roll of paper towels and raced for the kitchen.

"Hello?" She was breathless, wishing she could've found a way to be at the hospital instead of so far away.

"Very nice." A man chuckled on the other end. "You must've been waiting for my call."

At first Erin didn't recognize the voice. But as soon as she did, a chill ran down her spine and she shuddered. She grabbed the nearest chair and sat down. "Who is this?"

Another chuckle. "It's your good friend Dave." He cleared his voice and made a mocking attempt at sounding more official. "Oh, that's right; you know me as the birth father."

Erin clenched her teeth. "If you're looking for my husband, he's at work. You'll have to call back later."

"Listen—" his tone was suddenly gruff—"I'm a busy man, okay? You tell your hubby we're still a little short on cash; got it?"

A woman's voice sounded in the background, but Erin couldn't make out what she was saying.

"How short are you, Dave?" Erin hated herself for asking. They were out of money anyway. The cost of the adoption had depleted their savings, and now that they'd sold their car they had nothing left to sell. No money to scrounge up.

"Well . . ." Dave dragged the word out, toying with her. "Five thousand was too easy; know what I mean? Rich folks like you and your old man must have dough stashed away somewhere."

"How much, Dave?" Erin didn't have the patience for this. Her mother was being operated on fifteen hundred miles away. The last thing she was up to was another round of game playing with the slimeball on the other end of the phone. "What's the bottom line?"

He didn't miss a beat. "Ten thousand dollars. One final payment and the baby's yours. I promise."

Erin's mouth hung open. Ten thousand dollars? The amount screamed at her again and again.

"So what is it? Do we have a deal, or what?"

No words came from Erin. She couldn't speak, couldn't think about anything but the amount. Ten thousand dollars? For a moment her mind raced and she thought about calling her father, or Kari and Ryan. They might have that kind of money sitting in an account.

But bigger than the money or how she might get it was a truth that was only now becoming clear to her. The game Dave and Candy were playing was illegal. They couldn't blackmail them this way, raising the stakes each week in an attempt to sell their baby.

It was wrong for the two of them to ask for more money, but it was also wrong for Erin and Sam to pay it. Sam was right; they should've gone to the attorney and the social worker after that first meeting in the park. This wasn't about Candy needing a little extra money for diapers and vitamins.

It was extortion.

Sam had already told her that if the couple asked for more money, they would have no choice but to turn them in and risk losing the baby.

Dave was still talking as Erin clicked the Off button on the receiver. Then she did what she should've done a week ago. She dialed the number for the social worker and held her breath.

When the woman answered, Erin explained the entire story. She told her about the meeting at the park and their race to sell their car and give Dave and Candy the cash.

"The last phone call came a few minutes ago." Erin was tired, running on a strength that wasn't her own. All she wanted was to be in Bloomington, at her father's side in a hospital waiting room, praying for her mother. She willed herself to focus. "They want ten thousand dollars more or they won't give up the baby."

The social worker was outraged. She promised to contact both the attorney and the proper authorities. "People go to prison for this sort of thing, Erin. You made the right choice by calling."

The right choice, she thought. *But at what cost?* Certainly Candy wouldn't want to give her baby to them after they'd reported their scam to the authorities. When the conversation was over, Erin called Sam and told him what had happened.

His tone was heavy, but he was proud of her. "Can you imagine living like that, Erin? Even if they gave us the baby, they'd always be calling, looking for more money, making more threats."

By the end of the call, they agreed that God was behind what had happened today, that somehow this setback would lead to some sort of good. "Maybe the courts will take the matter out of Candy's hands. Maybe the baby will come early, with no possible chance for Candy to change her mind."

Erin wasn't hopeful.

Three hours later she got the call she'd been waiting for all day.

"Honey, it's Dad. She came through okay."

"How is she? I've been praying all day, I want to be there so badly."

"I know. Luke feels the same way." Her father's voice was thick. Nothing about it sounded upbeat or hopeful. "Your mother won't be able to have visitors until tomorrow, and then they're hoping to get her home pretty quickly. It's better that you're there, honey."

Erin hesitated. If she never asked the question, she'd never have to deal with the answer. But that wasn't realistic. She shaded her eyes with her free hand. "How is she, Dad? What'd the surgeons say?"

"They're concerned but hopeful, which is a good thing. They have to run tests to see if they got it all, but Dr. Steinman said she has a good chance of recovery." He hesitated. "They're recommending pretty intensive chemo and radiation for the next eight weeks."

Erin felt herself slump forward. "Eight weeks?"

"Yes." Her father sighed. "That'll take us to the middle of May, and then they'll run some more tests and see how she's responding."

The worst part was the waiting. Eight weeks? Eight weeks of recovery from surgery along with heavy chemo and radiation? All before they might have an idea about whether Mom was winning the battle? Erin worked her fingers into her brow. "That's all, Dad? Didn't they say anything else?"

Her father paused just long enough to make Erin suspicious. "We'll know more in eight weeks."

"What about today? They must have some idea if they got it all."

"You're right." He sounded resigned. "They have some idea."

"And?"

"And the cancer's very aggressive, Erin. They're not sure if they got it all."

Erin felt the floor move beneath her feet. Cancer was a terrifying thing at any level, but when doctors weren't raving with good news after a double mastectomy, the stakes were higher than ever before.

If they didn't get it all with the surgery, then her mother wouldn't be battling cancer any longer. She would be fighting for her life.

"I'm sorry, honey." Her father's voice was thick again. "You asked me to be honest."

"I know; I appreciate that." Erin's mind raced. "Have you told the others?"

"Yes." He drew in a shaky breath. "They were all waiting for my call. Everyone knows."

A chill passed over Erin, and she tightened her grip on the phone. "What's the plan, Dad? I want to see her."

"I've told everyone the same thing." He coughed. "Your mother wants everyone to get together this summer for a reunion. At Sanibel Island in Florida."

"Sanibel Island? Why there?"

"I guess she's always wanted an island vacation with her family." His tone said even he couldn't understand her request. "I'm not sure about Sanibel Island, but if things go well, she should be strong enough to get out a bit by the first of July."

"Ashley's wedding is July nineteenth, right?"

"Right." His tone was heartfelt. "Here's what I'm thinking."

Erin blinked back the tears. Whatever he was about to say, the request meant a great deal to him. Whatever it took, she would do her best to go along with the plan.

"Maybe set aside the month of July. I know Sam can't get a whole month off, but you can, right?"

"Definitely."

"Your mother would like everyone to fly into Fort Myers sometime after the Fourth of July for the reunion. Then maybe we can all fly home and use our house as headquarters as we get ready for Ashley's wedding."

Erin didn't want to say it, hated herself for needing to know, but she couldn't stop herself. "What if . . ." Her voice fell away.

"What if she isn't well enough to get away?" Sadness leaked between every word. "I can't think that far ahead, Erin. The others asked the same thing. All I can say is keep July open. Your mother wants everyone together, and if she has her way, we'll spend a week together on a beach in south Florida."

When Sam got home, Erin was in the nursery, sitting in the rocking chair thinking about the changes that had come into their lives in the past week. She heard him park his van in the garage and enter the house. The phone rang, and she heard him answer it. Whoever it was, he talked for only a few minutes; then she heard his footsteps in the hallway.

"Erin?"

"I'm in here." Her cheeks were tight, her makeup smeared from the tears she'd cried since talking to her father.

Sam stood in the doorway to the nursery, and the moment she saw his face she knew. Something was wrong, something other than Candy and Dave's attempts to blackmail money from them, something other than her mother's cancer and the fact that just possibly the doctors hadn't gotten it all with the double mastectomy.

Part of her wanted to cover her ears and run from the room. She'd had more bad news than she could take. But another part was drawn in, desperate to know what could possibly make Sam look so upset.

"What is it, Sam?" She pressed her back against the rocker and set the chair in motion. "Tell me."

"The social worker called." His tone was defeated. "They arrested Dave and Candy and another man named Larry. Apparently police found paperwork at their apartment detailing the entire scheme. It was pretty elaborate, Erin. They planned to take as much money from us as possible, and then skip town.

Dave had another couple lined up in Dallas willing to pay ten thousand dollars through a private attorney."

Erin's head was spinning. She stopped rocking and stared at Sam. "You mean . . . you mean they never intended to give us their baby?"

"No." Sam leaned against the doorframe and slid himself down until he was sitting on the floor. "Police contacted the attorney in Dallas, and of course they had no idea Dave and Candy had already arranged for us to adopt the baby."

"No, Sam. No . . . it isn't true." Erin bent forward. Black spots filled her vision and she felt light-headed, sick to her stomach, and faint. "Tell me the baby's still ours."

Sam let his gaze fall to the floor. When he found her eyes again, he shook his head. "Candy's changed her mind, Erin. She told the social worker she was coerced into the plan from the beginning. The whole thing: the adoption, the demands for money. She says she wants to keep her baby and be the best mother she can be."

Erin wanted to vomit. "She's lying, Sam. You saw her. She doesn't care a bit for the kids she already has."

"I know that." Sam dropped his head in his hands for nearly a minute. "How's your mother?"

"Not good." She started to tell Sam the details, how the doctors were afraid they might not have gotten all her cancer, and how her mother would have to face a rigorous round of chemo and radiation.

But instead she dropped from the chair to her knees. She crawled across the floor to Sam and knelt between his legs. "Hold me, Sam. I can't take another minute of this day."

He rose to his knees. His arms came around her, and they stayed that way as every sad thing about the day pressed in around Erin's heart. She was grateful for Sam, grateful that he cared enough to hold her, to rock away the sorrow that threatened to suffocate her. As night brought a merciful end to the day, Erin was sure her siblings were also bearing the pain of the news about their mother.

But hers was a different pain, more intense. Because she wasn't only dealing with the possible loss of their mother. She had lost a daughter, too.

All in one very awful March afternoon.

CHAPTER TWELVE

A WEEK HAD PASSED since his mother's surgery, and there were times when Luke still wanted to drop everything and head to Bloomington.

"I'll be fine," she told him every time he called. "Focus on your life there, Luke. We'll see each other this summer."

Luke opened his leather portfolio and slipped a stack of papers inside. He'd had two classes this morning and then an hour-long break at home. The law office was expecting him by one o'clock for a four-hour shift. Luke didn't mind; he loved his job. A professor at the university had arranged it, an internship with Morris and McKenzie, one of the top entertainment-law firms in Manhattan.

Three weeks into the job, one of the partners had pulled him aside. "You can clerk for us until the day we hire you, Luke. You're a hard worker and we like your style."

Luke was flattered. He had always figured he'd defend religious rights once he earned his law degree. But entertainment law was exciting, at least for now. Movie stars and television actors made regular appearances in the office, stopping by with their agents to go over the details of a contract or a pending deal.

Reagan was still excited about the names he dropped at the end of a shift, the entertainers who had stopped by and chatted with him while they waited for their agents and lawyers to hash out the details. But Luke wasn't that impressed. People were people, whether they clerked at a law office or made blockbuster films.

Still, the job was fast-paced and challenging, and Luke could hardly wait for the day—two years down the road—when he would have his law degree and the chance to jump into the middle of contract negotiations, arbitrations, and court cases.

Reagan entered the bedroom and smiled. Tommy was on her hip. "Your mother called while you were at school."

"Really?" Luke tucked the bag under his arm and put his free hand around Reagan's shoulders. "What'd she say?"

"She's feeling better. She wants you to call when you have a chance."

Tommy reached out and patted Luke's hair. "Da-da."

"Hi, little man." Luke brushed his nose against Tommy's. "How's the world's greatest baby today?"

"He took his first step." Reagan beamed. She was beautiful, not only because of her long legs and striking features. Ever since their wedding she hadn't stopped glowing. As if the sadness of losing her father and all the hard times that had followed had finally lifted from her heart.

"He isn't even ten months old!" Luke took hold of Tommy's fist and waved it in the air. "Champion baby of the world, right here. Yes sirree!"

Reagan giggled and sat on the edge of their bed. Tommy squirmed and she put him down so he could balance against the mattress. "How is your mom, really, Luke? Have you heard?"

"No." Luke stood near her. He worked his fingers into the base of her neck, massaging the knots that gathered there after a day of caring for Tommy. "My dad hasn't said much lately." He met Reagan's eyes and held them for a moment. "They're pretty sure they didn't get it all—we know that. Now it's a waiting game. To see how well she responds to the treatment."

"She's started, right?"

"Yes. A few days after the surgery."

Reagan winced. She swept Tommy back into her arms and stood again. "I'm sorry, Luke. I know how hard this has to be."

"Sometimes I think that's why I'm working so much. A full load at school and the hours I'm putting in at Morris and McKenzie."

"Could be." She leaned in and kissed him, a slow, seductive kiss square on the lips. Tommy cooed at them and grabbed a handful of Reagan's hair.

"That was nice." Luke tightened his hold on the portfolio. Another kiss like that one and he'd skip work for the day.

"Listen—" she drew back, her eyes tender—"I want you to know I support what you're doing. The hours at Morris and McKenzie, they're going somewhere. It's your future—our future. Don't ever think I expect you to miss out on an opportunity like this one, okay?"

"Okay." He kissed her this time and took a few steps toward the door. "I'll be home before dinner."

Luke took the subway to the law office, situated a few blocks from Times Square, in the heart of the theater district. He had barely settled in at his desk when he heard a commotion in the next room.

One of the secretaries popped her head in and giggled. Then in a loud whisper she explained what was happening. "Dayne Matthews! He's here. Can you believe it?"

Luke rolled his eyes and smiled. "Oh boy! Get an autograph for me, okay?"

The woman made a face at him and turned around, closing the door behind her. Luke chuckled to himself. Dayne Matthews was a household name, a rising star who was cast in lead roles because of his uncanny acting ability and his blond, boyish good looks. People compared him to a young Robert Redford, a heartthrob with timeless charm and a way of relating on-screen that kept him in high demand in Hollywood.

Luke had heard from one of the attorneys that Dayne was a client, but the guy spent most of his time in Hollywood, checking in with the offices Morris and McKenzie had there. He was probably filming something on location in New York City. Yes, that was it. Someone at the office had mentioned that the day before.

The commotion was dying down. The star gazers in the office had apparently found their way back to their work, and Dayne and his agent were probably getting down to business.

Luke studied the stack of contracts on his desk. Contracts made up the bulk of his work. The attorneys would write up an agreement—sometimes thirty, forty pages long—and attach it to a boilerplate, a contract that had already been approved. Luke's job was to go through both documents and find discrepancies. He would then yellow tag them so the attorney could go back and make sure the differences were intentional.

There was enough work to keep Luke busy ten hours a day, but he had agreed to just under thirty hours a week. Long enough to learn the business and figure out if entertainment law was his thing or not, but with time built into his schedule for classes and studying and his young wife and son. Them most of all.

He picked up the first contract and laid it out on the desk in front of him. Before he could reach for the boilerplate, the door opened and Joe Morris walked in with Dayne Matthews and another man.

Luke might not have been starstruck, but he knew enough to rise for the occasion. He stood and shook the partner's hand. "Mr. Morris, good to see you."

"You, too, Luke. I thought I'd introduce you to one of our clients." He stepped aside and nodded at the man on his left. "This is Dayne Matthews, and his agent, Chris Kane."

"Nice to meet you." Luke shook Dayne's hand and then nodded at the man's agent. He grinned at Dayne. "My wife's a big fan."

"Thanks." Dayne looked comfortable. He wore a pullover and a baseball cap, but he would've had to work hard to hide the face America was coming to love. "Joe tells us you'll be the next big entertainment attorney."

Luke smiled and gave a slight roll of his eyes. "As soon as I get my law degree."

Joe Morris and Dayne's agent started a conversation about some aspect of Dayne's current contract. They stood near the door, leaving Dayne no choice but to take the chair opposite Luke's desk. He shrugged his shoulders. "Looks like it could be a while."

This had happened before. Joe and an agent would get into discussions and leave Luke to talk to the client. With the two of them blocking the door as they talked, Dayne was right. It could be a while.

"You're on location, right? Filming something in Manhattan?"

"Yes." Dayne smiled. "They're going through technical shoots today, so we had some time off."

Luke felt himself relax a little. The office always made a big deal about the stars it represented, and many of them were high-maintenance, demanding the attention they felt they deserved because of their visibility.

Dayne was different.

From the moment they met, Luke felt something familiar about him, as if Dayne didn't quite believe the fame and attention people had awarded him. The air of pretense that surrounded most big names was simply missing with Dayne.

"So what's your story, Luke Baxter?" Dayne fingered the name-plate on Luke's desk. "You look too young to be married."

"Young but definitely happy." Luke chuckled and pointed to a framed photograph of him and Reagan with Tommy. "That's my family."

Dayne picked up the picture and studied it. "I can see why

you're happy." He set it back down and looked at the other pictures on Luke's desk. A photo of Tommy on his six-month birthday, one of Luke and Reagan at their wedding the previous Christmas.

Then Dayne's expression changed. "Who's this?" He picked up a small photograph of Luke's mother and father. It was taken when they were both students at the University of Michigan.

"My parents." Luke twisted so he could get a good look at the picture. "The way they looked in 1967, the year they met."

Dayne studied the photo a little longer, and then put it back. "They look nice."

"They are." Luke reached up and took another photo from the top shelf of his desk. "This is them now. They'll be married thirty-five years in August."

Again Dayne took special interest in the photo. "Thirty-five years." He shook his head. "That's just about unheard-of where I come from."

For a single instant, Luke felt sorry for the movie star seated across from him. For some reason, the man was giving Luke a glimpse of his heart, of the things that might've mattered to him if life were different. Almost as if Dayne longed for a desk like Luke's, one with a photograph of a pretty wife and an infant son and parents who had stayed married for thirty-five years.

Dayne leaned back and crossed his arms, studying Luke. "You're a Christian, aren't you, Luke?"

"I am." Again, Luke was struck by Dayne's transparency. "How did you know?"

"Your eyes." He laughed and flashed the smile that brought in millions at the box office. "And the eyes of your wife and parents. It's the same way my own parents looked."

"They're believers, then?"

"They were." Dayne sucked in a long breath and sat a little straighter in his seat. "I lost them a long time ago. They were missionaries; they died in a small-plane crash in the jungles of Southeast Asia."

The story triggered something Reagan had told him. She'd found a copy of *People* magazine in the doctor's office at one of Tommy's appointments and read that Dayne Matthews was raised in a boarding school, the son of missionaries. Luke kept the memory to himself. Instead he bit his lip and held Dayne's eyes for a moment. "I'm sorry. That must've been hard."

Dayne raised his shoulders. "They loved God more than me." He laughed, but it sounded practiced. "I was just a kid; I couldn't exactly compete with God, you know?"

Luke was hardly a psychiatrist, but even so he could read between the lines of what Dayne was saying. No wonder he was taken by Luke's family pictures. He had lost the people he loved most, and all because they had loved God more than him. That was how Dayne saw it, anyway, and his story explained much about his ability to express emotions on the big screen.

Luke wanted to keep the conversation going, find out more about the man sitting across from him. But everything he thought to ask, he already knew. Dayne had a reputation for playing the field, dating his leading ladies, and then walking away before things got too serious. His personal life was splashed across the cover of *People* magazine and every tabloid in the business.

"You know something, Luke Baxter?" Dayne leveled his gaze at him. He was a straight shooter, a man whose star status didn't figure into the conversation. Dayne pointed at the pictures on Luke's desk. "You're a lucky young man. That—" he nodded to the faces in the photographs—"that's what matters in the end, you know?"

"You're right." Luke looked at the pictures again. "I almost lost them all a year ago. But now—" he met Dayne's eyes again— "now I'm never letting go. Not for anything."

"Good." Dayne grabbed the arms of his chair and looked over his shoulder. His agent and Joe Morris had moved their conversation into a nearby room, so there was no longer a reason for Dayne to stay. He stood and stretched. Then he reached out and shook Luke's hand. "Nice meeting you."

"You too." Luke was struck by this guy, how easily they'd hit it off from the moment they were introduced. In another setting, they might've become friends, taken an interest in getting to know each other. But Dayne Matthews was, well, he was Dayne Matthews. People didn't just befriend big-time movie stars.

Dayne nodded at Luke. "See you around."

"Yeah." Luke did a small wave. "Good luck with your film."

"Thanks." And with that, Dayne turned around and walked out of Luke's office and down the hallway.

Luke didn't see him again that day, but he was sure of one thing: He wouldn't forget their conversation as long as he lived. Not because Dayne was a movie star, someone larger than life. But because he was human, just a guy caught up in the fast pace of life, wistful over the thought of normalcy.

Something about it made Luke sad, and he could hardly wait to share the story with Reagan. She would be bowled over, of course, asking him if he'd gotten the man's autograph or invited him for dinner. But when the silliness faded and she listened to the story, she would feel it, too. An ache for someone like Dayne Matthews, someone with limitless fame and talent and looks and money. But someone who was maybe missing the most important thing of all.

Family.

A few hours later, Luke finished up. He gathered his things and headed down the hall. On his way he poked his head into the office of Joe Morris. "Hey, thanks for introducing me. He's the real deal. Very down to earth."

Joe was about to say something, but he set his pen down and stared at Luke. "My word, Baxter, look at you."

Luke took a step back and shot a glance at the length of himself in Joe's mirror. "Did I spill pizza sauce on my shirt again?"

"No." Joe stood up, his eyes wide. "You look exactly like Dayne Matthews." He shook his head. "When I hired you I knew you looked like someone famous, but I couldn't put my finger on it." He chuckled. "Now I know."

"Really?" No one had told him that before.

"I mean, Baxter, you could be the guy's twin."

"I guess there are worse things you could say about me." Luke laughed and raised his portfolio in the air. "Maybe I should drop law and take up acting."

CHAPTER THIRTEEN

WITH ALL THAT was going on in her life, Ashley had asked the owner of Sunset Hills for six months off. Long enough to get them through the summer, the reunion their mother wanted, and her wedding.

She still had money in savings from the paintings she'd sold in Manhattan, and the occasional sale that took place at the local gallery. Taking time off was a good thing. It gave her time with Cole and Landon and her mother. Most of all her mother.

Two weeks had passed since her mother's surgery. Often in the afternoon Kari and Jessie joined Ashley and Cole in long conversations around their mother's bed. She was still weak from the operation, her incisions still healing. And the sickness had already kicked in.

She'd lost weight and hair and had trouble keeping food down. But at times like this, with the early April sun streaming through the bedroom window and her mother sitting up in bed smiling and laughing at the stories Kari told about little Jessie, it was easy to think her mother wasn't sick at all.

Elizabeth drew a long breath and pressed the blankets down

around her waist. "You tell the funniest stories, Kari. Sometimes I think you should've done stand-up work."

"Who knew two-year-olds could provide such good material?"

They all laughed again and Ashley remembered something. "I think I found the bridesmaids' dresses." She darted across the room and pulled a slip of folded paper from her purse. "I found this in one of those wedding books."

Ashley opened the advertisement and showed it to Kari. Their mother leaned closer, trying to get a better look. "Oh, Ashley, it's beautiful."

The dress was formfitting but not tight, a thin black satin with a single strap over the left shoulder.

"Oh, sure." Kari chased after Jessie and whisked her up onto her lap. "I'll be—what?—over four months pregnant." She traced the narrow waist of the model wearing the dress. "I'll be the general shape of a rectangle by then; keep that in mind."

Kari and Mom laughed, but Ashley was quick to accommodate. "We can have yours custom-made. That won't be a problem."

"Just give me a gunnysack. That way I can be sure the waist will fit." Kari set Jessie down, and they watched her skip across the room and stare out the window.

"Kitty, Mommy! Look!" Kari struggled to her feet and went to Jessie. As she did she looked over her shoulder. "Of course, if Jessie keeps up this aerobics program, I might actually fit into the dress."

Again they laughed, and Ashley savored the feeling.

This was what she'd always hoped for, wasn't it? Not just the fact that she was marrying the man of her dreams, a man who would be her best friend and the greatest daddy in the world for Cole. But that she had this, too. Unhurried conversations with her mother and sisters about dresses and fittings and all the other details that went into planning a wedding.

"Have you decided on the music?" Her mother reached into the top drawer of her nightstand and pulled out a pad of paper.

"You mean I'm not singing?" Kari kneeled beside Jessie, who was still caught up in watching the kitty through the window. "I thought for sure you'd have me sing."

Ashley and Mom winced at the same time. Kari had always been good in front of a camera, but never in front of a microphone. She was completely tone deaf. Everyone in the Baxter family knew that.

"Well—" Ashley played along—"I want people to dance, not leave early with a headache."

Kari made a face. "Ouch, little sister. Cut me deep."

Their mother studied the notebook on her lap. "Last time we talked, you were leaning toward a DJ; is that right?"

"Actually . . ." Ashley watched her mother and tried not to notice the way her lightweight cotton robe fell flat against her chest. "Landon's thinking about a live band. One of the guys at the fire station plays in one that does weddings. They can do seventies, eighties, country—pretty much anything that gets people on a dance floor."

Her mother thought about that. "It sounds lovely, Ashley. Would you like me to find out what they charge, or will Landon take care of that?"

Ashley's heart melted. "Landon'll do it, Mom. You're supposed to be recovering, remember?"

"My hands still work." Her mother held her chin up. "I hate just lying here when I could be doing something to help. Your wedding's in less than four months, honey. That's sooner than you think."

"Let's see, four months . . ." Kari studied the ceiling. "That means Jessie will be two and my morning sickness will be gone." She punctuated the idea by jabbing her finger into the air. "Let's hope it's sooner than we think."

"Ah, yes. I remember feeling that way." Their mother grinned, but she gave Kari a pointed look. "I thought I'd never have all you kids out of diapers, but it was over in a blur." Her voice was tender, her eyes suddenly damp. "Your little Jessie girl is a handful now, but savor every minute, Kari. Blink a few times and you'll be at her high school graduation."

Ashley was about to agree when the phone rang.

Elizabeth picked up the receiver and tapped the On button. "Hello?" A pause followed and she covered the mouthpiece. "It's Erin," she whispered. "Yes, I remember."

For several minutes their mother carried on a conversation with Erin, assuring her that yes, everything would be okay. Yes, God had a plan for her life and the life of the baby girl Candy had refused to give up. "He has a baby for you, Erin. I believe that much." A bit of silence. "Have you and Sam prayed about that?"

Ashley could hardly believe it. Here was their mother, fighting some awful, aggressive breast cancer, struggling to keep down even a glass of water, but her entire energy was focused on her children, on the events they were dealing with: Erin's loss of the baby she'd been waiting for, Luke's highs and lows at his new job, Kari's struggles with her strong-willed two-year-old, even the wedding she and Landon were planning.

All of it mattered more to Elizabeth than her own situation.

Their father had always been the strong silent type, the spiritual leader everyone fell back on when times were tough. But their mother was the family's heartbeat. Always she was at the center of their good and bad times, lending perspective or a kind word or a shoulder to cry on.

Never did any of them appreciate her more than they did now. Ashley talked to her siblings every day, and all of them were praying, praying with a kind of fervor none of them had known before. Not because they doubted God's faithfulness in hearing their prayers and answering. But because they appreciated her so much more now, appreciated everything she'd ever done, every perfect word or loving touch. Before they might've taken her for granted once in a while, the way kids sometimes do with their parents. But not anymore.

Now they savored every minute. And when they weren't doing that, they kept busy trying not to think about what would happen if God decided to take her home early.

Because none of them—Ashley most of all—had any idea how they'd survive without her.

❧

The girls had been gone for thirty minutes, and it was an hour before John would be home.

Elizabeth was glad. She hated getting sick in front of them, and the nausea hit her like clockwork every afternoon. Always she found a reason to say good-bye to whichever visitors had stopped by. Almost always Kari and Ashley were there, and often Brooke came by on her lunch break.

But come four o'clock, she would yawn and tell them she was tired; she needed her rest if she was going to kick cancer in the shins and send it on its way. But the truth was, she needed her privacy in order to hide her sickness.

The nausea came at her like a baseball bat, hard and swift and relentless in its accuracy. She would barely make it to the bathroom, grab the sink, and thrust her face toward the toilet.

This afternoon was worse than usual, the way Dr. Steinman had predicted.

"When will it go away?" she'd asked him the last time John had taken her in for a post-op checkup. "A few weeks?"

He'd sighed and shook his head sadly. "I'm afraid not, Elizabeth. It'll get worse before it gets better."

Indeed.

Elizabeth clung to the toilet rim. If she didn't hang on, she would fall to the floor and never get up. Her stomach twisted and convulsed until she had nothing left but dry heaves. Then, gradually, the nausea subsided and she slithered to the floor.

Sweat streamed down her face, and she ran her hands through her hair, trying to cool off. But the action left something strange in her fingers, and when she looked she gasped out loud. Her hands were full of hair—thick, dark clumps that stuck to her palms and twisted around her fingers.

The picture made her sick in a new sort of way. She pushed herself into a sitting position and grabbed a piece of toilet paper. Then she gathered the hair from her hands, wrapped it in the paper, and threw it in the trash.

From the beginning Dr. Steinman had told her what to expect, but nothing could've prepared her for this. At the rate she was losing her hair, she'd have to start wearing a baseball cap in the next few days. Not that she had to; she'd even told herself that it wouldn't matter.

It was just hair; it would grow back.

But now that it was falling out, leaving blank patches along her scalp, Elizabeth was horrified. All her life her hair had been part of her look, something she'd expected with each glance in the mirror. Watching it fall out was horrifying. She would either shave it all off or wear a cap. That way when she stumbled into the bathroom for another round of vomiting, her reflection wouldn't make things worse.

Minutes passed, and finally Elizabeth had the strength to stand. She was halfway out of the bathroom when she stopped and stared in the mirror. Dr. Steinman had been checking her incisions every few days, and he was happy with how she was healing. He had advised her not to look at herself until she was prepared mentally for what she would see.

Elizabeth pressed her robe smooth against her belly and winced at her flat chest. Her shape looked unreal, as if someone had placed her image in a computerized photo program and swapped her top with that of a man. The idea that her breasts were gone was something she couldn't quite grasp yet.

She turned sideways and studied her altered profile; then she faced the mirror again. Was she ready? Was this the time when she should lift her pajama top and see the damage cancer had wreaked on her body? Dr. Steinman had warned her that the sight—at first—could make her sick to her stomach.

But after spending twenty minutes hovered over the toilet, she didn't have anything left to lose. She might as well look now and get it over with. Not looking didn't make things different, didn't change the fact that she'd had a double mastectomy. The sooner she could stand looking at herself in the mirror, the closer she'd be to making a comeback . . . right?

Elizabeth narrowed her eyes and steeled herself to the image she was about to see. One button at a time she undid her light-weight robe and let it fall to the floor. Her thin cotton pajama shirt was all that stood in the way now. Her heart kicked into a strange double beat as she crossed her arms in front of her and took hold of the shirt bottom. Slowly, one inch at a time she lifted it until she had exposed her entire midsection.

For a while she looked at herself that way, with only her middle showing. *Not bad,* she thought. Not bad considering all the pregnancies and births her stomach had been through. She drew a deep breath and held it. One more inch and then another and another.

Her eyes grew wide, her expression frozen as she pulled the shirt all the way off. The flesh across her chest was pink and flat and stretched along the sides. The scar worked its way in a grotesque nonpattern around the perimeter of where each breast had been.

Elizabeth couldn't draw a breath, couldn't exhale, couldn't do anything but stare in horror at herself. She would never let John see her this way—never. The longer she studied herself, the worse she looked. Shocking, horrifying, a mutilated mass of flattened, scarred tissue where she once had looked feminine and attractive.

She'd seen this look somewhere before, and finally she remembered where. On a special about nuclear war and Hiroshima, she'd seen photos of people with massive chemical burns across their bodies. That's how she looked now. Like a burn victim, the sort of hideous look people turned away from in disgust.

With a sudden move Elizabeth turned her back to the mirror and slipped her pajama top back on. Dr. Steinman was right. She should've waited until she was ready, until the incisions had time to heal completely, until she was more used to the idea.

In the hours and days and weeks to come, she would feel sicker and lose more hair. Probably all of it. Life was going to get harder, more tiresome with every morning. That combined with how badly she'd been disfigured could've been enough to make her give up. But she couldn't do that, not when she had so much to live for.

Elizabeth shuffled her way to the bed, fell onto it, and stretched her legs out. *God . . . help me fight this battle. I can't do it without you. I look hideous, God. Even you must think so.*

The curtains rustled as a light breeze sifted through the bedroom window.

You are beautiful, daughter. I knit you together in your mother's womb.

The holy response came at her in the wind and spoke to her soul. "God?" She whispered his name, glancing about the room. He was here, wasn't he? Caring about her, loving her even if she looked like a monster. It was true. God had knit her together in her mother's womb, and that's still the way he saw her.

Whole and complete and beautiful.

Suddenly she knew the goal, knew how she'd have to see herself if she was ever to take the upper hand over cancer. God had given her a second chance with the surgery, and that could never be a bad thing, no matter how she looked. She would check her reflection in the mirror every day, praying not for a renewed body but for a renewed heart. She would know she was on the right track when she could look in the mirror and not be horrified. When her flat, misshapen chest was no longer a sign of defeat and disease and destruction.

But rather a sign of God Almighty's redemption and deliverance.

CHAPTER FOURTEEN

THE SOCIAL WORKER had tried to warn Erin what would happen if the adoption fell through, the sorrow she would experience. "You'll feel like your baby died," the woman told her. "Most people don't understand that."

Erin had let the comments pass. Her adoption wouldn't fall through. And if by some strange set of circumstances the adoption didn't take place, at least she would never have known the baby.

But the social worker had been right on.

The weeks and months of putting together the nursery, talking about names with Sam, and dreaming with her mother about the joys of raising a little girl. All of it had made the child a real part of their family, even though they'd never met her. She would probably have golden curls and big blue eyes like her sisters, and just before the meeting with Dave and Candy, they'd settled on a name.

Amy Elizabeth.

Erin had talked with her mother and Ashley and Kari and Brooke, and all of them said the same thing. The feelings Erin was having, the thoughts that occupied her mind, all of it was the same as if she herself were carrying the baby. That's how strong the maternal instinct was—whether the baby grew inside her or not.

Now she could barely force herself to go to work each day. The students didn't know what was going on, only that their teacher wasn't herself, wasn't the happy, creative, energetic person they'd come to depend on. Erin couldn't help it. Every little girl in her class seemed to have the face she'd assigned to Amy Elizabeth.

Questions assaulted her.

How come if God was so good, he'd denied them the chance to be parents? Would Candy's baby girl have a hope for a good life living between Candy and her mother, running around barefoot in dirty clothes and eating wildflowers while Candy smoked dope?

None of it seemed right, and in the month since Candy changed her mind, Erin was certain the baby had been born. With Candy's future hanging in the balance, the infant girl was probably being cared for by her grandmother—the one their pastor had told them about in the first place.

Erin and Sam's car-sharing arrangement wasn't working out. Sam usually pulled up in front of her school at about five-thirty, long after Erin had finished correcting papers and prepping for the next day. Most days she sat in the school's library staring out the window waiting for him, hating herself for making Sam sell their car.

The whole ordeal had been such a waste.

Police had promised to try to recover the money they'd given Dave, but a search of his apartment turned up nothing but the empty envelope and ample drug paraphernalia. The money was gone—smoked or sniffed or shot up the arms of Dave and his friends.

Thinking about it didn't make things any better, but Erin couldn't help herself. It was Thursday night after a long week, and as she and Sam walked through the garage door into their house they were both silent. That was something else, the way she and Sam hadn't talked to each other much since the loss of the baby.

That first night after they got the news had been good. Sam had held her and stroked her hair and helped her know she wasn't alone in how she felt. But since then he hadn't talked about the baby once, as if by ignoring the pain they were feeling it might somehow go away.

Erin wanted to talk about it all the time.

"Do you think she's had the baby yet, Sam?" she'd ask. Or "What would it take for Candy to change her mind again? You know, let us adopt her baby, after all?"

Sam would give her short answers, until finally she looked deep into his eyes and accused him of not caring.

He denied that, but still . . .

Erin put her bag away and returned to the kitchen. Sam was digging through the refrigerator. When he heard her come up behind him, he turned and gave her a half smile. "Any ideas for dinner?"

"Not a one." Erin flashed him a sarcastic smile and immediately let it drop from her face. "Maybe you can come up with something tonight."

Before the ordeal with the baby, Erin got home by four o'clock, early enough to make a meal. Now that they were down to one vehicle, she often used her slow cooker to keep a dinner simmering through the day. But this week she hadn't cooked once, falling back on tuna sandwiches, canned stew, and macaroni and cheese.

Sam released a long sigh, shut the refrigerator, and turned to her. "Wanna talk about it, Erin?"

"About what?" She poured herself a glass of water and leaned against the kitchen counter, facing him.

"About your attitude?" His tone was even. He didn't want to fight with her; she could see that much.

"I don't want dinner." She stared at her shoes, her eyes narrow. "I want that little girl." This time her eyes met his. "It's like I'm paralyzed, Sam. I'd do anything to make her ours again."

A tired look pulled at Sam's features, but he came to her anyway. "I owe you an apology."

"Why?" She angled her head. She'd expected him to be frustrated with her, tired of talking about Candy's baby.

"Because—" he rested against the center island and faced her, their toes touching—"every time you try to talk about what happened, I shut you down." He crossed his arms and shifted his gaze to the window behind her. "She's gone, Erin. I can't think what more we can say." He looked at her again. "But I was wrong; we have to talk about it. Otherwise we'll walk around like—" he gestured to the silent spaces between them—"like this, Erin. Silent and hurting and never connecting with each other."

"Somewhere in here—" Erin put her hand over her heart—"I don't feel like it's over, Sam. I feel like God still has a plan for that baby and for our role in her life." She let her hand fall to her side. "That's why I can't stop talking about her." Air found its way into her lungs and she held her breath for a moment. "But you're right, too. We have to move on, and that won't happen until I let it go. At least once in a while."

Sam reached out and took her hands in his. "Let's make a deal."

"Okay." Her heart fluttered with possibility. "What?"

"Every time you think about her, let's take it to God. Let's pray more, and maybe he'll show us why you still think he has a plan for this baby in our lives, okay?"

Prayer! Of course. She and Sam hadn't prayed about the baby since the day they'd found out. As if they'd taken the news and given up immediately.

She worked her fingers between his and drew him close. For a long time they stood that way, dinner forgotten, both lost in their own thoughts. She broke the silence first. "Can we pray now?"

"Yes." Sam closed his eyes and let his head rest against hers. "God, you know this little baby who may or may not be born yet, Candy's baby. Father, we still feel she's supposed to be with us, but we've failed to come to you every day and ask for a miracle. Forgive us, God. Please hear our prayers."

The rest of the evening was better than any they'd shared in the past month. They talked about Erin's mother and the plans for a reunion that summer.

"Does your dad think she'll be well enough?"

"He won't say." She was sitting beside him on the sofa. "But I know he's worried."

"Why?"

"Because my mom wanted the reunion in late August, around their thirty-fifth wedding anniversary, but we're planning the get-together in July. There can only be one reason for that."

Sam nodded, sympathy flooding his eyes, his voice softer than before. "Your dad's worried she won't be well enough if they wait too long."

Or worse, but Erin didn't want to say so. They read for a while, sharing an occasional bit of conversation, and then they turned in early.

The next morning they were awakened by a phone call just after six o'clock.

Erin sat straight up in bed, her heart racing. She answered it on the second ring. "Hello?"

"Yes, Erin, hello." It was the social worker. "I have some news for you."

Erin's heart stopped. "About Candy?"

"No, another baby."

Her heartbeat was back, twice as fast as before. "Another baby?"

"Yes. I don't know if you heard the news a few weeks ago. A teenage mother abandoned her newborn near the side door of a hospital in Dallas. The baby is mixed race. The mother is a sixteen-year-old African-American; the father is a teenage Caucasian. Anyway, the baby has been living with a short-term foster family while the courts decide what to do."

The facts swirled about in Erin's mind. She wrinkled her brow and gave Sam a gentle push. He eased himself up onto his elbow. "What is it?" he mouthed.

She covered the mouthpiece. "The social worker. She's telling me about another baby."

Sam sat up and hugged his pillow to his midsection, watching her, listening to her end of the conversation.

A bit of joy sang out in the social worker's voice. "The mother gave birth to the baby in her bedroom, snuck out the window, and walked two blocks to the hospital, where she wrapped her in a sweatshirt and left her with a note."

"A note?"

"Yes. Her parents are very strict, a Christian couple who never approved of their daughter's dating the young man. Apparently he was an athlete with a penchant for beer and fast cars. The young girl went out with him anyway, and that first night she believes she was date-raped. She was afraid her parents would disown her, so she left the baby at the hospital. Now that her parents know the truth, the family is in counseling. I think they'll be okay, actually. The girl doesn't want the baby and neither do her parents. The boy has already signed off any rights to the baby, so he isn't an issue."

"And . . ." Erin's body was tense, every fiber in her being waiting for the woman to get to the point. "What did the courts decide?"

"The mother was charged with abandonment—though I doubt she'll be convicted because of her age. And the judge declared the baby immediately available for adoption. I had marked your case a top priority because of what happened with Candy." The woman hesitated. "She's a beautiful, healthy little girl, Erin. The judge wanted her placed outside the Dallas area because of the publicity surrounding the situation." She paused. "Would you and Sam be interested?"

Erin's mouth hung open. "Interested?" She wanted to toss the phone in the air and jump around the room. Instead she gathered her emotions and swallowed, searching for her voice. "Yes, we're very interested. Can I call you back in five minutes?"

The social worker agreed. Erin hung up and stared at Sam. "God did it, Sam! We prayed last night and now . . . wait until you hear."

She told him the entire story and that the social worker was waiting for an answer. Race wasn't an issue because they'd discussed that a year ago when they first considered adoption. "Skin color isn't all we make it out to be," Sam had told her back then. "I think God must be up there shaking his head, wondering why we chose that as such a dividing line among peoples of the world."

"I never thought of it that way." Erin had looked at him, struck by the idea. "We could've divided ourselves by eye color or height or hair color just as easily."

"Right." He gave her a sad smile. "Can you imagine? You have blue eyes and I have brown. Our groups of people would've been at odds with each other through the centuries. One set of bathrooms and eating areas for brown-eyed people, one for blue-eyed. And since there're more brown-eyed people in the world, the blue-eyed folks would be the minority group."

The idea was ludicrous, the same way any discrimination based on color was ludicrous.

Of course, when they had learned about Candy, their thoughts about race were no longer an issue. Candy was white, and her children were white. But still Erin had expected that somewhere down the road they might adopt a biracial baby or a black or Hispanic child.

Sam wiped his eyes and stared at her, disbelief shading his expression. "You mean somewhere in Dallas there's a little girl who could be ours in a few days?"

"Yes." Erin bit the inside of her lip. "Can you believe it, Sam?" She looked up at the ceiling and shook her head. "How can this be anything but a miracle?"

The phone was lying on the bed between them. Sam picked it up and tossed it to her. "Call, Erin. Before something else happens."

Erin laughed and had the number dialed before she drew her next breath. She told the social worker yes, they wanted the baby girl. The two of them made plans to pick up the child the following weekend at the social service office in Dallas. The worker in charge of the case would be there all day Saturday.

When Erin hung up the phone, she was shaking. She shared the information with Sam, and they laughed and hugged and rehashed the details again and again. It was amazing, that just the day before they had wondered if they'd ever be parents and now, in a few days, they would bring home their first child.

"I can't wait to call my mom." Erin sucked in a quick breath. Her mother was having a hard time. She hadn't said so, but Ashley and Kari and Brooke had kept her posted. The treatment was rougher than any of them had expected. The news about the baby was bound to lift her spirits.

"I still can't imagine dropping your baby off and walking away." Sam climbed out of bed and stretched. "Angels must've been watching over that baby."

"Definitely."

For the briefest moment, Erin thought about Candy, about the newborn who was going to have such a different life now than the one she would've had with them. But just as quickly she put the thought out of her mind. God had given them a different little girl, one she was already starting to love and dream about.

Sam was getting dressed for work when he stopped and grinned at Erin. "We forgot one thing." He hopped a bit closer, his pants not quite on. "What do we call her?"

A feeling of sadness and far-off possibility wrapped itself around Erin's heart, and she tilted her head. "I'm not sure."

"What about Amy Elizabeth?" Sam's voice was tender, aware that the name they had planned for Candy's daughter might strike a nerve.

Erin smiled and shook her head. "No, Sam. Anything but Amy Elizabeth." She crossed the room and kissed his forehead as he finished getting dressed. "That name will always belong to a different little girl. Even if we never meet her this side of heaven."

CHAPTER FIFTEEN

DAYNE MATTHEWS WAS trying to concentrate.

"Okay, Matthews, let's have you in the stairwell. The scene starts with you running up and we'll take it from there."

"Got it." Dayne entered the building, sidestepped around three cameramen, and stood on the second stair.

"Places everyone," someone yelled. "We need it quiet."

Dayne went over his lines one more time. The movie was a thriller, and he was the lead. The scene they were filming involved his breaking into an apartment and rescuing his girl-friend from two criminals who had taken her hostage.

He was supposed to knock out the kidnappers, grab her, struggle with the handcuffs on her wrists, and then lead her through a hallway, out a fire escape, and down into an alleyway. There he was supposed to pick the lock on the handcuffs and then—with the bad guys firing guns in the distance—kiss her, fast and passionate, before they ran for their lives. He'd already messed it up three times. Twice he tripped on the stairs and once he ran to the wrong apartment door.

The scene was one of the most intense in the movie, and

though they had another week left of shooting in Manhattan, the expectancy on the set made it feel like the movie might make it or break it depending on how they pulled off this scene.

But all Dayne could think about was the photograph on Luke Baxter's desk.

"Ready Matthews?" the director shouted at him from the street.

"Ready." He bent his knees and locked his arms in a running motion. Next he worked on his expression. Intense and frightened and bent on revenge all at once, that's what the scene called for.

"And . . . three . . . two . . . one . . . action!"

Dayne sprang up the stairs, breathing hard, his footsteps quiet and stealthlike. Cameras followed his actions both from in front of and behind him as he tore down the hallway and stopped at the first door on the left. He put his ear to it, his hands shaky from the tension of the moment.

The subtle sound of voices came from inside, but Dayne pursed his lips and worked his face into a mask of determination. Then he grabbed the doorknob and shoved his shoulder hard into the door.

"Bill!" Sarah Whitley, his leading lady, shouted her line exactly on cue.

At the same time, two buff men wearing dark sunglasses came at him, but Dayne ignored them. He went straight to Sarah and grabbed her handcuffs, shaking them, looking for a way to release her hands.

"Cut!" The director shouted the word through the bullhorn. "Wait there, Matthews. I'm coming up."

Everyone in the room went quiet, and Dayne looked from Sarah to the actors playing the kidnappers. "What?" His eyes found Sarah again just as he remembered.

"The kidnappers," she whispered at him and made an apologetic face. "You're supposed to fight them off, remember?"

The director stormed into the room, his face beet red. "You're dead, Matthews. These are some of the toughest criminals in New York City and they're guarding your girl. You can't walk right past them and start fiddling with Sarah's handcuffs; get that?"

Dayne huffed quietly and rubbed the back of his neck. "Sorry."

"Yeah," the director barked at him and shot a look at the others. "It better not happen again. We're spending tens of thousands of dollars a day here, Matthews. You're a professional; now come on. Let's make it work."

"It won't happen again." Dayne lifted his eyes to the director. "Where do we take it from?"

"The top." The director spun around and marched into the hallway and down the stairs. He used his bullhorn to say, "Places everyone. Let's try it again."

Sarah squeezed Dayne's arm and gave him a nervous smile. "Where are you today?"

"Not here." He lifted his shoulders once, turned, and headed back down the hallway.

Cameramen followed, one of them finding his place at the far end of the hallway facing the stairs, the other at the opposite end in the corner, ready to capture Dayne's back as he sped past and headed for the apartment door.

Dayne headed down the stairs and took his spot again.

"Places, people!" The director's tone was still sharp, tense.

The sounds around Dayne faded.

Why had the photograph looked so familiar? And what was it about Luke Baxter that had caught his attention? Why was he still thinking about the kid a month after their meeting? Things like this didn't happen to him. He was a busy man, a person who avoided conversations like the one he'd had with Luke the last time he was in Manhattan.

But the memory of that time had stayed with him every day since. Even now, in the midst of the most important scene of a movie he was being paid millions to film, Dayne couldn't think of anything else. All he wanted to do was forget the shoot and find the law offices of Morris and McKenzie. Maybe he'd look at the picture again and the feeling would go away. Maybe those people in the photo would look like any other couple from the sixties. Dayne clenched his teeth and forced himself into position.

Or maybe not.

"Ready, Matthews?"

The question snapped him to attention. "Ready," he shouted loud enough for the street crew to hear him.

"Okay, quiet on the set. Three . . . two . . . one . . . action!"

Dayne darted up the stairs, fully intent on the scene now. He burst into the apartment and fought with the kidnappers. When they were on the ground, knocked out, he wrestled with Sarah's handcuffs for a few seconds. One of the men on the floor made a moaning sound.

Dayne grabbed Sarah's hand. "Come on." He pulled her behind him into the hallway.

"They'll come after us!" Sarah was perfect—her facial expression, her timing, all of it.

Dayne fed off her strength and doubled his effort at having the right expression, the right speed as they headed down the hall. At the fire escape, Dayne did as he was supposed to and shimmied down ahead of her, careful to help her since she was still handcuffed.

"You can do it; hurry." His timing was on. They would get it done this time around; he was sure.

They were almost at the bottom of the fire escape when the sound of bullets pierced the air. Dayne cast an intense look up toward the hallway. "We have to hurry!"

Just then in the corner of his eye he caught a glimpse of a familiar building. The building that housed Morris and McKenzie's law offices. *No, Matthews, not now.* He jumped to the ground and helped Sarah. Then he ducked her into an alcove and worked a bent paper clip into her handcuffs.

The scene was a mixture of passion and danger, and Sarah was playing her part perfectly. Her chest heaved as Dayne worked on her hands, and the whole time her eyes never left his face. He was her hero, her rescuer.

The moment the handcuffs were off, Dayne dropped them, grabbed Sarah's hand, and started running.

"Cut!" The director was closer this time, just fifteen yards away. "Am I seeing things or did Dayne Matthews just forget to kiss the girl?"

The kiss! Dayne wanted to slip into the nearest manhole. How could he have forgotten the kiss? He and Sarah had run lines the night before in his trailer and practiced the kiss for half an hour. She was gorgeous and he could feel her falling for him. Without a doubt the kiss figured to be the best part of the scene. How could he have forgotten it?

"Maybe we need more practice." Sarah elbowed him and bit her lip.

He could tell she wanted to laugh, but the director didn't appreciate laughter in light of mistakes. Especially during serious scenes. It broke the mood and robbed the shoot of the intensity that had to carry over into the film.

The two of them stepped into the alley and waited. Dayne could feel the sympathy from just about everyone else on the set.

The director took long strides in their direction. He looked at Sarah and clapped his hands. "You were perfect, Sarah. Right on." He nodded toward the catered food wagon. "Go get something to eat."

"Yes, sir." Sarah gave Dayne one more worried look, tossed her hair over her shoulder, and did as she was told.

"Matthews, what is it? What's eating at you today?"

"Nothing, sir." Dayne hated this, hated the way the director talked down to him. Everyone had an off day, didn't they? He looked at his watch and stifled a sigh.

"Right, go ahead and look at your watch. If you want to call it a day, you've got another thing coming." The director paused and his body relaxed some. "Look, Matthews, I don't know what's going on, but I know this. I've worked with you before and something's off." His voice came down a few notches. "Take two hours and meet back at the set. It'll be four o'clock then, and I plan to get this scene on the first run-through, okay?"

"Yes." Dayne breathed in long and slow through his nose. He found the corner of the familiar building and stared at it. "Can I leave the set?"

"Leave the city for all I care." The director brushed his hand through the air, still frustrated. "Just be back here at four o'clock, ready to shoot."

Dayne thought about finding Sarah and apologizing, but he changed his mind. He could do that later. He went to his trailer and pulled open a drawer of old clothes and hats—the things he wore when he didn't want anyone to know he was Dayne Matthews.

In spite of the early May sunshine, he slipped on a worn-looking gray hooded sweatshirt and a baseball cap. He slid the hood up over the cap, slipped on a pair of sunglasses, and stepped out of the trailer. Onlookers were gathered around the far edge of the roped-off area; he couldn't go that way. Instead he opened the door of the building they were using for the shoot, walked through it, and exited on the other side.

People milled about, wondering what was happening inside, why the streets were roped off. But no one recognized him as he made a sharp right turn and headed down the sidewalk.

This Luke Baxter thing had gone far enough.

If he didn't get his head back in the game, the tabloids would catch wind of the situation. He could just see it: "'Dayne Matthews Falling Apart.' Sources say America's hottest actor may be on the ropes. . . ."

He worked his jaw one way and then the other. His career was everything to him. After his parents died, he'd gone to an audition scheduled through the UCLA drama department, and that afternoon he'd taken a call from Jerry Lituzza, one of the top talent agents in Hollywood.

Jerry had been at the audition, scouting talent for bigger projects. At their first meeting Jerry promised Dayne the moon: an ever-increasing presence in the industry, a fan base that would grow with each movie, bigger and bigger parts, and one day the top draw for a Hollywood actor.

Jerry hadn't been wrong about any of it.

Yes, there were times when Dayne ran a little wild. Hollywood was a playground and he was a kid who never wanted to leave. But he remembered his parents' values, the principles they died for, and he never let his life get too out of control.

No matter how many young actresses came into his life, not one of them was as important as his career. Without his acting, he was nothing. A lonely man with no parents, no siblings, no family.

He would find Luke Baxter, prove to himself that the picture didn't look familiar in the least, and be on his way. He simply couldn't afford the distraction, whatever was causing it.

He kept his head low, his feet moving at a good pace. Dressed like this, even the paparazzi wouldn't recognize him. He looked up, but only long enough to make sure he was headed in the right direction. Yes, he'd take care of this strange distraction and then get back to the set, where he'd show the director and the cameramen and Sarah Whitley exactly what type of professional he really was.

He kept moving.

After several minutes, he saw he was at the right place. Then he ducked inside and slouched to the bank of elevators.

A heavyset woman was standing there, waiting. She looked at him and then took a step closer. "Hey, aren't you Dayne Matthews?"

A quick glance around the lobby told Dayne he had nothing to worry about. She was the only other person in sight, and she didn't have a camera. She looked nothing like a photo hound.

"Yes." He gave her a quick smile, but kept his face down, the hood still up over his cap. "That's me."

The woman gasped out loud and did a little scream. She covered her mouth with her hands. "Oh . . . my goodness . . . the girls at the office aren't going to believe this." She began rooting through her purse. She found a piece of paper and pulled it out just as the elevator opened up. "Can I get your autograph, please Mr. Matthews?" She rolled her eyes, shaking as they boarded the elevator. "The girls won't believe this."

She handed him the paper and dug around in her purse again for a pen. As they rode up he gave her his autograph, grateful no one had heard her. "There you go." He handed the items back to her.

Before the door opened she cocked her head. "You know what always surprises me?" She studied his sweatshirt and hat, his worn jeans. "How raggedy you stars always look." She reached out and took hold of his chin. Her accent was heavy New York. "With a face like that? The last thing I'd do is hide it."

The woman was still talking at him, still giving her opinion of his wardrobe, when he stepped off the elevator. The entire floor was taken up by Morris and McKenzie. Dayne was relieved when the elevator doors shut and he could no longer hear the woman's chatter. The woman didn't get it. He wore the old hats and clothes to avoid people like her.

He removed his hood and hat and smiled at the receptionist. "I need to see Luke Baxter. Is he working today?"

The young man behind the desk was flustered but professional. He checked a board and shook his head. "He's already gone home for the day."

Disappointment rocked Dayne, and he glanced around the office until an idea hit him. "I need to leave him a note." Dayne took a few steps around the reception desk and pointed down the hallway. "I know where his office is. I'll just go on down there myself and leave the message on his desk, okay?"

"By all means, Mr. Matthews." The receptionist looked proud

of himself. He had granted access to the great Dayne Matthews. "Is there anything I can do for you?"

Dayne stopped and thought. "Yes. Could you get me a bottle of water? I'll pick it up on the way out."

For reasons Dayne couldn't fathom, as he headed to Luke Baxter's office his heart beat hard against the inside of his chest. What was he doing, anyway? His director had called a two-hour break because he couldn't concentrate through a single action scene, and now he was strolling through his lawyers' offices looking for a clerk he'd met just one time.

Dayne pushed the thoughts from his head. The mission was perfectly sane. He needed to see the picture, needed to know if it was his imagination or if he'd seen something strangely familiar there.

Eyes were on him; eyes were always on him. Dayne didn't care. He kept a steady pace as he found Luke's office and stepped inside. He shut the door behind him and turned to the photographs. His eyes found it immediately: the old picture of a young couple, Luke Baxter's parents, taken the year they'd first met. Wasn't that what Luke had said?

Dayne moved to the edge of the desk, picked up the five-by-seven photograph and studied it. The feelings that made their way through him were the same as last time. A familiarity with the woman, especially. Something that defied both logic and explanation. Had he seen her picture somewhere? met her sometime back when he was a kid? He stared at the woman, her dark hair and delicate features. Had she been a missionary with his parents?

A memory came to him, distant and fuzzy. Somewhere in his past he had, indeed, seen a picture of the woman. The very same woman. But where . . . and why?

He lowered the photo just enough to see the other pictures on Luke's desk, pictures he hadn't noticed the first time. There was the shot of Luke and his wife and baby, of course, but there was something else. A picture of Luke and what must've been his siblings back when Luke was a teenager. His parents were at the center of the photo. Dayne couldn't decide which face was more haunting. Luke's mother's . . .

Or Luke's.

It hit him all at once why the photos had caught his attention, why the images had stayed with him since the last time he was in Manhattan. Luke Baxter was the mirror image of Dayne, a younger version whose teenage photograph looked exactly the way he himself had looked as a boy at boarding school in the mission field.

No wonder the woman looked familiar. Her face was Luke's face.

And Luke's face was his own.

The resemblance was strange, really. Far beyond the general way that people might look alike. Dayne lowered himself into the chair, the same one he'd sat in the last time he was in this office. Where had he put the box of pictures his parents left him? That whole awful summer was still a blur, even seventeen years later.

One day he'd been in algebra class, watching the minutes tick by at his boarding school in Southeast Asia, and the next he'd been in the headmaster's office, hearing the news about his parents: *Bad weather over the jungle, engine failure, no sign of the plane. Wreckage found, but no survivors.*

His parents had never spent enough time with him, preferring the mission field over being with him. But they loved him. They definitely loved him. And when they died, whole years of Dayne's life seemed to die along with them. Memories of the months and years after their deaths were almost dreamlike, with little substance or framework to remember them by.

He'd been given several boxes of their belongings; he remembered that much. Material goods were never something his parents cared much for, but still they'd kept the boxes in a storage unit. Important papers, keepsakes, and photographs. An official from the missions board had put his name on the storage unit.

The cost came out of his savings account automatically every month, and occasionally he remembered the things that were locked away.

It still felt like yesterday, the news about the crash, the reality that he was alone in the world. He'd gotten accepted to UCLA on a hardship vote, and immediately he'd fallen into drama. Dayne loved it because onstage he could express the emotions he kept bottled up; he could be angry and sad and passionate, and all anyone ever did was clap for him.

One thing led to the next and in no time he was busy making movies. The storage unit full of his parents' things was safe; it would be there if he ever needed a reminder of them. But never had he simply taken the time to go through it all.

Until now.

Now he wanted to sort through every last picture until he found the one he was thinking of. It was a picture of a woman by herself; Dayne was almost certain. He was maybe six or seven the last time he saw it, and the memory of it had all but faded from his mind. But something about the picture had been important to him. Even back then.

Maybe the woman had been related to his parents. The resemblance was certainly strong enough.

Dayne looked at the clock on Luke's desk and shot to his feet. He had thirty minutes to be back on the set, ready to film. He set the photograph back on Luke's desk. There. He'd satisfied his interest; he could put the image out of his mind now. At least until he found time to visit the old storage unit and find the picture he was sure would be there.

He was almost ready to turn around when he did something he'd never done before. Glancing once over his shoulder, he took the picture of Luke's parents and slid it beneath his jacket. Then he rearranged the photos on the desk so the empty spot wasn't so obvious, and he quickly left the room.

The photo frame jabbed into his ribs, but he pressed his arm even harder against it. One day he'd bring it back, after he had a chance to compare it to whatever lay in storage. Luke would never know it was gone, or if he did, he'd figure he must've misplaced it. No one would ever suspect that Dayne Matthews "borrowed" it for a while.

On his way out, the receptionist called after him. "Wait . . ."

Dayne's heart raced faster than before. He'd been caught! They probably had cameras in every office. He stopped, swallowed hard, and turned around. "Yes?"

"You forgot your water." The man held up a small bottle and smiled.

"Oh." Dayne willed himself to look at ease. Happy and relaxed. "Thanks anyway. I have to get back to the set."

CHAPTER SIXTEEN

ELEVEN O'CLOCK EACH MORNING was the worst and the best hour of the day for John Baxter.

Worst because that was when he took a break from his patients and met Elizabeth in the chemotherapy lab. Watching the technician disconnect her from the empty bag of poison hanging over her head was like somehow being a party to her torture.

But once he wheeled her out of the unit and down the corridor, away from the hospital and out to their car, the hour became almost magical. The nausea was different for every cancer patient, and with Elizabeth it didn't hit her right away. Her sickest hours would come later in the afternoon.

So from eleven to noon, she would hold his hand and believe along with him that everything was going to work out. It was the hour when she would share her heart with him, the hour when she told him her fears and dreams and deepest desires about the future—however long they had together.

But it was Monday, the middle of May now, the last week of her treatment, and when John arrived at the chemo lab he was struck by what he saw. She'd gotten worse over the weeks—

anyone could see that. Dr. Steinman had called him a few weeks earlier and hinted that he was afraid the new round of tests weren't going to be good.

Still, not until that moment did John see Elizabeth for what she had become. Whereas for most of her weeks of treatment she had sat in a chair and read a magazine, now she was stretched out on a table. Her frame was painfully thin, and when she recognized him standing there, she barely had the strength to smile.

The tech showed up, his voice pleasant. "Looks like we're all done for another day, Mrs. Baxter."

Elizabeth had a Pic-Line in her arm, a permanent opening to her vein. That way the technician didn't have to start a fresh intravenous line every time he transferred a bag of the toxic yellowish substance into her body. The tech unhooked the bag line from the tubing in her arm.

John stepped up and put his hand on her shoulder. "She . . . she doesn't look good. Did something go wrong today?"

"No. Her condition is fairly normal for someone at the end of a chemo run." A shadow passed over the tech's eyes, almost as if there was something he wasn't saying.

Not that he could hide much from John. He didn't need a chemo tech to tell him his wife wasn't doing well.

When Elizabeth rolled onto her back, panic punched John in the gut. She looked paler than before, almost gray. He leaned over her and searched her eyes. "What's wrong, honey? You don't look good."

A long sigh left her lips and she looked at him a long time. "I'm fine, John." She ran her tongue over her lips. "I wanna go home."

John wanted to carry her in his arms, run as fast and far away from the hospital and the chemo lab and the sad-faced technician as possible. Instead he brushed his fingers across her forehead. "Okay. I'll get the chair."

The tech offered to help transfer her from the table to the wheelchair, but John politely brushed him off. "I've got it." He lifted her, wincing as he felt her ribs and hipbones sticking out. He set her into the chair and didn't say another word to her until she was in the car.

"Maybe you're hungry." He slid behind the wheel and put his seat belt on. "Did you get breakfast this morning?"

"Yes, John." She pressed herself into the seat and stared out the window. "I told you, I'm fine."

But she wasn't fine; she couldn't fool him. He'd seen cancer patients who looked like Elizabeth before. They had a name for the way she looked: end-stage. John waited a minute before starting the car. He wasn't sure what to do, where to go. He wanted to race her back into the hospital and scream at someone, demand that Dr. Steinman or one of the other cancer specialists do something. How was he supposed to casually drive home when his wife was dying right beside him?

"Go, John." She turned to him and the corners of her lips raised. "I know what you're thinking. There's nothing you or anyone else can do." She stopped, exhausted from that small bit of conversation. "Please, John. Take me home."

John clenched his jaw and started the car. "I can't hide anything from you, can I?"

"Nope." She managed a small laugh.

They said little on the way home. John thought about calling Dr. Steinman and ordering the tests immediately. They had to know why she looked this way, why her color was gone and the pounds were falling off like autumn leaves.

But Elizabeth wouldn't let him. He held her hand as they headed up the stairs, and when she stopped to catch her breath, he swept her into his arms and carried her the rest of the way.

"How chivalrous, John." Her smile was weaker than before. She winced as he laid her in bed. "You haven't carried me into our bedroom in years."

John didn't laugh. "I should've done it more often." He pulled up a chair next to the bed and studied her, searching for some sign—any sign—that she was turning a corner, gaining ground on the enemy inside her.

There was none.

"When do I see Dr. Steinman again?"

"Next Wednesday. As soon as the eight weeks are finished." John's lips were tight, his body tense. The entire situation was so futile, and yet she was looking at him, waiting for him to say something positive. He reached for her hand. The words he dredged up were not even close to the truth. "I'm expecting good news; how 'bout you?"

"Definitely." She made a swallowing motion, but gave a weak shake of her head. "Can you hand me my water?"

John reached for her squeeze bottle, but the effort she needed just to hold it was more than he could stand to watch. Instead he cradled it near her mouth while she sucked down three mouthfuls.

"Really?" He set the bottle back on her nightstand. "You're feeling good about the appointment?"

"Yes." She exhaled and everything about her seemed to shrink a size. "We've been praying every day. Pastor Mark's been by to see me three times a week, you know. He says the church is praying." She gave him a lopsided smile. "Everyone we know is praying, John. Of course the news will be good."

"Right." John took hold of her hand again and ran his thumb along her knuckles. "That's how I feel, too."

The hour slipped away with more talk about the summer reunion and Ashley's wedding. John had long since made a reservation for three condominiums at a beach resort on Sanibel Island. Erin and Sam and Luke and Reagan would arrive in Bloomington on July third, spend a few days at the Baxter house, and the whole group would fly together to Sanibel on July sixth. They'd spend six days on the island and return home to get ready for Ashley's wedding.

"They have the band lined up, the group Landon found out

about through work." Elizabeth nodded toward her nightstand. "The florist is on board also. I have all the notes in there."

"That's good."

"Ashley brought the invitations by the other day." The conversation was making Elizabeth tired, but she kept on. "They look wonderful, John. Did she tell you about them? The words fall over a faded picture of the two of them with Cole. Did she show them to you?"

"No." John tapped his foot fast and steadily. He didn't want to talk about Ashley's wedding. Ashley was fine; the wedding would be beautiful. But if Elizabeth didn't turn a corner soon, she might not live to see them walk down the aisle.

"Only Sam has to return home for the week between the reunion and the wedding, but he'll come back that Friday night. Erin says he wants to be here for the big day."

"Mmm-hmm." He studied his wife's face, the features he'd spent a lifetime loving. "We don't have to talk about the wedding right now, honey. How are you feeling?"

"I told you, John—" she blinked, but her expression stayed calm—"I'm fine. I like talking about the wedding. That and how good Kari's feeling now that she's past the morning sickness, and how happy Erin is with her little girl, Heidi. It makes me feel better to talk about the kids."

"Okay." John stopped tapping. "I'm sorry."

"That's okay." She drew in a long breath, and the effort it took was both painful and obvious. "I can't wait to see that little baby. Heidi is such a beautiful name. She sounds like a little angel." Elizabeth's words were slurring. She was more tired than usual. Her eyelids looked heavier with every blink. "God is so good to us, John."

"Yes." The word felt bitter on John's tongue and he chided himself. He had to stay positive, had to believe she'd be okay. If he lost faith now, what would they have? What strength could he draw from? He steeled himself against the barrage of doubts. "Yes, God is very good."

Elizabeth did another weak smile and closed her eyes. They still had ten minutes before John had to return to work, but she was too tired to stay awake. Instead of rousing her, he leaned back and watched her sleep.

What had been different about this morning? Why had none of it felt real? He stroked his chin, replaying their conversation in his mind. Slowly it dawned on him. Not once had she mentioned her fears. Usually at least part of this hour together was spent with her looking deep into his eyes and admitting she was afraid, terrified actually. The chemo was her last bit of ground assault against cancer, her last chance to make headway in the battle for her life.

If it didn't work . . .

Elizabeth needed to talk about her fears. About how badly she wanted to live, so she could see her grandkids grow up, watch her children live out their lives now that they'd worked through so much. That was a large part of it.

"We've all come so far in the past three years," she'd say. "Now's when we get to sit back and watch them be happy. I don't want to miss that, John. Not even for heaven."

But today . . . today she'd said nothing at all about being afraid. She looked worse than he'd ever seen her look, yet all she talked about was how strongly she felt about her upcoming doctor's appointment, and how sure she was that everything was going to work out, how certain she was that their prayers were being heard and that God was going to answer them the way they wanted.

Elizabeth never would've worked through her fears this quickly. She needed time and tears and moments alone with God before she found peace in any difficult situation. In fact, when she was the most afraid—the way she'd felt about Luke when he left home, or the way she'd worried about Kari after Tim moved in with his girlfriend—Elizabeth shut down and pretended.

The kids used to accuse her of burying her head in the sand, but that wasn't it. She simply reached a point at times where she had to act like she was doing well so she wouldn't go crazy with fear.

Usually, once she shut down and stopped talking about being afraid, she met with God shortly after and worked through the situation. And since she hadn't had that sort of time since yesterday, John could only surmise one possibility:

Her fears were worse than ever before.

But then, he hadn't been exactly honest either. Because watching her now, the slow rise and fall of her flat chest, the gray-white coloring beneath her eyes and across her cheeks, the angled look of her ribs sticking out, he had just one emotion raging through his soul.

Complete and utter terror.

🌿

Ashley had been waiting for this moment all day.

She snuck into the house and set Cole up with a coloring book and a pack of markers. "Stay here, honey, okay?"

"Are you checking on Grandma?" Worry shaded Cole's expression. They came here often enough now that he understood his grandma was sick.

"Yes." She dropped down to his level and ran her hand over his pale blond hair. "I have to show her something, and then after a while you can come up."

Cole's face lit up. "I'll make her a picture!" He opened the coloring book and began flipping the pages, looking for just the right scene to color. "Teacher says I color in the lines bestest of all."

"Perfect." Ashley leaned forward and kissed the tip of his nose. "I love you, Cole. You have a good heart."

He took the compliment in stride, keeping his eyes on the coloring book and the markers and the task at hand. "Thanks, Mommy. You too."

Ashley studied him a moment longer. He was happier these days, more content. All he talked about was the wedding and how many more days and how glad he was that Landon was going to be his daddy.

"Okay, sport, I'll see you in a few minutes."

"Okay."

Ashley grabbed the bag with her dress in it and went upstairs to her mother's room. The lights were off, so she peeked in. "Mom?"

No answer.

Concern toyed with Ashley. She crept inside and tiptoed to the bed. "Mom? Are you okay?" The window was open and a breeze stirred the curtains. The smell of rose blossoms filled the room. Ashley flipped the light on. It was only four-thirty—too early for the lights to be off. "Mom?"

Her mother moaned and turned a few inches in each direction. "Hmmm?"

"It's me . . . Ashley." She sat on the edge of the bed and felt her mother's forehead. "Is today worse?"

No response. Gradually her mother opened her eyes and squinted at Ashley. "Oh, hello, dear. I guess I fell asleep."

"Was it a hard day?"

"Mmm." She made a face and rubbed her eyes. "It wasn't good."

"Want me to leave you alone?" Ashley had looked forward to this moment ever since she'd accepted Landon's ring. But not if her mother wasn't feeling well.

"No, dear." Elizabeth made a painful struggle to sit up against the headboard. "You sound excited."

"Well . . ." Ashley lifted her eyebrows, and her voice fell to a pinched squeak. She held up the garment bag. "I got my wedding dress! I haven't shown anyone yet."

"Oh, Ashley." She struggled again, but instead of sitting up higher, she sank back down. Her face was ashen, damp from the effort. "Can you help me, dear?"

Ashley tossed the bag over the back of the nearby chair and returned to the bed. She pushed four pillows behind and around her. Then she slipped her hands beneath her mother's arms and pulled her up higher. "There. Sunset Hills was good for something." Ashley kept her tone light, but she was shocked. No matter how sick her mother got, she'd never needed help to sit up in bed. She searched her mother's face. "You sure you're okay?"

"I'm fine." She folded her hands on her lap and nodded at the garment bag. "Will you try it on for me?"

The thrill of the moment replaced her fear. Ashley nodded, grabbed the bag, and headed inside her parents' walk-in closet. She had found the dress three weeks ago, and the seamstress at the shop had needed the extra time to narrow the waist and add a few feet of satin to the train.

She slipped it over her head and stood in front of the full-length mirror. The entire dress was white satin, accented with off-white satin embroidery. It was fitted at the bodice, with delicate sleeves that puffed slightly at the shoulders and then became fitted from the elbow down. Intricate appliqué ran the length of the arms and in a pattern along the skirt. The bottom half of the dress was neither formfitting nor full of flounce. Rather it fell gently in an alluring cascade that hinted at her figure but maintained a sense of propriety.

"Hurry, honey. I can't wait."

"Okay . . . just a minute." Ashley grinned at herself. Who would've ever thought she'd see herself in a dress like this? The back was covered with more appliqué and a row of delicate satin beads that served as buttons from the nape of her neck to her waist. Her mother would have to help her fasten them.

She shook out the train, opened the closet door, and presented herself to her mother. "Ta-da!"

Her mom took in the sight, and her lips parted. The color that had been missing from her cheeks returned in a rush, and she made a quiet gasp as she covered her mouth with her hand. "Ashley . . . you are absolutely gorgeous."

Ashley felt the glow from the center of her soul. She locked eyes with her mother and breathed in the smell of roses and springtime. As long as she lived she would remember this moment, cherish the fact that her mother had been the first to see her in her wedding dress, that despite her poor decisions and crazy choices, despite the times she'd broken her mother's heart, this glorious moment was one between just the two of them.

"You like it?"

Her mother held out her hand. "You are a vision, my dear. Landon won't be able to say a word with you looking like that."

Ashley gave her mother's fingers a gentle squeeze. "Look at the back." She turned around and spread out her train. "Isn't it something?"

"Yes, dear." Outside the open window, a flock of birds settled in the old oak tree and began to sing. The sound only added to the magic of the moment. "And that train . . . my goodness, it's breathtaking."

Ashley turned back toward her again. "I'll need help with the buttons, of course, but not right now. You get the idea."

"Come here." Her mother held out her hand again. "I can handle a few buttons. Let's see how it fits when they're all fastened."

Despite the color in her mother's face, Ashley wasn't sure. She looked too weak to do much of anything. Still, the glow in her eyes told Ashley she wanted to try. "Okay." Ashley turned the chair sideways and sat down, her back to her mother.

One at a time she felt the buttons come together, but when Elizabeth was halfway finished, Ashley felt her mother's hands drop away.

"Ah, Ash, I hate this."

Ashley spun around and saw tears in her mom's eyes. "It's okay." She stood and leaned closer, hugging her mom for a long time. Her tone hid the shock she was feeling. If Elizabeth was worn out after only a few minutes of buttons, then how could she be getting better? The answer shot a dart of fear through the moment.

"I'm sorry." Elizabeth wiped at her tears. "I don't have the strength for anything today. I almost fell asleep in the bathroom after I threw up."

The picture made Ashley shudder. She drew back and smiled at her mother. "Don't worry about the buttons; I told you we don't need to do them up today. Anyone would get tired with so many of them."

The door opened and Cole flew into the room. In his hand was a colored page from the book he'd been working in. He stopped and stared at Ashley. "Mommy!"

She grinned and did a small spin for him. "You like it?"

"Is that your wedding dress?" Cole's smile stretched from ear to ear.

"Yep." She fluffed out her train once more. "Whadya think?"

Cole came closer, circling her first one way then the other. "I think you look like a princess, Mommy. A fairy princess."

Elizabeth coughed a few times and then held her hand toward Cole. "What do you have there?"

"A picture for you, Grandma. So you'll feel better." Cole took a few steps toward the bed, but he kept his eyes on Ashley the whole time. He held the colored page out. "Here. You can keep it on the wall by your bed."

Ashley watched her mother admire the picture. At almost the same time, she felt Cole's fingers against her back, and she jumped. "Hey, mister, your hands are cold."

"How come it isn't buttoned, Mommy?"

"Because . . ." A lump formed in Ashley's throat. Cole's interruption had made her forget for a minute how sick her mother was. "Because Grandma was buttoning me up when you came in, but she got tired."

Cole's face lit up. "I'll finish it. I'm a good buttoner, right?"

"Yes, you're a very good buttoner." Ashley took Cole's hands in hers and checked them. He'd washed them after lunch, and they were still clean. "Okay, just go real slow, all right?"

"All right." He stood behind her and with her mother giving a few tips, he had the hang of it in no time.

"I can't reach the high ones." Cole was on his tiptoes, but she could feel his body wavering as he struggled.

"Sorry, buddy." She bent her knees. "How's that?"

"Perfect." He worked a minute more and she felt him back up. "There you go. All buttoned up."

"Good work, Cole." Her mother's voice sounded happier, less defeated.

"Yes. This is just how it'll look for the wedding." Ashley paraded around the room in a slow procession until she was a few feet from them. "Well?"

"It looks better now, Mommy. I'm glad we did the buttons." Cole's face was serious. "You'd get cold if you left them open for the wedding."

Ashley bent and slipped one arm around Cole and the other around her mother. The coloring in her mother's face was gone again, her complexion gray and lifeless. Hard times lay ahead for all of them; Ashley felt it in her bones. But here, now, with her mother and her son gathered around her, dressed in the gown she would wear when she became Landon's wife, Ashley wished just one thing:

That they could keep this moment for a lifetime.

Because in the months ahead, perfect days like this one might be hard to find.

CHAPTER SEVENTEEN

KARI WAS OUT SHOPPING for dinner, making sure she had plenty of food for that night. Jim Flanigan, his wife, Jenny, and their children were finally coming over for dinner.

But instead of concentrating on the menu, Kari couldn't stop thinking about her mom. It was Friday of Memorial Day weekend, the last week in May. Her mother's first batch of chemo was finally finished. Dr. Steinman had seen her, but so far they didn't have the test results back.

Not that they needed test results to see how she was doing. She was wasting away before their eyes. Her strength—which should've come back at least in part by now—was at its lowest point since the surgery. None of it looked good, but no one could seem to give them an answer.

She was halfway to the market when she made a right turn and headed for her father's medical office instead. Maybe he'd heard something this morning. It was worth a try; besides, she wanted to talk to her father alone.

Ten minutes later the receptionist ushered her back to her father's small office at the end of the hall. The woman had known the Baxters for years, and usually she was bright and cheerful. Not today. Her smile was sad, pained. She barely nodded at Kari and when she left, her voice was heavy. "He'll be right with you."

Kari sat in a hard-backed chair, stiff and straight. She was three months pregnant, starting to feel tight around her waist. Her doctor said the baby looked perfect, very healthy with a strong heartbeat. Kari clutched her purse to her waist and drummed her fingers on the soft leather. She willed him to hurry up, to have some kind of answer so she could stop guessing that her mother was doing badly.

Footsteps sounded in the hallway, and her father's muffled voice. He opened the door and stopped when he saw her expression. "Hi, Kari."

"Hi." She stood and hugged him. "I had to go to the store and I thought I'd stop by."

He nodded. "Have you been over to the house today?"

"Not yet. Ashley's there. I called and she said mom was more tired today than yesterday. Coughing more, too."

"Yes." John led her back to the chair, waited until she was seated, and then took the spot behind his desk. "I'm worried about her."

"Dad . . ." Kari waited until she had her father's complete attention. "Be straight with me, please. Why isn't she getting better?"

Her father gripped the arms of his chair, his eyes narrow, pensive. "We're still waiting for the results, Kari. We won't know anything until then."

"But you're a doctor, Dad." She huffed, the frustration spilling into her tone. "You must have an idea. Isn't she supposed to be getting better?"

For a long time John said nothing, just sat there and looked at her. His eyes began to shine and then tear up. He shrugged and gave a shake of his head. "It doesn't look good. I'm . . . I'm worried about her."

For the first time since hearing the news about her mother's cancer, Kari realized something. This wasn't merely another bout of cancer, another battle on the timeline of her mother's life. It was her life. Her very life was at stake, which meant that if something good didn't come of the tests, if she didn't start showing signs of improvement, she might die.

"Dad . . . I'm so afraid." Kari was too choked up to talk, so her words were a tinny whisper. She stood and moved around the desk. Then, like she'd done since she was a little girl, she sat on her father's lap and looped her arms around his neck. "We can't lose her."

"I know." Her father stroked the back of her head, her hair, and rocked her. "We have to keep praying, keep believing."

"Believing for what?" She wasn't being sarcastic, just matter-of-fact. "I keep asking God to heal her, but she's worse than ever."

John closed his eyes and blinked back the wetness. "Pray for a miracle, sweetheart. A miracle bigger than anything God's given us before."

A series of sobs lined up in her throat, but Kari refused them. She couldn't cry, not now when they still had a chance for good news. She clung to her father a little while longer, and then stood and faced him. "Let me know when you hear something, okay?"

He rose and hugged her. "I will."

"In the meantime I'll pray for a miracle."

❧

Dinner was better than Kari had expected.

After the conversation with her father, she hadn't felt like entertaining. She wanted to go to her mother, crawl in bed beside her, and wait for the miracle they were praying for. But life had a way of moving on, even when hard times were at hand.

Ryan found her an hour before the Flanigans arrived. "You

don't have to do this." He wrapped his arms around her waist and kissed her. "I know you're thinking about your mom."

Kari nodded. She loved Ryan, loved the way he always knew what she was thinking and just what to say to make her feel better. They'd known each other so long, he'd loved her mother almost as long as she had. She kissed him back and smiled. "It's okay. I want to meet Jim's family, and besides . . . having something else to think about will be good for a change."

The Flanigans arrived at six o'clock and almost instantly, the atmosphere in the house changed. Kari hadn't realized how gloomy she'd been over the past few days until the light and love and laughter that made up the Flanigan family spilled through the front door.

Jessie stood close to her and Ryan, batting her eyelashes, not sure what to make of the commotion.

Ryan welcomed them. "Hello!"

"We're here!" Jim and Jenny were first, Jenny balancing an oversized salad bowl in one hand and a gallon of apple juice in the other. Jim held a grocery bag full of what looked like potato chips. "Hi, everyone!"

They kept pouring in.

A striking girl followed Jim and Jenny, and Kari guessed her to be fourteen or so. She smiled sweetly at Kari and Ryan and Jessie. "I'm Bailey."

"Hi, Bailey." Kari patted the girl on the shoulder. "Come on in."

Next were a series of boys, each stopping and shaking first Ryan's hand and then Kari's. "Hello, ma'am; my name's Shawn." A small brown-skinned boy held out his hand and grinned at her. "Nice to meet you."

"Nice to meet you, too."

Next came Connor and BJ and Justin and Ricky.

Half of them were Haitian, half of them Jim and Jenny's biological kids. Every single one of them made a proper introduction. Kari hoped there wouldn't be a test. She would be lucky to remember half their names.

Dinner was a riot.

Kari served lasagna while Ryan poured apple juice for the kids and Jim and Jenny set about preparing plates. Two bags of rolls were ripped open, and Jim had them buttered at a speed that Kari was sure set some sort of record.

"Two rolls or three?" he yelled out.

The boys lined up as if they were used to getting their food this way. As they filed past Jenny, they took a heaping plate of lasagna and held up two or three fingers for Jim, depending on how many rolls they wanted.

Kari watched the entire process with her mouth open. She came alongside Jenny and leaned close enough so she could whisper. "You do this every night?"

Jenny laughed. "Only if we want to eat." She handed out another plate. "It's a circus, but we love it."

Finally, when even little Jessie was served, they sat at the table. Ryan had added two extra leaves for the occasion, and with the addition of the folding chairs from the basement everyone fit around the table.

Ryan prayed over the meal. A half dozen quiet conversations began as soon as he was finished.

"Pass the salt, please, Shawn."

"I'm gonna use it first, okay?"

"Okay."

Jim took a big bite of lasagna, chewed twice, and swallowed. "We love lasagna in men's town. Lasagna and beans and spaghetti. Those are the best, right, guys?"

The five boys giggled.

Across the table, Kari saw Ryan stifle a chuckle. "Kari doesn't know about men's town."

"Believe me—" Bailey rolled her eyes and grinned at Kari— "you don't want to know."

"I don't?" Kari tore a roll into small pieces for Jessie. "Okay, someone give. What's men's town all about?"

Connor was the oldest Flanigan boy. He put his fork down and cleared his throat. "Sometimes when Mom and Bailey are gone shopping or if Mom has a writers meeting and Bailey's at her friend's house, we have men's town." He giggled and looked at his brothers. "Dad makes frozen lasagna or beans and we . . . well . . ."

Jenny raised her eyebrows at Connor. "And the dinner table takes on a locker-room atmosphere," she concluded. "Let's just say we need a can of air freshener to get back in the house."

"I see." Kari covered her mouth to keep from laughing out loud. She shot Ryan a look. "Glad we don't have men's town over here, right?"

Ryan tried to look serious. "Right, honey. Couple town, that's us."

"That's okay, Taylor." The men were sitting next to each other, and Jim elbowed Ryan. "You can join us in men's town anytime you like. Okay, boys?"

Cheers went up around the table.

Bailey gave a slight shake of her head. "Brothers are disgusting."

"Oh, yeah?" Ricky was the youngest. He was a towhead with big blue eyes like his mother's. "Then how come you always wanna give us yucky kisses, huh?"

"Look out!" Bailey pretended to get up from the table. "I might come over there and give you one right now."

Everyone laughed. Jim suggested they play a game. "Any suggestions?" He looked from Kari to Ryan.

Jessie took a drink from her sippy cup. It was the quietest Kari had ever seen her.

"Games?" Ryan's face was blank. "A dinner game?"

"Sure." Jim looked at his kids. "Pick one guys; we'll teach the Taylors how to play."

"The alphabet game," someone shouted out.

"No, the what-am-I? game."

A round of agreements followed and Jim waved at them. They were quiet instantly. "Okay, the what-am-I? game it is." He looked around the table. "You all know the rules. You give us a bunch of clues and we have to guess what or who you are. Whoever guesses gets to go next."

BJ went first. "I'm thinking of something brown and flat and roughish."

Hands shot up around the table, with some of the kids so anxious to be picked, they bounced up and down in their seats.

BJ picked Justin, who proudly exclaimed, "You're a tree."

"Nope." BJ pointed at Bailey. "You pick."

"A picnic table?"

The boys giggled, as if only a girl might give such a lame answer. "Definitely not." BJ looked at Connor. "You."

"Brown and flat and roughish . . ." Connor scratched his forehead. "The roof of a house?"

"No, not a roof."

"Come on, BJ, give us more clues." Bailey took another bite of her lasagna. "You can't expect us to get it on that."

BJ grinned at the others. "Give up?"

A general consensus passed around the table that they had, indeed, given up. "The answer is me!" BJ pointed proudly at himself.

"That's my brother over there." Bailey pointed her thumb at BJ. "Captain Obvious. Brown? Flat? Roughish? Of course it's himself. How could we have missed it?"

Wild laughter and loud moans went up around the room, and Jim rubbed his knuckles on BJ's head. "Brown and flat and roughish? Come on, BJ, you forgot to mention the stinky-socks part."

"Dad . . ." BJ was still laughing. "I'm brown and flat." He patted the top of his head. "And when I forget lotion, my elbows and knees are roughish."

"Of course." Jim smacked himself on the forehead. He looked

at Ryan and shrugged. "Now you know how to play the what-am-I? game."

The joy and laughter continued until the meal was over and Jim excused the kids. Each of them cleared his or her own plate and thanked Kari for the dinner. Bailey held out her hands to Jessie, who grinned and went along without a complaint.

When they were gone, Kari stared at Jenny, awed. "That was absolutely amazing." She looked to Jim and back at his wife. "I've seen polite kids and I've seen silly kids, but I've never seen both. Your kids are wonderful."

Ryan leaned back and crossed his arms. A smile had hung on his face for the past ten minutes. "I told you they were great."

"How in the world does it work so well?"

"What? The numbers?" Jenny pushed herself back from the table and crossed her legs. She chuckled and reached across the table for Jim's hand. "I know it looks crazy, but we have a good time."

"The numbers, the manners, the laughter, the adoption . . . all of it. I've never seen a family like yours."

"The adoption was easy." Jenny winked at her husband. "Well, not completely easy."

"It was three months of adjusting, because the boys spoke Creole. But after that, it was great." Jim shrugged. "I feel like we've always had them."

Kari was dying to know more. "What led you to look at Haiti to adopt?"

"We didn't start there." Jenny took a sip of water. "We wanted to adopt domestically, but we had young kids in the house."

Jim nodded. "It's sad, really. So many of the kids you can adopt in the U.S. are physically abused in a number of ways. Our social worker told us it wouldn't be safe to bring them home until our biological kids were older."

"Then someone told us about this orphanage in Haiti. We went online, checked it out, and sent away for the video."

Kari slid closer to Ryan and took his hand in hers. Their story was fascinating.

Jim picked up where Jenny left off. "The video came and we waited until the kids were in bed to watch it. There were all these kids, laughing and singing and hugging each other. It looked like our family." He flashed a crooked grin. "Well, sort of."

"We didn't say a word through the whole video, and when it was over Jim turns to me and says, 'Looks like we need a bigger house.' "

"Hmmm." Ryan leaned closer to Kari. "Amazing. Weren't you worried about the culture differences? What if they got here and felt too strange to ever adjust?"

"We could tell from the video that everything would work out." Jim looped his arm around Jenny's shoulders. "Besides, whenever we prayed about it we got the same feeling. Those kids would be different, for sure. Different color, different country, different culture. But we would all have the same Christ. In the end that's all that's ever mattered."

They went on to talk about the adjustment period.

"The worst day was when I took them in for shots." Jenny let her head fall back against the chair and stared at the ceiling. "I wasn't sure any of us would survive."

"What happened?" Kari could already feel herself beginning to laugh.

Jenny looked at her. "I get the bright idea that they should all three get shots at once. Our own youngest, Ricky, isn't in school yet, so he can come with me. Just to help keep them occupied when it isn't their turn."

Jim chuckled, apparently remembering the recap of the day, and picked up the story. "They get in the car and Ricky starts to get sad. 'Mommy, are they going to get shots today? Why, Mommy?' That sort of thing." He laughed again. "So here's these three boys who don't speak a word of English, but they know Ricky's their brother. They start patting Ricky on the arm and comforting him, because for some reason, Ricky's not happy like before."

"They had no idea what was happening even after we got into the doctor's office." Jenny shook her head. "They were so excited, pointing at the artwork on the walls and the floating model airplanes in the doctor's office."

"Right up until the nurse walked in with a tray of needles."

"In the blink of an eye it became the craziest scene you could ever imagine. Shawn started screaming in Creole, '*Y Bondye, Y Bondye?*' which means 'Why, God, why?' "

The story got funnier the longer it went on. By the time the shots were given, all three boys—each between the ages of five and six at the time—were sobbing and holding their arms and straggling in a show of angry defiance. Ricky was crying, too, out of pity for his new brothers.

"People were staring at me like, 'Come on, lady, can't you control your day-care kids?' "

Kari laughed out loud. She could've sat there all night listening to stories, but the mood changed when Ryan asked Jim about Cody Coleman, one of the football players on Ryan's team.

"Is he living with you?" Kari leaned her head on her husband's shoulder but directed her question at Jim and Jenny.

"He never was, really." Jim's eyes grew softer, and Kari could see a pain there that defied the silly side of the man she'd seen earlier. "He slept on our couch for a few nights, but then he went back home and we haven't seen him since."

Kari was struck by the sorrow in both Jim's and Jenny's eyes. Almost as if they cared as much for Cody as they did for their own kids.

Jenny caught her attention. "He dropped out of the passing league at school; we think he's drinking again."

"I hate that." Ryan pursed his lips and gave a hard shake of his head. "The kid's got so much talent, so much inside him."

"He needs the Lord, but I think right now God scares him."

Jim exhaled hard. "As if he knows God's chasing him, and he's determined to run until he hits a brick wall."

"Exactly." Ryan leaned back and stretched his legs. "Anything we can do?"

"Pray for him. Pray he'll trust us enough to come back and listen."

The conversation shifted again, this time to the twenty-seven-year-old woman who had moved into their house a few months back. "Her name's Katy Hart." Jenny smiled. "Isn't that pretty?"

Kari nodded. "She's here to start a Christian theater? for kids?"

"Actually, she's already got it up and running. Sixty kids auditioned for the first play—*Charlie Brown*. The show will be sometime in July."

"That's great." Kari thought about Jessie, how dramatic she already was. "Kids need something like that."

"Our kids sure do." Jim gave his wife an easy smile. "The four youngest boys are sports crazy, but not Connor."

"Since he could walk he's wanted to be on Broadway, singing and dancing and entertaining an audience." Jenny looked over her shoulder. The kids were watching a movie in the next room, so she continued. "He's wanted to be part of a theater group forever, but many of the options are downright frightening. The Christian Kids Theater puts on three plays a year, and Connor's determined to be in every play until he's too old to try out."

"And the fun thing is that Bailey's interested, too. She sees how much fun Connor's having, and she's already decided to try out for the next play."

Kari thought about Katy Hart. "How'd she wind up living with you?"

"For months before she got here, the folks at our church who helped organize the theater group were asking for someone to give her a room. Back then we were too caught up in getting settled. We didn't even know she was coming out." Jim paused. "The position doesn't pay much, if anything, and she didn't know a soul in Bloomington. We have an apartment over the garage, so as soon as we realized she needed a place, we volunteered."

"She's a delightful young woman, beautiful and great with kids," Jenny added. "Quirky enough to make the commitment fun for everyone."

"No guy in the picture, huh?" Kari always imagined a love story when she heard about someone single doing something crazy like moving to Bloomington to start a children's theater.

"No guy." Jenny gave a few slow nods of her head. "She left something behind in Chicago. I'm sure of that. But so far she hasn't shared whatever it was."

Connor came running into the room, his eyes bright. "Guess what? They have *Fiddler on the Roof*; isn't that great?" He looked at Kari. "That's one of the greatest musicals ever."

"See—" Jim motioned to his oldest son and grinned—"I told you."

They talked a while longer, but then it was time to go. Jim made the announcement and without a single complaint, the kids slipped their shoes back on and thanked Kari and Ryan for having them over.

"Let's do this again," Jenny said, hugging Kari as she left. "Next time you come to our house."

Kari smiled. "Absolutely. I can't wait to see where all these kids sleep."

The couples said good-bye to each other. After the Flanigan family was gone, Kari put Jessie to bed and found Ryan in their bedroom. "They were just like you said. What a great family."

"They have their struggles. Yesterday the athletic director told Jim he can't pray with players anymore if he wants to keep coaching at Bloomington High."

"You're kidding?" This was the first Kari had heard of the situation.

"No, but neither of us is worried. As long as the kids lead the prayers, no athletic director can stop us. Besides . . ." He made a funny face and pointed to the wall where his NFL plaques hung.

"Yes, you're right." Kari laughed. "He could hardly get rid of two former NFL players. The community would have a fit."

"Yeah, Jim's a great guy. I knew you'd love his family." Ryan came up to her and pulled her into his arms. He searched her eyes and she felt the familiar tickle in her stomach, the feeling he had given her since she was twelve years old and met him at a backyard barbecue.

She kissed him and drew back, enjoying the closeness. "Now I know what you mean."

"About what?"

"When you picture us down the road, you picture us like them."

"Mmm." His lips found hers. "Exactly."

"They're sort of like we were, us Baxters, growing up."

Ryan thought about that. "They are, aren't they?" He nuzzled his face against hers. "No wonder I like them so much."

It wasn't until an hour later, when they were both falling asleep, that Kari realized just how wonderful the evening had been. Not only because she'd had a chance to meet the Flanigan family, to witness their loving children and hear some of their funny stories, but also because for an entire evening she didn't have to worry about the one thing that stayed with her night and day.

Whether or not her mother was getting better.

CHAPTER EIGHTEEN

ERIN HAD FOUND a substitute teacher to take over the rest of the school year for her. Now that she had a baby, a daughter, the last thing she wanted was to place her in day care. Her principal wanted to know whether she'd be back in the fall, and the answer was an easy one.

"I've wanted to be a Mommy ever since I got married," she told the woman. "Next time you see me looking for work, my hair will be a lovely shade of gray."

Being a mother to Heidi Jo was a greater experience than Erin had ever imagined. Heidi was a happy baby with olive skin and eyes that were already turning green. Erin had settled into a wonderful routine, one that included hours of feeding Heidi, changing her, and standing over her crib while she slept. Twice a day she put Heidi in a stroller and walked her through the neighborhood.

But most of all, Erin loved sitting with Heidi in the old Baxter rocking chair and singing to her. The way her mother had said she used to sing to each of them.

Often, when Heidi fell asleep, Erin would call her mother and marvel over the amazing feelings her tiny daughter evoked in her. "It's like this is what I was created to do," she told her mother this afternoon, the first Monday in June. "Did you ever feel that way?"

"Always." Her mother paused. "Every time I brought a baby home from the hospital I felt that this was the reason God had given me life. So I could raise my babies and give my family a life they would always remember, a life that would teach them to do the same thing for the people they loved one day."

The answer seemed to sap the energy from her mother, and Erin wondered, as she had often in the past week, how well she was really doing. "Did you get your test results?"

"No." Her answer came quickly. "We should hear any day."

"But how do you feel, Mom? Isn't that the real test?"

The silence at the other end made Erin stop rocking. She wasn't sure, but it sounded like her mother was crying. Not loud sobs, but a soft kind of tired weeping that would've been easy to miss over the phone lines.

"Mom?" Heidi was asleep, so she held the phone between her shoulder and cheekbone, and laid her daughter down in her crib. She waited until she was out of the nursery to ask the next question. "Are you okay?"

Her mother made a few light sniffs. "I'm okay." She sighed and it sounded almost like a sob. "I hate feeling tired all the time. I never got my energy back and Dr. Steinman is worried. Everyone's worried."

Erin hated this, being so far away and not having the chance to look at her mother, to see for herself how bad off she was. She'd asked her sisters and always the answer was the same: "Mom's battling it, Erin. She's fighting back. She's praying for a miracle." But unless Erin could see for herself, she'd never know for sure.

She stared out the window at the storm clouds gathering in the distance. "Should I come, Mom? Is that what you're saying?"

"No, dear." The sorrow shifted just a bit, and Elizabeth uttered a sad laugh. "Don't get on a plane. You'll be coming in four weeks. Better to wait until that angel of yours is a little older, anyway."

"But what about you?"

"I'm fine. It's probably just my age. Anyone would have a hard time coming back after eight weeks of chemo, but at fifty-four it's bound to be tougher."

"Fifty-four is young, Mom. Especially for you." Erin hesitated. "Is your hair growing back?"

"Actually, it is." Her mother laughed again, and this time her tone sounded lighter. "I look like a porcupine, pokey pieces of dark hair sticking straight out from my bald head."

Erin didn't smile. She couldn't stand the thought of her mother looking anything but beautiful. "At least it's growing back."

"Yes. Now, dear, go get some rest. You know the adage . . ."

" 'When the baby sleeps, you sleep.' " Erin relaxed some.

"Right. That was especially true for you, Miss Erin. I swear you didn't sleep more than two hours at a time until you were a year old."

"Heidi's a lot better than that. She gives us six-hour stretches every night, but you're right. I'll go lie down for a while; Sam won't be home for another few hours."

"Okay. Call me tomorrow if you get a chance."

"Mom . . ."

"Yes."

"I love you." A sudden rush of emotions made it hard for Erin to speak. "These past few months, before Heidi and especially now, I feel closer to you than ever. I just . . . I want you to know how much these talks mean to me."

Her mother didn't respond, and Erin understood why. Neither of them knew how many of these talks they had left. Finally her mother coughed several times and in a small voice racked with emotion, she said, "Thank you, Erin. I love you too."

Erin hung up and drifted down the hallway to their bedroom.

Things were so good here at home. Not just with Heidi and the light she'd brought into their lives. But with her and Sam and their faith and everything about their new lives together. Only two black marks smudged the perfect picture, and as Erin lay down she determined to pray about both of them.

First for her mother, that God would give them the miracle they needed and let the test results be hopeful. And second, as she had every day since the awful call from the social worker, she prayed for Candy and her baby.

A little girl Erin still thought of as Amy Elizabeth.

※

The screaming was incessant.

Ever since she'd brought the kid home, all she'd done was scream, the same way she was screaming now. Candy went to the cupboard, found a cracked bottle and a nipple that looked clean enough. Then she mixed up four ounces of formula and shoved the bottle in the microwave. *Fifteen seconds—that oughta be long enough to heat it up.*

She pulled it out, shook it up, and then noticed something she hadn't seen before: a perfectly good joint sitting on the edge of the ashtray at the center of the coffee table. How great was this? She hadn't gotten high in three days, mostly because money was tight. But people must've come by last night, because sure enough, someone had left a marijuana cigarette just lying there.

Candy set the bottle down and looked across the room at the dresser drawer in the corner that was doubling as a crib. "Just a minute, crybaby. I'll get ya . . . I'll get ya."

She took the roach, lit the end with a lighter sitting nearby, and inhaled until her lungs wouldn't hold another bit. The longer the hold, the better the high, so Candy held in the smoke until she was about to pass out. Slowly she exhaled, and already she could feel the buzz, feel the way it clouded every bad thing about her life.

The screaming wasn't as loud now, but it was still going on.

Candy looked around the room. Where had she put the bottle? In the refrigerator? She stood and walked around the apartment until her trail led her back to the still-smoking joint. She pinched it between her fingers, held it to her lips, and lit the end again. This time she sucked in even more of the sweet, pungent smoke.

The feeling was working its way through her body, numbing her, lulling her into a rhythm that would take her away from the rotten apartment and empty refrigerator, to a place where she couldn't care less if the kid was screaming.

Candy put the roach down and looked across the room again. The kid. She'd almost forgotten. Her eyes made a lazy circle around the room and there, a few feet from her on the very same coffee table, was the bottle. It was probably cold by now, but so what? At least the kid wouldn't be hungry.

She took the bottle, crossed the room, and finally exhaled the smoke. It seemed to settle over the dresser drawer, where her latest baby was still screaming.

"Whadya want, kid?" Candy swept the baby up and into her arms. "You've got a nice bed, warm blankets." She pressed the bottle against the baby's lower lip and right away she began sucking. "Hmmm." The buzz was growing stronger. "Didn't I feed you this morning?"

The baby sucked at the bottle with all her might, so urgent and desperate that the sight of her made Candy laugh. Or maybe it was the pot making her laugh. Either way she was glad the kid had stopped screaming.

Candy laid her on the sofa and used a worn-out pillow to prop up the bottle. The joint wasn't half gone, and Candy wanted to finish it. Better to get a good solid buzz than drag it out over a couple hours.

She took drag after drag, and suddenly she realized the baby was crying again. "What is it now?" Her words were slurred and the floor was no longer steady. She turned and saw what was wrong. The bottle was on the floor, empty, and the baby had worked the old pillow up over her face.

Candy laughed. "Still hungry, huh?" She moved the pillow, picked up the baby, and put her over her shoulder. "You and me both, kid."

She grabbed the bottle and walked the baby into the kitchen. The buzz was intense now, one of the better highs she'd had that month. But still she was able to mix up another four ounces of formula. She stared at the microwave and tried to remember. Fifteen seconds? Or was it twenty-five?

The kid was screaming again.

Candy lowered her to the crook of her arm. It must've been twenty-five. The baby liked her milk warm. She heated the formula, headed back to the sofa, and put the bottle to the kid's lips. As soon as the formula touched her mouth, she jerked back and screamed even louder than before.

"Okay, so I was wrong." Candy chuckled and shook the bottle for a minute or so to cool it down.

This time the baby made only a few faces and uncomfortable squirms, but she took the milk. Candy grabbed a bag of chips from the counter and put the baby back on the couch, the bottle propped by the pillow again. She almost finished the bottle when she started fussing and arching her back.

The moment Candy picked her up, a stream of vomit came from the baby and splashed across Candy's shirt. Candy swore out loud and set the baby back on the couch. "Now look what you've done, ya brat."

She left the baby and went to the closet to find a clean shirt. While she was cleaning herself up, she heard the baby making sick sounds again. "Hold on," she shouted. "And don't get any on the couch!"

The weed was still working its magic on her, but who could enjoy a good buzz with a fussy baby? Candy mumbled a few more choice words and headed back to find her.

She was lying on her back, a pool of vomit gathered around

her lips and chin. A gurgling sound came from her throat, and suddenly fear knocked the wind out of Candy. "Hey!" She grabbed her and smacked her back.

After a few seconds, the baby did several loud coughs. Once she was breathing right, the screaming started up again.

Candy took off the kid's damp undershirt and used it to wipe her chin and neck. She shouted over the child's screams. "Bedtime for you, little girl." Then she marched her across the room to her bed in the dresser drawer.

Candy couldn't possibly have been more frustrated. Everything about her situation was Dave's fault. Dave's and Scary's. But still, here she was, with a month before her oldest two kids would be dumped at her front door and a newborn screaming in the corner.

It was enough to make her crazy.

Things had gone from bad to worse so fast Candy wasn't sure what to do. Her mother had taken the older girls, but she'd made things clear to Candy. They could stay with her only for a month. After that she was joining some Christian cruise line, where she would work in the kitchen and travel the Bahamas for the better part of a year.

"I love those girls, Candy, but they deserve a real family," her mother had said the last time they were together. "Get yourself a life, Candy. Clean up and make a home for those babies. Otherwise do the right thing and give them to someone who will."

Candy hated her mother's lectures.

They were her kids; she could do whatever she wanted with them. The thought rolled around in the stoned areas of her mind. Of course, she couldn't really do whatever she wanted with them. She couldn't sell them, that's for sure.

What had they been thinking, anyway? You couldn't blackmail people into giving you money for a kid. The plan had been doomed from the beginning. For a while there, it looked like she and Dave and Scary were all going down. They'd sat in jail almost two days before the judge made up his mind.

Dave had pinned the whole scam on Scary, and Scary, well, he pinned the whole thing on Dave. Candy gave the judge a teary-eyed song and dance about wanting the best life for her baby and about how Dave and Scary had convinced her they could find a better home for the child if they asked for more money.

The judge looked like he wasn't sure about her, but being that she was eight months pregnant, he told her to go home and take care of herself until the baby was born. He left her with a warning: "If I see you in court again or hear you're putting your baby in jeopardy in any way, I'll take her away from you and prosecute you to the fullest extent of the law."

The judge's warning played in her head again, swirling about and climbing the walls of her brain the way thoughts sometimes did when she was high. He was all talk; he wouldn't take her kid away.

Though he'd been pretty serious about Dave and Scary. They were still in the slammer facing trial later that month. Whatever happened, they better get out soon. Without them, she had no idea how she'd get the drugs she needed.

Candy put her hands over her ears.

The screaming lessened, but it still gave her a headache. What she needed was more weed, something to pass the time until the kid got old enough to farm out. If her mother wouldn't take the girls, someone would. She could get connected with that church her mother was always going to. Someone there would watch the girls—at least during the daytime. There were always nice old grandma-types at churches, right?

An idea started to grow in Candy's brain.

A grandma-type lived right next door. Maybe if she took the kid there now, the old lady would take care of her for a while. Until she could figure out what to do next. She stood up, swayed a few times, and made it across the apartment to the bathroom. Her vision was blurred a bit, but she squinted and got a decent look at herself.

She was heavy and her T-shirt and jeans didn't fit great. Also, her skin still smelled of baby puke. But she didn't look like a pot-head. Not really. Potheads had narrow, bloodshot eyes, and hers looked pretty normal. It was important that she not look like a pothead if she was going to ask the neighbor for help. She would have to make up some sort of story, something about needing a job and trying to make a life for herself and her kid.

Now that Candy knew what she was going to do, a sense of freedom and purpose came over her. She held herself a bit straighter as she went back to the dresser drawer, picked up the baby and a half-empty pack of disposable diapers, and knocked on the neighbor's door.

The old woman answered after the second knock. She stared at Candy and the baby. "Yes?"

"Hi. I'm Candy." Her words sounded right to her, but Candy wasn't sure if the old lady would think so. Words would have to be at a minimum. She pointed to her right. "I live next door and . . . well . . . I need to get out and find some work." She smiled. Grandma's liked it if you smiled. "Trouble is, I can't bring my little baby, and I was wonderin' if you'd watch her for me for a while."

The woman was wearing a necklace with a cross on it. Just like Candy had hoped, a churchgoing lady. How could she say no? Candy tilted her arms so the woman could get a good view of her kid. She was a screamer, but she was also a looker. Every-one who had seen her said so.

"She's a beautiful baby." The grandma-type brushed her knuckle against the baby's cheek. "What's her name?"

"Her name?" A chill ran down Candy's spine. What had she named the kid? She'd written something down in the hospital, something with a *C* in it. But now . . . now she hadn't used it in a few weeks and she wasn't sure. She smiled at the old lady. "Clara. Her name's Clara."

"I'm Nancy." She looked at the baby again and held out her arms. "Here, let me have her."

Candy turned the baby over to her neighbor and started

backing away but Nancy stopped her. "How long? Two hours? Three?"

"Yes." Another step backward. "Thanks. I'll get so much more done now."

The minute Candy was back in her apartment she flopped down on the couch and savored the sound.

Silence. Pure, wonderful silence.

Another plan began to form and she sat up to think it through.

An hour later she had her things packed into a duffel bag. She walked to the closest bus stop and climbed into the first bus that came by. The buses were easy in Austin, and after she got to the main station, she'd bum a ride to Dallas. One of Dave's friends was there, some guy who dealt for a living. Lots of space, lots of drugs, lots of free time.

She pictured the old grandma trying to find a way to keep the kid quiet. Two or three hours? Candy laughed to herself. The woman wouldn't see her for two or three days. Maybe longer. And by then Clara—if that was her name—would've gotten over the stomach bug or whatever was making her cry. If so, Candy would consider taking her back.

Welfare paid better the more mouths you had to feed.

CHAPTER NINETEEN

THE SCENE WAS eerily similar to the one back in March, when Elizabeth and John first found out about her cancer. But this time, the stakes were higher.

Elizabeth was exhausted, with barely the strength to sit in the chair beside John. "Why do we have to be here?" She leaned her head on his shoulder. "Can't he just call us with the results?"

"It's easier this way." John eased his arm around her shoulders. His tone told her there were things he wasn't saying. "We can talk about a recovery strategy better in person, with all of us here."

"I wish he'd hurry."

John kissed the side of her face. "Me too."

The worst part about fighting cancer was the waiting. Eight weeks of chemo, then two weeks of waiting. A day of testing, ten more days before the results came. She was thin and tired and achy all the time, and the cough that had come on a week ago was worse than ever.

Still, they were praying for a miracle, and the test results were the only way they'd know if one was being worked in her body

or not. Elizabeth hated herself for doubting, for fearing whatever
tomorrow might bring. But the longer she felt sick and the worse
her symptoms grew, the more terrified she became.

Certainly God knew that. He had to know that she wanted to
be planning a reunion and a wedding, not a recovery. And since
the answers she and John were praying for weren't coming easily,
Elizabeth was more afraid than ever. So afraid that she'd slipped
into a denial, a way of telling everyone she was feeling fine, that
everything was going to be okay.

But she wasn't fooling anyone.

A door opened behind the big wooden desk. Dr. Steinman
entered with a folder under his arm. A strange sense of déjà vu
came over Elizabeth, and she glanced at the door behind her, the
one that led to the hallway and the outside world. If she could
only get up and run out the door, tear down the hall and never
stop, maybe she could keep this moment from happening.

"Elizabeth . . . John." Dr. Steinman took his place at the desk
and laid open the file.

She gave a last look at the door and turned to face the doctor.
John tightened the grip on her hand.

"I'll get right to the point." He sighed and held up a single
sheet from the file. "I'm afraid the results aren't what we were
hoping for."

Not what they were hoping for? Panic shot a burst of adrenaline through Elizabeth's system, and she leaned forward. *Breathe,*
she told herself. *Just breathe.* Beside her, a moan sounded deep in
John's chest, but he said nothing.

Dr Steinman shook his head. His eyes met hers and held.
"Elizabeth, your cancer has spread. We did a biopsy of your
lymph nodes, as you know, and every test came back positive
for cancer."

"No . . ." She said the word so softly no one heard her, not
even John. The scene kept playing out before her, the doctor's
words coming at her like so many bullets. She closed her eyes,
desperate for a way to outrun the news, to stop the doctor's pro-

nouncement before it got worse. *No, God . . . no! Why is this happening?*

"Elizabeth?" The doctor sounded tired, as if the blow he was delivering was aging him several years in as many minutes.

She opened her eyes. "Go ahead."

Beside her, John was staring at his lap, his eyes vacant.

The doctor sighed. "On top of that, we compared the ultrasound and X rays we did the Monday after your treatment ended with an ultrasound and X rays we did yesterday." He set the first piece of paper down and picked up another. "We knew after the surgery that your cancer was in your lymph system. With this type of aggressive cancer, the lymph system often deposits cancer cells throughout the body. It appears that's what has happened in your case, Elizabeth. The cancer has spread to your lungs and possibly to your liver and pancreas as well." He pursed his lips and met her eyes again. "The CAT scan looked clean, so that much is good news. So far the cancer hasn't spread to your brain."

Good news? Elizabeth wanted to throw something at him, pound her fists on the wall, and break something on the floor. The cancer hadn't spread to her brain? That was the good news? She sucked in a quick breath and then another. The panic swelled within her, suffocating her. Another inhale and another.

"Elizabeth, breathe out, honey." John had his hand on her shoulder. He gently pushed her head down, the way she'd seen him do for the kids before. "It's okay, Elizabeth, breathe out. Blow on my hand."

She pursed her lips and tried, but only a whisper of breath came out.

Dr. Steinman was on the other side of her now, pressing a cool cloth to her forehead. She was hyperventilating, letting panic have its way with her. She sucked in another breath, and then, above her pounding heart, above the sound of Dr. Steinman's voice, above the panic screaming at her from all sides, she heard the only sound that could possibly restore her sanity.

The sound of her husband praying.

"Dear God . . ." His words were hushed, meant for her ears and God's alone. "Please . . . give Elizabeth your peace, a peace that passes all understanding. Let her remember that you are a God of miracles, that you haven't ever stopped loving her and that you have a plan, even now."

John's words wrapped themselves around her like a shield, a cocoon. One breath at a time she could feel a change coming over her. The muscles that had refused to exhale only a moment earlier could now do so. *Breathe out,* she told herself. *Out . . . out . . . out . . .*

"How're you doing, Elizabeth?" Dr. Steinman had returned to his place at the desk.

How was she doing? Didn't he realize how ludicrous he sounded? Hadn't he just answered the question himself? She wasn't doing very well. She was dying, in fact, right? Wasn't that what he had told her? She lifted her head and looked at him. Why was she mad at him? It wasn't his fault. She felt her anger melt away like April snow. He was simply the messenger and he was waiting for an answer.

She gripped John's knee as she sat a little straighter. "Better, I guess."

"Good." The doctor put the file back together. Then he looked from her to John. "You understand what I'm saying, right?"

The muscles in John's jawline flexed twice. He inhaled sharply. "I assume you're going to give us a treatment plan?"

Elizabeth wanted to kiss him. That was her John. *You tell him, honey.* Neither of them would ever settle for a death sentence— not now with Ashley's wedding and Kari's baby and Erin's and Luke's visits on the horizon. Definitely not.

"I . . . uh, well . . ." Dr. Steinman's face went blank and he fumbled a few seconds more. "Look, John, don't make this harder than it has to be."

"I want a treatment plan." John's tone was sharp, pointed.

"We didn't come here to make funeral arrangements, so please, tell us what to do next. That's your job."

Dr. Steinman lifted his hands a few inches off his desk and dropped them again. "We could operate on her lungs, and possibly her pancreas." He opened the file again. "The liver isn't operable without a transplant." His eyes scanned the sheet. "Any surgery would mean more chemo and radiation—" he looked at John again—"which her cancer isn't responding to, frankly."

Elizabeth glanced at John, waiting for his response. But he was quiet, tense. He had one hand over hers and the other clenched in a tight fist. When he spoke again, some of his earlier fight was gone. "We'd like a day to talk it over, if that's all right."

The doctor released a slow breath. Exasperation showed in his eyes, and his voice was filled with a quiet pleading. "Please, John. Think it through. Quality of life has to mean something."

John made a tighter grip on her hand and squeezed his eyes shut for a moment. When he opened them, Elizabeth met his eyes and a pain took up residence in her heart. No matter how confident and authoritative John sounded, he was dying inside, dying every bit as much as she was.

He spread his free hand out on the doctor's desk and leaned forward. "If we didn't operate . . ." His mouth hung open. The next words seemed to take all his effort. "How long would she have?"

It was the question Elizabeth hadn't wanted to address, not now or ever. But there it was. Out on the table for the doctor to pick up and run with. She leaned into John, praying for a miracle. Begging God for another chance, a different diagnosis.

"Whether we operate or not . . ." Dr. Steinman closed the file and angled his head. His eyes were damp. "Three months, John. Maybe four. Not more than that."

Three months? Four? The numbers swirled in Elizabeth's mind, and she buried her face in John's shoulder. Panic, fear, desperation, none of them could reach her. Not when her entire existence was numbed by the figures. Sixteen weeks? At best? Was that all she had left?

Tears filled her eyes and spilled down her face, making the sleeve of John's shirt wet. She wasn't crying, not really. She was too numb to cry or feel or react. Rather her body was grieving all on its own, the tears leaking from her eyes without any weeping or sobbing or emotions.

Sixteen weeks?

John was saying something, going on about taking a day to decide and not giving up, about wanting the best for Elizabeth, and how they were willing to fight the cancer whatever the cost. And the doctor was responding, something about recovery time and weight loss and statistics.

Elizabeth let their words blur together.

In the aching, desperate places of her heart she was no longer sitting in a doctor's office receiving a death sentence. She was eighteen, dancing in John's arms at the University of Michigan summer mixer. But then the image blurred and she wasn't wearing a summer dress, but a simple white wedding gown and John wasn't teaching her to dance, but telling her he loved her. Forever and ever and always, he would love her.

But they weren't in a church anymore; they were in a hospital and Brooke was in her arms. Tiny and red-faced and making the small bleating sounds of a newborn. Elizabeth held her close yet when she looked again it wasn't Brooke at all, but Luke, and John was saying, "I knew God would give us a son one day, a son we could call our own."

John's words were still filling the room, but the two of them weren't in a hospital; they were walking beside a Realtor, leading all five kids through a freshly painted farmhouse just outside the city limits with views of trees and creeks and rolling hills and wheat fields as far as the eye could see. And John was saying, "We'll take it!" And he was framing her face with his hands and whispering, "We'll raise our children here, Elizabeth, and when they're grown, we'll have grandchildren here—the Baxter house. And one day we'll be buried—"

"Elizabeth." John's tone was sharp, flooded with concern.

She blinked and looked at him. His eyes were intense, his expression fearful, the way it had been when Erin got lost at the mall one December. She glanced around and gave her head a slight shake. Where were they? Why was John . . . ?

The answers came at her almost in sync with the questions.

"Elizabeth, can you hear me?" He wasn't angry, just afraid. The way he looked so often these days.

"I'm sorry. I . . . I guess I didn't hear you." She sat up straighter and rubbed her eyes. "I was thinking back." She looked at the doctor's desk. "Are we done?"

"Yes." John breathed out and took both her hands in his. "Did you understand what the doctor was telling us? About the cancer?"

She didn't answer, couldn't. Instead she looked into his eyes. "We need to go home."

He angled his head, looking straight into her soul, telling her what his words could not. That he was sorry, that this was never how he'd pictured it ending, that he would do anything to change the facts, to turn back the hands of time and find a way to the place where she was well and the tomorrows spread out before them like the never-ending stream behind their house.

After a minute, John's voice strained, he pointed toward the door and said, "I'll get you a chair." He had turned to leave when she stopped him.

"John!"

He spun around, more fear in his eyes.

"No chair." She met his eyes. "I want to walk with you, beside you."

At first he looked as if he might disagree, insist on the wheelchair because of her condition. But he knew her heart even now. He went to her, looped his arm through hers and, as always, he led her. Through the office, down the hallway, outside and toward the parking lot.

They were halfway to the car when she stopped and hung her head. "I can't, John."

"Okay, stay here." He was about to run back for a chair when she shook her head.

"No." She turned to him and searched his eyes. "I can't be dying, John. I'm not ready. I love you too much."

As he studied her face, Elizabeth watched his expression fill with frustration, regret, futility. Then, in painful slow motion, he took her face in his hands the way he'd done so often over the years. His eyes grew watery as he gave the slightest shake of his head. "I'm so sorry, Elizabeth. I wish it were me."

"John . . ." She clung to him, grabbed handfuls of his navy pullover, and pressed the side of her face against his. The tears started up again, and this time they came from a place in her heart even she hadn't known about. A deep, anguished place that had somehow always known their story might end this way, a room Elizabeth had never dared to enter, with feelings so raw and terrifying they threatened to take her life there on the spot.

He smoothed his hand over her knit cap, down her back along the bones that stuck out more all the time. "Elizabeth, hear me." His words were determined, spoken through clenched teeth. "We can't give up. You have to fight it."

She sobbed, and the sound was louder than she intended, more like a series of deep coughs, each one shaking her, hunching her over as she held on to John. "I'm sorry. I . . . want to. I don't . . . know how."

They stood there that way, holding each other so they wouldn't fall, until her sobs became shallow jagged breaths, until the tears gave way to a round of sputtering coughs, and John started them moving toward the car again.

The feel of his body at her side, his legs still strong as they moved in rhythm with hers, brought a strength Elizabeth hadn't felt all morning. But still every step seemed to rattle off her prognosis. *Cancer. Spread. Other organs. Liver. Pancreas. Three months. Four.* All the while the doctor's words acted as a backdrop, a running feed that colored every other aspect of her condition. *Whether we operate or not . . . whether we operate or not . . . whether we operate or not . . .*

The tears still fell from her eyes, but a new sort of peace filled her heart. Why would she agree to a surgery if half her organs were already affected with cancer? She was already bone thin. More surgery? The ordeal might leave her bedridden for the remainder of her days.

An image grew in her heart and filled her mind. Ashley on her wedding day, standing at the altar in their family's church, Pastor Mark marrying Ashley and Landon while everyone they knew or loved filled the building. And where would she be? In a hospital bed, too weak to even get dressed?

No, she wouldn't have it. Yes, they'd asked for a miracle, and God could still give them one. She was still afraid to die, still certain that somehow she'd survive even this type of cancer. But they'd also prayed for wisdom, hadn't they? As long as she was breathing, God could change her condition. But the doctor had given them all the wisdom they needed at this point.

Whether we operate or not, three months . . . maybe four.

They reached the car, and John helped her inside. When he climbed in beside her, she searched his eyes. *God . . . let him understand what I'm about to say. Please, God.*

"John . . ."

"I know." He slipped the key in the ignition and started the engine. "We can talk at home."

"No." The calm in her voice surprised even her. "Please. I have something to say."

He shifted sideways and slipped his fingers between hers. "Okay." A knowing filled his features, and he almost winced as he waited.

Elizabeth tilted her head and willed him to see it her way. "I don't want another operation, John."

His shoulders fell an inch and his expression wilted. "What if the doctor's wrong about the liver? Lots of people function with one lung, and the pancreas can be removed."

"It's in my lymph system. You and I both know that means cancer cells could show up anywhere, anytime." She lifted her chin and gazed at the sky for a moment. "Open me up now and I might never get out of bed again." Her eyes locked on his. "I can't have that happen. God can cure me with another round of chemo or radiation; he can give us the miracle we're praying for. But we asked for wisdom, John, and Dr. Steinman gave it to us. The surgery won't make a difference, so why have it?"

John exhaled and dropped his head into his free hand. For a moment he rubbed his thumb and forefinger along his brow, his anguish echoing with each breath. "How . . . how can you give up?" His hand fell away and he looked at her. "Lung cancer, Elizabeth." The fight was gone from his voice. "Surgery isn't optional. It's the only way around it."

"If it was only in my lungs I'd agree." Her words were slow, tender, revealing none of the fear that still tore through her. She gave his hand a gentle squeeze. "You heard him, John. Surgery won't help."

"But . . ." The word hung on his lips and died there. His arms came around her, pulling her close once more. "You're not giving up?"

"No." She whispered the word against the side of his face. "Never, John. I'm not ready to go. I'm still scared to death." Her throat felt thick and she waited until she could speak. "I told you, after a few weeks I'll do more chemo, radiation. Whatever. But don't—" her voice broke—"don't let them operate. Please."

His hold on her grew tighter, but after a minute he relaxed and breathed against her hair. The way his body felt against hers, the tone of his voice, all of it told her he'd known all along that this was the logical decision. But he spoke none of that and said only, "Okay."

When they pulled apart, Elizabeth studied his features. His expression shouted of resignation and defeat, but deep in his heart she could see that he agreed. That he was almost relieved by her decision.

"One more thing." She held her breath. This request was maybe even more important than the first one.

He looked at her, waiting.

"I don't want the kids to know."

John raised one eyebrow and stared out the windshield. "How?" He looked at her again. "They'll find out. They've been asking about your tests since the day you finished the chemo."

She was determined. "We tell them we're optimistic, that I'm going in for more chemo in a few weeks, and that we should all keep praying."

"You think that'll be enough for Brooke? Come on, Elizabeth, she's a doctor. She'll want specifics and so will the rest of them."

"We'll tell them the truth; the surgery went well, but they didn't get all the cancer, and they're not sure how far spread it is."

"The truth?" John bit the inside of his cheek and narrowed his eyes. "The truth is you could be dead before the end of summer, Elizabeth. How can we not tell them that?"

Dead before the end of summer? Before their thirty-fifth anniversary? Elizabeth swallowed, grabbing at her next breath. Fear and panic joined hands and suffocated her, but only for a few seconds. "It is the truth." Elizabeth leaned against the car door. She lifted her hands and blew out through pursed lips. "They didn't get all the cancer, and they're not sure how far spread it is."

He sank back. "If we tell them that much, we might as well tell them the rest."

"I can't have them know the whole truth, John. That I could die." Sorrow mixed with anger, and her tears came again. "How can Ashley plan a wedding when you and I are planning a funeral? Tell me that, John. Tell me one good reason why I should tell them I have three months when God could still take the cancer away tomorrow. Or don't you believe God can do that, John?"

"Yes, I believe." For a single heartbeat he remained motionless. Then everything about him softened and his jaw dropped. "Elizabeth, I'm sorry."

"It's the same way I felt about our son, the boy we had to give up." Sweat beaded on her forehead and she was exhausted. But she had to explain herself. "Why tell the others, when to do so would only cause confusion and pain? If we couldn't find him, they never would've found him either. They'd spend a lifetime wondering about the brother they didn't know."

He nodded. "You're right."

She sobbed twice and squeezed her eyes shut. "So why would we tell them? For what? We had no choice about that child, John; he belonged to someone else long before he was even born." Her eyes opened and she searched his heart, his soul. "We have no choice now, either. None of us knows the number of our days. This—" she waved her hand about the inside of the car—"this is Ashley's season of love and happiness and everything she's ever dreamed of. I . . . will . . . not . . ." She sucked in three quick breaths. "I will not ruin it for her, John. I won't."

"Elizabeth—" he cupped her hand with his—"I won't either."

His words told her he agreed with everything she'd just said, that comparing this to what had happened thirty-five years ago was the quickest way to make him understand. They hadn't had a choice about the boy, and they didn't have a choice about this. Telling the kids would only borrow tomorrow's pain, and there was no sense in that.

John pulled out of the parking lot and headed for home, silent, probably as struck by what she'd said as she was.

Plotting and planning and family discussions wouldn't be enough to find the child they'd given up, any more than plotting and planning and family discussions would be enough to make her cancer mysteriously disappear.

It would take a miracle.

Elizabeth corrected herself as she settled into the seat and stared out the window at the busy street. It wouldn't take one miracle at all.

It would take two.

CHAPTER TWENTY

ASHLEY COULDN'T PUT her finger on it.

She'd spent the past hour having tea with her mother, sitting at her parents' dining-room table going over details of the wedding. It was the second week of June, and her mother looked better than she had in months, more color in her face, more energy.

But something wasn't right, the same something Ashley had sensed a dozen times since their father told them the test results. The surgery was successful, but they hadn't gotten all the cancer; they weren't sure how far it had spread. The information had felt a bit hazy at the time, but her mother was committed to taking more treatment. At first she'd planned on starting the chemo next week, but because of the wedding she was waiting until the end of July.

"That way we can have our reunion on Sanibel Island," she'd told them.

Ashley had compared notes with her sisters and Luke, and all of them were nervous. Nervous about the idea that somewhere the cancer still remained in their mother's body, nervous about her postponing her treatment, nervous about taking a trip to Sanibel Island, so far from her doctors.

But they kept praying, and every day she seemed to get a little better.

"Okay." Her mother made a check mark on the notebook she'd been keeping. "You've got a cake picked out and ordered." She leaned back in her seat and took a sip from her teacup. "How 'bout the RSVPs? Do we have a head count?"

"That was next." Ashley sorted through a portable file she kept for the planning of her wedding. As she did, she caught another glimpse of her mother, relaxed and drinking tea.

Despite the unsettling concerns in her heart, Ashley smiled at the image her mother made. If only she had a canvas and a paintbrush handy.

When Ashley drank tea she liked it in the biggest mug she could find, steaming hot and half full of cream.

Not her mother.

Elizabeth collected teapots, dainty china containers with intricate ribbons of gold and other precious metals. She never made just a cup of tea; she brewed a pot. And when it had steeped the proper amount of time, when it was neither "too hot nor too tepid," as Elizabeth said, she would pour a fine brown stream into a delicate teacup.

In some ways the picture of her mother reminded her of her friend Irvel from Sunset Hills, and her love for tea, even until the end. But that was the only similarity. Her mother was still young, still vibrant, still fighting the disease and winning—if her improved appearance was any indication.

Ashley pulled out a stack of small white cards and laid them on the table. "More than two hundred people coming so far."

"We invited three hundred." Her mother set her cup down and flipped a few pages in her notebook to a list of names.

"Right. But they have another week to get their responses back."

"True." She ran her finger along the edge of the paper. "How about the Cummins family, your father's partner?"

"I doubt it; they're busy with family issues. At least that's what Dad said."

"Fine. I'll put *doubtful* by their names." Elizabeth ran her finger down a bit farther. "Landon's Aunt Kathy from Indianapolis and her family—any word from them?"

"Landon says they're coming for sure."

"Good." She made a mark by the name and continued down the list.

They kept up that way until they had a rough idea that two hundred and fifty guests would attend the event. But all the while, Ashley couldn't shake the feeling that somehow they shouldn't be talking about wedding guests and cake designs, but whether her mother needed more tests, more treatment. Not after the wedding, but before it.

The angst stayed with Ashley even after she left the Baxter house. Landon had the day off. He was picking Cole up at school and they were meeting at the park. He was already there with Cole when she pulled into the lot and climbed out of her car.

She started toward them and stopped.

With all the worrying about her mother and the details of the wedding, she hadn't stood back and realized the miracle their lives had become, the three of them. Her two men hadn't spotted her yet, so she watched them unnoticed.

Cole was on an old lopsided merry-go-round, clinging to the metal bars while Landon ran alongside it, picking up speed. After a few seconds, he stood back, grinning. Then, when Cole passed by the next time, Landon jumped on and scooped Cole onto his lap. Together they held on as the merry-go-round circled another ten times before slowing to a stop.

When they climbed off, Cole held his hands up and Landon swung him onto his shoulders. They were laughing about something, but Ashley was too far away to make out what. They barely made it out of the sandpit and onto the grass before they spilled onto the ground, giggling and rolling around.

Ashley's eyes stung as she watched them.

God . . . I doubted you all my life. And now . . . She breathed in
sharply through her nose and lifted her eyes. *Now I'm healthy and
I'm marrying Landon and my little boy has a daddy; all my dreams
are coming true.*

She wanted to fall to her knees, to beg God to forgive her for
every time she'd ever doubted him. But she'd already done that
so many times before that here, now, she looked across the park
to Landon and Cole and grinned. *Thank you, God. I'll spend the
rest of my life being thankful.*

A verse flashed in her mind, so real, so distinct she wasn't sure
if she'd heard it or just remembered it. *"In this world you will have
trouble. But take heart! I have overcome the world."*

It was a Scripture from John, Ashley was sure. She'd taken to
reading a chapter in her Bible every night before bed. The verse
about trouble was one she'd come across a week ago.

But why would it come back to her now?

Cole bounced to his feet and began running from Landon, but
Landon was quick. He chased her son, and several yards away
he caught him and spun him around a few times before setting
him back down.

Suddenly it dawned on her why the verse had come to her
here as she watched Landon and Cole. In this world she'd had
plenty of trouble. Paris? Jean-Claude? Her resistance to Cole, to
Landon? Her determination to fight her family's faith?

A sad chuckle came from her. Yes, she'd had trouble in this
world. But God had overcome all of it.

She sauntered toward them, and after a few steps Landon
spotted her. He tapped Cole and in no time her son was running
toward her, his short blond hair flying in the wind. "Mommy!
You came!"

"Of course, silly." She swept him into her arms and kissed
the tip of his nose. Landon was smiling, drawing closer, his eyes
intent on hers. Her stomach flip-flopped the way it always did
these days when Landon was near. The wedding couldn't come
soon enough.

"Good, let's go swing!" Cole slid down, grabbed her hand, and closed the distance to Landon. "We're gonna swing, Landon. Wanna come?"

"Sure." He came up alongside her, slipped his arm around her waist, and kissed her. Then in a voice for her ears alone he said, "You look beautiful, Ash."

"Thanks." She grinned and felt her cheeks grow hot. "You too."

"How's your mom?" He moved slowly, his long legs in step with hers.

"Better, I think. She looks stronger, healthier. Still talking about that crazy reunion on Sanibel Island." She thought for a moment. "I'm worried about her, Landon. But I think she's winning the fight."

"No one's too crazy about Sanibel, huh?" His voice was tender, understanding.

"Not this year." She blew at a wisp of her hair. "We want to stay home, around the Baxter house, remembering the good times and helping Mom get better."

"Makes sense."

"Hey!" Cole ran a few steps ahead. "You guys are taking too long. Come on . . ."

"I missed you, Ash." Landon spoke near her ear.

"Me too." His closeness sent shivers down her spine. "What're we doing tonight?"

"Nothing alone." He gave her a crooked smile. "I can't take it."

She giggled and let herself melt against his side as they walked. "Definitely nothing alone."

They'd imposed guidelines on their engagement dating. A curfew if he was at her house and an agreement not to be alone together. Whereas before they could kiss and no matter how difficult, still walk away, now the desire between them was more than either of them could take. Especially since she was healthy.

Cole jumped onto the first swing he came to and looked at them, wide-eyed. "Ready, guys. Someone push me, please."

Landon leaned in and kissed her again. "I called Kari. She'll watch Cole at your parents' house. How 'bout dinner near the university and a walk near the art gallery?"

She caught his eyes and her heart dissolved. He loved her so much, knew her so well. The week before she'd finished a painting, a piece detailing a little boy and a puppy playing in the front yard of a country home. The local gallery had it in the front window, and Ashley had wondered if they had sold it yet. And what else had the gallery taken in?

But with the wedding plans and worries over her mother, she hadn't had time even to call.

This time she leaned up and kissed him on the cheek. "You'll never know how much I love you, Landon."

He grinned. "I'll take that as a yes."

"You know what?"

"What?" He turned and faced her, ignoring Cole's cries for a push.

"I can't believe we're getting married." She brought her voice down to a whisper and brushed her cheek against his. "I was thinking of a Bible verse before I walked out here. It's in John, when Jesus is talking: 'In this world you will have trouble. But take heart! I have overcome the world.' "

Landon's face was inches from hers, and he looked straight to her heart. "That's just what he did with you and me, Ash. He overcame every single thing."

"As long as we live—" she tapped her nose against his—"even when we're old and gray, he always will. He's that kind of God."

"Guys, come on!" Cole swung his feet and made a half-hearted attempt at getting the swing in motion. "Someone push, please!"

Ashley gave Landon one more look, a look that said she couldn't wait to walk down the aisle and become his wife, couldn't wait for their first night together and their first year and every other wonderful thing that would happen after that. She whispered another, "I love you" and then turned to Cole.

She darted around behind the swing and tickled Cole. "Okay, mister, get your feet out. This is gonna be the best under doggie you've ever had."

✥

All he could think about was the photograph.

Dayne Matthews pulled the baseball cap low over his eyes and climbed in behind the wheel of his Navigator. He had a house on the beach in Malibu, and for now, a leased apartment in Manhattan as well. The movie cast and crew had the weekend off, so he'd taken a flight home and arrived at his beach house late last night.

Today, a long jog on the shores of Malibu, tennis with his neighbor—an MTV video producer—and lunch on his balcony overlooking the water. Through all of the day's activities he looked to this moment, to the time when he would leave the house behind and head for the storage unit. He grabbed a grungy sweatshirt from the backseat, pulled it on, and backed onto Pacific Coast Highway. The tinted windows helped, but he needed the cap and sweatshirt. He wouldn't take any chances of being recognized. Not today.

Tomorrow he had to catch a flight out of Burbank, one that would change planes in Chicago and land at New York's LaGuardia sometime after midnight. He was due back on the set Monday morning, so he had no time for autograph seekers or paparazzi, no time to think about anything but finding the picture.

The storage unit was off Ventura Boulevard near North Hollywood, and after forty minutes behind the wheel, he saw the sign up ahead. He pulled into the parking lot, turned off the engine, and fingered the key. After spending an hour looking for it, he'd found it in a drawer in his Malibu kitchen.

The unit number was taped to the key ring. Unit fourteen.

He glanced at the office, but the woman inside was busy on

the phone. Keeping his face down, he raised one hand in her direction and kept walking. Unit fourteen was easy to find. He turned the key in the lock and lifted the door.

The place was dark and musty after years of never being exposed to fresh air or sunlight. He flipped on the light switch and stared at the contents. Thirty or forty boxes, some bigger than others, stacked eight feet high in what had to be the smallest unit the office rented out.

A step stool sat against the inside door, and Dayne grabbed it. He was six-two, but the top boxes were out of reach without some help. The stool wobbled and a cloud of dust billowed out as he took down the first box. He coughed and waved his hand in front of his face. Dreaded dust, bound to kick up his hay fever. He'd be sneezing and coughing straight through Monday's shoot if he didn't be careful.

The second box brought just as much dust, and Dayne breathed into his sweatshirt. This was why he'd thought about hiring someone for the job. But that wasn't possible either. He couldn't trust anyone. Regardless of what they found in his parents' archives, the tabloids would hear about it within a week.

Dayne couldn't take that chance.

When half the boxes were spread in rows across the floor, Dayne started with the first box on the left. "Tax Documents" the box read. He opened the lid, peered inside, and verified that the contents were, indeed, tax documents.

Then he moved to the second box, which was marked "Support Letters." Inside were letters from churchgoers who had supported his parents over the years. He picked out one and opened it.

> Dear Bob and Andrea Matthews,
> Enclosed please find a support check for $1,100, collected last Sunday at a special offering for your jungle work in Indonesia. We approve of your efforts at getting out the Word of God, and we pray that the love of Christ and his saving truth will spread and gain acceptance in the places where God has put you. . . .

Dayne stopped reading.

The places where God has put you? If God was so good at put-ting people in the right places, how come he didn't put his par-ents in the same village as he was? Four hundred miles away at boarding school couldn't possibly have been God Almighty's idea of good placement, could it?

Dayne shoved the letter back in the box and shut it. When his parents died he'd told himself the same thing he'd always told himself every day since: It was their choice. They loved mission work. Flying in small planes over jungle areas was just one of the risks they were willing to take.

He could shake his fist at God or hate his parents for tak-ing a job that kept them away from him most of the year. He could walk around angry at the irony of his parents' spending a lifetime telling other people about God while their own kid didn't get it.

Or he could simply accept the facts, the way he'd worked to accept them every day since their plane crashed.

His parents had followed their hearts, given their lives to something they loved. If they died doing it, so be it. At least they were happy. If they were in his business, they could've died on location for a film. He wouldn't have spent a lifetime hating them if that had been the case. Just because their work involved a God he didn't believe in didn't mean he'd spend a lifetime hat-ing them.

Rather, he had spent his years trying to remember the good times, the summer months and furloughs when they were together. His parents had been wonderful, totally focused on helping people and tending to the needs of others.

No, they hadn't exactly tended to his needs. Boarding school had never been his idea of a perfect family setup. But as long as Dayne lived he would respect them for the kind of people they were, and for following their beliefs. Still, enough of the support letters.

He worked his way through the boxes as one hour became

two. Finally, scribbled on a box stacked near the back, second row up from the floor, he saw words that made his heart miss a beat.

"Adoption Information."

Adoption.

The word landed in Dayne's gut like a rock, and for a moment he could only let it sit there. *Adoption?*

"Adoption?" He whispered it out loud, and it felt foreign on his tongue.

Suddenly memories jumped out at him and came to life.

He'd been what, six? seven? He and his parents were on furlough back in Chicago, Illinois, staying in an apartment leased by one of their supporting churches. They had called him into their room and sat him on the bed.

"We want to be honest with you. No matter what, you're our son. You've always been our son, and you always will be."

The memory grew more vivid, the details sharper.

Dayne had pulled his feet up and sat cross-legged on their bed. His stomach hurt because where in the world was the conversation going? "I know all that," he told them.

"Yes, but there's something you don't know." His mother angled her head; her eyes looked watery.

"A different woman carried you and bore you, Dayne." His father gave a serious nod. "She was too young to have a baby so she made up her mind long before you were born to give you to us."

"Because you were our son, honey. Does that make sense?"

Not a word of it made sense, but Dayne nodded anyway. A few more times over the years, they had mentioned something similar, something about praying for the woman who had given birth to him. But never in that time did they use the word *adopted.*

He was their son from the start, end of story.

What would a kid know of things like that? He had been what, eight?—nine maybe?—the last time he'd even considered the idea that someone else had given birth to him? Middle school came and then high school, and even at a boarding facility a kid has more to think about than whether he was adopted. Especially when his parents never came out and said as much.

Another memory hit Dayne then, almost knocked him back on the storage unit's cement floor.

The week before his parents' plane crash, his mother had called him and asked the usual. How was he doing in class? What were his study hours like? Which play was he working on? How was his relationship with Christ? Being missionaries, his parents were always asking how his relationship with Christ was.

And being a missionary kid, his answer was the same each time: "Fine." What else could he say? That he hadn't a clue how to have a relationship with someone invisible? If that someone even existed in the first place.

Anyway, his mother had said something else at the end of the conversation, something about the pictures. Dayne closed his eyes now, and he could almost hear her voice, hear her end of the conversation as if it were playing again in his mind.

"Now that you're a senior, there are some things we want you to have," she'd told him. "Photographs, things you've already seen but things that should be yours now."

They made plans to look at the pictures next time they were together. But the plane had crashed before they had a chance, and his parents' belongings were shipped to the storage unit in North Hollywood.

One of the men from the missions board at their supporting church in Chicago had met Dayne at the airport and told him about the storage unit. He had offered to take Dayne there, help him sort through his parents' belongings. But Dayne had put it off.

He'd applied to UCLA, sending in thirty minutes of highlights from plays he'd starred in at boarding school. Because of his tragic situation and his high promise, he earned a full-ride scholarship. Since then he hadn't had either the interest or the time to go through their things. They were gone; nothing in the boxes could bring them back or give him a family where he had none.

But now . . .

Now, looking at the box, with a lifetime of memories tak-ing shape in his head, Dayne realized something he hadn't ever fully acknowledged. He wasn't merely a kid who'd had a dif-ferent woman give birth to him than the one who raised him. He was adopted. His parents would always be his parents, but somewhere out there was a woman who had given birth to him, who had struggled in some way or been unable to raise a baby. A woman who had loved him enough to give him to the people he called his parents.

Never in all his growing-up years could Dayne remember his mom and dad using terms like *adoptive parents* or *birth mother.* They never said, "Dayne, you're adopted." Rather they walked around the issue and lived with the fact that Dayne never con-nected the dots. Why would he? There were no family members around to remind him of his background, no reason to talk about it at all except when he was interviewed by a variety magazine or a TV talk-show host.

"Orphaned at the age of eighteen" was what they usually said. Once in a while they went a little deeper. "Reared in a board-ing school while his parents were missionaries in the jungles of Indonesia until a plane crash took their lives." That sort of thing. The story never got deeper than that because Dayne didn't let it. Never had he mentioned that "oh, by the way, another woman gave birth to me."

It wasn't something he thought about, wasn't something he acknowledged or admitted on a conscious level.

Until now.

Slowly, not sure if he should turn and run or open the box, he headed toward it. The contents were heavier than some of the oth-ers, and when he set it down he heard the clank of glass. Picture frames. The box had to contain pictures. But why would framed pictures be in a carton marked "Adoption Information"?

He opened the flaps and took a step back, as if the documents and pictures might take the form of a rattlesnake and bite him.

But there was no turning back; now that he'd come this far there was nothing to do but look. His jeans-covered knees hit the ground, and he slid the box closer.

One look inside told him the box didn't contain pictures. Rather it contained framed documents of some sort. He lifted the top frame, a cheap brown metal one, and under the glass was a document declaring "Dayne Matthews the son of Bob and Andrea Matthews, residing in Chicago, Illinois."

The one beneath it was similar, but the document had some sort of official seal. He looked closer and realized it was his birth certificate, at least as far as he could make out. But in the section marked "Birth Mother" the name was x-ed out. At least three times across, so that the entire line was a smeary black mess.

One more frame remained, and now that the top two were removed, Dayne saw it was smaller than the others. Much smaller. It was facedown, but even before he turned it over, he knew. It wasn't a document like the other two.

It was a photograph.

He reached into the box, but he couldn't bring himself to turn it over. Not when his little-kid memories were coming back again. Something about that first time, the day his parents had asked him into their room at the church-leased apartment. They'd told him about the woman who had given birth to him—even though they said they'd been his parents even before he was born.

But they'd showed him something, too.

"Dayne we have a picture of the woman who gave birth to you." His mother had taken a framed photo from her bottom dresser drawer and held it out for Dayne to see. "She was very young and very kind. Because she knew God wanted us to be your parents. She left us this picture, and we saved it for you. In case you ever want to see what she looked like."

The memory was so clear now it was spooky. Why, after all these years, would everything about that time come back to him? And if the woman had left a picture of herself, why hadn't his parents showed it to him again, when he was old enough to make a conscious decision about it? Like, "Hey sure, I'll take it," or "Gee, whadya know; I sorta look like her."

Dayne sat back on his heels and felt in his oversized sweatshirt pocket for the picture, the one he'd taken off Luke Baxter's desk. He pulled it out and set it up on the floor a few feet from the box. If his director could see him now, he'd think Dayne Matthews had lost it for sure. Never mind messing up an action scene or forgetting to kiss Sarah Whitley. Here he was in some dank storage unit performing a ritual with some photograph he hadn't seen since he was six or seven years old.

Talk about wacky.

But still he couldn't stop himself, couldn't keep from finishing what he'd started. And without waiting another minute he reached into the box, grabbed the frame, and pulled it out.

It was the photograph, the one he remembered his mother showing him.

Dayne's hands began to shake and he set the photo down. His heart was beating wildly, and in a blur of motion he shut the box lid, set the Baxter photo on it, and placed the picture of his birth mother beside it.

The trembling worked its way through his body. He couldn't draw a deep breath. His eyes focused first on one picture, then the other, until there was no denying the resemblance. Not because the woman who bore him looked like him.

But because she looked exactly like Luke Baxter's mother.

CHAPTER TWENTY-ONE

ELIZABETH WAS ALONE in the house and, as usual, fear was having its way with her.

A week earlier she'd been sure God was answering her prayers, that the miracle everyone was praying for was actually taking place. She'd been able to sit with Ashley and discuss the wedding over tea, take walks around their property with John, and most of all, start her special project—the one she'd been wanting to do since her surgery.

But now it was late in the third week of June, and for six straight days she hadn't had the strength to get out of bed. She was achy and tired, with not even a little appetite. But worst of all, she couldn't stop coughing. A cold, she called it, or flu or maybe bronchitis.

John went along with her. He agreed that several bugs were going around and that certainly her hacking cough could be attributed to something viral. But shouting at her all the while were the facts, the ones she had tried to leave back at Dr. Steinman's office the day they got the test results.

The cancer was in her lungs.

Wasn't that what the X rays had shown? Wasn't that at least as viable an explanation for her cough and weight loss, for her lack of appetite?

At her request, they still hadn't told the kids those details. That first week, when her strength seemed to be coming back, there seemed no need. She was getting stronger, better, more able to get around, and clearly God was healing her. Even as late as a week ago, the conversations between her and John were always anchored on that truth. Of course God would heal her. The cancer would be gone by fall, no doubt.

But now, just after noon as she lay in her bed, her body aching, lungs burning, ribs sore from coughing, she was too scared to do anything but stare at the door and wish for a visitor: Ashley with wedding plans, Kari with stories of Ryan's coaching buddies, Cole bringing her another colored picture, John stopping in to check on her.

Anything to interrupt the building anxiety, the raw terror at what was seeming more and more obvious. That maybe she really was dying.

The thought tried to lodge in her throat, tried to stop her from drawing another breath, but she wouldn't let it. Lying there feeling afraid was no way to live, no matter what was happening to her.

Her mind reeled with the possibilities. *Cancer . . . cancer . . . cancer . . . spread through her lungs . . . spread through her . . .*

The idea was so frightening she lay frozen and stayed there, eyes unblinking. Imagining being ripped from her family in three short months was bound to make her more frightened, more ridden with anxiety.

What she needed was something to distract her. The project, yes, that's what she needed. A moment to work on the project. No matter how sick she felt, she needed to continue working, plodding away until she was finished. It was the only thing that took her mind off the terrifying possibilities.

She reached for the portfolio she kept beneath her pillow. It was easier that way—no need to worry about climbing out of bed or even opening the drawer of her nightstand. For a while, her chest heaving from the exertion, she stared at the leather binding, then opened it. The inside cover had a pocket and three envelopes. They were in order, one for John, one for the kids, and another that read simply "Firstborn."

She was writing letters to all the people she loved, the people who had made her life something to sing about. The man she'd fallen in love with so many years ago, the one she fell more in love with all the time. The five kids who had given her the greatest life a woman could ever have.

And one more.

For the son she never knew. Not because she had any reason to believe God would give her a miracle and let her find him. But because one day he might find her; and if he did, she wanted to have something for him, some words that would tell him how she felt, how she hadn't forgotten, no matter how hard she'd tried.

John knew nothing of the letters. She kept them hidden at night, and tucked beneath her pillow in the daytime. The letters would worry him; she was supposed to be gearing the family up for the Florida reunion and Ashley's wedding, not writing farewell letters.

Elizabeth coughed three times straight and held her breath. Sometimes holding her breath warded off more coughing, and this time it worked. She was finished with John's letter and working on the one for the kids. Each child would be mentioned, and right now she was writing the part specifically for Kari.

Elizabeth took a sheet of floral paper from the back pocket of the portfolio and laid it across the cardboard writing surface inside. The paper was something she'd picked up at the Christian bookstore in town. Each piece had a different floral pattern and a Scripture verse printed across the top. She held her pen near the top of the page and looked up a few inches at the verse.

"Not my will, but yours be done."

Elizabeth stared at the words. She'd read the verse a hundred times in her life, but now . . . now it held new significance. Was God trying to tell her something, trying to adjust her perspective?

Ever since the diagnosis, she'd been praying for her will, and hers alone. *She* needed a miracle because *she* wanted to live, wanted to stay with her family a full hundred years before heading off to heaven. Her prayers had been entirely focused around that idea. *Please, God, heal me. Please let me live; don't let me die, God, not now.* Hour after hour, day after day, she'd prayed.

Not once during that time had she prayed for God's will, and now, as she stared at the verse, Elizabeth knew why. She didn't want to pray for God's will. Praying like that meant that maybe, just maybe, his will might not match up with hers. His will might be to take her home before summer was over.

Rather than risk that, she had simply prayed for her will. The will of everyone she loved. Everyone except her Savior.

A piercing remorse cut through her and her face grew hot. She drew in a deep breath and the air rattled in her chest, sending her into a coughing spasm that seemed worse than any before it.

She gasped for air, her lungs screaming within her. Another series of spasms and she coughed again, and again. Usually she coughed in bursts of three or four, but this time her body fell into a rhythm she couldn't break. She dug her elbow into the mattress and worked herself up onto her side.

Another cough and another. Her hipbone hurt from having to bear her slight frame, so she struggled and worked some more until finally, still coughing and exhausted, she was sitting up.

Tears welled in her eyes and she stared at the bedroom door. "Someone, come . . ."

All of the kids had told her to call, to say the word and they'd be there for her, but she had brushed away their offers. "I'm fine," she would tell them. "Come visit, but don't worry. I'll be all right."

Two more deep coughs. She pressed her hand against her chest, willing her body to regain control.

If she could reach the phone, she'd call them now, ask one of them to come and help her. But what good would it do? She needed help now, needed someone to get her up and take her to the bathroom so she could stand against the counter and catch her breath.

Her body relaxed some, but she felt another wave building in her lungs, pushing her to cough again.

Out of the bed, Elizabeth, she told herself. *Now . . . out.*

She swung her legs over the edge and allowed two short coughs. *Give me the strength, God . . . I can't do it alone.*

Her feet made contact with the floor, and she pushed her hands against the edge of the mattress to give her the momentum to stand. Then, as though a pair of unseen hands were guiding her steps, she made it to the bathroom. She stared at herself in the mirror and her heart caught in her throat.

She was deathly gray, the skin around her lips a translucent blue. Her hair wasn't growing back as well now, and bare patches still stood out along her scalp. Besides all that, her sweatshirt and sweatpants hung on her. She looked nothing like the woman she'd been only two months earlier.

The urgency in her lungs built again, and she gripped the bathroom counter. This time the coughs came from a deeper place than before, shaking her body and leaving her nauseous and on the verge of collapse. Elizabeth wasn't sure how much time passed before finally, mercifully, the coughing subsided.

Something filled her mouth, and she reached for a tissue. Was she vomiting? Had the strength of her coughing brought up the few bites of oatmeal she had been able to stomach for breakfast? Whatever it was, it tasted strange and bitter.

She spit into the tissue, pulled it back, and stared.

Her heart skipped a beat and then flipped into a strangely irregular rhythm. The entire tissue was filled with thick, bright red, clotted blood. She stared at it, studied it, until gradually the truth began to dawn.

Viral infections didn't make a person cough up blood; neither did the flu or bronchitis or even pneumonia. Only one thing would bring up the thick blood she held in her tissue.

Advanced lung cancer.

Elizabeth wadded up the tissue, tossed it in the trash can, and rinsed her mouth. Then, with a strength that came from God alone, she made her way back to the bed and sprawled out against a stack of pillows. There, for the tenth time since their last meeting with the doctor, Elizabeth considered something she hadn't before.

What if she didn't get her miracle?

What if everything Dr. Steinman said was right? Her cancer had spread through her lungs and internal organs, and with or without a second surgery, she would die in three months?

Her breathing came quicker, and more coughing with it. She gripped the bedspread, digging her fingernails into it until her knuckles were white. *Take it away, God; make my lungs better. You know me . . . you knit me together in my mother's womb . . . take the cancer from every part of my body, please, God. Please . . .*

The silent words became a whisper, and the whisper a desperate cry for help. "Please, God . . . I beg you, make me well."

Don't be afraid, daughter. Remember . . . not your will, but mine be done.

The whispered response blew across her heart and she fell silent. Her eyes opened and she stared out the window. It was windy; thunderstorms were forecast for later in the afternoon. A gust hit the house and the roof creaked.

"God?" Elizabeth coughed twice and watched the sky. Dark clouds were rolling in.

The response had been more real than anything she'd ever heard before. Not a gentle feeling or a sense of peace but loud enough to echo through her very soul. Gentle and firm, the response could've come from only one place.

"Not my will, but yours be done."

It was the verse on the floral paper, the one she was going to use to write the letter to the kids before her coughing attack. And suddenly, her entire body went limp with wonder. Was it possible? Had God put the Scripture before her eyes as a way of getting her attention? And then when she'd fallen prey to fear and resorted to her same old prayers, had he brought the verse to mind again?

"Not my will, but yours be done."

And what else had she heard? *"Don't be afraid, daughter"*? Yes, that was it. *"Don't be afraid."*

Tears stung at her eyes. But she *was* afraid; she was scared all the time, torn between living in the moment and making mental calculations of how little time she might have left. Three months meant she might not live to see most of her kids and grandkids have another birthday. It meant no more Christmases or Thanksgiving dinners or Easters. The more she thought about those horrible possibilities, the more frightened she felt.

Until now.

Now, with storm clouds gathering outside her window, Elizabeth felt a burst of sunlight in her heart, a warmth that had been missing since before her surgery. Peace flooded her being, warding off what had become a permanent chill.

"Do not be afraid. . . . Not your will, but mine be done."

Something beyond peaceful filled her at the thought of God's will. She remembered when she first heard about God's will as a little girl. Her father had lost his job at the factory and for the first time Elizabeth could remember, the strong, unyielding man she had always counted on was broken.

That night, after he'd dried his eyes, her father told her, "Sometimes things just aren't God's will."

And then he'd given her a word picture she remembered still. "God's will," he told her, "is a little like taking a Sunday drive with God behind the wheel. God's driving.

"He might turn where you don't expect a turn or go through a valley that feels too dark," her father said. "But you don't have to worry about a thing, because you're just the passenger. What-ever happens, God will get you home in the end as long as you let him drive." He patted her on the head. "That's God's will."

The memory hadn't come back to her in decades, but now it was as large as life, bigger than the thunderheads gathering outside.

A flash of light lit the outdoors, and almost at the same time a clap of thunder shook the house. An hour ago, the storm would've made Elizabeth feel worse, more frightened, less in control.

But now with her father's words and the gentle answer from God echoing through her being, Elizabeth sank deeper into her pillows, utterly relaxed. God was in control. Wasn't that the bottom line, the message he was trying to tell her? Not her will, but his be done. That meant that yes, maybe she would die soon. But she wouldn't die afraid and alone with no hope. She would die with her family gathered around her, certain of her place in heaven, convinced that one day they would all be together again.

God had created her, and he knew the number of her days.

Fretting about her situation, begging God to change his mind, would only color her remaining time in fear and panic—whether she had days or years left to live.

The change of heart worked its way through her conscious and her subconscious, her sinews and bones, and even to the cancer-ridden places of her body. God was driving; she was not.

Yes, she would like a miracle.

"God . . . you know my thoughts." She whispered the words, staring at the dark sky and the occasional bolt of lightning that shot through it. "Of course I want you to heal me . . . but I hear you . . . for the first time since I've been sick I hear you."

Elizabeth coughed again and once more something filled her mouth. She reached for a tissue from her nightstand and spit. More bright-colored blood. But this time she wasn't surprised. More than that, she wasn't afraid.

And as another clap of thunder rattled the windows, a knowing came over her. Yes, they would pray for a miracle. But the family also needed to be aware of the very real possibility that she might not survive. It wasn't fair to keep them wondering, guessing. She glanced at the tissue again and folded it. Not when all the signs pointed to one fact and one alone.

Footsteps sounded in the foyer and outside her bedroom door. John burst into the room, his face a familiar mask of fear and concern. "Hey . . . sorry, honey. I meant to stop by earlier." He headed for her bed and sat at the edge. His eyes searched hers and he leaned in close, kissing her with all the tenderness the years had given him. "Kari and Ashley called, and I guess they've been out looking at shoes for the wedding. They didn't want to call and wake you. Anyway, I was talking to Dr. Steinman earlier and he says . . . Elizabeth . . ." He dusted his fingertips along her cheekbone. "What is it? You look . . . different."

"I feel better, John. God and I had a talk. I'm not afraid anymore."

"That's great." Relief softened his eyes. "I've been praying all day that maybe it really has been just the flu or bronchitis, and that even this afternoon you'd start to feel better. And if you've talked to God, then—" he looked at her nightstand and his expression became a mix of horror and shock—"Elizabeth . . ."

She saw out of the corner of her eye what he was looking at. It was the bloody tissue, the one she'd used just before he got home. "Yes." Her voice was calm, measured. "I've been coughing up blood."

"But I thought—" he looked at her and then back at the tissue—"I thought you felt better?"

"I do." Her heart ached at the look in his eyes and she felt a certain understanding. The fear was gone, yes, but this journey would still be marked with sorrow. It would be her job to help John and the others feel the same peace God had given her.

She reached for his hand and searched his eyes, praying he might find the peace she'd found. "I'm getting worse, John. We need to tell the kids."

"No!" He stood up, staring at her. "What's this about?" He brushed his hair back, paced to the door, and turned around. "This morning you were sure you had the flu, and now you're dying? Is that all the fight you've got?"

Thunder rocked the room; she waited until it died down. "I'm still fighting, still praying for a miracle. But the truth is, unless God changes something fast, I don't have long." She paused. "That's what God and I talked about."

"So that's it?" John tossed up his hands and huffed. His voice was tense, fearful, bordering on angry. "What about chemo or a second opinion or radiation? We can postpone Ashley's wedding, Elizabeth, but you can't give up."

She held out her arms and waited.

Minutes passed while the storm outside raged every bit as hard as the one raging within John. Then finally the clouds in his eyes broke. First anger, then fear fell from his expression, until all that remained was sorrow. He went to her, dropped onto the bed beside her, and took her in his arms. "I'm sorry."

"It's okay." Her eyes stung, but she wasn't going to cry. Not now when she was still basking in the peace of surrendering her will. A series of hard coughs shook her body, while John soothed his hand along her back.

"How long—" he lifted his eyes to hers and waited while she coughed again—"how long have you been coughing up blood?"

"Like that?" She looked at the tissue on the nightstand. "Just today. But it's happened twice in the last hour."

John gave a slow nod. Then he buried his face in her shoulder and stretched out alongside her. "Tell me about you and God."

"It was a verse I saw today." Three more coughs tore at her. "A verse from Luke: 'Not my will, but yours be done.' "

She felt him stiffen. "Earlier . . . after you got sick again I saw that verse and thought of you."

"Yes, well . . ." She inhaled slowly. Her lungs rattled in a way John could certainly hear, too. "I read it today and I remembered something my dad said."

KINGSBURY / SMALLEY

235

"Your dad?" He cuddled against her, clinging to her. "You mean the man who hated me?"

She managed a sad, small laugh. "This was before he hated you."

"Okay, go ahead then."

"Anyway—" another cough—"he told me that knowing God's will was like getting in the car and letting God do the driving. You, the passenger, never have to worry about a thing because God's at the wheel. No matter how scary the ride gets, God's in control, and in the end he'll get you home safely."

"Hmmm." John hesitated. "Lots of wisdom for a mean guy."

"Right." She breathed in the smell of him, the sensation of his body against hers even with her sweats and the lumpy sheets and his clothes separating them. "That's what I thought."

They were quiet, holding on to the moment. "The Scripture? That's why you felt better today?"

"Mmm-hmm." Her bones ached again, and she made a slight shift of her body. "I'm not afraid anymore." She exhaled and let herself relax against him. "You can't believe how good that feels."

"I'm glad."

She could feel his heartbeat, feel it pick up speed. "What are you thinking?"

"You think you're dying, Elizabeth? Is that why you want to tell the kids?"

"Thinking something doesn't mean I'm giving up." Again her words were slow, filled with a peace that had been missing for so many weeks. "It means God's giving me a glimpse of the road ahead, and I think the kids should know."

He slid back so he could see her. "You didn't answer my question."

"About dying?"

"Right." His voice was no longer urgent, but clearly he wasn't satisfied with her first answer. He pursed his lips and then relaxed them. "Do you think you're . . . you're . . . ?"

The answer became more certain in her heart as he searched for the right words. But the strangest thing was this: She felt even more at peace now than before. She lifted her hands and framed the sides of his face. "I still want to pray for a miracle, and I promise, as soon as Ashley's wedding is over I'll go for another round of chemo."

"But . . ."

"But yes, John, I think I'm dying. And I'm not afraid even a little; you know why?"

Tears flooded his eyes and his chin quivered. He cleared his throat so he could find a way to speak. "Why?"

"Because no matter what happens now, God's driving."

⁘⁘⁘⁘⁘⁘

CHAPTER TWENTY-TWO

THE MEETING TOOK PLACE the last Friday in June.

John invited them for seven o'clock and from the moment they arrived, he was sure they knew something was wrong. They never received an invitation to visit without an invitation to dinner. Their conversations with each other were short and hushed, and John saw Kari and Ashley exchange curious looks more than once.

After everyone was there, John said, "Let's have the kids go upstairs for a movie."

Ashley led the way, and Cole, Maddie, and Jessie traipsed up the stairs behind her. "Let's watch *Cinderella*, okay, guys?" Maddie was the leader among the three cousins.

"*Cinderella*'s for girls." Cole's voice trailed as they reached the top of the stairs and turned down the hallway.

"'Cept the prince!" Maddie's voice squeaked with sincerity. "He's a boy!"

The happy noises faded and John gestured toward the family room. "Let's all sit down."

Kari and Ryan took the loveseat near the window, and Brooke

237

and Peter sat at one end of the sofa; Landon saved a spot for Ashley at the other. John helped Elizabeth to the front of the room, where he eased her into one of two overstuffed chairs near the fireplace.

He took the chair next to Elizabeth's and sucked in a quiet breath. *God . . . give me the words.* Elizabeth had asked him to do the talking, and he was of course willing. Now it was a matter of getting through the night without breaking down.

Normally with this many of them gathered together, conversations would be breaking out across the room—laughter and the sharing of anecdotes from the week. Not tonight. If anything, they each seemed lost in their own world, nervous about whatever the meeting might involve.

Ashley bounded down the stairs and ran lightly through the dining room. She took her spot beside Landon. "Did I miss anything?"

"No." John made a light cough. "Kari could you call Erin and Luke three-way, please. You know their numbers, right?"

The tension in the room doubled. "Sure, Dad." Kari did as she was asked.

John caught a glimpse of Elizabeth. Her cough was worse, but she was using the sleeve of her sweater to muffle the sound. When she looked up, he tried to see past the gaunt hollows of her cheeks and the dark smudges beneath her eyes. He focused on her eyes, eyes that were as filled with peace and serenity as they'd been four days ago.

She was coughing up more blood with each day, and he'd had a phone conversation with Dr. Steinman. "The blood . . . it's related to the cancer, right?"

The doctor sighed. "John, you know the answer. She's end-stage. I don't know how else to say it."

"What about chemo?" Again John had known the answer, but he had to ask, had to know if there was something they could do, something other than watching the days pass knowing they were her last.

"We could try it; it might buy her a few weeks."

"But she'd be sick, right? The whole time?" He pinched the bridge of his nose.

"Worse than before. She'd be bedridden the whole time."

The memory of the conversation faded and John looked at Elizabeth again. She was up, able to walk beside him still, though not as fast as a week ago. But this had to be better than putting her in bed, violently ill. Especially if the miracle they were praying for didn't come through.

And John had his doubts. Not about whether God heard them. He did, of course. A dozen miracles in their family alone proved that much. But what about now? The idea that God would let her get worse even after the surgery was hard on him. Too hard to spend much time thinking about. It was enough that Elizabeth felt peace; his would have to come later.

Kari held up the phone. "I have them both on the line."

"Good." John leaned forward. "Put them on speaker, okay?"

Kari pushed a button on the phone. "Hi, guys. You there?"

"I'm here." Erin sounded anxious, her voice giving expression to the way they were all obviously feeling. "Hi, everyone."

A round of halfhearted hellos passed around the room, but Elizabeth hung her head and bit her lip.

John took her hand in his. "Luke, you on?"

"Yeah." He hesitated. "Reagan's here beside me." A muffled sound came across the line. "What's up, Dad? Everything okay with Mom?"

"I was about to ask the same thing." Erin paused. "It's hard not being there in person."

"Yes. I'm sorry about that, too. I just felt we couldn't have this meeting without all of you here. And this—" he looked at Elizabeth, checking on her, making sure she was holding up okay— "this is the only way we can all be together for now."

"Dad . . . we'll all be there next week, right? Getting ready for Sanibel Island."

John held his breath. There was no turning back now, no way to let them go on believing everything in their world was going to be okay. The truth had to come out, and after the next few minutes, nothing about their family would ever be the same again. He exhaled. "That's what we need to talk about." He tightened his grip on Elizabeth's hand. "Your mother and I have decided to hold the reunion here at the Baxter house."

Relief flashed in Ashley's eyes. "I think that's a good call. We have a lot going on this month, and with Mom still getting her strength back—"

"Ashley." John held his hand up. He had to get the next part said or he wouldn't say it. He'd run from the room and down the driveway or behind the house and across the stream, as far as he could get away from the stark reality of what he was about to say. "We didn't cancel the trip to Sanibel for convenience."

The room was silent.

Elizabeth inhaled and coughed twice.

When she was finished, John met the eyes of each of his kids and their spouses. "Your mother's cancer is . . . it's worse than we hoped, worse than we told you before." Every word felt like a blow to his gut, a crippling blow that threatened to drop him to his knees. It wasn't really happening, was it? He wasn't really telling them that Elizabeth was dying, that they were about to lose their mother. He squinted for a moment and then looked around again. "They didn't get all of it when they operated."

"We know that, Dad." Kari dug her elbows into her knees and looked from him to Elizabeth and back. "What's changed?"

"Her tests show the cancer's in her lungs." John's voice was raspy now, strained with the emotion.

Around the room he measured their reactions. Kari hooked her arm through Ryan's, her mouth open but silent. Ashley hung her head and gripped Landon's knee as his arm went around her. Brooke folded her arms and hunched forward some. Peter's hand was on her shoulder.

Elizabeth coughed again and kept her gaze down somewhere near her feet.

"Anyway . . ." John massaged the muscles in his neck. His head was spinning and he felt sick to his stomach. "Her doctor thinks it's even worse than that. He thinks maybe it's spread to her pancreas and her—" His voice broke. An ocean of sorrow welled in his throat and he couldn't say another word. He planted his elbow on his thigh and placed his fist against his brow.

As he did, he felt Elizabeth beside him, felt her hand on his shoulder, her soothing fingers near the base of his neck. She meant to comfort him, but her touch only made him sadder than ever. Not because of the news they were telling the kids, but because the news was true. And in far too few days, her hand on his shoulder wouldn't be a comfort to him.

It would be a memory.

The moment her husband's composure broke, Elizabeth made a decision. No matter how hard it would be to tell the kids the truth, it would be worse to watch John suffer through the process. She closed her eyes for just a moment. *Okay, God . . . it's me. We can do this.*

"What your father's trying to say is that the cancer's throughout my body." She looked around the room and gave each of her daughters a sad smile. "We've made some decisions and we want you to know."

A stream of tears started down Ashley's cheeks.

"Mom . . . can you talk a little louder; it's hard to hear." Erin's voice was high-pitched, as if she was crying, too.

"Yes, sorry." Elizabeth cleared her throat. "Dr. Steinman says it doesn't matter what I do at this point. He sees my condition as terminal."

There it was. The *death* word out there for all of them to hear, in case they had any doubts where this conversation was headed.

"So, what's the treatment?" Luke's voice was less urgent than matter-of-fact.

Elizabeth felt a tug in her heart. He was so like his father. "Any treatment we'd do would leave me very sick and bedridden until the end. It wouldn't save my life. Do you understand that, Luke?"

"I understand, but what if they're wrong?"

"Mom, you know they've got lots of options now." Brooke slid to the edge of the sofa, eyes pleading with her. "There must be something they can do."

"There is."

"Good." Kari dabbed her fingertips beneath her eyes. "Tell us what it is."

"It's the same thing I'd like each of you to do from this point out."

John let his hand fall to his legs and he looked at her. He was more composed now, ready to field questions if she couldn't. She gave him a quiet nod; she could do this. Since her moment of peace with God, she could do it maybe even better than he could.

The room was silent, each of them waiting for whatever it was she wanted them to do. She coughed once and then willed herself to stop. "I'd like each of you to honor my decision not to seek treatment. The cancer is in my lungs, my pancreas, my lymph system, probably my liver. It's an aggressive cancer."

She paused but not long enough for any of them to protest. "Dr. Steinman said my condition is terminal either way—with or without surgery or chemo. The difference—" another cough— "the difference is how I'll be able to spend my time." She gestured to the chair and each of those sitting around her. "Sitting up and in conversation with you." She looked at John and put her hand over his. "Taking walks together, sharing memories." Her eyes found the others again. "Or sick and flat on my back, too weak to leave my bedroom."

Brooke's eyes were red. Hayley sat in her wheelchair a few inches away, quieter than usual, as if even she understood how serious the situation was. "When they say terminal, what are they meaning? Two years? Three?"

Elizabeth felt her expression soften. "The doctor gave me three or four months."

"Three or four—" Kari covered her mouth with her hand, her eyes betraying her shock.

"Mom . . ." It was Luke's voice. "Did you say three or four years?"

Ashley answered for her. "Months, Luke. She said three or four months."

Kari was the first to move. She crossed the room and knelt near Elizabeth's feet, holding on to her legs and hanging her head. "Mom . . . no! Please, no."

A few seconds later Ashley and Brooke joined the small circle, and Elizabeth felt their grief like a wall around her. Across the room, Peter and Landon and Ryan stayed motionless, staring at the ceiling or down at the floor. Anywhere but at Elizabeth and her daughters, clinging to each other, crying.

Elizabeth closed her eyes and savored the moment, memorizing the way it felt to have her arms around her daughters, remembering how they'd always come to her when they were upset ever since they were little girls. They clung to each other now, comforting one another as the reality settled in. Elizabeth had expected more of an argument, an insistence that she have surgery or seek treatment, whatever might buy her more time.

Instead they had honored her request, believed that if their doctor father hadn't seen a benefit in surgery or medication, neither could they. She was dying; the facts were out in the open for all of them to deal with.

Erin's voice broke the silence. "You could still respond to chemotherapy . . ." Erin was obviously crying. Her nose sounded stuffy, her voice tinny.

"No, dear. Dr. Steinman doesn't think it'll do any good." Elizabeth ached to hold her, to have her be part of the cluster of girls gathered at her feet.

"Okay, but—" panic colored Erin's tone now—"but they have other drugs, newer drugs, right?"

"Erin, dear?" She spoke loud enough so both Erin and Luke would hear her. "The only thing that would change my diagnosis now is a miracle."

"Then we'll keep praying." The sound of Erin's sniffing came over the phone.

"Let's pray now." It was Landon, and he looked around the room, then bowed his head. After a minute he opened his mouth and the words came. "God, you're a miracle maker. We know that; we've all seen it happen right around us. Ashley, Luke, Peter . . ." His voice filled with sadness. "Even Hayley. So, God, heal Elizabeth please. She's everything to this family, the heart and soul of who the Baxter family is. John needs her; we all need her. Please, God . . . give us a miracle."

A chorus of amens passed around the room and over the speakerphone.

"Thanks, Landon." John nodded to him. "We're nothing without our faith."

"Yes, thanks, Landon." Elizabeth looked around. "Thanks to all of you who are praying for me. I know it's helping; I can feel it."

"Really?" Ashley looked up at her, her cheeks tearstained.

"Really." Elizabeth didn't mean it in the way they would take it, but it was true. Her physical condition wasn't better, but mentally, spiritually, she was doing very well. Even now. And it was the most positive thing anyone had said that hour.

"Okay, I need to change the subject." Elizabeth steadied herself, forced her lungs to remain calm despite their constant tendency to slip into a spasm. "Erin and Luke, I'm asking you to keep your plans to come here on the third of July, but we'll have the reunion here instead of Sanibel Island, and then on the nineteenth we'll have Ashley's wedding. Will that work for you?"

"Of course." Luke was quick to answer. His voice was thick and again Elizabeth's heart hurt. She hated telling them this when they were so far away. But it was more important that Luke and Erin hear it firsthand—the way their siblings were hearing it.

Erin's voice was muffled for a moment. "Sam can't be gone that long, but he'll join us on the eleventh and stay for the wedding."

"Perfect." The now-familiar peace from the past few days worked its way over the raw edges of Elizabeth's heart. July would be heavenly, time for conversations and board games and walks near the backyard stream. They would get to know Erin's new daughter and talk about the upcoming wedding and take pictures of everything. They would laugh and, yes, maybe a time or two they would cry.

But at least they would be together in the place she loved better than any other. The old Baxter house.

"I love you, Mom." Luke's tone was strained. "Reagan says she loves you, too. We'll be there on Thursday, and we'll keep praying." He hesitated. "You can beat this, Mom. You're strong that way."

"He's right." Erin sounded more determined. "Sam and I will keep praying, but you have to believe you can survive, okay, Mom? I love you. We all love you."

"Okay." Elizabeth stroked her hands over the heads of her girls, still gathered around her—Kari's and Ashley's and Brooke's. "I love you, too."

John held his hand out to Ryan, who had been holding the phone. Ryan stood and handed him the receiver, and John pushed the Speaker button off. "Luke and Erin . . . you're off speakerphone now." He walked with the phone into the kitchen and talked in hushed tones.

Ryan leaned over and said something to Peter and Landon, something Elizabeth couldn't quite make out. Almost at the same time, the guys all nodded, stood, and crossed the room toward her. One at a time they hugged her and uttered words of hope and quiet promises to keep praying. Then the three men went together into the foyer to wait.

Kari came closer and hugged her, keeping her face close while she said, "I love you, Mom. I'm . . . I'm sorry about all this." She took a step back. "It's late; Jessie needs to get home. We'll talk more tomorrow."

"Okay."

Brooke hugged her next, stood, and nodded. "God isn't finished with you yet, Mom."

"I know, honey."

Ashley waited until Kari and Brooke were halfway up the stairs, then huddled a little closer. "Now I know why I've been feeling strange around you. I knew something was wrong, Mom. Something you weren't telling us."

Until now, none of the kids had mentioned that fact. They had looked past the idea that they'd been kept in the dark for a few weeks. But because of the wedding, because of the time they'd spent together lately, Ashley was bound to be more perceptive than the others. Elizabeth ran her fingers over Ashley's hair. "I'm sorry. I wanted to wait until after the wedding."

"I guessed that." Ashley hugged her and held on for a while.

With Ashley in her arms, Elizabeth was overcome by more emotion than at any other time tonight. She would miss her children so much, miss the closeness she had with each of them. She held on tighter, longer, trying to imagine saying good-bye to Ashley for the last time this side of heaven.

It was tragic, really, that Ashley had no idea how much the two of them actually had in common, how often she looked at Cole and thought of her own firstborn, the young man who had been on her mind and in her prayers since her diagnosis.

No wonder she felt a special connection to Ashley, especially in the past few years since Landon had worked his magic on her heart. They had lost too much time after Paris, back when Ashley felt like an outcast. Maybe if she'd been honest with Ashley about her own past, they would've made peace years sooner.

Elizabeth cast the thought from her mind. Time was short for all of them; backtracking would never make a difference now. She pressed her cheek against Ashley's. "I love you, honey. I always have. So much."

"Me, too."

They held on a while longer, and then the sound of the children—groggy and overtired—came from near the front door.

Ashley got up. "I'll be by tomorrow." She dabbed at the runny mascara beneath her eyes and looked more serious than before. "Don't hide things from me, Mom. We can get through anything together, okay?"

Elizabeth nodded. She was exhausted, too tired to move. She stayed seated, watched John follow Ashley into the foyer, listened while they spoke with him in hushed voices. When he returned he held up the receiver and put it back on its base. "They said they'll call you later."

She looked up, worried. "Are they okay?"

John stopped, and his frame seemed to wither some. His expression told her he couldn't answer the question. "Of course not," he whispered. "None of us are. We can't lose you, Elizabeth."

She held out her arms to him. "John . . ."

Looking beyond weary, he worked his way closer and sat on the arm of her chair. "It's true." His chin quivered. "We'll never be okay again."

"Yes, you will, too." She kissed his cheek and brushed a piece of his hair off his forehead. "You know why?"

He exhaled and seemed to summon a bit of strength he hadn't had before. "Why?"

"Because God loves you even more than I do."

CHAPTER TWENTY-THREE

ERIN CRADLED HEIDI in her arms and stared at the stacks of clothes on her bed. It was Tuesday, July 1, and she'd kept as busy as possible since the phone call with her family. She shopped for the trip one day, bought a bigger suitcase and ran errands another, and spent an entire afternoon at the park with other moms from church.

Not once did she talk about her mother to anyone.

It was simply more than she could believe, more than she could take in. The last time she'd seen her mother, she'd been fine. The picture of health. Slim and fit and cancer-free. Now she had three or four months to live.

No, Erin wouldn't believe it.

All her life she'd wanted children, and more than that, time to share them with her mother. She was the youngest daughter, the one who had stayed at home longer than any of the other Baxter girls. Now that she was grown up and married, nothing had changed at all. She still called her mother when she was upset, still spent hours on the phone with her, asking her for advice about diaper rash and formula and the merits of various baby toys.

Since her mother's surgery, Erin had called less often. She worried that her mother needed her sleep, her time to recuperate.

But never did she worry that her mother was dying.

Heidi squirmed and began to cry. She was a quiet baby, with none of the health problems that can accompany a child who hasn't had prenatal care. The only time she cried was when she wanted a bottle or a nap. At the moment, it was the bottle.

The crying became more incessant.

Erin gave one last look at the stacks of clothes, then turned and headed for the kitchen. "Okay, sweetie, just a minute."

She started preparing the bottle, thinking the whole time not of her mother and the cancer and the death sentence she'd been given, but rather about what she was going to pack.

She and Heidi would be gone three weeks, at least. They would need summer clothes, warmer outfits for the sometimes-cool nights, and church clothes. Heidi would need her car seat and her swing and a bag of squeaky toys and rattles. She'd have to pack several bottles and burp rags and blankets.

The list seemed never-ending.

With the bottle warm and ready to go, Erin sat down at the table, cradled Heidi close, and began to feed her. At the same instant, a few feet away the phone rang. Erin stared at it for a moment, not wanting any more bad news. Finally, she slid her chair closer and without disturbing the baby, she balanced the bottle until she had the phone on her shoulder.

"Hello?"

"Yes, hello, Erin." It was the social worker. "I have some interesting news for you."

Erin's heartbeat stuttered. She stood and walked to the nursery. "Yes?"

"Candy Santana is in jail in Dallas facing a life sentence."

"What?" A burst of adrenaline rushed through her. She sat in the old rocker, the phone pinned between her shoulder and her cheek. Heidi was content, taking the bottle as fast as she could.

The social worker released a deep sigh. "Apparently she ran out of drugs. She left her baby with a neighbor woman and took a bus to the house of some drug dealer in Dallas. The two of them dealt together and did drugs for the past few weeks. Then late one night the guy she was with took her to a rival drug dealer's house. I guess the rival owed him money. Anyway, he gave her a gun and told her to wave it around so the other drug dealer would take them seriously."

Erin could hardly believe what she was hearing. She closed her eyes, anxious for the social worker to get to the point of the story.

"So Candy was high on drugs, waving a gun around, and somehow it went off. The bullet ricocheted off the ceiling and hit the man she was with, hit him right in the chest." The social worker paused. "The man bled to death before help could arrive, and Candy's facing half a dozen charges."

She went on to list the things Candy faced: manslaughter, certainly; reckless use of a handgun; intent to deal, since police found bags of marijuana and vials of cocaine in her purse. The list went on, and in addition to everything else, she was being charged with abandonment of her children.

"Abandonment?"

"Yes. The neighbor woman had the baby all this time. We didn't find out about Candy's arrest until the neighbor finally called our department and wanted to know what to do with the baby."

Erin held Heidi close, trying to imagine Candy's baby left behind like an old sweater. But her sinking feeling gave way to a burst of sudden joy, a feeling that maybe there was another reason why the woman had called. Maybe she and Sam were going to have a second chance at the baby, but if so, how would they handle two newborns at the same time?

The questions pelted Erin's heart like hail, but only one found its way to her lips. "What are you doing with the baby?"

"Well . . ." The woman's voice fell a notch. "That's why I'm calling. Here's the situation. . . ."

It was Luke's last day of work before summer.

Since the job was an internship, he'd arranged with his boss to take off all of July and part of August. When he started back up before the fall session at school, his position would no longer be connected with the university but rather a part-time job. One Luke hoped would turn into something full time as soon as he had his law degree.

"Take a break, Baxter." His boss stuck his head in the conference room and grinned. "You work too hard."

"Okay." He'd been comparing contracts ever since he came in, just before lunch. But that was a good thing. Busy meant he wasn't thinking about his mother, about the fact that she might be dead by Christmas. Even sooner.

He stretched, grabbed a bottle of water from the office lunchroom, picked up a stack of documents from the secretary's desk, and headed for his office. He had a few phone calls to make before he started on the next contract. Odds and ends his boss liked him to take care of.

But once the door was closed behind him, Luke sat at his desk, caught a glimpse of their family photo, and suddenly it hit him.

His mother was dying.

As healthy and vibrant as she looked in the picture, her body was not healthy anymore. It was riddled with cancer. The trip he and Reagan and Tommy were about to take wasn't a reunion at all; it was a farewell tour. He closed his eyes and tried to imagine all of them gathered around the Baxter house, finding separate ways to tell their mother good-bye.

Prayer, right? Wasn't that their only hope? Luke swallowed, nodding to himself. Of course it was. They would all pray until

God answered them. Beg God night and day, if they had to. That was the answer, wasn't it?

Luke stared out the window at the building across the courtyard. What about the last time he'd begged God for something? It had been September 11, almost two years ago. Reagan's father, Tom Decker, had been working near the top of the twin towers when the terrorist attacks happened, and Luke had begged—absolutely begged—God that somehow Mr. Decker would live.

But that didn't happen.

Reagan's father died along with three thousand other people, and the reality had shaken Luke to the core. He'd made so many bad decisions since that awful time; every one of his rebellious choices had come after that.

In some ways, Luke wanted to warn himself now, that begging God for a miracle would only set him up to fall again, to spiral into another dark chasm of unbelief and bad choices. How was this time of desperately begging God any different from that time?

A sense of peace washed over him.

It was entirely different. God had taught him so much since September 11, so much about the hard truths of life. That it was a fallen world, that terrorists had free will the same way any believer in Christ had free will, that death happened even to nice guys like Tom Decker.

Maybe even to his mother.

But still he would pray, because otherwise he had no hope at all. He would ask, because God loved him, and God heard his prayers. In the end, God would decide the number of days his mom had left. But no matter the outcome, Luke would never again lose faith in God. Never.

He shifted his gaze to his desk and the ten or so pictures he kept there. His father had been nothing but strong on the phone, but he had to be struggling. Short of a miracle, his wife of thirty-five years was about to leave him alone. And then what? Would his father stay in the big house by himself? Sell it and take an apartment in Bloomington?

Luke shuddered.

It was impossible to think of his parents separated, one without the other. Yet that was the way of life, wasn't it? One day, decades down the road, he and Reagan would have to face that type of loss the same way any couple who stayed together faced it.

Time was a thief; that much was certain.

He let his eyes skim over the photographs, taking in the pictures one at a time. It took a while, but eventually he realized something wasn't right. The black-and-white picture of his parents was missing, the one taken back when they first met. Maybe it fell off his desk and got stuck along the wall.

He stood and pulled the desk out a few inches, but it wasn't there. The drawers, maybe? Sometimes things fell off his desk and into his drawers. He sat back down, pulled open the top drawer, and searched inside. Nothing. The second and third drawers turned up nothing either.

Luke lowered his brow. Why in the world would one photo of his parents be missing? And who would've come into his temporary office and taken it?

The answer was obvious.

No one. No one would go to his desk, sort through his pictures, and take just the black-and-white photo of his parents. Obviously it had fallen or gotten knocked over. He slid his chair back. The picture had to be somewhere.

Dropping to his hands and knees, he scanned the floor beneath his desk, and even the narrow bit beneath the bookcase. The picture was nowhere.

Slowly he lifted himself to the chair again and looked once more around the office. Only then did he notice the trash can. It sat just beneath his desk, directly below the place where his photos were arranged. Suddenly it was clear what had happened. The night cleaning crew must've been dusting his desk and knocked the picture into the trash can. Then, when it came time to change trash bags, they must've wrapped it up with the garbage without ever realizing that the photograph had fallen inside.

A sick feeling came over Luke.

The photo wasn't a copy; it was the real thing. A keepsake his mother had given to him when he moved to New York. She had told him that she wanted the picture to remind him that his parents had loved each other a long time. And that in some ways as a young couple they were very much like Luke and Reagan.

The picture was gone, lost in the trash, probably in a landfill by now.

Luke opened the bottle of water and drank half of it down. He needed to make the phone calls and get home. That way he could pack and start counting down the hours until their flight back to Indiana. He could hardly wait to see his mother, to know for himself that most of what he'd already heard was exaggeration, the way a house full of women often exaggerate.

He could go through his parents' photo albums, find another photo like the one his mother had given him, and make a copy. The picture could be replaced; at least he hoped so. Time with his mother, that was priceless.

Especially now.

CHAPTER TWENTY-FOUR

THE MANHATTAN SHOOT was just about wrapped up, and Dayne Matthews could hardly wait. After his quick trip to Los Angeles, he'd placed both photos on the top shelf of the coat closet in his Manhattan apartment.

Out of sight, out of mind.

At least that's what he told himself when he showed up for work that Monday and every day after that. He had no idea what to make of the strange resemblance in the two photos. They couldn't be the same person; things like that simply didn't happen. The fact was, everyone had a twin. He'd heard people in show business talk that way more times than he could remember. Casting directors would want a Robert Redford type or a Ben Affleck look-alike. And always they could find them. Why? Because everyone had a double out there, someone who looked just like them.

That had to be the explanation for why his birth mother looked so much like Luke Baxter's mother. It would also explain the strange way he and Luke looked alike. After all, Luke had to be ten years younger than him, at least. There was no way the resemblance was anything but coincidence.

His birth mother was probably in Alaska somewhere, not New York City.

Either way, as soon as he hid the photos in his closet he felt better, more able to concentrate on the matter at hand—a multimillion-dollar picture in which he was the star. At this point in his career he couldn't afford to be anything but right on. As much as he was the media's golden boy today, they would turn on him in a heartbeat if he churned out a flop.

And it was up to him. He owed it to the director, the producer, the supporting cast, his leading lady, Sarah Whitley. All of them were depending on him, and he wouldn't let them down.

He had decided one thing. The day the shoot was over, before he headed back to Malibu and his place on the beach and the other shooting they still had to do in California and in British Columbia, he would go to Luke Baxter's office once more. He would return the photo he'd taken and explain the strange way Luke's mother looked like the woman who had given him birth. He would ask a few questions, just in case maybe the two women were related somehow. And then he'd put the entire ordeal out of his mind forever.

Today was that day.

Shooting would wrap up any minute, and Dayne had heard from everyone on the set that this picture was going to be his strongest yet. He glanced at his trailer. He had the photo tucked inside his leather portfolio, waiting just inside the door.

"Okay, people." The director stood up and brushed his hands together. It was the first time he'd smiled all week. "I'm happy to say that's a wrap." He pointed at a group of extras milling about a few yards away. "We need to take another go at that alley shot, the one where you're the patrons running out of the back entrance of the bar. It wasn't clean the first time, but I'm sure we'll get it in the next hour or so." His grin inched its way up his cheeks. "The rest of you . . . you're all invited to a dinner dance at the Marquis at seven o'clock tonight. You'll need your ID badge at the door." He clapped twice. "Good work, people." His eyes worked the area until he found Dayne. "And you, Matthews. Best work I've seen from you yet. Congratulations!"

Dayne pumped his fist in the air. Sarah Whitley was standing beside him, and he looped his arm around her waist and swung her in a circle. "We did it, baby!"

The others began milling off the set in different directions, but Sarah worked her fingers into his hair. "Yes, we did!" She kissed him square on the lips.

A few people hooted and howled as the kiss continued, but when Dayne drew back, he and Sarah were both laughing. "Wow." He gave a shake of his head.

"That'll teach you to forget to kiss me." She raised her eyebrows, sultry and suggestive, as she turned and walked toward her trailer. Looking back over her shoulder, she winked, and her come-on look was replaced by the gold-mine smile he was more familiar with. "See you tonight."

Dayne lifted one hand and held it there, watching her go. No question Sarah Whitley had been playing with him these past few weeks. She would linger next to him after a scene was over, flirting with him, teasing him, pushing him on to his best performance. The director frowned on relationships during the shoot, but now that it was over . . .

"Hmmm," he muttered. Then he turned and headed for his trailer.

Sarah was the hottest leading lady in Hollywood and maybe, if he played his cards right, after tonight she'd belong to him. At least for a while, a few months, maybe six. As long as most of his Hollywood relationships lasted.

No matter how great she was, his thoughts of Sarah vanished as soon as he opened his trailer door. He'd had his agent call ahead earlier to make sure Luke's office would still be open early tonight.

"Okay." His agent hadn't sounded suspicious, just curious. "What's your interest, Matthews?"

"Nothing." Dayne had managed a lighthearted chuckle. "Just

a personal touch. Wanted to thank Joe for making that last contract come together."

"I see." His agent clearly approved. "Public relations, then; is
that it?"

"Right."

The arrangement was made for five o'clock, assuming the
shoot was wrapped up by then. Dayne only hoped Luke Baxter
would still be there. He could hardly have had his agent ask for
Luke, when Joe was his attorney. He grabbed the portfolio and
considered changing clothes. His black T-shirt and jeans weren't
so bad, but he didn't have a hat handy.

He shot a look at his watch. Four-fifteen.

Forget the hat. He grabbed the portfolio, stepped around the
side of the trailer and out onto the streets behind it. His personal
assistant would box up his things and make sure they were sent
to his Manhattan apartment. He didn't have time for a hat or
any other disguise. If he wanted to find Luke Baxter, he had to
go now.

His feet moved fast, keeping to the pace of commuter traffic
along the busy street. Halfway to the attorneys' offices, three
women walking toward him shrieked, "Dayne Matthews! Look,
it's Dayne Matthews!"

He looked up, flashed his standard grin, and tried to keep
walking. But across the street a group of tourists heard the cry
and jaywalked over for an autograph. They were scrounging
pieces of paper from their purses and wallets and looking for a
pen when he realized it was better to stop and cooperate than to
lead a parade of fans through Manhattan.

"Hi." He smiled at the women first.

"Sign something for us, Dayne." One of the women jumped
up and down and grabbed his arm. "You're more gorgeous in
person than on the big screen."

"Thanks." He felt his cheeks get hot. No matter how often
this happened, he could never get used to the idea of perfect
strangers coming on to him, acting as if they were old friends. He

signed a receipt from the lady's shopping bag and looked around at what had become a small crowd.

All the people waiting had something to tell him, opinions about which of his films they liked best, and questions about his current movie, the one they'd just wrapped up.

The encounter took twenty minutes, and Dayne motioned to the nearest doorman when it looked like more people might cross the street to see what the commotion was. Above the small crowd he mouthed the word, "Help!"

The doorman nodded, parted the group of fans, and took Dayne by the elbow. "You're needed inside, sir."

"Yes." Dayne shrugged at the people still approaching. "Sorry."

Once inside, Dayne pulled a twenty-dollar bill from his pocket and tipped the doorman. "You saved my day. Thanks."

The man was older, probably in his fifties. He pulled a slip of paper and a pen from his pocket and handed it to Dayne. "For my daughter?"

Dayne uttered a single laugh. "Sure."

When he was done, he made his way through the lobby and out the other side of the building. The move saved him a bit of walking, but it was almost five o'clock. He kept his head low and walked even faster.

This time when he arrived at the office, he merely nodded to the receptionist and gestured with his chin toward the back rooms. He never broke stride. "I have an appointment with Joe Morris."

"Very well, Mr. Matthews. I'll tell him you're on your way."

"Thanks." Dayne turned down the hall, passed the office belonging to Joe Morris, and continued on to Luke Baxter's. He knocked once at the door, and then a second time, more sharply. When there was no answer, he opened the door and his heart sank.

Luke was gone, and his desk was completely cleared.

Maybe the guy didn't work there anymore, or maybe he was gone for the summer. Either way Dayne wasn't sure what to do with the photograph in his portfolio. He couldn't very well leave with it or mail it back to the office later. After today he didn't want to think about Luke Baxter or the photo he'd taken from the guy's desk. Dayne glanced out the office door and down the hallway. No one was watching, no one was expecting him to be working a covert, possibly illegal, operation in the empty law office of some seasonal law clerk.

Moving quickly, he set the portfolio on Luke's desk, opened the flap, and pulled the picture out. He started to put it on the edge of the desk, where it had been the day he took it. But he stopped. It would look strange, standing there by itself. Strange enough that someone might connect his visit with the return of the photo. After all, Luke must have noticed it was missing. The entire office might be on alert looking for the picture of Luke Baxter's mother.

The shelf, that's where it would look more hidden. If he was lucky it would seem as if Luke had misplaced the photo, forgotten it in his attempt to clean out his office. Dayne checked the hallway once more and took quiet steps around the desk toward the shelf. He was breathing fast and he chided himself. The picture wasn't actually stolen—more of a loan, really.

He set it up on the shelf and started to back away.

"Dayne?"

He jumped back and turned around. Joe Morris was standing in the doorway looking at him. "Morris!" Dayne hurried around the desk toward the door. "Hi . . . we wrapped up the shoot."

"The receptionist said you were coming back to talk to me." Joe looked past Dayne toward the desk, the shelving. He gave him a curious, partly comical look. "I thought maybe you got lost. My office is back down the hall."

"I know." He forced another laugh. "I kinda hit it off with that Luke guy . . . thought I'd catch up with him."

"Oh." Joe shrugged.

"Yeah, we had a pretty good talk the other day." Dayne studied his attorney. If the man was suspicious of Dayne's actions, he didn't say so.

"Luke's a great kid." Joe hesitated. "He's accepted a part-time job with us in the fall. Off for the summer though. I guess he's got a lot going on back at home."

"Hmmm." Dayne's heart rate picked up. "A lot good or a lot bad?"

"I don't know." Joe waved his hand toward Luke's empty desk. "A family wedding, and I guess his mom's pretty sick."

"His mom?" Dayne pressed his portfolio against his side. "He didn't mention that."

Joe uttered a strange chuckle. "You only knew the guy for ten minutes."

"Yeah, but . . ." Dayne caught himself. The whole thing was crazy. Why was he here at the office of some law clerk, and why had he taken the kid's photograph? Maybe Dayne needed a beach vacation, some time on a sunny stretch of sand without any directors or deadlines or movie shoots, no autograph seekers or paparazzi or any other distractions.

That way he could forget about the photograph and his birth mother and any resemblance she had to some stranger's sick mother.

Dayne gave a shake of his head and led the way out of Luke's office. "Anyway, I thought I'd stop in and thank you for the work on that last contract." He patted Joe's back and grinned. "Brilliant, man. Absolutely brilliant."

"Thanks." Joe rubbed his knuckles on the lapel of his suit coat. "That's my job."

The conversation shifted to the party tonight and Dayne's plans to hold on to the Manhattan apartment. After ten minutes, Joe gestured toward his office. "Another hour of work before I can go." He gave Dayne a light punch in the shoulder. "Keep it up, Matthews. You're at the top of your game."

Dayne could hardly wait to leave.

Once out on the street, he kept his head low but he didn't care if he was spotted, not really. As long as he hadn't been spotted putting the photograph back, the rest of the day couldn't be anything but gravy.

He took long strides as he headed for his apartment. It was ten blocks away, and he considered a cab. But he needed to think. Was that the last he'd know of Luke Baxter or his sick mother? He gazed up through the spaces in the buildings and wondered. What if by some strange twist of fate, the woman wasn't merely a look-alike? What if she was his mother, too?

The sun must've been lower because the air had cooled and the streets were covered entirely in shadows. No, the woman couldn't have been his mother. The pictures looked alike, but not exactly alike. Besides, it was only his imagination wanting there to be a connection.

If only he'd never met Luke, never seen the picture and felt that strange feeling, that somehow he'd seen the woman before. He had enough on his mind—endorsements and appearances and movie offers and romance—without the mind-boggling idea that maybe, just maybe, he'd found his birth mother.

Dayne made it back to his apartment without incident. He put thoughts of the sick Baxter woman out of his mind and changed for the dinner dance. It was time to party, time to celebrate the hard work he'd put into the film.

He was talking with one of the sound guys in the buffet line at the party when he felt someone breathe into his ear. He turned and Sarah Whitley was standing next to him. She wore a slinky white tank top and tight black jeans. On the set she'd played a plain girl from a small town, but here that image was gone completely. She was stunning, and Dayne felt himself react to her presence. "Hey . . . look at you."

She dropped her chin an inch or so and batted her eyelashes at him. "I was just thinking the same thing." She let her gaze move slowly down the length of him and back up to his eyes. "Be my date?"

He gave her an easy smile. "You mean I might be so lucky?"

Her arm slipped around his waist and she snuggled close to him. "Definitely."

They shared dinner and laughter and two large bottles of Dom Perignon, and when they left in his limo sometime after midnight, Dayne had no doubt how the night would turn out. The entire location shoot had been like one giant session of foreplay. A little flirting, intentional eye contact, casual touching and hugging and tickling. And of course the kiss. Though he'd messed it up, they'd found a dozen times to practice, times when he would step into her trailer, catch her from behind, and give her a liplock that took her breath away.

Then earlier today when she'd kissed him in front of the entire cast . . . yes, he knew where the night was headed.

Sarah helped him into his apartment, both of them stumbling and laughing and feeling the effects of the champagne. By the time they reached his bedroom, most of their clothes were strewn along the hallway.

When he opened his eyes in the morning, his head was pounding and Sarah was sitting dressed in the chair beside the bed. "Hey," she said.

"Hey." He rubbed his face and moaned. "What a night, huh?"

"Yeah." She smiled, but he couldn't read her eyes.

He hated this part of his lifestyle. She was a beautiful movie star, a girl any guy would love to chat with for an hour, let alone share the night with. The drinking and partying and getting together parts were always easy, but this . . . this awkward morning-after feeling was always uncomfortable.

Questions hung in the air between them.

Okay, so they'd slept together. Did that mean they were an item now? committed to each other somehow? ready to move in together? And because of their celebrity status, there were other issues. Had anyone from the media seen them together after the party, photographed them in the limo, or watched them head up to his apartment?

If so, it would be on the covers of the tabloids within the month.

Sarah pursed her lips and drew in a long breath. "I guess we got kinda crazy last night, huh?"

"Yep." He sat up in bed. Last night he hadn't cared a bit for modesty, but now he felt uncomfortable without a shirt on. He adjusted the sheets and rested his arms on his knees. "You okay?"

"Sure." She gave a thoughtful nod. Her smile didn't quite make it to her eyes. "Dayne, I need to tell you something."

"Okay." His heart thudded harder than before. What was this? Surely she was on some sort of birth control. "What's up?"

"I liked working with you." She uttered a sad laugh and looked at the ceiling. When she met his gaze again, she shook her head. "It was great, really. But . . ." A short breath crossed her lips. "What I'm trying to say is, I've got a guy back in Hollywood. A director. We're sort of—" she moved her hand about in the air— "sort of exclusive."

"Oh." A strange mix of rejection and relief washed over Dayne. Relief because the news could've been worse. She could've told him she hadn't used birth control, or that she had some sort of disease. But rejection because what? She was exclusive with someone? So why was she climbing out of his bed this morning?

"Don't be mad, okay?" She wrinkled her nose, looking irresistible despite the hard night. "I like you a lot, Dayne. It's just . . . the guy I'm seeing wants a family someday and, well . . ."

He understood. A bitter laugh worked its way through his chest. "I'm a playboy, right?"

"Kind of." She shrugged daintily. "Lots of fun for a few nights or a few months, but not much of a family guy."

Dayne wanted to point out that if she could enjoy his bed for a night, she probably wasn't much of a family girl herself. But he didn't. Instead he cocked his head and gave her a mock salute. "Glad to be of service. Anytime I can bring a little entertainment to an otherwise boring night."

Sarah's cheeks reddened and she looked at the floor for a few beats. "Hey." She looked up, her eyes filled with concern. "Don't say anything about last night, huh? My guy wouldn't understand."

Her guy? Dayne wasn't sure whether to laugh out loud or tell her to leave. In the end he decided on the latter. He pretended to zip his lips together. "It's our secret." He nodded his chin toward the door. "Go ahead, Sarah, but use the back door. I'll stay another few hours so no one thinks anything."

Her expression softened. She stood, kissed him on the cheek, and tousled his hair. "You're a good sport, Dayne." The corners of her lips lifted, and she winked at him. "Last night was awesome."

She was gone before he had time to sort through his feelings. Last night was awesome, but see ya later? What had she said? The guy she was exclusive with was more of a family type? And guys like Dayne were better for a night or a few months? Was that really what people thought of him?

He slid back beneath the covers and stared out the window. Ten years of Hollywood living flashed at him in as many minutes. Leading lady after leading lady, he'd gotten together with them and walked away when the thrill wore off. If that was his reputation—and it obviously was—then he'd done everything in his power to earn it.

His frustration at Sarah passed.

She had her own issues, certainly; otherwise she wouldn't have come home with him. But he couldn't be angry with her. Her thoughts about him were right. In a sense what she was telling him was "hey, thanks for the fun night, but a season of wild living is just a little too much for me."

She didn't want a playboy; she wanted a family guy.

The word *family* filled his mind and took up every bit of his consciousness. *Family.* A mom and dad, brothers and sisters. Wasn't that what he'd always been missing? A family to call his own?

A memory began to form. He was sixteen, a sophomore at the Indonesian boarding school while his parents were on the mission field. A girl in his math class asked him how long until he'd see his parents again.

"Three months, maybe four," he'd told her.

"Don't you hate it?" She tipped her head, pensive.

"Hate what?"

"Not having a family." She leaned forward on her forearms. "At least most of us have brothers and sisters, but you . . . you're always alone." A sad look flashed in her eyes. "I'd be mad at my parents if they did that to me, you know, made me an only child and then stayed away so much."

The memory lifted.

Even as a kid Dayne hadn't been a family guy. He didn't have the first idea how to be one. No wonder he hadn't stayed with anyone longer than a few months. He'd been alone, independent, as far back as he could remember.

He rolled onto his side and stared at the photo on his dresser, the only photo he kept visible anywhere in his apartment. It was a picture of his parents, dressed in khaki pants and tops, surrounded by village people, somewhere deep in the outback areas of Indonesia.

How come he hadn't remembered that he'd been adopted? In the back of his mind he'd always known, hadn't he? After his mother had shown him the picture of the woman who birthed him, the truth was out. He hadn't belonged to his parents from the beginning.

But somehow in his little-boy heart he hadn't wanted to believe anything but what was comfortable. His parents were his parents. Period. Never mind about some strange picture of a woman who had given birth to him. Not once until he went to the storage unit had he thought of her as his birth mother.

He studied the faces of the village people surrounding his parents. The people in the mission field were more family to his parents than he had been. His parents lived with those people, cared for those people, prayed for those people. All while he lived at the boarding school year after year after year.

Maybe he did have a right to be mad at them.

The picture of Luke Baxter's mother came to mind. What if by some strange, bizarre coincidence she really was his birth mother? If so, then the pictures that covered Luke's desk were pictures that could've been his own, pictures that would've lined his dresser even now.

The thought exploded in his mind, tearing at his lifelong belief that he hadn't missed out on anything by not having a real family. Of course he'd missed out.

Sarah's words came back to him: *"Not much of a family guy . . ."*

Unless maybe he did have a family somewhere. If not Luke Baxter's mother, then someone else. Whoever she was, she'd be in her midfifties now, something like that. According to the papers in the box, the adoption had been closed. She might've tried to find him and been unable to. Or maybe she was looking even now.

Maybe fate had brought him into Luke Baxter's office that day, so that he'd be driven to the storage unit. Otherwise he never would've faced the fact that he had a birth mother or that maybe she was someone he wanted to find.

Dayne sat up in bed and stared at the telephone on the nightstand. Maybe if he found his birth mother, he would find a family at the same time. Then he might have a reason to give up his independence, settle down with a girl who had no ties to Hollywood whatsoever.

Before he had his mind made up, before he was certain this was something he really wanted to do, he picked up the phone and dialed his agent. "I need the number of a private investigator, someone I can trust."

His agent hesitated. "Dayne?"

"Yeah, sorry." He leaned back against the headboard. The clock on his dresser read nine-thirty. "It's a little early."

"Right." Concern rang in the man's tone. "Why do you need a PI, Dayne? You can't afford to be in trouble, not now."

"No trouble." Dayne wondered how much he should say. Nothing, probably. If he did find his birth mother, the last thing either of them needed was publicity. He drummed his fingers on his thigh. But if he couldn't trust his agent, whom could he trust?

"So what is it, Dayne? Be straight with me."

"Listen—" he pursed his lips and blew out—"I was adopted, man. I guess in the back of my mind I always knew, but last time I was in L.A. I did a little research. Found some papers my parents kept."

"Okay." His agent sounded relieved. "So why the PI?"

There was no turning back now. He closed his eyes and worked his fingers into his brow. "I wanna find my birth mother. It's important to me."

A silence followed. "Look, Dayne, I'm not sure that's a good idea."

"Why?" Dayne leaned forward and rested his elbows on his knees.

"Because you're Dayne Matthews. That means whatever woman gave you up for adoption has no idea her biological child is a famous multimillionaire."

Dayne tried to make sense of his agent's argument. Then, gradually, a light began to dawn. "You mean she might want money?"

"She might want a lot of things. Fame, a slot on the nighttime talk shows." He made a sound that expressed his frustration. "What if she's a drug addict or locked away in some insane asylum? That would look good, wouldn't it?"

Dayne hesitated. His next words came slowly, laden with emotion. "What if she's got a beautiful family and all she's ever wanted was to meet me."

"Touché." His agent waited, his voice softer than before. "You really want to find her?"

"Yes." This time when Dayne said it, he had no doubts. If his birth mother was alive—and he maybe even had a family out there—he wanted to know about it. "I want it quiet, though. That's why I need your help."

"You have some papers; is that what you said?"

"A whole box of papers. They're in storage in North Hollywood."

"Okay. Sit tight. I'll make a few calls and see if I can find someone who'll help you."

Dayne showered, got dressed, and made himself some eggs. The whole time he couldn't stop thinking about the chain of events that had led to this moment. Finally, just before noon, the phone rang. Dayne grabbed it on the first ring. "Hello?"

"I found someone. The guy works for entertainers, promises complete anonymity. He's been around, Dayne; he keeps his word."

"Can he find birth mothers?" Dayne's heart pounded so hard he thought it might come through his chest and bounce about on the kitchen floor. "Does he do that?"

"Yes. He's very good. Let me see here . . ." A rustling sound filled the phone lines. "Yes, adoption is one of his specialties. I put him on retainer for you, and he says he'd like the box of documents as soon as possible."

"Then what? How long will it take?"

"No guarantees, Matthews. All he can do is try."

"Okay." Dayne paced across the kitchen and back again. He thought of his attorney's words yesterday, how Luke Baxter's mother was sick. Of course, she was probably not his birth mother, but still. Whoever she was, he wanted to find her. Now, before another week went by. "But he's good, right? He has a good chance of finding her?"

"Yes, Dayne. He's good and very expensive."

"I don't care." He worked the muscles in his jaw. This was a new feeling, this determination. Strong and unyielding and bent on getting his way. "Whatever the cost, I've got to find her. I want to know who she is and why she gave me up and if she ever wishes she hadn't done that. I want to know how my parents wound up with me, and what arrangement my birth mother had with them. I have dozens of questions."

"All while keeping the whole thing out of the press, right?" His agent sounded doubtful.

"Right."

"All we can do is try." He hesitated. "But in the end, if some-one ends up getting hurt over all this, Dayne, don't say I didn't warn you."

Dayne dropped to the closest chair and hooted out loud. "Thanks, friend." He hung up.

Dayne spent the rest of the day cleaning his apartment and packing for his flight back to Hollywood. The excitement bub-bling within him was different than any he'd ever felt in his pro-fessional life. Better, somehow, than getting an Oscar nomination or a raving review in *People* magazine. Better than knowing he could command top dollar for a film.

He was about to find his birth mother. How amazing was that? And how great that his agent had found a PI who would keep things confidential. That way he could find out her identity, set up a meeting, and get to know her—if she was willing, that is. All without ever having the press find out about it.

No one would get hurt by this strange and unusual search.

Dayne was completely convinced.

CHAPTER TWENTY-FIVE

THE KIDS WERE ARRIVING and no matter how bad she felt, Elizabeth couldn't be sad or sick or tired or anything but happy. This was the reunion she had dreamed about since Erin and Luke moved away. No, they wouldn't go to Sanibel Island to bask in the sun, but at least they'd be together at the Baxter house, the way they hadn't been in nearly two years.

The very thought of it made her feel stronger than she had in a week.

And another good thing—they already knew about her cancer. After telling the kids about her sickness, Elizabeth had at first doubted herself, wondering if she should've waited until she had them in person before explaining the situation. But now that it was behind them, she was relieved.

Now they could focus on having fun together, making memories, and getting ready for Ashley's wedding. Yes, she was sick; she was probably dying. And there were entire days when the sorrow of leaving her family was so suffocating she could barely breathe.

But she wasn't afraid. Not since that day in her bedroom, the day God used a simple Scripture to speak so loudly to her heart. And as much as possible, she wouldn't be sad—not while the kids were around. The tears could come late at night or closer to the end—if this was the end. But for now she wanted to celebrate her family, every wonderful moment they'd ever had together.

Elizabeth was sitting in a chair in the living room, watching out the front window. Ashley was at the airport picking up Luke and Reagan and Tommy. She tilted her wrist and checked her watch. It hung on her bony wrist these days, but she wore it anyway. It was a gift from John, an anniversary present he'd given her seven, maybe eight, years ago. Even cancer couldn't make her take it off.

She looked out the window again and strained to see down the long country road that led to their house. It was two-fifteen, just about the time Luke's plane was to arrive. Ashley should be back with them no later than four o'clock. Brooke was going to pick up Erin and Sam and Heidi in two hours, and that carload would show up around six.

Elizabeth folded her hands on her lap. They were having the Spanish casserole tonight, the one that had been a Baxter family favorite since Brooke was a little girl. Earlier Elizabeth had mixed together the filling—tamale sauce, sour cream, black olives, salsa, mushroom soup, and cooked chicken. The mixture was in the refrigerator, and all she had to do now was fill the tortillas, cover them with more sauce and grated cheese, and bake it.

For days, Elizabeth had been praying that she'd have the energy to fix dinner tonight, their first night home. Now, though she was somewhat tired, she was half done and grateful for the chance to cook for them again.

Funny how she was progressing, really. Her body was still recovering from the initial chemo, which meant that in some ways she felt better every day, more able to stand or take a short walk with John. But at the same time, the cancer was gaining ground, taking its toll on her breathing, most of all, and causing her to lose what little weight she still had.

A flock of birds drifted from one tree to another, soaring and dipping in unison across the field out front. How wonderful to sit here, looking across her property, waiting for her children to come home. What if she'd gone ahead with the second surgery? Elizabeth shuddered and pressed her arms against her sides, warding off the sudden chill. She would've been lying in bed, drugged to ease the severe pain, suffering through a minute-by-minute existence. The entire visit would've gone by without her ever enjoying a bit of it.

For what? Dr. Steinman was one of the top oncologists in the state—John had known that much. If he was certain a second surgery wouldn't have helped, then there was no question she'd made the right decision.

Elizabeth smiled to herself; it was the only decision, really, since her cancer was progressing so quickly. Of course, she was still praying for a miracle, but God—in all his mercy—had been placing something new on her heart recently. Miracles didn't always come in the shape of a dramatic healing. Maybe her miracle was having this time to quietly ponder the wonderful life they'd all shared together, the joy of being married to the man of her dreams all these years, the reward of being Mom to each of her kids.

And of course the miracle of this reunion, the chance to be together even if it was the last time.

Elizabeth reached for the portfolio, the one she carried with her whenever she had a chance these days. The letters were almost written, and that was another miracle. That she'd had the time and energy and health to put on paper her thoughts for each of those she'd spent a lifetime loving.

She opened the cover and pulled out the letter for the children; she was working on Erin's part now. John was at the store getting food for the weekend, so she could write for an hour or so. Write and gaze out the window and look forward to seeing Luke and Erin and their families.

Life couldn't be much better than that.

Ashley recognized them even from far away, her handsome brother and his pretty wife. She waited near the front of a crowd of people gathered near the airport security system, her eyes stinging. It hadn't been that long since she'd seen him. Except for Brooke's husband, Peter, they'd all been together last December for Luke and Reagan's wedding.

But so much had changed since then.

No matter that they were getting together to celebrate her own wedding this time; they couldn't kid each other about the bigger situation. Unless God granted them the most extraordinary miracle, their mother wouldn't live through the summer; this would be the last time they'd all be together with her.

Ashley watched her brother draw closer, watched him search for her, and then spot her. He smiled big and Ashley felt a tug in her heart. She would always feel a special connection to Luke, despite their hard years after her time in Paris. He was the kid brother who had spent most of his waking childhood minutes with her.

Luke had one hand on Tommy, who was snuggled in a front pack against Luke's chest, and his other hand around Reagan's waist. She reached Ashley first and gave her a quick hug. "Ashley! You look great!"

It was Luke's turn. Because of the crowd milling past, his hug was rushed also. "Look at you!" His eyes were shining, telling her how happy he was for her. "You're going to be a stunning bride, Ash."

They started walking, but Ashley reached for Tommy's finger. "My goodness, he's huge." Her nephew had turned one the month before and he seemed twice as big as last time they were together. She smiled at Reagan. "What are you feeding him?"

"Everything we can get our hands on." Reagan laughed. "He's a chunker all right."

"Yep." Luke made a silly face at his son. "He'll be a football player like his Uncle Ryan."

"Where are Landon and Cole?" Reagan peered around Luke and the baby.

"They stayed home. Landon was off today; he took Cole looking for a tux for the wedding."

"I always knew he'd make the perfect dad." Luke patted Ashley's back. "It's about time you figured it out too, big sister."

Ashley loved the small talk, the way it felt to simply be together again. But her stomach hurt because she knew what was ahead. They made their way to the luggage area and found a quiet place off to the side. Reagan took Tommy from Luke and rubbed her nose against his blond head. "Off for a diaper change." She made a crooked smile. "My favorite part of being a mommy."

They chuckled as she and Tommy headed toward the restroom. When they were alone, Luke turned to her and his smile faded. "Okay, tell me, Ash. How is she? Really?"

This question had been coming since he stepped off the plane; Ashley could tell that. She had planned to smile and nod and give some sort of reassuring answer. But this was her Luke, her brother, the one who could look into her eyes and see straight to her soul. Ashley opened her mouth, but no words came. Her eyes found Luke's and held them.

Grief and sorrow and fear came together and shaded his expression. "It's bad, isn't it?"

Without warning, the tears came. They spilled from her eyes down her face, and all she could do was go to Luke, hold him close and tight so her heart wouldn't break in half. Of all the Baxter kids, Luke was the one who understood her best, and now that they were losing their mother, he was the one who would know her pain better than anyone.

"Luke . . ." She spoke his name against his chest. "She looks awful. You . . . you won't recognize her."

He held her close, stroking her hair and rocking her. "I should've come sooner."

"No." She sniffed and pulled back enough to see him again. "Actually it was worse before, during her chemo." Ashley dropped her gaze for a moment before looking at him once more. "It was awful, Luke. She was so sick."

"So . . ." His eyebrows raised a bit, hopeful. "She's getting better? That has to be a good thing."

Ashley shook her head. "She's not getting better. She's recovered from the chemo, but she's wasting away." Her chin quivered. "You'll see, Luke. It scares me how bad she looks."

He searched her face. "What are we going to do?"

"I don't know." She hugged him again. "I really don't know."

They were quiet as they found the luggage and met up again with Reagan and Tommy.

"Are you hungry?" Ashley pointed to a snack stand nearby. "It's a long drive; we can pick up something if you want."

"I'm fine." Reagan cradled Tommy in her arms.

"Let's go straight home." Luke's tone was somber as they headed for the parking lot. "Mom's probably got dinner going."

"She does. She's definitely waiting for us." Ashley dried her eyes and uttered a soft laugh. "Counting the minutes."

"Well, then, let's hurry." He slipped one arm around Reagan, the other around Ashley. "I don't want to waste a single one."

He picked up the luggage and started walking. His steps were purposeful, almost fearful, and Ashley hurt for how he would feel when he saw their mother. But despite all the sorrow and potential loss ahead of them, she couldn't help but feel a ribbon of excitement weave itself across her heart.

They were all going to be together, just like old times. The kids would laugh and run and play together in the field in front of the old Baxter house. The adults would talk about the past and share long hours of silliness and conversation. And after they'd spent a couple weeks together, the greatest thing of all would happen. The thing that kept her going despite her mother's sickness.

All of heaven would sit back and smile and she, Ashley Baxter, would really and truly marry Landon Blake.

❧

Elizabeth was in the kitchen with John when she heard voices at the front door. The casserole was in the oven, and she was watching John prepare the salad.

He looked up from the salad. "They're here." He gave her a questioning look. He knew how badly she wanted to seem well tonight. "You ready?"

She frowned and smoothed her hands over her apron. The sound of the grandchildren in the background doubled her energy, but she was still worried. Luke hadn't seen her since she'd lost her hair. The navy beret and matching bulky sweater and pants did the best job yet of making her look like her old self. But still her appearance had changed; there was no hiding that fact.

John took a step closer and kissed her on the lips. "You look beautiful, Elizabeth." He took her arm in his. "Let's go say hello."

Elizabeth rounded the corner and stopped short. They looked so happy, so healthy and full of life. Ashley had stopped to get Landon and Cole, and now Cole was jumping up and down trying to make his little cousin laugh. Right behind them were Kari and Ryan and Jessie.

And Tommy . . . the boy was huge, the exact image of Luke at that age.

Luke noticed her first. "Mom . . . hi." His expression went from thrilled to shocked in as much time as it took him to tell her hello. But Ashley had obviously prepared him for the moment. He managed a smile despite the conflict that showed in his eyes. "I like your hat."

"It's not a hat, Luke." Ashley bopped him on the shoulder. She grinned at Elizabeth. "It's a beret, right Mom? The French would be appalled."

"Hi, everyone!" John crossed over to Reagan and Tommy and hugged them both at the same time. Then he shook Luke's hand and pulled him into a long embrace.

Whatever John was saying to Luke, Elizabeth couldn't quite make out. She came a few steps closer, trying not to look tired or worn out. "Reagan, you look lovely, dear." She hugged her daughter-in-law and blinked twice to keep her eyes from tearing up. "Thanks so much for coming."

Reagan angled her head, her own eyes glistening. "We wouldn't have missed it."

"And look at Tommy." She kissed her grandson on the forehead and held out her hands.

"He's a brute, huh, Mom?" Luke helped transfer the baby from Reagan's arms to Elizabeth's.

Up close, Tommy looked even more like his father. Elizabeth slid him onto her hip. The weight of the child sent a sharp pain through her torso, but she ignored it. Nothing was going to keep her from holding her grandson. Tommy pointed to her hat and smiled, showing off four little teeth. With her free hand, Elizabeth hugged Luke. "This is exactly how you looked at his age."

"Was I a chunker like him?" Luke pulled back, but just a bit.

"Definitely." Elizabeth laughed and looked back at Tommy. As she did she saw the resemblance again, but this time not to Luke. To her firstborn, the one she was still praying daily for. "Yes, he's a Baxter."

Cole skipped up and tugged on Elizabeth's sweater. "I'm not the only boy now, Grandma. Isn't that the bestest thing you ever heard?"

She tousled Cole's hair and smiled at Ashley and Landon nearby. "The absolute bestest thing, Cole. You'll like him even better in a few years when you can teach him how to catch frogs."

The group fell quiet as sorrow seized the moment. If her doctor was right, Elizabeth wouldn't live to see Tommy grow up, or to cheer when Cole taught him how to catch his first frog.

"Okay." John gave a light clap and turned toward the family room. "Let's come on in and get settled. Dinner's in the oven, and Brooke'll be here with Erin and Sam and Heidi around six."

Time flew as they sat around, catching up on Luke's work at the entertainment-law office and hearing about the online courses Reagan had been taking. She wanted to work as a copy editor for one of the publishers in New York City—a job she could do from home on a part-time basis.

"And what's the situation at the law firm?" John sat next to Elizabeth, his hand in hers. "You have the whole summer off, but they want you back in the fall?"

"Right." Luke was on the floor holding his hands out to Tommy, who was just learning to walk. Reagan sat in the closest chair, ready to catch the boy if he fell. Cole was trailing behind him offering words of encouragement.

"Sounds like a nice group of people." John gave a single nod. "And entertainment law, of all things. So interesting."

Luke picked up Tommy's pacifier from the floor and set it on the table. "The job started out as an internship, but I connected real well with the attorneys." He shrugged. "They want me to work on a more regular basis starting in September, and after I have my law degree, they're talking about giving me a chance with some of their clients."

"Are they all movie stars?" Elizabeth loved this, loved hearing her grown son talk about his career, loved watching him interact with his wife and son. Things were so different than they could've turned out. So different from the way they'd been in the months after the terrorist attacks.

"Most of the clients work in the industry, but they're not all movie stars." Luke grinned and looked at Ashley. "Did I tell you Dayne Matthews came in a while ago?"

Ashley laughed and leaned a little closer to Landon. "The Hollywood playboy, huh?"

"Actually—" Kari slid forward, bouncing Jessie on her knee—"he's not too shabby."

"Hey . . ." Ryan gave her a gentle elbow in the ribs. "What's this now?"

"Don't worry, honey." She laughed and winked at Ashley. "Dayne Matthews doesn't hold a candle to you."

"He sure has a bad reputation with the women." Ashley gestured to Cole, and he came running over, cuddling between her and Landon.

"Yeah, I guess." Luke caught Tommy, turned him around and sent him toddling toward Reagan. "In person, he's not that bad, really. Stopped in to meet me and the two of us got to talking. He's just a regular guy when you're one-on-one with him."

"Is he tall or short?" Elizabeth hadn't ever seen one of his films. She wasn't taken much by celebrity status, but if it involved Luke or his job, she was interested. "Most actor types are short; isn't that right?"

"He's actually pretty tall." Luke caught Tommy by the back of his sweatpants, tossed him in the air a few times, and set him back down again. "About my height, I'd say."

"And did Luke get me an autograph?" Reagan held Tommy's bottle in the air in mock exasperation. "Of course not. Has one of the most famous guys in Hollywood in his office and forgets to get an autograph."

They all laughed, and the conversation shifted to Ashley and Landon's wedding, where everyone could go for a tuxedo fitting, and how the reception was going to play out. Time passed quickly, and before long they were interrupted by the sound of more voices at the front door.

"Erin!" Elizabeth raised her eyebrows at John. "Now I can see that little Heidi Jo."

Before John could help her, Luke was at his mother's side, easing her to her feet. He hadn't been maudlin or emotional, but he was fiercely protective of her. Even though it was another reminder of her illness, Elizabeth enjoyed his attention. She looped her arm through his and moved with the group into the foyer.

Even before she got there, she heard quiet gasps coming from the others. Brooke and Peter were in sight, standing there with Maddie beside them and Hayley in Peter's arms. The commotion must've been about Erin's new baby. That had to be it. When Luke and Elizabeth rounded the corner, they both stopped short.

Erin and Sam were standing near the door, but each of them was holding an infant. Between them stood two gorgeous little girls with blonde curls, wearing matching play clothes.

Elizabeth's head began to spin and she held more tightly to Luke's arm. "Erin . . ." She searched her daughter's face. Her words were breathy, capturing the feeling of the moment as the other Baxters stood in a circle, grinning, teary-eyed, too stunned to talk. "What's going on?"

"Mom . . ." Erin's eyes were wet. She uttered a nervous laugh as she approached Elizabeth. "This is Heidi Jo."

"She's beautiful." Elizabeth reached out and took the infant in her arms. John came up along one side, and with him and Luke supporting her, she lifted her eyes to Erin, waiting.

"This is Amy Elizabeth." Sam held the infant in his arms so they could all see her sweet face. Then he grinned at the little girls, both shy and quiet, who had taken up positions on either side of him and were now clinging to his legs. "And these two are Chloe and Clarisse."

Elizabeth's knees felt weak. She handed Heidi to John and held her hands out to Erin. Her throat was so thick, the words would barely come. "You have . . . *four* babies?"

They fell into each other's arms, hugging and rocking and hearing six conversations strike up around them. "Erin . . . ," Elizabeth whispered into her youngest daughter's ear, "I'm so happy for you. I didn't think—" she swallowed, willing herself not to break down—"you always wanted a big family. I didn't think I'd live long enough to see it happen." She sniffed. "God is so good to us."

The group stayed that way, each of them meeting the new

children and making introductions with Maddie and Hayley and Cole and Tommy and Jessie. Kari and Ryan took turns talking to Chloe and Clarisse, and then the group shifted and Ashley and Brooke knelt down to meet them.

All the while, Elizabeth held on to Erin, listening to the story: how the social worker had called a few days ago, and how the girls' grandmother had become the legal guardian because of Candy's arrest, and how the older woman had called social services to find out if Erin and Sam were still interested. Not only in the baby, but in the other two sisters too.

Erin wiped at her eyes. "If we were willing to take all three girls and still give her chances to visit them, the grandmother was willing to sign over her rights. She wants to work on a cruise ship and travel." Erin gave a disbelieving shake of her head. "She said she thought the girls needed a real family, and that Sam and I could give that to them better than she could."

"So . . ." Elizabeth brushed her hand against Erin's cheek. "You have four daughters." She snapped her fingers. "Just like that."

"Yes, Mom." She hugged Elizabeth close again. "Just like you."

"Just like me."

The group started migrating toward the kitchen. Elizabeth called out in the happiest voice she could muster. "John . . . I think we'll need a few more plates at the table."

He grinned at her and nodded his approval. "That's what reunions are all about."

CHAPTER TWENTY-SIX

THEIR MOTHER'S DECLINE happened right before their eyes, and quicker than any of them had expected. Least of all Ashley.

Those first few days of being together, Mom was her old self: upbeat, energetic, the one starting conversations and keeping them going. And there was so much to talk about. Erin's new girls, Kari's pregnancy, Hayley's progress, the wedding. And all the changes and stages the kids were going through.

The one thing their mother hadn't wanted to talk about was her health. "We can talk about that later." She'd give them a partial smile. "Besides, without more tests, there's nothing new to talk about. Right now I feel good, and that's all that matters."

The day before had been Elizabeth's roughest since she'd gotten sick. She couldn't get through a sentence without coughing, and twice she'd disappeared into her bedroom for a few hours.

Ashley had gone to check on her once and met her father coming out of the room. "How is she?" But the question wasn't necessary. Her father's face was a mask of sorrow and fear, a look Ashley had never seen him have in all the years she was growing up.

"Not good." He'd closed the door quietly behind him. "She's coughing up a lot of blood."

"No!" Ashley's stomach tightened. "We can't let that happen, not now. She wants to be with us so badly." She took her father's hand. "Let's get her to the hospital, Dad. There's gotta be something they can do."

He shook his head. "There's nothing. Cancer like your mom has is so wicked, it literally takes over the body and suffocates a person." He slumped against the hallway wall. "We have to keep praying, but it's time to make some hard choices."

"Choices?" Ashley's heart had slipped into an irregular beat. They weren't really talking about her mom this way, were they? Not when she had been perfectly fine a few months ago.

"Pain meds." Her father'd hung his head and rubbed the back of his neck. "She's in a lot of pain, Ash. The cancer's tearing up her insides. That's why she's been spending time in her room. Praying . . . trying to tolerate the pain without resorting to medication."

"That's crazy." Ashley worked to keep her voice low. "If she needs medicine she should take it."

"It's not that easy." Her father had led her away from the bedroom. "The medication would make her sleepy, too groggy to get out of bed most of the time."

Ashley felt sick to her stomach. No wonder her mother hadn't said much that day. She'd been trying so hard to mask her pain, she had worn herself out.

Now it was Monday morning. Today's plan was for everyone to meet at the house before noon and have a picnic on the back lawn. Ashley had intended to use the morning to work on a painting for her mother—one based on a photo of the Baxter family taken at Luke's wedding. But as soon as she woke up, Ashley had wanted to be only one place.

At the Baxter house with her mother.

She and Cole had a quick breakfast and arrived at the house at nine. Her father, Landon, and Peter were scheduled to work that day, so other than Ryan and Luke and Sam, the picnic would involve the women and kids. But when she pulled into the driveway she saw her father's car.

Before Ashley had time to think it strange that he'd still be home, she knew. Her mom must be worse; there was almost no other explanation. She pushed back her fears, parked the car, and followed a bouncy Cole into the house.

"Hi, everyone! We're here!" Cole leaned his head back and made the announcement. He looked around, then turned to Ashley. "Mommy, yesterday there were a hundred people here. Now where are they?"

She caught her son's shoulder and whispered to him. "Let's be quiet, Cole, okay? Grandma might be sleeping."

"Oh." His eyes got wide and earnest. "But where's all the people?"

Ashley smiled. Cole would've done great as the oldest in a family with eight kids. He was loving the commotion and crowded conditions of the reunion. Lots of aunts and uncles and cousins; Landon always around; Grandma and Papa taking it all in. He knew nothing of how sick his grandma was, only that this time with family was the best thing in the world.

She dropped down to his level. "Maybe they're still asleep."

"Who's here?" Cole was whispering now, but his excitement still ran through him.

"Aunt Erin and Uncle Sam and their girls are in the guest rooms upstairs; Uncle Luke and Aunt Reagan are sleeping with Tommy in my old room. Everyone else is still at their own houses."

"Oh." Cole took a few steps toward the stairs. "Can I go wake up Aunt Erin's girls? I think they wanna play."

Ashley was just about to tell him no, that they'd watch something quiet on TV and head outside to wait for people to wake up, when her father walked into the room. He had obviously showered and shaved, but he looked weary. As if he'd been up all night.

"Papa!" Cole shouted his name, but then dropped his tone to a loud whisper again when his grandpa smiled and held his finger to his lips. "What's everyone doing?"

He hugged Cole to his leg and ran his fingers over his hair. "Hi, Cole. Everyone's up." His eyes met Ashley's. "They're just trying to keep quiet for Grandma. She didn't feel good last night."

"Oh." Cole's expression fell. "Does she have a tummy ache?"

A sad smile tugged at the corners of her father's mouth. "Something like that."

"Can I watch cartoons?" Cole looped his hands around his grandfather's forearms.

"Yes, Cole. That's a very good idea." He took Cole's hand and got him situated in front of the television set.

Ashley watched her father and son, touched. With Landon marrying her, Cole would have a father now. Something he'd wanted as long as she could remember. But Cole's time with her father, with his "papa," would diminish some. The thought was both comforting and sad. Her father had never intended to raise a grandson, but during the early years, until Cole was four, her father had treated Cole like his own.

The idea that their relationship might change had never hit Ashley before.

Once Cole was distracted, her father gestured for her to follow him into the kitchen. He filled the kettle and put it on the stove. "Some tea?"

"Sure. Thanks." Ashley leaned against the island countertop and studied her father. Something was wrong, worse even than yesterday. She waited until she had his full attention, until he was leaning against the opposite counter, looking straight at her. "You're supposed to be at work; what's going on?"

The sigh that came from her father rattled every nerve in Ashley's body. "She's worse, Ash. She's in a lot of pain."

Ashley clenched her teeth and stared out the kitchen window. "Why all of a sudden? Why would cancer do that?"

"Because . . . it's spreading so fast her body can't handle it."
Her father crossed his arms. "I called Dr. Steinman today and he
said . . ." He was choked up, unable to speak.

She crossed the space and stood beside him, arm to arm. Her
heart raced just beneath her T-shirt, and she wasn't sure whether
to cover her ears or ask more questions. "What, Dad?" She laid
her head on his shoulder. "What did he say?"

"I told him her symptoms, about the blood and the cough
and the pain." Her dad looked at the floor. "He said she doesn't
have long."

"But we know that already." Ashley bit her lip and willed him
to make eye contact. "Three or four months, right?"

"No, Ashley." His arm came around her shoulder, the way he
used to hold her when she was a little girl. "It could be much
faster. Weeks, maybe."

Ashley met his eyes, as shock and panic took turns kicking
her in the gut. "Weeks?"

"She doesn't have long, Ash." He drew in a shaky breath. "And
since we don't know, we need to think about the wedding."

Ashley couldn't believe she was having this conversation. She
closed her eyes. *God . . . what's happening? Help me, here, please.*
"Dad . . ." She looked at him again. "You're that worried? You
want me to postpone the wedding?"

He released his hold on her and took her hands in his. "Yes,
I'm that worried." He looked straight into her heart, more serious than he'd ever looked. "But I don't want you to postpone
it. I want you to consider moving it up. Getting married this
weekend instead of next."

Ashley's head began to spin. Her mother was so sick she
might not survive another ten days? Was that what her father
was telling her? And how could they move the wedding up a
week? "From the nineteenth, to the twelfth? Is that what you're
saying?"

"Yes." John dropped his gaze to the floor for a moment. When
he looked up, it was clear he was trying not to cry. "Your mother

has spent years wanting to see you and Landon get married. I couldn't—" he struggled with his composure—"I couldn't stand the thought of her dying before your big day, Ashley. She has to be there."

Ashley was too shocked for tears. The idea of shifting the wedding was overwhelming, but nothing to the awful realization that her mother had such little time left. She wanted to run from the kitchen, down the hall, and into her mother's room. Wanted to crawl into bed with her and hold on to her so she couldn't ever leave them.

But the matter at hand was too pressing to do anything but face it. "How, Dad? We've spent all this time getting ready. How would we change it now?"

"I called in to my office and told them I wasn't coming in for a month or so. Your mother needs me, so I'm staying home. I can help." He took a slow breath. He'd been thinking about the idea of changing the wedding date for some time; that much was obvious. "I figure everyone will be here today; most of us have cell phones. We can call Pastor Mark at church and then the banquet coordinator at the lake club. I've been praying about this all night, Ash. I have a feeling God will open the doors and let us do this. Even at the last minute."

Ashley nodded, dazed. She felt like she was dreaming, going through the motions, that her heart and soul and mind were really only on autopilot. "So we start there, and then call the florist and the bakery and the tuxedo places? the alterations woman and the band we hired? the photographer and video guy? All of them?"

"All of them." Her father sounded more determined the longer he talked. "You and I can make a list and split it up when everyone's here."

Even though it felt overwhelming, the idea was starting to make sense. "What about the guests, Dad? We have more than two hundred and fifty people coming. People can't switch their plans this late, can they?"

"If you explain the situation, you'd be surprised." Regret and sorrow mixed in his voice. "For something like this most people will go to amazing lengths to do their part to help."

"So we break up the list of guests and call each one?"

"Right." He reached across the counter, took the kitchen phone from its base, and handed it to her. "The first call is to Landon. He needs to know what's happening."

It wasn't until Ashley heard Landon's voice that she broke. Emotion welled up in her heart and throat, and all she could say was his name.

"Ashley . . . what is it?" His concern was immediate. "Honey, is it your Mom? Tell me."

"Yes." She allowed two sobs, and then she took control again. The tears could come later; there was too much work to do to break down now. "Mom's sicker than we thought, Landon. Dad wants us to change the wedding date."

She explained the situation, how they would divide the phone calls and pray for a miracle—that somehow everyone involved could change their plans so the wedding would take place in five days. Landon was completely agreeable, of course, and worried enough that he wanted to come over.

"No, Landon. Stay there at work; we'll make the calls." She hesitated. "Could you make one call, though?"

"Anything, Ash." His tone was filled with sadness, and she wanted to hold him more than she wanted her next breath.

"You made the honeymoon plans, so could you call the travel agent?" It was a part of the arrangements that would be most difficult to change. The part that would make the nightmare more real than any other. She still had no idea where Landon was taking her, but now maybe it would be better to cancel the trip.

"When—" Landon paused, his tone heavy—"when should I reschedule it?"

Ashley couldn't think of an answer. Giving him a date meant guessing when her mother would be dead and gone. Finally she found her words. "Let's cancel it, Landon. We'll take a honey-moon later, okay?"

"I was thinking the same thing. We can't pick a date."

Her father had cancelled the trip to Sanibel Island and gotten a full refund. Hopefully Landon would be able to do the same thing. She walked to the family room with the phone, where Cole was still watching TV. "Maybe we could take a trip on our one-year anniversary."

"I like that." Landon's voice was tender. "I'll get off work as soon as I can and meet you there, okay?"

"Okay."

"I'll be praying, Ash."

"Thanks. Me, too."

But as she hung up she realized something. In the past twenty-four hours her prayers had changed from asking God for a miracle healing to asking him for a different kind of miracle for her mother. A miracle wedding. Because at this point, all they could ask the Lord was that the wedding and its many details be changed to the twelfth, and that her mother be well enough to attend.

That, then, would be miracle enough.

❧

Elizabeth still wasn't afraid.

As sick as she was, as awful as she felt, fear was not one of the emotions running through her heart and mind. Instead the feelings inside her were familiar ones. Like those she'd felt when she and Kari took a trip to New York City the summer before Kari's senior year of high school.

In the weeks before the trip, Elizabeth had felt a slow buildup of nervousness and concern, a sense of wanting to be ready and at the same time a commitment, a knowing that once they stepped foot on the plane there would be no turning back. At the gate the feelings had been more intense than ever, and when

John had taken them to the airport she felt a sorrow and longing and yes, excitement, mixed with the other feelings. Not because she was afraid; she was never afraid to fly.

But because the journey would separate John and her for a season.

Somehow dying was like that. A sense of nervousness and finality and sorrow because for a season, they wouldn't be together.

It was just before noon and John was helping her get dressed. She didn't care about the pain or the coughing or any of it, as long as she spent the days with her family. She sat forward as John lifted her hand, placing it through the arm of her sweater. It was supposed to be eighty-five degrees this afternoon with almost as much humidity, but she was freezing cold.

"Is everyone here for the picnic?" She winced as he helped her slide the sweater over her frame. Bruises had started appearing all over her torso, another sign of the progression of the disease.

"Yes." John gave her a pained look. "They don't mind coming in here to visit. Maybe you should rest."

Elizabeth wanted to get frustrated, but the action would take too much effort. Instead she kept her tone patient. He meant well; he just didn't understand her urgency. "No, John. Get my beret, please, and then let's get out there."

He did as she asked, and together they made their way toward the family room. "Are they making the calls?"

"Yes." His steps were slow, and she could sense a helplessness in him. John Baxter, strong in every sense of the word, the one whose faith and character had been a rock for this family since its beginning, couldn't do anything about her cancer. Couldn't pray it away or will it away or fight it with knowledge and determination.

She could tell by his tone, his frequent sighs and edgy mannerisms, that the fact was taking its toll on him.

When they reached the family room, Ashley rushed to her side. "You won't believe it!" She had a list in her hands. "The church and reception are both moved to this Saturday. The church was open and the banquet coordinator was able to move a few smaller parties to other rooms, so the main dining hall is ours."

Elizabeth squeezed John's hand and smiled at Ashley. "God's working with us; he knows what we need."

The others stopped what they were doing and watched her. The looks of fear and concern in their eyes were almost more than Elizabeth could handle. She let John help her to the over-stuffed chair, the one that was most comfortable for her now. Her eyes traveled around the room at her five children and Ryan. "Where are the kids?"

"Upstairs." Ashley glanced around the room. "They're watching a movie, sort of a quiet time. I told them they could run through the hose later. Sam's trying to get the babies to sleep in the other room."

Elizabeth nodded. John took a few steps back, and the silence around her grew more awkward. "Thank you for doing this." She met the eyes of each of them. "I'm sorry it has to be this way."

"Mom, don't be sorry." Erin came to her and took tender hold of her shoulder. "We're worried about you; that's all."

"Well, don't worry." Elizabeth ran her tongue over her lower lip. Her mouth was constantly dry lately. "I'm actually feeling a little better."

It was a lie, and she could see by their faces that all of them knew it. But it was enough to let them, one at a time, return to the job of making phone calls. Elizabeth watched them pouring their energy into helping Ashley, and the love she felt in that one room was so strong it was a physical force.

She hated being the reason they were changing the wedding. Everyone would know, and she would have as much attention at the ceremony as Ashley and Landon, maybe more.

But inside she was secretly glad they'd made the change, glad she'd at least be able to be there. That evening when they discussed the day over pizza, the reports were all good. The band had another event scheduled, but they recommended a wonderful disc jockey who happened to have a cancellation for Saturday.

The florist couldn't switch his date, but he worked out a deal with a competitor who had the day open. Nothing about the floral arrangements would change at all, and neither the original company nor the new one would charge them for the confusion.

All the guests but four could make the switch or were willing to rearrange their schedules to accommodate the new plan. Along the way, well wishes and promises of prayer were passed on to Elizabeth from everyone. The group was exhausted as they turned in or returned to their separate homes for the night, but it was a good kind of exhaustion.

The Baxters had done what Baxters do: they'd faced a hard situation and pulled together.

That night Elizabeth's pain was worse than ever. Tylenol was the strongest drug she would take, but she ached everywhere her body made contact with the bed. She tried thinking about the wedding and the way her family had worked so well together today, but still she couldn't fall asleep.

Finally she had an idea.

She allowed herself to go back in time to the night at the University of Michigan mixer in 1967, and from that point on, she worked her way through the years, reminding herself of every miracle God had ever granted her. Her plan was to be so comforted by the host of blessings she'd been given that when she reached the current day she'd be able to fall asleep.

But sleep took her much sooner than that, for one very wonderful reason.

The list of miracles in the Baxter family history was so long and detailed, one night never would've been enough time to recall them all. Very simply, God had always been faithful to them. Even now, in her final days, Elizabeth had just one request, one crazy prayer that she lifted day and night before the Lord.

That one day her firstborn would know her, or know of her. That he would understand deep in his being how much he was loved, how she had longed for him all of her life—even during the years when she had promised not to talk about him with anyone.

And somehow, as Elizabeth fell asleep, the pain dimmed from the joy of her memories. She was certain deep in her heart that one day—when God knew the time was right—he would answer her prayer about her oldest son, the one whose name she didn't even know.

God had been faithful time and time and time again. That was the type of God the Baxters served. No, they didn't always get the answers they wanted. But they always got the right answers, even now with her cancer.

If her firstborn needed to know about the Baxter family, God would direct his steps until that happened. God was always faithful.

He would be faithful in this, too.

CHAPTER TWENTY-SEVEN

ASHLEY WAS NOT SURPRISED when she looked out the window the morning of her wedding day. The skies across Bloomington were bluer than she'd ever seen them. As if God himself had peeled back the cloud layers so the angels would have a better view of today's events.

She lifted the window and breathed in the sweet summer air. Most of the time she did her praying at night or while she painted. But the slow and wondrous realization that today she would marry Landon Blake, that her mother would be at the ceremony, that all of them would be there together, was more than she could hold in her heart.

There was nothing she could do but drop to her knees, and she did so, staring into the blue and knowing that every moment, every second of that day would be forever etched on her soul.

God . . . you did it. All those weeks and months when I thought I couldn't have Landon, when my past hung over us like a dark cloud, and yet here we are. You and me, God.

Tears filled her eyes, tears of joy and certainty and a glorious feeling she'd never known before. She'd always wondered about heaven, and as she stared into the sky she thought about Irvel. Was she watching even now? Did she have a front-row seat to watch Ashley give her heart to Landon the way she, Irvel, had once given her heart to Hank?

Ashley hoped so.

She liked thinking that people in heaven had a window to earth, a way to see what they needed to pray about, but through the tearless veil of heaven's understanding. If that was the case, then her mother was certainly not going to leave them one of these days. She would watch over them forever. Not in the way of an angel, of course, because people and angels were entirely different. But in a prayerful way that would stand as a reminder to each of the Baxters that their mother could go, but she could never quite leave.

Ashley smiled. Irvel would be one of the first people to find her mother, once she passed from this world to the next. They would share tea, no doubt, and talk about the joys of loving one man for all their earthly days.

A breeze sifted through the window and dried her cheeks. It would be the best day ever, a day when for just a little while longer they could all be together, the day when God in all his loving mercy would have the last word in the drama that had been her and Landon.

Lord, thank you. I know you'll be smiling on us today; I can already feel it. Please, God, let my mother feel it, too. Take away her pain so she can enjoy every moment. You say to ask anything in your name, according to your will, and you will hear. Please, God . . .

She glanced around the room and saw it standing in the corner. The painting she'd been working on since she found out the good news about her health. In the foreground were the backs of her and Landon—she in a flowing white dress, he in a dark suit. Between them was Cole, his little-boy, towheaded look, the one he was losing a little more each day. The three of them were holding hands, walking toward a brilliant sunrise that took up most of the painting. The colors were breathtaking, bright oranges and stunning yellows, colors that represented the future they would have together.

She would give it to Landon tonight, when they were alone after the wedding. It would be one more moment to spend a lifetime remembering.

She rose to her feet, her eyes still on the brilliant blue sky. Then, as if she might burst if she didn't take action, she sprinted into Cole's room, threw her hands in the air, and squealed.

Cole moaned and the sound became a giggle. "Mommy, you look silly." He sat up and rubbed his eyes. "What are you doing?"

Ashley did a little circle dance and raised both fists into the air. "Come on, Cole, get up! We're getting married today!"

꧁

It was the strangest thing.

Elizabeth was sitting in the chair near her bed, watching her daughters slip on their dresses, listening to their sweet conversation, and still she couldn't get over it. Ever since she'd awakened, the pain in her body was gone. Not diminished or lessened, not that she was merely getting used to it.

Rather it was completely gone.

She was tired and weak; no doubt she'd lost more weight. That much was obvious when John helped her into her gray linen dress, the one she'd picked out sometime after her surgery. She was dressed, ready to go, but with none of the pain she'd expected to feel. She could sit there with the girls, watching them get ready for Ashley's wedding, without feeling anything but complete joy.

Ashley was the first to ask her about it. "You look better today, Mom."

"I am." Elizabeth lifted her hands and let them fall back to her lap. "I can't explain it, but I don't hurt like I did yesterday."

The expression on Ashley's face changed. "Really?"

"Really." She ran her hands over her arms and legs. "The pain is gone."

"Well, then—" Ashley bent down and kissed her cheek—
"let's have the best day ever."

Kari and Brooke and Erin and Reagan all had their dresses on.
They worked each other's straps, helping with adjustments and
making sure no undergarments showed. Earlier in the morning,
a hairdresser from a small shop near the university had come and
put the bridesmaids' hair up.

Each one of them looked like a vision, but none of them compared with Ashley. Her hair was a cascade of ringlets, pinned up in
a way that was soft and delicate, with tendrils framing her face.

"Okay," Kari made a final shift of her dress. "It's your turn,
Ash."

"Right." Ashley pulled a white garment bag from Elizabeth's
closet, unzipped it, and took out the dress. She held it out as
each of the girls gathered around, touching the skirt and admir-
ing the needlework on the bodice.

Elizabeth coughed twice and held her hand out toward Ashley. "I'm feeling well enough; can I help you, dear?"

The room fell quiet for a moment, and Kari sniffed.

"I'd love that, Mom." Ashley and the others moved the dress
closer to Elizabeth.

At the same time, Erin was at her mother's side, helping her
to her feet. They all lifted the dress and eased it over Ashley's
hair. But Elizabeth wanted to do the buttons. She'd been thinking about this, practicing the move in her mind. Since her hands
didn't hurt, she set to work on the bottom button and gradually
worked her way up.

"Can you believe it, Mom?" Ashley had her back to her, but
she angled her face so they could see each other.

"I know I can." Kari dabbed at her eyes. "Landon has loved
you since the first day he met you."

Brooke smiled. "Sort of like you and Ryan."

"Yes." Kari's cheeks glowed and she smiled at Ashley. "You're
beautiful, little sister. Wait till he sees you."

Elizabeth kept working the buttons, steady by Erin's side.

"When you left for Paris, Ashley, I didn't know if you'd ever come back." Her words were thoughtful, drenched in the memory of those long-ago emotions. "And when you came home, I wondered the same thing."

"I'm sorry." Ashley held her fingers to her eyes and uttered a sad-sounding laugh. "Glad my makeup's not on yet."

"No, I don't mean to make you sorry." Elizabeth struggled with the buttons. She was tired, but nothing was going to stop her. She had dreamed about this moment too long to let anything get in the way. "I just mean look at how amazing God is. He kept Landon from going to New York City too early. If he would've gone when he was supposed to, he would've been in the twin towers that day."

"Like my dad." Reagan's eyes were damp also.

"Yes." Elizabeth paused and held her hand out to Reagan. "Like your dad."

Ashley breathed in and straightened herself. "I've thought about that."

"You see . . . God had a plan for you all along." Elizabeth looked at the other girls. "He always has a plan for us; either to give us a hope and a future here in this world. Or—" she smiled and waited for her emotions to level out—"or in the next."

"It is amazing how things work out." Brooke sat on the edge of the bed near Elizabeth. "Hayley is doing so much better. Drinking from a cup, eating solid food. We could've lost her, but God wasn't finished with her yet."

"That's what it comes down to." Elizabeth worked the last few buttons together. She stopped to cough, but only for a moment. "He alone knows the number of our days, and until that moment, he always has a plan for us."

She fastened the last one and then held her breath. "Okay, turn around."

Kari picked up Ashley's train and fluffed it out behind her. Ashley made a slow spin to face Elizabeth. As she did, she smoothed out the front of the skirt and their eyes met. "Well . . ."

Elizabeth covered her mouth, but only for a few seconds. "Ashley . . . you're absolutely gorgeous." She gave a slow shake of her head and put her hands on her daughter's shoulders. "Remember what I said about God having a plan for us?"

"Yes." Ashley's eyes glowed, much like the rest of her. "You've always taught us that. God has a plan for his people as long as they draw breath."

"This—" her voice grew tight and almost too soft to hear— "this is my miracle, Ashley. Seeing you get married. I'm still alive because God allowed this day to be part of his plans for me." She kissed Ashley's cheek. "What else could I ask for?"

Even as Elizabeth said the words, the answer came to mind. She could ask God to help her find her firstborn. But she quickly dismissed the thought. Here and now, seeing Ashley marry Landon would be more than enough.

The girls were talking at once again, marveling over the dress and the way Ashley looked in it. Whereas at one time in her life Ashley had worn beatnik clothing and refused anything even slightly mainstream, now she looked like she'd stepped off the cover of a bridal magazine.

They were all saying so when Cole burst into the room. He stopped when he saw Ashley, and suddenly his steps became slow and dreamy. "Mommy . . . you look like a princess."

"Thanks, honey." Ashley lowered herself to his level. "And look how handsome you are!"

The wedding was an hour away, and John had already dressed Cole in one of the upstairs rooms, the one where all the guys except for Landon were getting ready.

"I know. Papa says I look good in grown-up duds." His face fell some. "'Cept I'm a little nervous about my wedding."

Around the room the girls did a good job of hiding their smiles. Of course Cole would think it was his wedding. He'd wanted it even longer than Ashley had.

Ashley crooked her finger and rubbed it against Cole's chin. "What are you worried about, sport?"

He angled his head and blinked. "I don't have the words yet."

Kari, Brooke, Erin, and Reagan gathered closer. Ashley lowered her brow. "What words? You're the ring bearer, honey. You don't have to say any words at all."

Cole nodded his head emphatically. "Yes, Mommy. Landon said so."

Elizabeth pressed herself back into her chair, trying to keep from giggling.

"What did Landon say?" Ashley stood and took Cole's hands in hers.

They were a vision, facing each other that way. Cole drew circles on the floor with the toe of his shiny dress shoe. "He said after we say the vows, he'll be my daddy forever." Cole paused. "So what if I don't know the vows, Mommy. I haven't practiced like I practice my ABCs."

"Cole . . ." Ashley pulled him into a hug. "Landon and I say the vows, silly. You don't have to do anything but walk up with the ring pillow and stand there looking cute."

"Really, Mommy?"

She kissed the top of his head. "Really."

"Goody!" He raised a fist into the air, all boy despite the fancy clothes. He started to turn around, but he stopped himself. "After the vows part, can I call Landon my daddy?"

Elizabeth felt a rush of tears, but she held them back. Name or not, Landon had been Cole's father for years now. Ashley had told them that Landon already had the papers filled out to officially adopt Cole once they were married. He couldn't have loved Cole more if the boy had been his own.

"Yes, Cole." Ashley's voice was thick when she finally found the words to answer him. "Yes, you can call him Daddy."

John could feel the presence of God around them.

It had been that way since this morning when Elizabeth first reported that for no reason at all, her pain was gone. But it was more than that. In some ways, Ashley's wedding represented a coda on the past years of Baxter life. Just four years ago there were more questions than answers making up their family. Questions concerning Kari and Luke and Brooke and Erin. Even the harder questions regarding Ashley. Now the questions had been answered. God had come through on every front except one.

Elizabeth was dying. She wasn't getting the miracle they'd prayed for, and one day—when the wedding was over, when everything was over—he would spend some time with God and try to figure out why. Why it was necessary for her to die when everything in their lives had finally worked out.

The questions he had for God didn't leave John angry, just confused.

But that time would wait. For Ashley was getting married and in spite of all the ways he couldn't understand what God was doing with Elizabeth, John could feel his presence all around them.

The ceremony was set to start in twenty minutes. All the other guys had gone on to the church, so just the women remained. John had hired a limousine for the occasion, a stretch that would seat him and Elizabeth, the bridesmaids, and Ashley and Cole.

He stood near the front door and cupped his mouth. "Time to go." Familiarity surrounded the moment. This was how he'd felt when Kari and Erin and Brooke got married. This rushed, exhilarated feeling that they'd entered a countdown. That in less than an hour he would give away his daughter, that when the day was over, she would bear another man's name.

And now he was doing the entire routine for the last time.

Erin led the way down the stairs with Elizabeth on her arm. "We're all coming."

A trail of his daughters and Reagan followed, each of them stunning. His eyes locked on to Elizabeth's and held. They had always been able to speak without words, and this moment was no different. As beautiful as the girls around her were, Elizabeth was the most striking. With her fashionable beret—this one blue-gray like her dress—and her delicate features, she was still the only woman who could take his breath away.

But her looks were nothing compared to her eyes, full and emotional and as intently aware of the significance of the moment as he was.

"Elizabeth . . ." He held out his hand and she came to him.

"You look wonderful, John." Her steps were slow, but her smile spread from one cheekbone to the other. The bridesmaids passed by them, hurrying along with Cole out to the car, giggling and remarking about the limo and how fun the ride to the church would be.

Ashley was last. She took both his hands and Elizabeth's and looked from one of them to the other. "If I've never said this before, I need to say it now." She bit her lip and her chin quivered. "Thank you for putting up with me, for believing in me when I didn't believe in myself."

"That's what parents do." John leaned in and kissed her cheek. "You look stunning, sweetheart."

"Thanks." She squeezed their hands. "We have to go. I just had to tell you that. Every time you prayed for me, God heard you." A grin flashed across her face and she gave a light shrug. "Can you believe it? I'm really getting married!"

She was gone in a flash, leaving John and Elizabeth alone. He angled his head. "Look at you, Elizabeth. Mother of the bride again and still pretty enough to make the bride jealous."

"You always know what to say, John. You always have." A light blush came into her cheeks. "Let's go. I don't want to miss a minute of this one."

❧

The final minutes felt like an eternity.

After all the time Landon had waited for Ashley Baxter, these last moments were almost more than he could take. He shifted from one foot to the other, staring every few seconds at the back door, willing the music to start so he could finally see her.

The church was packed. Half the church was filled with his family, his parents' friends, and two dozen guys from the fire department. There were people he and Ashley had attended school with and doctors who worked with John Baxter.

Every one of them was obviously aware of the circumstances. That despite the happy occasion, the wedding had been changed because the bride's mother was dying. Luke had already ushered his mother in, and she was sitting serenely in the first pew. No matter the illness that ravaged her body, the look on her face was pure, untainted joy.

How long had he loved Ashley Baxter? Many guests were aware of their history, how he had pursued her even when she seemed not a little interested. There were doctors from the hospital who remembered his injury in the Bloomington fire, the way Ashley had stayed by his bedside, proclaiming her love to him, and then taking it back when he woke up.

Back then she was always so afraid to love.

But God had changed all that, and now, here they were.

The music changed and Landon felt his heart skip a beat. He swallowed hard and clasped his hands behind his back, the way Pastor Mark had instructed last night at the rehearsal.

The bridesmaids and groomsmen came first, each of them wearing a look that was deeper than mere happiness. These were people who had prayed for him and Ashley, people who knew what they'd been through and how far they'd come, the obstacles God had removed to bring them to this day.

Landon had thought about asking some of his buddies at the fire department to act as ushers, but with Elizabeth sick, somehow it didn't seem appropriate. Instead he'd chosen the spouses of Ashley's sisters, and for his best man, Luke, the Baxter he'd gotten closest to during his time in Manhattan.

Erin and Sam were first down the aisle, followed by Brooke and Peter, and then Kari and Ryan. Luke and Reagan were last, and since Kari was Ashley's matron of honor, she swapped places with Reagan so she'd be in the right spot. Luke caught Landon's eye and gave him a thumbs-up.

Landon grinned and looked at the rear of the church again. Cole was the ring bearer, and Maddie and Hayley were the flower girls. A lump grew in Landon's throat as he watched the tender procession. Cole pushed Hayley in her wheelchair. She was dressed in a white-and-pink dress identical to Maddie's. Cole's pillow was on her lap, and the flower basket on top of that. Maddie walked alongside the chair, taking small handfuls of rose petals from the basket and sprinkling them along the aisle runner.

Hayley didn't hold her mouth open the way she had for months after her drowning accident. Watching her now—the smile on her face, the way her blonde hair fell in ringlets around her head—it was easy to believe she might actually make a full recovery one day.

When the children reached the front, Cole pushed Hayley to a place along the front row near Elizabeth. He waved big and said, "Hi, Grandma. Did I do good?"

A few feet away, Pastor Mark stifled a giggle as a round of quiet laughter fanned out across the first few rows. Elizabeth leaned close to Cole. She looked beautiful, much like Ashley. But she was too thin. Much too thin. "Yes, Cole," she said in a loud whisper. "You did great."

He nodded, proud of himself. Then he took the ring pillow and the flower basket from Hayley, handed the basket to Maddie, and led her to her place in front of Brooke, the way he'd been taught to do the night before.

Finally he spotted Landon—as if maybe he hadn't actually noticed him before because of his responsibility of pushing the wheelchair down the aisle. Cole gave a big wave, tucked the ring pillow under his arm, and took a few running steps toward him. Just then, Ryan gestured him over, and Cole stopped short, gave another wave to Landon, and went to stand with Ryan.

The music changed again, and "The Wedding March" rang out through the church. People stood and faced the back door, and Landon watched Elizabeth. She didn't have anyone sitting near her to help, but she was able to stand on her own. The look on her face was one Landon would remember all of his days.

And then, like a vision, Ashley was there. Holding gracefully to her father's arm, she started down the aisle. Landon had been to weddings—even Baxter weddings—where the bride glances at the guests while she walks down the aisle, taking in the family and friends who were there in support.

But Ashley did nothing of the sort.

She found Landon's eyes the moment she stepped into the aisle, and her gaze didn't waver once while she walked alongside her father. Even from seventy-five feet away, he could read her look, feel how the truth was hitting her, the way it had been hitting him all day.

They were really here, really getting married.

Though she had run from him, hidden from him, refused his ring the first time around, and told him to fall in love with someone else, here they were. In love and determined to share every day of forever, thanking God for allowing them to find a way to be together. And now—looking more beautiful than she'd ever looked before—she was about to become his wife.

He prayed he could make it through the ceremony. Because the look of love and awe and adoration in Ashley's eyes was enough to bring him to his knees.

*

The entire walk down the aisle, Ashley couldn't stop thinking about the past. Yes, there was Landon, standing at the front, shoulders squared, eyes locked on hers. But at the same time he was coming into a coffeehouse, spotting her and telling her she should call him sometime. He was playing Frisbee with her on the shores of Lake Monroe and sitting beside her at a campfire listening to her tell him details about her past that she'd never told anyone.

He should've been long gone by now, right? Wasn't that what people did when they found out someone they cared about had a sordid past? They disappeared—fast. But not Landon. She blinked, her steps slow and in time with her father's.

The image in her mind changed, and Landon was lying in a hospital bed, half dead, and her father was telling her to say something to him, to give him a reason to live, a desire to hang on; and then he was recovered and she was telling him she wasn't sure, didn't know if she could love him the way he wanted her to love him, and he was telling her he was leaving for New York City.

The pictures in her head blurred, but Ashley kept her eyes locked on Landon's. The same eyes that had loved every painting she'd ever created, the eyes that had held hers that night in Manhattan and asked her to be his wife. How was this happening after she'd told him no, after she'd rejected him so many times?

And it was Landon at Luke's wedding last December, dancing with her, telling her he loved her no matter what happened with her health; Landon coming up behind her at Irvel's funeral service and telling her he'd taken the matter out of her hands. He was back in Bloomington, and there was nothing she could say to make him go away. Landon . . . picking her up and swinging her around and around when he got the news that she wasn't sick after all.

Always Landon, every time. Loving her and bearing with her, putting up with her when no one else would've.

What kind of love was that, anyway? A crazy, life-defining type of love that would see them through whatever the road ahead held. Even her mother's sickness.

They reached the front of the church, and her father tightened his hold on her. She gave him a quick squeeze and looked at Pastor Mark.

"Who gives this woman to be married?" He smiled at Ashley and then at John.

Her father stood a little straighter. "Her mother and I do." He lifted her veil just long enough to kiss her cheek and whispered, "Love you, Ash."

"Love you, Dad."

He circled behind her and took his place beside Mom. At that, Landon stepped forward, took her arm, and the two of them stood together in front of the pastor and faced each other.

This was the part where Pastor Mark would talk, and Ashley was sure he did a great job. Every now and then she caught something he was saying, something about knowing the Baxters and learning from the Baxters and realizing that they defined the way a family was supposed to be.

But she didn't catch every word; she was still too busy looking at Landon. He mouthed the words, his whispers just loud enough for her to hear. "Did anyone ever tell you . . ."

She lowered her chin so no one would see her giggling beneath her veil.

"You have the most beautiful hair." He gave her hands a gentle squeeze and mouthed one last thing. "We're getting married!"

She felt chills down her spine, her arms. The moment was surreal, like something she might've painted. Here they were getting married and whispering like schoolkids. "I love you, Landon."

Finally it was time to say the vows. Like most of her sisters before her, Ashley had chosen to write her own. Landon, too.

He went first. "Ashley, you are my other half, the part God gave me before I even knew your name." He looked deeper at her. "Come with me, stay with me, dance with me, play with me. Love me all the days of our lives. No matter what happens, be my wife and my friend, the piece my heart can't live without."

Seconds passed, and she couldn't speak, couldn't think of what to say or do. Landon loved her! They were here, getting married. What more was there to say?

Pastor Mark made a quiet coughing sound and gave her a pointed look. It was enough to snap her into action. She caught Landon's look again and began reciting the lines she'd written the day he gave her the ring.

"I belong to you, Landon Blake. God directed my steps even when I was running, so that one day you would find me and you would find my son, and we'd never, ever be apart again." She paused and out of the corner of her eye she saw Cole take a step closer. "I see life as a painting, a picture to be savored. And you, Landon, are my reds and oranges and brilliant golds. In my life you are the sunrise and this is only the beginning. My heart was locked up tight when you came to me, and now you will forever hold the key. Be my husband, Landon, and walk forever with me and God Almighty."

"And me!" Cole spouted the words before Ryan could slip a hand over his mouth. Again a tittering worked its way across the church.

Ashley grinned at Cole and gave him the okay sign. "That's right. And Cole, too. Because we both love you and we always will."

Landon's eyes shone and he let loose a quiet chuckle. He wanted to kiss her; his eyes told her that much. Instead it was Pastor Mark's turn again. He led them through the various statements, the promises to be true in good times and bad, the exchanging of rings. Finally he pronounced them husband and wife and gave Landon permission to kiss her.

The moment was brief, with only a hint of the passion they would share with each other later. The guests clapped, and Pastor Mark said the traditional words Ashley had asked him to say: "I'd like to introduce to you . . . Mr. and Mrs. Landon Blake."

Ashley spotted her mother sitting in the front row, looking straight at her. And somehow she knew that God had answered their prayers after all, that he'd given them a miracle the last time she had cancer all those years ago. That she'd been living on borrowed time ever since, going along year after year so that she might be here to see each of her children get married.

She felt Landon take her hand and lead her down the aisle. And though the clapping came from the family and friends that filled the church, she was sure she heard a distant clapping, too. A clapping of all the angels in heaven and earth who knew that a moment like this could only come from one source.

Their loving, faithful Almighty God.

CHAPTER TWENTY-EIGHT

THE END WAS COMING FAST. John knew better than he let on. But since Ashley and Landon had postponed their honeymoon, the reunion continued unabated. There were picnics in the backyard, game nights, and conversations that lasted until all hours of the morning.

Elizabeth was there through most of it.

She hid her pain as best she could and did most of her coughing into a handkerchief, which she kept with her. But on Tuesday morning, three days after Ashley's wedding, he could see in her face, in the whites of her eyes, how quickly she was fading.

"You aren't feeling well, are you?" He walked around the bed to meet her.

She looked almost green, as if she might not survive the effort it took to get out from underneath the covers. "I'm . . . I'm a little queasy."

He helped her into the bathroom, but before she could reach the sink, she called out his name and collapsed in his arms.

"Elizabeth!" he shouted at her, suddenly terrified that the end had come without any traditional warning, without any parting words, or last-minute chances to tell her how much he loved her, how much he would miss her.

She was limp, so he stretched her out on the bathroom floor. Adrenaline coursed through him and his heart raced. He had to force himself to stop shaking long enough to feel for her pulse. "Elizabeth?" His fingers found the spot on her neck. It was slow and thready; she needed immediate help. "Honey, wake up. We need to get you to the hospital."

When she didn't show any signs of responding, John raced into the bedroom and dialed 9-1-1. *God, let them hurry. Don't let this be it. . . .*

"9-1-1, what's your emergency?"

"This is Dr. Baxter from the hospital." It was a detail he didn't need to mention. His information would, of course, come up on the screen of the operator as soon as his call went through. But he was desperate, hoping maybe they'd come faster if they knew it was him. "My wife's collapsed; please . . . please hurry."

"Yes, I'm sorry, Doctor." The woman's voice was familiar, probably someone he'd seen in the emergency room before. She sounded alarmed at the news. "We'll have someone there in five minutes."

He thought about waking the others or calling Brooke or Kari or Ashley. But he couldn't leave her side. Her arms were pale and clammy, same as her neck and chest. This time he got down low to her face. "Elizabeth, it's me . . . honey, wake up."

Still there was no response.

Sirens sounded in the distance, but the driver must've turned them off as he got closer to their house. He was at the door, ringing the bell, before John could get down the stairs. He flung open the door and pointed upstairs. "She's up there."

At the same time, the other bedroom doors flung open. "Dad, what's happening?" It was Erin, and she pulled a robe around her as she darted down the stairs.

"Your mother collapsed; I can't rouse her." He looked up and saw Luke in another doorway wearing sweats and a T-shirt. His mouth hung open, face pale from the sudden shock. "Please, one of you call the others. We can meet at the hospital."

"Dad . . . is she . . ." Luke clearly couldn't bring himself to say the words.

John shook his head. No, she wasn't; she couldn't be. "She's breathing, Luke. Maybe she just needs some fluids, but they have to take her in. Please . . . stay calm. We'll get through this, okay?"

"Okay." The old Luke would've gotten angry or shaken his head or stormed off, doubting God for not giving them the answer they wanted. But the look Luke had in his eyes now was that of a grown-up, a young man ready to face whatever the day held.

And John was fairly sure whatever it held, it wouldn't be good.

❧

Dayne was on location in British Columbia when he got the call.

His pager had a distinct sound when the message was from his agent. It was Friday, and the director was blocking a scene that didn't involve him, so he waved at one of the assistants. "I've got a call; okay to take it?"

The woman nodded and smiled at him.

His playboy image was still intact, but only because he hadn't had the chance to prove otherwise. Sarah Whitley was on location with him, but the two had kept their distance. Meanwhile, all Dayne wanted was to hear back from the private investigator. In some ways, his entire life felt like it was on hold while he waited.

He'd spent some time dating since he'd been filming in Canada, but very little. The assistant director was hot for him; he could tell that much. But nothing interested him. He'd lived the wild life so long it had lost its appeal. Beautiful Hollywood women all looked alike to him now, and he found himself looking at families who stopped by to watch the filming. Not people in the business, but everyday families who had only stopped by out of curiosity to see what was happening.

Dayne would see a couple, hand in hand, with a few children gathered around them and he'd stare, wondering the same thing he'd wondered so often since meeting Luke Baxter. What would it have been like to grow up with brothers and sisters, to know the tangible presence of his parents day in, day out?

Funny, he would think as the family got bored and wandered off. He had everything the world considered important: money and fame and talent and looks. But none of it would buy him the one thing he'd never really had.

A sense of belonging.

These thoughts flashed in his mind as he stepped off the set toward his trailer and called his agent. "Hey, it's me." Dayne turned to block out the noise. "What's up?"

"I heard back from the PI this morning."

Normally, nothing made Dayne anxious or nervous or surprised. But suddenly his palms were sweaty. He looked around and found a stump to sit down on. "Shoot."

"What was that kid's name, the one who worked at the law office in Manhattan?"

"Baxter." Dayne's heart rate tripled. In the distance, the director was barking at someone. He covered his other ear with his hand so he could hear better. "Luke Baxter."

"No wonder you hit it off with him."

The ground beneath Dayne's feet felt suddenly unstable. His head spun and he used a tighter grip on the phone so he wouldn't drop it. "What's that mean?"

"According to the investigator, your birth mother's name was Elizabeth, and about three months after you were born she married your father—a John Baxter. John and Elizabeth went on to have five other children: Brooke, Kari, Ashley, Erin," he paused. "And Luke. Dayne, the guy's your brother."

Dayne couldn't talk, couldn't think. The woman in the photograph on Luke Baxter's desk was his birth mother? She really was? The idea was crazy, insane. He'd dreamed tens of times that Luke's framed photographs were pictures he could share one day, a nice family, siblings who cared about each other, loving parents.

Everything he hadn't known before.

A single question worked its way past the shock. "Why? Why'd she give me up?"

"The records are pretty clear on that, too. Elizabeth and John met in Michigan, attending the U of M. I guess when she got pregnant, her parents sent her to a girls home in Indiana. They insisted she give you up or they wouldn't support her." The agent paused, and Dayne heard the sound of loose papers being shuffled. "I guess she got smart at the girls home, because after they took you from her, she lived with her parents for less than a month before marrying John Baxter."

"What about Luke and the other kids?" He held his breath. He hated having to ask the next question. The answer could determine exactly what he would do from this point on. "Do they know about me?"

"Well—" more shuffling—"the PI talked with some people at their church in Bloomington, Indiana, and apparently not. Everyone interviewed said John and Elizabeth had just five children. Churchgoers, pretty clean folks. Sounds like you were their one secret."

Anger stepped into the ring and threw punches with the other emotions fighting it out. "They never looked for me, never cared to find me?"

"Don't be too hard on them." His agent took a few seconds. "Back in the 1990s, they filed some papers with the court, trying to locate you, but the records were closed. It was a dead end." He was quiet for a beat. "And look where they wound up living, Dayne. Back in Indiana, where you were born. Makes me think they've always hoped they'd find you."

Dayne hung his head, trashed by the feelings in his heart. No wonder he and Luke Baxter looked alike. They were biological

brothers. The idea was more than he could grasp, sitting there
on the outskirts of the shoot.

"Matthews!" It was the director, waving a rolled-up script and
scowling at him. "Off the phone; we have a movie to make!"

Dayne waved his hand, signaling that he'd be finished in a
minute. He closed his eyes and concentrated on his agent's voice.
"Anything else, anything important?"

"Yes." The man's tone grew somber. "This is the worst part.
Your birth mother is sick, Dayne. She has terminal cancer. She's
in the hospital there in Bloomington. Her records show she
doesn't have long; it could be anytime."

Dayne thanked the man, clicked the phone off, and stared at
the ground. He hadn't come this far to miss his only chance to
meet her. Maybe she hadn't told his siblings about him; maybe
he would never tell them either. But he wanted the chance to
see her, to look her in the face and tell her he'd turned out okay.
That the couple who had been his parents were nice people—
misguided, maybe, but nice all the same.

"Matthews!" The director was heading his way, his steps long
and angry. "What're you doing? This isn't break time."

"Sir." He let the cell phone drop to his side. "An emergency
has come up; I need the weekend."

"Right now?"

Dayne doubled his determination. "Right now. I can be back
Monday morning."

The director wasn't known for his compassion, but he must've
seen something in Dayne's eyes. He huffed and kicked up some
dirt with the toe of his boot. "Go. We'll work on some of the
technical shoots." He started to turn away, but looked back
again. "I hope everything turns out okay."

"Thanks." Dayne was already dialing the charter jet service
he used. If he caught a flight this evening, he could probably fly
straight to Bloomington. That way he could get to the hospital
before lunch tomorrow. "Me, too."

Elizabeth had no idea where she was or how long she'd been there. She opened her eyes and after what felt like several minutes, the shapes around her began making sense. She was lying in a bed, but it wasn't her own.

Something was different about her body.

She wasn't in pain the way she'd been before the wedding, and she wasn't pain-free the way she'd been during and afterwards. Her body felt like it was floating in some sort of half-asleep state, and she felt numb all over.

Her vision cleared a little more and she saw the IV bag hanging by the bed. Suddenly alarm wrapped its arms around her. She was in the hospital! Something must've happened to her, but what? Her mind tried to drift back, tried to remember where she'd been last, but her memory wasn't working right. Thinking back felt like trying to grope her way through a cloud of fog. Hard work and nothing visible to grasp hold of.

She'd been at the wedding, right? memorizing every moment. And then she was at the reception, watching her children dance with their spouses, enjoying the babies in their car seats beside her, watching Cole and Maddie and Tommy and Jessie entertain everyone with their own version of the "Hokey Pokey." Hayley had also been by her side, cooing occasionally and pointing at the others.

And there were Ashley and Landon, young and in love, and Cole was dancing between them, running around the room shouting, "I have a daddy! Guess what? I have a daddy!"

And John was helping her to her feet so they could sway right there next to their table in the sweetest slow dance she'd ever had. And Kari and Ryan and Brooke and Peter and Erin and Sam and Luke and Reagan were all in a circle, holding hands and dancing the "Twist and Shout" with Ashley and Landon in the middle.

Wasn't that just a few minutes ago?

How had she gotten here? Elizabeth blinked and looked at her arms, her hands. The IV was in the crook of her right arm, so she slipped her left forearm under her head and glanced around the room.

She was in the hospital, but where was everyone? Where was John?

She scanned her bed and a small table beside her and found a call button. Maybe someone could help her find them.

"Yes, Elizabeth?" The voice was tinny, not one she recognized. "Are you awake?"

"I feel sort of funny." She smacked her tongue against the roof of her mouth. "I need water, I think."

"We'll get some water for you right away. Would you like to see your husband?"

"Is he here?"

"Yes." She paused. "You've been asleep for quite a while."

Asleep? "How long?"

"You know, Elizabeth, I'm going to let your husband and the doctor explain things to you. They'll do a better job than I could."

Elizabeth stared at the plastic control. "Okay . . . I guess."

She heard John in the hallway a few minutes later, his steps fast and anxious. She knew the sound of him, the way he sounded when he was in a hurry. He rushed inside, stopped, and met her eyes.

"Elizabeth." He was scared to death, his mouth open as if he wasn't sure if she was really there looking at him. "You've been . . . you've been sleeping."

Her arms felt heavy and numb. "I think they've got me on drugs."

"Yes." His expression told her that was an understatement. "A few drugs."

She held out her hand. "I woke up . . ." Her eyes made another pass around the room. "I didn't know where I was or what had happened to me."

John came to her, cradling her arm against his waist, running

his fingers over her palm, the back of her hand. "I'm sorry. I was visiting with the others. Everyone's here; we've been waiting for you to wake up."

Her head hurt, and she couldn't concentrate the way she'd like to. "How long have I been asleep?"

"Since Tuesday morning."

"What time is it now?" Her words were slurred some. She hated the fact that she was on drugs without ever wanting them.

"It's Friday afternoon."

It took a minute to sink in. Elizabeth calculated the days in her head and stared at him. "I've been sleeping for three days? straight?"

"Yes." John leaned over her and kissed her on the cheek, the lips. "Do you remember where you were when you collapsed?"

She thought about that. "At the wedding?"

"No." He couldn't hide the concern in his face. "At home. We were heading for the bathroom, but you never made it. You passed out and, well, here you are."

Suddenly, as if the fog might be starting to lift, her situation became more clear. She was at the end stages of cancer, and this—this hospital stay might very well be the end. Fear wanted to say something to her, but she refused it.

Instead she looked out the window and whispered a quiet thanks to God. For letting her wake up, for letting her have this time with John and her family. She turned to him and smiled. "I have something to give you."

He looked concerned again, as if maybe she was delusional. She did a soft, sick-sounding giggle. "It's in the nightstand beside my bed at home; it was a surprise."

"A surprise?" He was still leaning over her, bracing himself on his elbow. He searched her eyes. "What sort of surprise?"

"A letter." She tried to turn onto her side, but the effort was too much.

John hurried to help. He grabbed two extra pillows from a cupboard near the door and used them to prop her up. "Better?"

"Yes." She exhaled, exhausted. "I wanted to write you each a letter, but instead I wrote three."

"Three?"

"One for you, one for all the kids, and one for our firstborn. In case he ever finds you, John." She paused. "After I'm gone, I mean. That way—"

"Elizabeth . . .." He wanted to tell her not to talk like that; she could tell by the tight way his lips stayed frozen, partially open. But the fight left him almost as quickly. "Go ahead." He pulled a nearby chair closer to the bed. "I'm sorry; I shouldn't have interrupted you."

He took her hand again, and she ran her thumb over his fingers. "That's okay. I'm sorry, John." Her heart ached for what he was going through, what they were all going through. "I hate talking about being gone from you; I'm not afraid to die, but I can't imagine a week without you, let alone years and decades. But still . . ."

"You have to talk about it." He dug his fingers into his hair and when he looked up, there was a weariness in his eyes. A weariness Elizabeth had never seen before.

"You're right; I have to talk about it." She inched a bit closer to the rails at the side of the bed. "Anyway, have them play my favorite hymn at the service, please, John."

" 'Great Is Thy Faithfulness'?" He was trembling, but his eyes were dry.

"Definitely."

"Okay. I'll make sure."

"John." She looked at him and felt her expression soften. "You know something?"

"What?" His voice was tender, his eyes deep into hers.

"I don't think I've ever loved you more than I do right now."

His eyes grew damp and he blinked three times. "What else, honey? What about the letters?"

"Right." Elizabeth tried not to feel lost in his eyes so she could focus. It was harder with the medication. "After my service, have everyone come to the house. You can read their letter to them then. I say something for everyone, but a lot . . . a lot of what I wanted to say was meant for everyone to hear. That's why I stuck to one bigger letter."

"And you want me to read it out loud?"

"Yes. And make sure they each get a copy, please, John."

"I will." He was on his feet again. The bed rail was raised like a prison wall between them. He released a latch and it fell down below the bed. "There." He brushed his nose against hers, and with careful hands he hugged her for a long time. "What else, Elizabeth? I'd do anything for you."

"Hold me, John. That's all. Just hold me." Her voice was a whisper, full of equal parts passion and pain. Not the sort of pain that had sent her to her bedroom before Ashley's wedding. The kind that came from seeing the look in his eyes, from hearing his voice. A pain that knew the hour for good-byes was drawing near, pain that meant her heart was breaking in two.

After ten or fifteen minutes, he stood and looked at her, his eyes full of questions. "Do you think . . . do you have a sense about when?"

She kept her eyes locked on his and gave a slow, sad nod. "Soon." A single tear slid from her left eye and down the bridge of her nose. "Could you do me one more favor?"

"Anything."

"Get the kids for me. Every one of them. Please, John."

It was a reunion, exactly the way she'd pictured it.

Only instead of lying on the beach or even picnicking on their front yard back at home, they were here, in the hospital. All Friday evening and again now that it was Saturday, the hospital staff had allowed them to pack out the entire room. Elizabeth didn't have a roommate, so the conditions were crowded but manageable.

She'd already asked to go home, and they were saying maybe Sunday afternoon. The bottom line was exactly what Dr. Steinman had told her from the beginning. They could do nothing for her, nothing but keep her hydrated and on constant pain meds. Since she'd agreed to take special protein drinks and take the pain pills at home, Dr. Steinman was more than willing to let her go home.

"If I had a family like yours, I wouldn't want to be any other place."

He was right, especially now, with her family still here. But until she could go home the hospital room would do. Even now, propped up on half a dozen pillows, with John sitting by her side holding her hand, Elizabeth was taking in every moment of her time with them. Kari and Ryan and Brooke and Peter were talking about the fact that Jessie's adoption had gone through. After Kari's first husband was murdered, Ryan had married her and promised he'd adopt Jessie. The process had taken longer than he'd expected, but she was legally his now.

"And we have this little one." Kari patted her rounded tummy.

Ryan gave her a light tap and put his face near her midsection. "Hello, in there. You're my little linebacker, right, baby? Enough pretty girls running the place, right?"

They all laughed and Elizabeth shifted her attention to Erin and Sam and Reagan, sitting together with the babies. Tommy was toddling about Reagan's knees, and Erin was saying, ". . . so then the pastor at our church tells us there's a woman in the congregation whose daughter is pregnant with a baby she doesn't want, and . . ."

Elizabeth looked to the other side of the room where Luke and Ashley and Landon sat near Hayley in her wheelchair. Cole and Maddie were on the floor coloring with Clarisse and Chloe. Every now and then Cole would lift the coloring book up so Hayley could see. "Like it, Hayley? I'm coloring it for you."

And she would coo a little louder, happier than before.

Landon was saying, "She was crazy, remember? Thinking

somehow Reagan's baby was mine? A little wacko if you ask me."

"Stop!" Ashley giggled. She had a new glow since she'd married Landon, a peace and serenity that hadn't been there before, but a deep sense of happiness that only true love could bring. She gave Landon a mock punch in the arm. "I only thought it for a minute or two."

Landon raised his eyebrows at her.

"Okay." She gave Luke the punch this time. "Maybe an hour at the most. It was jet lag, I tell you. Or maybe too many paint fumes."

"You were painting a lot back then." Luke tilted his head. "You have to keep painting, Ash. You're too good."

"What's this? This coming from my doubting little brother, the one who once watched me sketch a tree and thought it was a Russian building?"

Luke held his hands up, bringing them together in a strange shape. He cocked his head one way and then the other, as if he were trying to figure out what it was. He looked at Landon and shrugged. "I'm still not sure; it had the exact look of one of those government buildings you see in those Russian photographs."

"It was a tree!" Ashley nudged him and they both laughed.

Elizabeth felt the corners of her mouth lift. All her life she'd loved music: classical, country, slow songs, and movie sound tracks. But here, under the fluorescent lights of a hospital room, the blended sounds of their voices was the most beautiful song she'd ever heard.

John leaned sideways so she could hear him. "You're liking this, aren't you?"

"I am." She yawned. "I could listen to them all day."

He ran his fingers through her short hair. She no longer wore the beret. They'd all seen her patchy hair, anyway. "Maybe it's time you get a little rest. You'll need your energy if you're going to come home tomorrow."

"Not yet." She drew in a breath. The rattle in her chest had gotten so loud it stopped the conversations near her.

"How are you feeling, Mom?" Kari stood and stretched. "I saw you smiling."

The kids played off to the side, but everyone else was quiet, listening for her answer. "I was smiling at all of you." She let her eyes meet each of those in the room. "Listening to you talk about the past, laughing together. This was why I wanted a reunion in the first place. I could sit here all night watching you visit, hearing your stories."

Luke seemed to catch a signal from John. It was five o'clock and none of them had eaten yet. "You know, I was thinking we ought to head out for something to eat, maybe let the kids run around the park across the street for a little while and get them situated with the sitters before we come back."

Pastor Mark had arranged for three young women from church to be at the Baxter house by seven o'clock so the children could get to bed. There were nine in all, and with Hayley's special needs, Elizabeth figured it would take at least that many sitters.

She looked at John. He was serious about her getting some rest, and if it was just for a few hours, she could manage the separation. "I guess I could take a nap. But you'll all come back?"

"Of course, Mom." Erin sauntered over and took hold of her foot sticking up under the hospital blankets. "It's a good time to take a break."

The kids each came by, Cole and Maddie taking turns scrambling onto the bed and snuggling with her for a minute or two. Kari helped Jessie, who was not quite big enough to climb up, and next Luke held Tommy up so she could kiss his cheek. The babies were being rocked by Sam and Erin, and Clarisse and Chloe were still fairly shy. They wriggled their fingers at her and gave her timid smiles.

Elizabeth watched them go and looked at John. She could only imagine the lives those girls had led before coming to live with Erin and Sam. How blessed that they might get four daughters in as many weeks. How sad that the girls would never know her well enough to jump up next to her like the other kids.

When everyone else was gone, John bent low and touched his lips against hers. "Have them call me if you need anything."

"I will." She understood what he meant; if something went wrong, if she took a turn for the worse, he wanted to be there. It was all he could do to leave even for a few minutes. Two or three hours? He never would've gone if it weren't for the kids. "John, do you see it?"

"See what?" Another bit of worry splashed across his expression.

"How special this reunion is. None of them will ever forget it."

He straightened, but his shoulders stayed slumped. "You're right; it's very special."

After he was gone, she closed her eyes. John was right. She was exhausted; a nap would do her good. Before she fell asleep, she thanked God for every good thing he'd done for them that past week.

There's just one more thing, Lord. I've asked before, but you and I both know my time is running out. Right now, right this minute you know where he is, the boy I gave up. If he's close by or far away, you see him. God, how much I'd love to talk to him just once before I die, to tell him we never forgot about him.

She blinked and looked out the window. A robin lighted on the windowsill, cocked its head, and peered into the room. Then it hopped twice and flew away. Elizabeth closed her eyes again. *That's all I want, Lord. A quick visit like that robin just now. I know it looks crazy and impossible, but you're the God of impossibilities. That's how come Ashley has a wedding ring on her finger. So please, God, if it be your will, lead him here. And if not, let him find the others after I'm gone.*

Sleep took her then, deep and restful, and she dreamed about the reunion, about all of her family—every single one—together in one place. Together, the way she liked them best.

✦✦✦ ✦✦ ✦✦✦

CHAPTER TWENTY-NINE

AIR TRAVEL HAD NEVER BEEN SLOWER.

Dayne was used to placing a call with the charter jet company and having a Gulfstream meet him within a few hours. He had a standing contract with them, and always they'd been reliable—whether his assistant gave them two days or two hours to line up a plane. But this weekend the entire fleet was booked so Dayne had to resort to a public airline.

Now that he knew the information, that his birth mother was Elizabeth Baxter and that she was dying of cancer in a Bloomington, Indiana, hospital, Dayne couldn't wait to get there. But his six o'clock flight out of British Columbia had been delayed because of a thunderstorm, causing him to miss his connection in Los Angeles.

His only option was to spend the night in L.A. and take a flight to Indianapolis the next morning. He walked to a hotel across the street, registered under a false name, and was back at the airport at five Saturday morning for the six-thirty flight. The whole time he wore his baseball cap and sunglasses to avoid being recognized.

It was a good thing. He was so focused on getting to Bloomington, he wouldn't have been able to sign his name without checking his watch.

The nonstop flight from Los Angeles was delayed because of storms in Indiana, but the plane finally took off at nine and arrived at two in Indianapolis. Thirty minutes after landing he was at the car-rental lot, and by three-fifteen was pulling out of the lot in an SUV.

No question the people at the car-rental agency recognized him. But that was okay. They took his information, but let him register under a different name. He had a brand-new Chevy Tahoe with dark tinted windows, OnStar, and a navigational system at no extra charge. He had hoped to arrive at the hospital by four o'clock, and even after the ground delays by no later than four-thirty. But an overturned semitruck on the main highway caused a delay, and he didn't pull into the hospital parking lot until just before five.

He chose a spot near the back, away from passersby. Not until he turned off the engine did it hit him.

Okay, so he was here. Now what?

Dayne stared hard at the building. Inside was his birth mother, dying of cancer, probably with all the other Baxters gathered around her. All he'd known when he took the call from his agent was that he had to come, had to find a way to see her, to meet her before she died.

But now that he was here, in the fading sunlight of a warm July evening, the logistics seemed suddenly outrageous. What was he going to do, walk through the door and introduce himself? Maybe she didn't want to see him, didn't want him to find her. Especially now.

He let that thought sit for a minute.

No, that wasn't the case. She wanted to meet him; otherwise she wouldn't have tried to find him back in the 1990s. The trouble was with his siblings. If the PI was right, the five of them were biologically related to him, but not one of them knew he existed.

He tried to think back to his discussion with the attorney, Joe Morris, before he left Manhattan last time. What had the guy said? Luke Baxter was off for the summer because he had some family matters to take care of. His mother was sick, yes, but something else.

Then it hit him. Luke's sister was getting married; wasn't that it? Dayne gripped the steering wheel. Yes, absolutely. That's what it was.

A big group of people, adults and children, came through the double doors of the hospital and stood in a cluster, talking and keeping track of their little ones. Dayne pushed a lever near the base of his seat and moved into a reclining position. He couldn't afford to be noticed. Bloomington was a small town; if he attracted a crowd he would never be able to make it up to see his birth mother.

The visit would raise too many questions, and the tabloids would find a way to splash it across the headlines.

His thoughts returned to his siblings. If they were gathered together for a wedding, and at the same time facing the loss of their mother, then no doubt they had enough on their plates. Besides . . .

Dayne sucked in a hard breath and filled his cheeks with the air. Besides, his birth parents had chosen not to tell them. What right did he have to tell them now? And what good could ever come from it?

They lived in Small Town, America. Bloomington was nothing more than a quaint college town where everyone probably knew everyone else. If he connected with these people now, their lives would forever be in the limelight. The paparazzi would spout about "Dayne's sister this . . ." or "Dayne's nephew that . . ." Whatever lifestyle they knew and loved now would be changed forever if he entered the picture.

The large group milled into the parking lot and headed

toward him. He lowered his seat back farther, but only enough so they wouldn't see him. It was an attractive group, several couples and—

He sat up a few inches.

One of the guys was Luke Baxter—no doubt about it! After spending months thinking about the guy, he would've recognized him anywhere. The group was moving slowly, talking, still heading his way.

And suddenly Dayne felt his heart rise to his throat.

There, walking toward him, was the family he'd never known. Luke and his wife and a baby, four other couples—obviously his sisters and their husbands. And more kids than he could count. At the center was a tall man in his late fifties, early sixties. A man with his own stance and shoulders and gait.

The man who was his biological father.

Dayne glanced sideways and saw five cars parked fifteen yards away. The Baxters were headed for those cars, and Dayne wasn't sure what to do. A part of him wanted to jump out, run to them, and introduce himself. He would meet them and hug them and learn the names of the children. And in a matter of minutes he would have the family he'd always wanted.

They were walking closer . . . closer.

The tint on his windows would keep them from seeing inside his car; if he didn't want them to spot him, they wouldn't. They were too involved in conversation, and as they came still closer he was able to make out their faces.

One of his sisters had short hair and a businesslike look. From far away it had looked like she was pushing a stroller, but now he could see he was wrong. It was a wheelchair, and inside was a beautiful blonde girl whose eyes and expression looked distant and slow.

Other than Luke and John, the other men had to be the guys married to his sisters; he didn't pay close attention to them. His eyes moved quickly to the shortest of the four women. She had a plain look, a type of wholesome look directors were always

searching for. She was definitely pushing a stroller, and inside—
if Dayne was seeing it right—were two babies. His other two
sisters were drop-dead gorgeous. Both were tall, with big husbands at their sides.

They were still headed straight for him; Dayne gripped the
door handle. He could do it; he could approach them and tell
them who he was, and John would back him. John knew the
truth. And since they were out here at the back of the parking
lot, no one from the media would have to know.

He could make out their expressions now. They were sad—
that much was clear. But they were smiling, touching each other's shoulders, chatting about something, and taking their time.
As if they loved being together.

Dayne watched, mesmerized. He belonged with them, didn't
he? Wasn't this the time to make himself known, so that forever-
more he would have a place with them? Even a borrowed place?
He opened his car door, put his feet onto the pavement, and was
just about to stand up when he heard the sound of a camera.

Instantly he slid his feet back inside, shut the door, and locked
it. That's when he saw a man crouched beside a burgundy sedan
two rows in front of him. The man had a full-size camera aimed
straight at him.

Dayne looked around the lot, dazed. The man was paparazzi;
Dayne was sure. But how had he followed him here? He stared the
man down, glaring at him, and the answer became obvious.

The man at the rental counter had informed OnStar; through
some manner he must've told OnStar he needed to track the
vehicle's whereabouts, maybe under the guise of additional safety
or security. Then, for a price no doubt, the rental-agency guy
must've alerted the tabloids that Dayne Matthews was parked at
the hospital in Bloomington, Indiana.

He wanted to punch the photographer in the face.

But his family was getting away. They were veering toward
the parked cars, and most of them had their backs to him now.
He took hold of the door handle one more time. Forget the

paparazzi; they could say what they wanted about him. No one would have to know the identities of the people he was talking to. There was still time to introduce himself, to find out where they were going and join them for the evening.

He tore his eyes from them and spotted the photographer again. The camera was still aimed straight at him. In a practiced manner, he pretended to be looking at something else. If the man knew he was onto him, it would be harder to get away later on.

But what about the Baxters? Dayne shifted back to his family and held his breath. They were opening the doors, getting kids into car seats.

Quick, Matthews . . . they're going to leave!

But then he saw something move near the photographer's car. The man was standing up, watching the Baxters with a curious eye. Obviously he had seen Dayne's interest through the high-powered lens of his camera. And now he wondered if the people getting into the five cars might hold the reason why America's hottest movie star was sitting in a rented SUV in the parking lot of a hospital in Bloomington, Indiana.

And in that moment Dayne did the only thing he could.

He let go.

He took his hand off the door, leaned back in his seat, and watched his family climb into their cars. His earlier thoughts had been right on. If he met his family now, the media would figure it out. The tabloids would hire some crack investigator, and the entire story would make headlines by the end of the month. Every one of them would have their story smeared across the headlines.

The car doors were closed now, and one at a time they pulled out of their parking spots and drove away. The family he had never known. His family.

Dayne gritted his teeth. He could've killed the photographer, but there would always be another one. Paparazzi went along with the territory. But in that moment he would've given any-

thing to undo the fame he'd earned. To be a teacher or a lawyer
or a doctor, someone who could meet his family without the
whole world knowing.

His eyes stung and he gave a sharp sniff. He'd been independent this long. What did it matter if he never met them, anyway?
He'd only just found out about them yesterday.

As dusk was falling over the city, Dayne looked again at the
hospital. The photographer might've kept him from his siblings,
from the chance of getting to know his family. But he wasn't
going to keep him from his birth mother.

He started his car and zipped out of the parking lot. This time
he spotted the burgundy sedan easily. The guy was good. He
stayed back, with one or two cars between them.

But Dayne had an idea.

Driving at an average speed so the photo hound wouldn't be
suspicious, he traveled until he spotted a supermarket stuck in
the middle of a strip mall in what looked like the busiest part of
town. He parked near the middle of the lot and slipped on his
baseball cap. Walking with his face down, he headed into the
store. He was too far away to hear the camera, but the clicking
sounded in his mind anyway.

Click-click. Click-click-click-click.

How could they live with themselves? Human maggots, that's
what they were. So he went to a supermarket in Bloomington?
Big deal. Dayne swallowed his disgust. He picked up his pace
once he got inside and headed straight for the back of the store.
The only way it would work was if he could find a side door.
He'd used this trick before; most markets had another exit.

He spotted a sign that said Restroom and headed for it. Sure
enough, the bathrooms were down a hallway, and at the end was
a single door with an Exit sign over it. He darted outside and
found himself in an alleyway. Beyond it was a car dealership, and
he headed for it at a slow jog.

Once in the lot, he spotted a restaurant a few shops down to
the left. The walk took three minutes and a tired-looking cabbie

was parked just outside. Dayne was careful to keep his face down, not that it mattered so much now. People weren't expecting to see Dayne Matthews walking down the boulevard in Bloomington, Indiana.

He tapped on the cabbie's window.

The man jumped, startled. He folded a newspaper that had been on his lap and gestured to the backseat. Dayne climbed inside and shut the door. The entire scene felt more intense than anything he'd ever filmed.

"Where to?" The guy was in his sixties, probably retired and looking for a little extra income. He didn't even turn around.

"The hospital. The one near the university."

The driver gave him a wary look in the rearview mirror. "You must be new around here."

"Yes, sir."

"That's the only hospital in town."

Dayne stayed slightly slumped during the ride and gave the driver a ten-dollar bill when he dropped him off near the entrance. "Keep the change."

He started to walk off, but the driver called out. "Hey . . . you need another ride when you're done here?"

"Yeah." The old guy didn't recognize him. Probably didn't get out much. Dayne looked both ways, scanning the parking lot and the lobby area. No sign of the burgundy sedan or the photographer. "I don't know how long I'll be."

The cabbie shrugged. "I ain't got nothing going. I'll be here unless I get another call."

"Great."

Dayne headed into the hospital and tugged on his hat, keeping it low over his eyes. It was warm out, but he wore his sweatshirt, the one with the hood that bunched up around his neck. He stopped at the front desk and asked about Elizabeth Baxter.

"Elizabeth Baxter . . ." The woman was young, in her mid-twenties. She searched a computer screen and then seemed to find it. "She's on the third floor. In room 318."

Dayne's knees shook, but he stayed calm, his words relaxed. "Does she . . . are there any other visitors here?"

The woman was chewing gum. She worked it for a few seconds. "Let me call the nursing station on that floor." Taking her time, she punched a series of numbers into the phone by her elbow, spoke to someone in hushed tones, and hung up. "She's by herself, sleeping by the sounds of it."

He took a few steps toward a bank of elevators nearby. "So it's okay if I go up?"

She narrowed her eyes at him and angled her head. "Why do you look so familiar?"

Before any realization could dawn on her, Dayne gave her a sad smile. "I've been up here a lot. I'm Elizabeth's son." The words felt foreign on his tongue, but he didn't blink.

"Oh." She gave a knowing nod. "That must be it." She pointed to the elevators. "Yes, go right up. Family can stop in anytime."

Her words stayed with Dayne for the next few minutes. *"Family can stop in anytime . . . family . . . family . . ."*

He stepped out of the elevator onto the third floor and kept his face low again. It was one thing to claim to be Elizabeth's son. But the people working directly with her would know he wasn't Luke Baxter, even if they did look alike. He wanted to get in before anyone asked any questions.

The nursing desk was empty, and he crept past, careful not to make any noise as he walked. Up ahead he saw her door: room 318. His heart was pounding so hard he wondered if he should stop and get a grip. But he couldn't; he had no time. It wouldn't be long before the photographer would figure out he'd been ditched, and then it would only make sense that he'd return to the hospital.

Dayne held his breath, knocked twice on her door, and waited. No response. Slowly, carefully, he opened the door, stepped inside, and closed it behind him. He was in. The lights were off except for a soft bar light above her bed. It took a few seconds for his eyes to adjust, and then he saw her. She was sound asleep, hooked to machines and an IV, and making gentle snoring sounds.

Without taking a step in her direction, he stared at the woman in the bed, and he knew: It was the same woman as in the pictures. The pictures on Luke Baxter's desk, and the picture he'd kept in storage all these years.

His birth mother was a few feet away, and he didn't know what to do next.

Mesmerized, he walked toward her, stood over her, and searched her face. They shared the same cheekbones, the same brow structure. But she was way too thin, and her hair didn't look right. Probably the effects of chemo.

He took the chair next to her bed, keeping his back to the door. At that instant someone walked in, and Dayne's heart stopped. "Oh, it's you, Luke." A big nurse strode around the bed, checked the IV bag, and wrote something on a chart. "Everything going okay?"

"About the same." His heart stumbled back into a racing rhythm.

"Good." She patted him on the shoulder as she passed by. "You're a good son, Luke."

He hesitated but only for a second. "Thanks."

Then the woman was gone.

Dayne hung his head on the rail that separated him from Elizabeth and let the adrenaline rush pass. What had he just done? Pretended to be Luke? Surely someone would hear about that, make a comment that Luke had been by, when really Luke was out somewhere with his family.

He had to hurry, had to make the most of the moment while he still could.

It was time to wake her up, but what would he call her? How could he explain why he was here, especially if she was half asleep? He felt for a latch near the railing and released it. Then he slid closer and gave her arm a gentle nudge. "Elizabeth?"

She turned her head and mumbled words he couldn't understand.

"Elizabeth?" He shook her a little more this time. Any minute he expected the other Baxters to return, or worse, the photographer to burst into the room and start snapping pictures. He leaned closer. "Wake up, Elizabeth. I'm your son. I've come to meet you. I'm your—"

She blinked a few times and squinted at him.

"Hi." His voice cracked and he couldn't speak. They had so much to talk about, so many years to make up for. However many minutes he had now, by her side, they would never be enough. She was very sick; that much was clear. Whatever happened in the next few minutes, this would not only be their first visit.

It would be their last.

CHAPTER THIRTY

ELIZABETH HEARD THE VOICE, heard it calling her name.

But when she opened her eyes, she knew she had to be dreaming. The face just inches from hers was as familiar as it was foreign. Sort of a mix between John and Luke, but at the same time neither of them.

She squinted at him and tried to make out what he was saying.

"Elizabeth . . . can you hear me?"

"Yes." She coughed and tried to sit up, but her body wouldn't let her. "Help me, please."

The young man had tears in his eyes, but he was kind. He did as she asked, taking the pillows from the foot of her bed and placing them under her head and back so she could see him better.

"Is that good?" The man took a step back.

"Yes. Thank you." What was it about him? He was more familiar than anyone other than her own family, yet she was sure she'd never seen him before. She was awake now—at least it felt that way in her dream. Her eyes found his and searched for some sort of connection, a reason why he might be in her hospital room. Was he one of Luke's friends? one of the kids who had once hung out at the Baxter house?

He seemed to read her mind. His head moved from side to side, and he touched her hand. "You've never seen me before."

"I haven't?" She studied his face, his frame.

"Not since I was a baby."

A baby? Elizabeth sat up some, her eyes glued to him. "You . . . you remind me of someone."

He came closer, taking her hand in his. Tears glistened on his cheeks. "Elizabeth, I'm your son."

The moment the words were out, Elizabeth felt the room start to spin. Her son? The one she'd been praying about, begging God for a chance to meet? She ran her thumb over his hand, her voice suddenly weak. "Is this . . . is it a dream?"

"No." He kept his eyes on hers. "My name's Dayne, and . . . well, I found out you were sick." His tone was pained. "I wanted to meet you before . . . before it was too late."

She looked straight into his heart and, as surely as she knew God existed, she was sure this was her son. Her prayers had been answered, and now the boy she'd spent a lifetime missing was standing there before her. "Dayne, that's what they called you?"

"Yes."

There was so much to ask, so much to tell him. But she needed to tell him one thing first. "I never wanted to give you up, Dayne. I was young; they made me do it."

He nodded, his eyes swimming. "I know. The investigator told me."

Investigator? Elizabeth put the thought from her mind; those questions could come later. "Were they good to you, your parents? Do they still live in Indiana?"

"No." He swallowed, struggling to stay composed. "They died when I was eighteen. In a small-plane crash."

The news cut her like a knife. His parents were dead? So who did he have in the world, no one? "Brothers and sisters? Did they ever adopt other kids?"

He angled his head. His expression told her he wasn't angry, wasn't bitter. "They were missionaries. I spent most of my childhood in Indonesia, at a boarding school. My parents were wonderful people, but we didn't have much time together. They died out on the field."

Elizabeth let the information rip through her. There was nothing she could say, nothing that would erase the fact that the young man standing before her had lived through a lonely childhood. When no words would come, she held out her hands to him. "Dayne . . . I'm sorry."

He hugged her then, shaking from the tears, holding her as if he never wanted to let go. The same way she had held him thirty-five years ago before they came to take him away. "Don't be sorry," he whispered near her ear. "I had a good life."

"But we missed you." She snuggled her face against his, her firstborn. "You belonged with us. Every year on your birthday . . . or when you would've had your first day of kindergarten, your first day of high school—all the milestones—I thought of you. I had to give you over completely, Dayne. I had to trust God that you'd be okay." A few sobs made their way up from her throat. "But I never stopped missing you, never stopped loving you."

They stayed that way, hugging, holding on until finally he sat back down on the edge of the chair and searched her face. "I never really thought of myself as adopted. My parents—" he sniffed and dragged the back of one of his hands across his cheeks before taking hers—"my parents told me there was another woman who had given birth to me. They even showed me your picture when I was a little boy, maybe first grade. But we didn't talk about it much after that. They never—" he looked out the window, his eyes distant—"they never used the word *adoption* around me."

The questions were back. Elizabeth savored the feel of her

hand in his. "How did you find me, Dayne? I tried—" her voice broke and she shook her head, waiting for her body to cooperate with her—"I tried to find you the last time I was sick. In the early 1990s."

"I know that, too. The records were sealed."

She raised an eyebrow. "Your investigator is good."

"Yes." He nodded. "I wouldn't have come if I hadn't found out that you'd tried to find me back then."

"John and I used to promise each other we wouldn't talk about you." She felt herself drifting. How many times had they stuffed the truth about their oldest son, buried it, forbidden themselves to talk about him even with each other? And what if they'd used that same energy to hire an investigator—the way Dayne had done?

The answers were too sad to think about. She met his eyes again. "Why now, Dayne? What made you look?"

For a moment, he hesitated, as if he was trying to decide how much to say. "I found a box in storage marked 'Adoption Information.' Your picture was inside."

"My picture?" Her eyes welled up again. She had asked the director of the girls home to pass on a picture of herself to the adoptive parents so that her son would have something to remember her by. "Did you open it, pull it out?"

Dayne wrinkled his brow. "I . . . I left it in the frame."

"I wrote you a letter on the back. Read it sometime, okay?"

He nodded, his chin quivering.

"So . . ." Elizabeth coughed two more times. Every breath was a struggle, worse even than earlier today. The end was coming; she could hear the plane taxiing to the gate. "You turned the paperwork over to an investigator, and here you are. Is that it?"

Again he hesitated. "Yes."

An idea hit her. Maybe God had allowed him to come now because of the reunion! Because they were all together. What better time to tell their children about the past, to let them know that she and John had a boy before Brooke, and that they'd had no choice but to give him up for adoption?

She tightened her hold on his hand. "Dayne . . . what time is it?"

"Six-forty."

"Good." She could feel her eyes dancing. "The rest of the family will be here around seven. I'd like them to meet you."

"I can't stay long, because—"

Pain filled his eyes, a pain that hurt her worse than him. "What, Dayne?" Her voice was gentle, the voice she used with all her children when they came to her upset about something. "What is it?"

"You never told them about me, did you?"

It was the hardest question she'd ever been asked. She drew in a slow, painful breath and willed him to understand. "From the beginning they told me to forget about you. We could never look for you, never find you. The director at the girls home said it was better to pretend you'd never been born."

Dayne said nothing, but his eyes held a sympathy that took the edge off the ache in her soul.

"When we started having children, John and I talked and—" she glanced around the room, desperate for the right words— "and we decided we couldn't tell them about a brother they would never know, never find. It was enough that we missed you, without them missing you, too."

Dayne nodded, the muscles in his jaw flexing. "How would they feel now? After so many years?"

Elizabeth looked down for a minute, thinking. When she looked up, she had something she needed to know before another minute passed. "Do you have a relationship with God, Dayne?"

Something hard flashed in his eyes. "Not a relationship, maybe. I haven't given God a lot of thought, I guess. My parents were in the God business, but they never talked with me about him much." He gave a light shrug. "I guess they figured my faith was an automatic thing. Because they believed."

"Okay." Elizabeth ached at the news. Her oldest son had not

only grown up lonely and without the Baxter family support, but he didn't share their faith. "So maybe that's why God let us meet. Can I tell you something, Dayne?" She loved the sound of his name on her tongue. It was a name she might've given him if she hadn't given him up.

"That's why I'm here."

"I've been begging God that you would find me. Ever since I found out I was sick, I ask my Jesus every day, 'Please . . . bring me my firstborn. Before I die, let me meet him.' " She stroked the top of his hand with her fingertips. "I thought it was because I needed to tell you that I never forgot about you, never stopped loving you. But maybe . . . maybe it's so you can find a heavenly Father in God."

Dayne shifted in his chair. "Maybe."

The conversation about God seemed to be making him uncomfortable. "Just something to think about, okay?"

"Okay."

"Now . . . I know about your childhood." Elizabeth worked the corners of her mouth up. "What's your life like now, Dayne? Are you married? Do you have children? What's your line of work?"

He seemed surprised by the questions, but his expression relaxed noticeably. "I'm not married; no children." He paused. "I'm an actor."

She felt her heart swell. Her children had always been interested in the arts. Brooke had played the piano as a young girl, Kari with her modeling, and Ashley, the painter. Luke and Erin had sung in the church choir all through high school, and now . . . this young man who had missed out on every bit of life as a Baxter was also involved in the arts. "Tell me about it."

"Well . . ." He gave a soft chuckle. "I've been doing it for a while. I've been in some movies."

"Really?" Pride mixed with regret and made her throat tight. She had missed so much of his life, all the important years. And now . . . now they had only a few days at best. "Big movies?"

"Pretty big." He paused. "That isn't important. Tell me about your other kids."

She noticed that he kept from calling them his brother and sisters. "Okay . . . okay . . . well, we had Brooke first . . ."

Over the next ten minutes she gave him a sketch of each of his siblings and caught him up on their adult lives as well. Who they'd married, how many kids they'd had, what struggles they'd overcome. Her coughing grew worse as she talked and when she finished, Dayne stood and looked at his watch.

"I should go."

"But the others . . ." She was exhausted from talking, and the IV must've pumped a fresh dose of medication into her. It was all she could do to keep her eyes open. "Dayne, you have to stay."

He touched her forehead and took her hand again. "Maybe I'll come back and meet them tomorrow."

His answer made her relax some. "Okay." She forced her eyes to stay open. "I'm really not dreaming, right?"

"Right." He tightened his hold on her hand. "Thank you, Elizabeth."

Something in his tone brought her around again, made her more alert despite the exhaustion coming over her. "For what?"

"Thank you for having me, for praying that I'd go to a good family." He smiled, even though his eyes were watery again. "Thanks for never forgetting me."

She couldn't speak, could barely draw in a breath. Instead she held out her hands and once more he came to her, embracing her. When he pulled back, she forced herself to speak. "This wasn't enough time."

"No." A single tear slid down his cheek.

"Dayne . . . there's only one thing I want you to do for me."

He sat on the edge of her bed, holding her hand against his chest. "What?"

"Find God. Find your faith." She bit her lip. "Things didn't work out the way I wanted them to; we couldn't all be together here. But in heaven—" she smiled—"in heaven we can all spend eternity together." She felt the smile fade. "Please, Dayne."

He didn't answer her. Instead he hugged her once more and whispered near her ear, "Something was always missing in my life until now." He straightened and gave her one last smile. "I'll never forget you, Elizabeth."

The tears blurred her vision, but she blinked them back. "I love you, Dayne. I always have."

"Me, too."

He held up his hand, took a few steps back, and turned around. He was gone before she could call his name. She wanted to tell him that he was wrong about one thing. The something missing hadn't been her or John or any of the Baxters. Yes, that was a part of it, but the bigger part was his faith.

And until he found that, he would never really be whole.

But she couldn't tell him, because he was gone. Maybe he would come back tomorrow, or maybe he wouldn't. Elizabeth's head was fuzzy, sleep coming over her fast like a tidal wave. If he didn't come back, none of the others might ever see him. But maybe he wasn't even real. Maybe the whole thing *had* been a dream.

But if it were a dream, then how come her arms still remembered the feel of him against her? And how come the ache in her heart was so familiar?

The same as it had been thirty-five years ago.

CHAPTER THIRTY-ONE

THE CABBIE WAS STILL OUTSIDE WAITING.

Dayne looked around, but the burgundy sedan was nowhere nearby. He climbed inside and pressed himself against the back-seat. "The supermarket, the one near the restaurant where you picked me up."

The driver made no small talk, and Dayne handed him a twenty. The cabbie thanked him and pulled away, and this time Dayne held his head high. He spotted the photographer in his burgundy sedan still, but he'd changed parking spaces. Dayne glared at the man, looking right at him. When the photographer saw him, he sprang to life and began shooting pictures.

Dayne didn't care. Let him take pictures now. He'd no doubt been driving around the past hour trying to figure out what sort of clandestine deal Dayne Matthews was involved in.

But the photographer would never find out. Dayne had already made up his mind. He would drive back to Indianapolis tonight and take the first flight back to Los Angeles. No use staying in Bloomington another day, not when the paparazzi were already onto him.

His family, the Baxters, were nice people. He could tell that much after an hour with Elizabeth. He wouldn't subject them to the type of scrutiny he would bring into their lives. No, they'd gone all their lives not knowing about him; they would never know the difference.

He gave a final look at the photographer, climbed into his SUV, and drove off. This time he did a little fancy driving and lost the guy. It didn't matter now; he had no more reason to hide. Still, he didn't want the jerk having the satisfaction of taking any more pictures.

Dayne studied the area around him. He'd turned into an older part of town. Probably closer to the university. Since it was Saturday evening, the little shops and businesses were closed.

Everything in him wanted to turn around and find Elizabeth Baxter again, wait for the others to come, and then figure out a way to make a place among them. Even after all these years. The visit had been amazing, much better than he'd ever dreamed. But every detail was pressing near the surface of his heart, ready to burst through and overtake him with emotion.

She hadn't recognized him; that was the best part. She didn't know he was Dayne Matthews the movie star. Only that he was Dayne, her son. The one she'd spent a lifetime thinking about and wondering about and never quite forgetting.

He drummed his fingers on the wheel of the Tahoe and kept driving. There would be time to remember his visit later on the plane. For now he wanted to soak in all he could about Bloomington.

This would've been his hometown if she'd been allowed to keep him, if he'd grown up the oldest Baxter son. He took his time, looking down the side streets and imagining. It was small and fresh and nothing at all like Manhattan or Hollywood. The kind of town where a kid could play football and race his sisters to the local park. A place where families would share Sunday picnics and spend a lifetime believing that life really was something out of *Mayberry R.F.D.*

He kept driving until he spotted a crowded parking lot ahead.

Though the rest of the area looked shut down for the night, in front of him was a large, ornate structure. A church maybe, or an arts building.

Dayne leaned forward and squinted. A marquis in front of the building read "Academy of the Arts." Beneath that it said "CKT Presents *Charlie Brown.*" A list of dates and times followed. Dayne pulled over. He checked his watch; the final performance was tonight at six o'clock. It would be almost over, but still he wanted to go inside.

Community theater . . . in Bloomington, Indiana.

Acting didn't get much more small-town than that. He parked, donned the baseball cap, hunched his sweatshirt around his neck, and headed for the front door. A ticket table was just inside, but no one was manning it. He walked past, slipped into the dark theater, and took a seat in the back row.

Positioned across the stage was a group of clean-cut kids dressed in Peanuts costumes and singing. Some were holding hands. The song was vaguely familiar, something he'd heard back in boarding school, maybe. It was a song about happiness and being together with people you cared about.

" 'Happiness is . . . three kinds of ice cream . . .' "

This was what drama was about, wasn't it? Not the wild, Hollywood life; not waking up in bed with your leading lady wondering how either of you got there; not hiding from the public and deranged photographers; and not making millions of dollars for a single film.

How real was any of that?

The song continued. " 'Happiness is . . . having a sister . . .' "

Having a sister?

He thought of the women he'd seen in the parking lot earlier. He would never know that feeling. He brought his hands together and remembered how it had felt. Holding hands with his birth mother, knowing that she had loved him all his life. That she had wanted to keep him and even now, on her deathbed, her one regret was giving him up.

The song was ending, the kids were singing, " 'Happiness is . . . coming home again.' "

Dayne felt his eyes grow wet and he cursed himself. He'd cried more today than in all his life combined. The scene onstage ended and after a few more minutes the play came to a close. At that point the entire cast filled the stage, took a bow, and began shouting, "Katy . . . Katy . . . Katy . . ."

The houselights came on and Dayne kept his face hidden by the bill of his cap. The kids onstage were relentless, grinning and waving and shouting at this Katy person, whoever that was.

After a few minutes, a young woman sprinted down the side aisle and up the stairs onto the stage. The kids in costume circled her, jumping up and down and calling her name. Finally, when they settled back to their places, she motioned for them to quiet down, and they did.

When she faced the audience, Dayne felt his breath catch in his throat. She was gorgeous. Fresh-faced with layered blonde hair and blue eyes that shone even from where he was sitting.

"Hi, everyone." She waved and shaded her eyes, trying to see the audience past the bright lights. "I'm Katy Hart, director of Christian Kids Theater. Let's hear it for the kids who made our first show such a success!"

The crowd clapped wildly, bigger than Dayne had heard crowds clap at the Academy Awards. They rose to their feet and clapped some more until Katy motioned for them to sit down.

Dayne couldn't take his eyes off her. She was maybe twenty-six, twenty-seven, with the sort of beauty Hollywood had forgotten about. If she wore makeup, it wasn't much. She had on jeans, a silky pale blue blouse, and a black fitted blazer. But nothing about her shape or her looks compared with the glow on her face.

Katy Hart loved what she was doing. That much was obvious.

She was about kids and acting and making magic happen on the stage. No multimega contracts, no autograph seekers, no fame or fortune. Community theater . . . teaching kids about acting, and that was enough.

It hit him then, exactly what he was looking at.

If he'd been raised in the Baxter family, he might've been working right alongside her. Maybe they would be friends or lovers. Maybe she would've become his wife. His heart felt strange, as vast and empty as the Grand Canyon. Yes, perhaps this would've been his life, the one he would've lived if Elizabeth's parents hadn't sent her away when she came home pregnant.

He'd been robbed of a normal lifestyle, a loving family, a brother and four sisters, and now this. The chance at a normal life with a beautiful girl who would never see her name in lights, a life that certainly would've filled the emptiness inside him.

As he slipped out of the theater, as he made his way back to the rented SUV and headed for the freeway, he remembered something Elizabeth had said: *"Find your faith, Dayne . . . find your faith."*

He tightened his grip on the steering wheel. Why bother? God—if there was a God—had left him out of the life he would've loved. He'd been given a window to all he might've had, but no door to get to it. And God had allowed it to happen.

Elizabeth was wrong. He didn't need faith; he needed a family.

And one day—even if it took a decade to figure it out—he would find them again and tell them who he was. One day when he was washed up in the business, when the paparazzi no longer cared about who he was or what business he might have in Bloomington, Indiana.

Until then, he would work and carry on the best he knew how. Carried by the memories of his family as they walked toward him in the hospital parking lot; his birth mother holding him in her arms, telling him she had never stopped thinking about him, never stopped loving him.

And the memory of a small-town girl named Katy Hart, who represented everything he had missed out on along the way.

Katy saw him from the stage, saw him sitting in the back row watching the last part of the show. This was closing night of their first play, and the guests in attendance were family members and friends of the theater troupe.

Strangers stood out, especially strangers who showed up near the end of the play and left after ten minutes.

The strike party was about to begin. Katy had a dozen kids tugging on her, asking her questions about the awards and the strikes—silly spoofs on the play that the kids wanted to perform. Tim, the teenager who had played Charlie Brown, brought his guitar for the event. He was going to lead them in a few worship songs before they got started with the silliness of the evening.

But Katy couldn't get the stranger from the back row out of her head.

She'd seen him somewhere before, but where? Was he an uncle, maybe? Someone affiliated with the Arts Center or the university? She was about to forget the whole thing, when Rhonda— the dance instructor—came running up.

"Can you believe it? Did you see him?"

Katy searched her friend's face. "Who?"

"Dayne Matthews!" Rhonda took hold of her shoulders. "He was here; I promise!" She pointed to the back row. "He sat right there for ten minutes and watched the end of the play."

Dayne Matthews? The famous actor? The Hollywood playboy who had dated almost every one of his leading ladies? No wonder he looked familiar. But the guy couldn't have been Dayne Matthews. "It wasn't him." She turned and headed back to the stage.

Rhonda stayed close by her side. "It was. Bethany followed him out when he left. She called his name and he turned around." Rhonda did a few jumps and a bell kick. "Dayne Matthews came and saw our play! Who'd have thought?"

Katy was needed onstage. She held up her hand, stopping further conversation about famous actors coming into the Bloomington community theater building. Tim was already onstage with his guitar, warmed up and ready to sing.

The group of parents and kids involved in CKT was amazing. Dozens of families who had come together to help get the theater troupe off the ground, and who were thrilled that their children had a chance to explore the arts in a Christian environment. Katy had never felt more full in all her life.

People took their seats, and a silence fell over them. Tim—a talented fifteen-year-old with a gift for leadership and a heart for God—led them in prayer. "Lord, thank you for letting us finish our first show. Thank you for Katy and for a Christian theater group in Bloomington. . . ." He kept on, praying about the performance and asking that it might have been a light to the community.

But as he prayed, Katy began her own private conversation with God. *Lord . . . Dayne Matthews? Here in Bloomington? If it was him, God, then maybe you brought him by for a reason. Let him find that reason, God. And bring him back if you can use our group to touch him.*

A gentle breeze stirred in her soul.

Daughter, you will see him again. I know the plans I have for him and your place in those plans.

The response rippled through her, making her tremble inside. Once in a while when she prayed, she could feel God answer, practically hear his voice. But this time the answer was more specific, as if maybe God really had a plan to bring Dayne Matthews back to their theater.

The idea was crazy, but the things of God often were.

She let the thought pass and tuned back in to Tim's prayer.

"And so, God, bless Katy and CKT and everything about our group. And most of all make your purpose known to all of us involved. Especially Katy. In Jesus' name, amen."

℣

John had taken the call while they were all still at the Baxter house. Elizabeth wasn't feeling well; her vitals weren't as strong as they'd been earlier. He told the kids, and the group gave hurried instructions to the babysitters and left.

Now they were back at the hospital, and Elizabeth was barely conscious.

Dr. Steinman met them in the hallway and pulled John aside. "It could be anytime, John." He shook his head. "She was doing well an hour ago, when Luke was in with her, but she's taken a turn for the worse."

"Luke?" John glanced at his kids and their spouses, standing a ways from him. "Luke was with us for the past two hours."

Dr. Steinman made a face. "That's strange. The nurse said Luke was sitting by her side for the past hour." He lifted one shoulder. "Anyway, the point is she's getting worse." He hesitated. "I don't think she'll make it through the night."

The truth suffocated John like a plastic bag. He had so much left to tell her, so much more to talk about. Everything about the moment felt stilted and robotic, as if his body knew how to go through the motions, even if his heart didn't.

He pulled his kids together—all five of them and their spouses—and one at a time he met their eyes. "Your mother is leaving us." Tears came, but his voice stayed steady, on some type of autopilot John hadn't known he possessed.

"You mean now?" The question came from Luke, and even before John could answer, his son was taking steps toward Elizabeth's room.

"Yes." John held out his arms, and all of them formed a group hug. "Dr. Steinman says it could be tonight."

It was time for good-byes, and John organized it as best he could. "I'll sit on the far side of her bed, and each of you take a turn visiting with her. One couple at a time, okay?"

There were tears and quiet nods of approval. The kids clung

to their spouses as John entered the room first. Elizabeth's mouth was open. Her chest rose several inches with each inhalation, proof that her lungs were filling up, that death was at hand.

"Elizabeth." He took her fingers in his and searched her face. "We're here, honey."

She opened her eyes, and after a few seconds recognition filled her face. "John . . . you came."

"The kids want to talk to you, okay?"

He released her hand, circled around the bed, and took hold of her other arm. Brooke and Peter were the first in. Peter said hello and then stood back while Brooke took her place near Elizabeth.

"Mom . . . I love you."

"Brooke." Elizabeth's face was pale, but she had her wits about her. Her words came slowly, with much effort. "Don't be sad. We'll all be together again. The greatest reunion of all, okay?"

"I'm going to miss you so much. Hayley's going to miss you; you always take such good care of her."

"I'll never stop praying for her." A smile tugged at Elizabeth's eyes. "I have a feeling . . . she's going to be okay."

Brooke nodded, too choked up to speak.

"You're a wonderful mother, Brooke. I know . . . I know you doubted that after Hayley's accident. But don't." She coughed, but the effort was so weak it barely made a sound.

"Mom . . ." Brooke hugged her, placed her cheek against Elizabeth's.

John wiped at his eyes and memorized the scene.

"I love you, Brooke." Elizabeth's words were muffled because of their embrace.

"You'll never know how much you taught me."

Brooke said good-bye, stood, and touched Elizabeth's cheek once more. Then she turned and fell against Peter. He led her from the room, and after a few seconds, Erin and Sam entered the room.

The scene repeated itself over and over again. Ashley and Landon were last. Landon took hold of Elizabeth's hand. "You're a special woman; the things you've brought this family will live on long after you're gone."

Elizabeth gave him a weak smile. "Thank you, Landon. I'm so glad you didn't give up on Ashley. She needed you. She always will."

"I know." Landon's eyes were watery. He stepped back and Ashley took his place.

"Mom . . . how are you feeling?"

"I'm fine." She gave a slow shake of her head. "No pain. Just in here." Her fingers rested above her heart. "I don't want to leave you."

"I . . ." Ashley dabbed at her eyes. "I don't want to say good-bye, Mom. I don't know how."

"You don't have to, honey." She took Ashley's hand and brought it to her lips. "We'll be together again; this is just a so long."

"But it's too long." Ashley hung her head before looking at Elizabeth again. "I was your black sheep." She sniffed and struggled for the words. "But you never gave up on me."

"That's what real love is about, Ash." Elizabeth looked past her to Landon. "But you already know that now."

"Yes. I'm beginning to understand."

"Ashley . . ."

"Yes?" Her tears splashed on Elizabeth's hospital gown.

"Don't let Cole forget me, okay?"

"No one will ever forget you, Mom. You and Dad were the reason everything turned out okay."

"And God most of all."

"And God." Ashley smiled through her tears. "Of course, God."

"You know what I want to do when I get to heaven?"

John felt a wave of sobs building inside him, but he kept strong, letting Ashley have her moment.

"What's that?" Ashley lowered herself closer.

"I want to start planning the next reunion. The one that will last forever and ever."

"Oh, Mom." Ashley hugged her. When she pulled back, the sorrow in her eyes wasn't as heartbreaking as before. As if maybe Elizabeth's words had eased some of the pain. "I can tell you one thing; we'll all be there."

🌿

Finally, he was alone with her.

The kids had all had their turns, and Ashley informed him of their plans. They were going back home to be with the children, and he was to call them if anything changed.

He took the better chair, the one closer to her bed. Every breath was a struggle, and the rattle was worse than before. Dr. Steinman was right; she didn't have long before she left them.

"Elizabeth . . ."

"Mmmm." She opened her eyes, and despite her condition, a knowing look shone through. "I'm not doing too well, am I?"

John smiled. He wanted to be strong, wanted to enjoy this last time with her. The grieving could come later. "You're doing fine."

She swallowed, and the effort made her wince. "I have . . . to tell you something, John."

"Okay." He cradled her arm against his chest, wishing he could cuddle up next to her but knowing she was too weak for that.

Her eyes opened wider than before. "I met him; I met our firstborn." She searched his eyes. She looked more lucid than she had all afternoon. "His name is Dayne."

John felt his stomach drop. What had the doctor said? Something about his son being here, sitting by Elizabeth's side for the past hour? It was impossible, wasn't it? Wherever their oldest son was, he never could've found them now, on Elizabeth's dying day. "Honey, what are you saying?"

"He came here, John." She sank back into the pillow and closed her eyes for a moment. When she opened them, she looked confused again. "Unless it was a dream."

A dream. That had to be it. John felt himself relax. "Tell me about it."

"He was handsome, a lot like Luke. He said he was an actor, John. And that his parents were dead and he has no brothers or sisters." Her words were slurring and she struggled to keep her eyes open. "It didn't feel like a dream until the end. I thought he said he'd come back tomorrow."

An understanding passed over John. It wasn't a dream; it was the pain medications. Hallucinations were common for people dying of cancer, especially at the end. The combination of the body shutting down and the medications made people hear and see things that defied explanation.

That was obviously what had happened to Elizabeth. An actor named Dayne? She must've been thinking about Dayne Matthews, the man Luke had met at his office. Somehow bits and pieces of the past few weeks had come together to give her the impression she'd met him and that he was her son.

She was definitely hallucinating.

"I'm glad you met him, honey. That's what you prayed about." He decided to go along with her, so that these last few moments they had together wouldn't upset her. "Thanks for telling me."

Her eyes opened big again. "Do you think I'm crazy, John?"

"Not at all." He thought of the doctor's words again. That someone had been in with her for the past hour. Probably someone from church, maybe even Pastor Mark. "I'm sure he came by, and I'm glad. Maybe I'll meet him when he comes back."

"Yes." A wonderful peace came over her expression. "That would be nice."

"You're tired, aren't you?"

"Very tired."

John's mind raced. He still had so much to tell her. Ten years' worth of things at least. "You know what I wish?"

"What?" She looked at him, and despite the sickness and the medication and the exhaustion she was feeling, it was the same look she'd given him at the University of Michigan mixer, the same look she'd given him a thousand times since. A look of love that would stay with him even after she was gone.

"I wish—" he brought her hand to his lips and kissed it—"I wish I could go with you."

She shook her head, her eyes never leaving his. "The kids need you, John. Besides . . ." A choking sound came from her, and she waited until she'd caught her breath. "God wants me to go ahead and help get things ready."

"For what, sweet Elizabeth?"

"For what?" Her smile was timeless, one he would keep with him always. "For the greatest reunion ever."

"I love you." He'd told her that every day, several times a day, since the August morning when they married. But here, in her last moments, he couldn't say it enough.

"I'll never really leave you, John." Each word was an effort. "You know that, right?"

"I know." He held her hand to his heart again. "You'll be right here, woven into the center of all I am."

"That's not all." Her eyes shone. "I'll be in Cole's grin and Jessie's silly dance steps and Tommy's bright blue eyes. You'll see me in Erin's mothering and Ashley's artwork and Luke's determination to do right." She exhaled and the rattle echoed through the room. "You'll feel me when you hold Maddie's hand and when any of them gives you a hug." She paused, gathering her strength. "If you listen, you'll hear me in Kari's laughter and Hayley's gentle cooing and Brooke's moments alone at the piano. I'll be there, John. I'll always be there."

She fell quiet then, and though he told her he loved her every minute or so, after a while she stopped responding. For hours he watched her, watched every painful rise and fall of her chest, listened to her lungs shutting down, her life draining away.

Sometime around midnight, she drew her last breath, and John tightened his grip on her hand. But he couldn't hold her, couldn't keep her from going, from leaving this world and taking the sweet and wonderful trip into the next.

Relief filled his heart, flooded him with a feeling that was indescribable. She wasn't in pain anymore, wasn't sickly or wasting away or dying. She was with Jesus, because that was his promise. That those who love him will never taste death. John had expected to feel cut in half. Since she completed him, he had known that her loss would leave him feeling broken, as if he'd never be whole again.

Instead, he felt his heart swell with a fullness it had never known before, because Elizabeth was right. Her body was gone, but she would never leave him. She would live on in the memories he would cherish, in the years and decades his family still had left together.

She would be around them always, and at the same time she'd be working on the special plans she'd talked about earlier tonight. The greatest reunion of all, one that would see Hayley running the streets of heaven, and no more tears for anyone. One where all of them were together, healthy and happy, and praising the God who had given them eternity.

Forever and ever and ever.

CHAPTER THIRTY-TWO

THE SERVICE WAS OVER.

John had gotten through it on strength that wasn't his own. Each
of the kids had been there, of course, bidding their mother good-
bye, remembering her for the strong, graceful, loving woman she'd
always been. According to her wishes, they had sung her favorite
hymn: "Great is thy faithfulness, O God my Father, there is no
shadow of turning with thee."

And there wasn't. God had been faithful to the end; John had
no doubts, no questions. Pastor Mark had said some profound
things at the service, bits of truth that would stay with John
forever.

"Human suffering is too big to get our arms around." His face
had been earnest. "Don't try to figure out what God's teaching
you by this, don't try to understand it, and don't try to understand
God. If he could fit into your idea of him, he'd be too small for
any of us."

John had sat mesmerized as the message continued.

"All I want you to do today is run to Jesus. Being God, he
alone fully understands both God and suffering. And right now

all he wants to do is let you cry." Pastor Mark's eyes shone. It was hard to imagine that ten days earlier he had married Ashley and Landon. "We never own the people in our lives. We love them, yes, but they are on loan from God. We have them for a moment and then they're gone. Go ahead and grieve, because you'll miss Elizabeth. We all will. But while you're grieving, don't get mad at God for the minutes you'll miss with Elizabeth. Thank him for the minutes you had."

That last part was the best of all.

Every time John was tempted to wonder why God would take her now, he would remind himself of those words and be thankful. Because the minutes he had with Elizabeth were the most wonderful of all.

They were back at the house now, gathered in the family room. The grandchildren were playing upstairs with a babysitter, and only Hayley was down with the adults. It was the moment John had been waiting for, the moment he'd told the kids about.

"Your mother has written you a letter, one that each of you will get a copy of." He stood near the fireplace and looked around the room. The eyes of his children were somber, tearstained. But they were not without hope. "I'm going to read it to you now, because that's what your mother wanted me to do."

In his hand he held a manila envelope, the one Elizabeth had told him about. Three smaller envelopes were inside, just as she'd said. One had his name on it, one was labeled "For the kids," and one read "Firstborn."

John took out the one for the kids and opened it.

"What about the other letters, the ones still in the envelope?" Ashley cocked her head, staring at the package in his hands.

"Uh . . ." John felt the blood leave his face. He hadn't counted on his kids noticing the other letters. "Those are for me."

He'd already read his letter three times; it was beautiful of course, more of what she'd told him her last night in the hospital. As for the other one, the one marked "Firstborn," he'd thought about throwing it away. But he couldn't. It was important to Elizabeth, and what if one day—by some miracle—their son found them?

The letter would belong to him, in that case.

John made a mental note to keep the manila envelope well hidden. Maybe in the box of things Elizabeth had kept on the top shelf in their closet. If any of them ever found the envelope, he wouldn't have any idea how to explain it.

John looked at the letter in his hand and started reading: " 'Dear children, if you're hearing this, then I'm already gone, already off in heaven. This has probably been a hard day for you, but please . . . for a minute, try not to be sad. I want you to know some things that are on my heart, things I don't ever want you to forget.' "

John paused. His throat was thick, but he felt a strength inside him, a sense that somehow Elizabeth was cheering him on from heaven, urging him to continue. " 'You are all so different, but now—as I near the end of my days—God has shown me a theme to our years together. That theme is redemption.' "

Looking around the room, John saw Brooke and Kari close their eyes. Erin and Luke and Ashley stared off into the distance, intent on listening. John resumed reading. " 'Time and again this theme has come up in our lives. Brooke and Peter, what happened with Hayley was devastating. The strain nearly tore you apart, but here you are. Together, stronger than ever before.' "

Peter reached for Hayley's hand and brought it to his lips. He took hold of Brooke's knee with the other and gave her a sad smile.

" 'Kari, your life hasn't been without sorrow. Tim's unfaithfulness, his murder, all of it might've had a tragic ending, but God brought hope to every part. Tim died knowing his Savior; and God led you to Ryan, a man who will care for you and cherish you all the days of his life.' "

John saw Ryan put his arm around Kari and hold her close.

" 'Ashley, you thought you were the black sheep but, honey, you never were. You had lessons to learn, and God used all sorts of people to teach you. Irvel and Cole and especially Landon. You are a living illustration of God's mercy and forgiveness, of the truth that he has a plan for each of his children.' "

Ashley let her head fall on Landon's shoulder. John saw her shoulders shaking just a bit, but she kept her tears quiet, to herself.

" 'Erin, you couldn't have a family, couldn't bear children and you wondered if God had forgotten you. Then you show up for our reunion with four beautiful little girls. Can you ever doubt God again, sweet daughter? You were made to be a mother, and a mother you will be. No matter how dark the night, morning always comes, Erin. That's the message in Lamentations, chapter 3. The basis for my favorite hymn. The dark valleys are not where life ends. Not for you and your desire to have a family, and not for me.' "

Erin looked at the ceiling. Her eyes were damp, but a soft smile tugged at the corners of her lips. John saw her whisper the words, "Thank you, God."

John stared at the letter and found his place. " 'Luke, I watch you, and it's like seeing the Scriptures come to life. Your faith wasn't real for so many years. Yes, you talked about believing, but until you were tested, until you realized that suffering is part of a fallen world, you couldn't take Christ as your own. But here you are, and all of us see what God's doing in your life, what he's already done. I said it to you once before, and one far-off day I'll say it to you again: Welcome home, Son. Welcome home.' "

Luke tightened his hold on Reagan's hand. He clenched his jaw, trying to stay strong, but finally he hung his head. Two teardrops fell onto his dress pants, and with his free hand he covered his eyes.

John's voice was still strong, but his eyes were blurred. He blinked and looked around the room. Elizabeth was right. He could see her in them, feel her in them. In the way they talked and hugged and laughed and loved. She was still with them, the way she always would be with them.

His eyes focused on the last paragraphs, and he finished the letter. " 'So you see, the theme is very clear. In life we have choices, choices all of us must make. I'm hardly perfect; your father and I know what it is to go against God's plan for our lives. Everyone breathing knows that awful feeling. In life there will be consequences for our bad choices, and there will always be suffering. Some of it, like my cancer or Hayley's accident, we'll never understand.

" 'But this is the part I want you to keep, the part you've illus-trated with the stories of your lives. With Christ there will also be hope and forgiveness and faith and love.

" 'And most of all, because of what he did on the cross, there will always be his amazing, unlimited, perfect redemption. Remember that, okay? I love you more than you know. And when you come home, I'll be here waiting for you. Then we'll have the greatest reunion of all.' "

MORE ABOUT THE BAXTER FAMILY!

Please turn this page for a bonus excerpt from

F A M E

the first book in the

FIRSTBORN SERIES

by Karen Kingsbury

CHAPTER ONE

THE PART SHOULD'VE been easy to cast.

Dream On, the romantic comedy that would star Dayne Matthews, called for a small-town girl, an upbeat, outgoing type, with dreams of the big city and a genuine innocence that overshadowed everything about her.

Dayne had spent the morning watching half a dozen top Hollywood actresses file through the room for an interview and a quick read, and so far none of them fit the bill. They were talented actresses, friendly, beautiful. Two he'd starred with in other films, two he'd dated, and two he'd hung out with at some party or another.

He'd shared the night with three of the six.

They were girls whose faces decked the covers of every gossip rag in town, and in theory, any one of them could play the part of a small-town girl. How hard could it be? The actresses Dayne had seen today could be upbeat and outgoing, and they could certainly pull off the role of a dreamer.

But something was missing, and by three that afternoon Dayne knew what it was.

The innocence.

Dayne leaned back in his chair and crossed his arms as the last of the six read through her lines. A person couldn't fake innocence—not even with an Academy Award performance. Innocence was something that grew in the heart and shone through the eyes. And it was the innocence that was lacking with each of them.

Mitch Henry, casting director, was pacing near the back of the room. He finished with the final actress and bid her good-bye.

On her way out she looked at Dayne and gave him a teasing smile. "See ya." She was one of the ones he'd dated. Actually, he'd lived with her off and on for a month or so. Long enough that their pictures made the tabs a couple of times. Her eyes locked onto his. "Call me."

"Yeah." Dayne pretended to tip an invisible hat, but his grin faded before she left the room. He turned to Mitch. "Who's next?"

"Who's next?" Deep lines appeared between Mitch's eyes, his tone frustrated. "Do you know how hard it was to get six A-list actresses in here on the same day? The part doesn't even require the kind of talent we had in here, Dayne. Any one of them would knock it out of the park."

"They're good. They're all good." Dayne uncrossed his arms and tapped his fingers on the table. "But something's missing." He paused. "I'm not seeing innocent, Henry. Sophisticated, flirty, take me to bed, yes. But not innocent."

"Fine." Mitch tossed his clipboard on the table and yelled at a passing intern to shut the door. On the table were the files belonging to the six actresses, and when the door was shut, Mitch took a few steps closer. "We're on a schedule here, Matthews." He gripped the edge of the table and leaned in. "Hollywood isn't exactly a stable of innocence."

"Okay." Dayne pushed his chair back, stood, and walked to the window, his back to Mitch. He stared out through the hazy blue, and a face came to mind. A face he hadn't forgotten in nearly a year. He held the image, mesmerized by it, and an idea started to form. It was possible, wasn't it? She worked in theater. She must've dreamed of the silver screen somewhere along the way, right?

Dayne felt Mitch's eyes on him, and he turned around. "I have an idea."

"An idea?" Mitch scratched the back of his head and strode to the door and back. "We don't need an idea; we need an actress. Filming starts in four months. This film is too big to wait until the last minute."

"I know." The idea was taking root. It was definitely possible. What girl wouldn't want a chance like this? Dayne sucked in a slow breath. He couldn't get ahead of himself. "Listen, Mitch, give me a week. I have someone in mind, but she's out of state." He leaned against the windowsill. "I think I can have her here in a week, by next Monday."

Mitch folded his arms, his expression hard. "Some girl you met at a club, Matthews? Someone you made drunken promises to? Is that what you want me to wait for?"

"No." Dayne held up his hand. "She's the real deal. Give me a chance."

A moment passed when Dayne wasn't sure which way the casting director was leaning. Then Mitch swept up the six files and the clipboard and shot him a look. "One week." He was halfway out the door when he turned once more and met Dayne's eyes. "She better be good."

Dayne waited until he was alone to look out the window again. What had he just done? Buying a week meant putting the other talent on hold. It meant playing with a budget of tens of millions of dollars so he could find a girl he'd seen just once and ask her to read for a starring role opposite him in a major motion picture.

All when she might not have the interest or ability to act at all.

The idea was crazy, except for one thing. In the past year the only time he'd seen genuine innocence was when he'd watched this same girl light up the stage at a small theater in Bloomington, Indiana, directing the chaos of a couple dozen kids in costumes at the close of what was apparently the theater troupe's first show.

He remembered most of what he'd seen that day, but still the details were sketchy. The location of the theater was easy, something he could definitely find again. But he had almost no information on the girl except her name.

Dayne gripped the windowsill and leaned his forehead against the cool glass. He could fly out and try to find her, but that would bring the paparazzi out of the woodwork for sure, make them crazy with questions about why Dayne Matthews was in Bloomington, Indiana.

Again.

A WORD FROM KAREN KINGSBURY

 AND SO WE HAVE COME to the end of the Redemption series.

Sort of. I'll explain more about that later. First let's go back; let's revisit the journey of not only *Reunion,* but the entire Redemption series.

In writing *Reunion,* I felt again and again the faithfulness of God, working in me, going before me, speaking to me in the plot and story line. But it wasn't just his faithfulness in writing *Reunion,* but his faithfulness in seeing the entire Redemption series come to an end.

Everything the Baxter kids had to work through over the past several years had seen a transformation because of God's redemption. Not without consequences or sorrow, but always with his love and grace and hope.

I have to tell you, I hated outlining *Reunion,* because I couldn't imagine saying good-bye to the Baxter family. After writing five books with these characters, they felt more than real to me. I'd find myself talking about our weekly church service and referring to the pastor as Pastor Mark.

I also struggled with letting Elizabeth die, but God reminded me of something in the midst of writing *Reunion.* It isn't the number of our days that counts, but the life in our number.

Many of you know personally the pain of suffering. Whether you've lost a job or a friendship, or worse, a spouse or a child. Maybe someone you love has walked out of your life the way Tim walked out on Kari in *Redemption.*

Your situation might be overcoming a shameful past, the way it was for Ashley in *Remember.* Or maybe you've walked away from your faith and just need to understand again that God's still waiting for you, the way Luke had to understand that in *Return.* Perhaps you've been caught up in a tragedy, the way Brooke was

in *Rejoice*. If so, then the lessons there are yours also. That joy
always comes in the morning, that only by keeping your attitude
of worship and praise will you ever survive a tragedy.

Or maybe you're in the season of losing a parent, the way the
Baxters were throughout *Reunion*. The sad experience of watching a parent die, or getting the call that a parent has passed
suddenly, is one that most of us will experience. That's why I
included it here.

It is my prayer that in reading Elizabeth's story, you might find
strength for your own. That you would understand that God's
will is always best—even when it doesn't line up with your own.
And that yes, trouble will come into our lives, but still, God
wins. In the end, he always wins. I'm so grateful for that.

People write to me every day telling me that I've captured
their story in the lines of one of my novels. I don't think that's
a coincidence. God has given me stories like the ones in the
Redemption series so that each of you will know you're not
alone. Whatever you're going through, other people around you
have gone through the same thing.

Sure, we can fight God. We can get angry at him for our suf-
ferings or our circumstances or even our consequences. But in
the end, we must be like the disciples of Christ, who once wit-
nessed dozens and dozens of people walking away during one
of our Lord's priceless messages. Jesus waited until only the disciples were left. Then he turned to them and said, "What? Aren't
you going too?" They answered the same thing you and I must
answer, regardless of our situation: "Where would we go? To
whom would we turn?"

Another theme I hope you've picked up on in the Redemption series is that God has great plans for your life. He loves you
because you belong to him, because he made you. And as such,
he knows the plans he has for you. Jeremiah 29:11 tells us that,
and it's a truth you can stand on forever.

Things aren't moving as quickly as you'd like? Ryan knew that
feeling in *Redemption*. Confused about the place God has you in?

Landon understood that while he was digging through the rubble of the collapsed World Trade Center. Certain that morning will never come again? Peter knew that sort of darkness after Hayley's accident. Figuring God has forgotten about you? Check in with Reagan and the way she felt raising an infant by herself, a thousand miles from the man she loved. The verdict's in, the diagnosis is made, the casket's closed? John knows how it feels to think all of life is behind him.

But the truth is that for each of these—and for each of you—God still has a plan. A good plan, to give you a hope and a future.

From the beginning, when Gary Smalley asked me to consider writing a series of books that might illustrate his teachings about relationships, my hope and prayer have been not only that you would be entertained. Certainly I want you to feel that the Redemption series is good, clean, moral fiction. But my prayer is that these books have been so very much more.

I love hearing from you, so many thousands of you, who have written to tell me that the books in this series have changed your lives. Marriages have been restored, relationships have been healed, love has been brought back to life. And many times you have told me that the Redemption series introduced you to God, or better still, brought you back to him.

Because of your letters, I know God has abundantly blessed my prayers about these books. The end result of the Redemption series is so much greater than I ever could've dreamed way back when Gary and I had our first meeting.

On that note, yes, I've agreed to write more books for Tyndale, books that will branch off the one you're holding in your hand. Five of the books will be part of the Firstborn series, and four will make up the Sunrise series. All of them will be set in Bloomington, Indiana.

The Firstborn series will involve Dayne Matthews and his search for meaning in his life, and Katy Hart and her role as director of the Bloomington Christian Kids Theater. New families and situations will be introduced, but Dayne's search—and other issues facing single people—will stand at the center.

The Sunrise series will involve the Flanigan family, Ryan Taylor's assistant coach, his wife, and children. This series is very close to my heart because in many ways it mirrors the lessons about love and life I've learned in these first fifteen years of being a wife and mother.

Like my own family, the Flanigans have six children, three who are adopted from Haiti. Two of the kids will be involved in the Christian Kids Theater, and Katy Hart, the director, will live in a garage apartment at the Flanigan house. So there will be a tie from the Sunrise series to the Firstborn series. The other four kids will be athletes. Dad is a coach, Mom is a writer, and people of all ages tend to wind up on their doorstep looking for hope and a new life in Christ.

Expect me to deal with situations involving a host of family issues including learning disabilities, teenage eating disorders, children who are picked on by their peers, teens at the beginning of dating and driving, teens who enlist to fight for our country, and the effect these types of issues have on a couple in love with God and with each other.

This is the life I live—and though there will be dramatic plot changes in the Flanigans' lives compared with my own—it is still my thrill and honor to use my family as a platform to bring you those four books in the Sunrise series.

The Firstborn series will be first, though. *Fame, Forgiven, Found, Family,* and *Forever* will be the titles in that series. Then I will bring you the Sunrise series—*Sunrise, Summer, Someday,* and *Sunset.*

Please pray for me as God brings the story lines into finer detail, as he makes clear to me the types of situations I should address in each of these eight books. I am truly thrilled and honored by this opportunity. I pray you will find these books as life-changing as my Redemption series.

As always, I would love to hear from you. Those of you who

have book clubs, please know that if you choose to read one of my books and would like me to "drop in" at your get-together, e-mail me at **Karen@KarenKingsbury.com**. I will try my best to arrange a phone conversation with your group at a meeting time that works for all of us (on speakerphone, of course). Or I will e-mail you a response that can be read aloud to your group.

This is one more way that I can stay in touch with you, the reader, the one I have prayed for as often as I have put my fingers to the keyboard.

By the way, my Web site has become something of a ministry. Please visit the Guest Book, the Reader Forum, the Prayer Ministry, or the Dear Karen section so you can share thoughts, make friends, get connected with a prayer partner, and find other people like yourself who are being touched by what God is doing in their lives.

Contact me at **www.KarenKingsbury.com**, or write to me at my above e-mail address.

Blessings in his light and love,

Karen Kingsbury

A WORD FROM GARY SMALLEY

HOLDING A REUNION is something most families do from time to time. But have you ever considered why it's important to get together, to gather in one place for a set-apart time? The reason is honor.

We show that we value our relationships when we make them a priority. That is what honor is all about—making the people we love a priority in our lives. The message Pastor Mark gave the Baxter family at the end of *Reunion* is one that stands for all of us. We don't own the people in our lives; rather we borrow them. They are gifts from God that we have for just a moment.

Since they are gifts, it is even more important that we realize how much our special people need to be honored. Yes, reunions can be chaotic. They can be costly, crazy, and sometimes corny—depending on who's telling the jokes. But the fact is, when people you love grow up and move away, getting together for a reunion is crucial. The following is a brief list of the benefits that can come when you go to the trouble of honoring those you love with a family reunion.

THREE BENEFITS OF HOLDING A FAMILY REUNION

1. Renewed Closeness

   One way to honor someone you love is by listening to them. When that person lives far away, phone calls and letters—even instant messages—are rarely enough to maintain a strong bond. It is honoring to a family member to make the time for a family reunion, because then whole days can be spent sharing the experiences that have happened since the last time you were together.

2. Revitalized Memories

Since most reunions involve hours of talking, not only are experiences shared, but memories are brought up. People at reunions tend to take the past, dust it off, and hold it up for everyone to laugh and cry and marvel at all over again. In doing so, this keeps the sense of family alive and well, not only for your generation but for the one to come. It is honoring to everyone in the family to make your memories and your heritage something worth investing in.

3. Rekindled Love

There's nothing like taking someone in your arms and holding them to let them know they are loved. The best part of a family reunion is the time spent simply being close to the people you care about. Holding hands with your son or daughter, bouncing a grandbaby on your knee, getting reacquainted with an aunt or uncle. All of it shows that you have made family a priority. This is honoring to everyone involved.

Reunion shows the importance of taking time for each other. This, of course, is just one aspect of keeping strong relationships in your family. The other Redemption series books illustrate many others.

If you or someone you love needs counseling or other resources to improve a key relationship, contact us at:

Smalley Relationship Center
1482 Lakeshore Drive
Branson, MO 65616

Phone: 800-84TODAY (848-6329)
Fax: (417) 336-3515
E-mail: family@smalleyonline.com
Web site: www.smalleyonline.com

DISCUSSION QUESTIONS

Use these questions for individual reflection or for discussion with a book club or other small group. They will help you not only understand some of the issues in *Reunion* but also integrate some of the book's messages into your own relationships.

Note: Those of you who have book clubs, please know that if you choose to read one of my books and would like me to "drop in" at your get-together, e-mail me at Karen@KarenKingsbury.com. I will try my best to arrange a phone conversation with your group at a meeting time that works for all of us (on speakerphone, of course). Or I will e-mail a response that can be read aloud to your group.

1. How did you feel when you realized Elizabeth Baxter's cancer had come back? Explain.

2. Describe a time when you received bad news. How did you handle that news?

3. Describe how Elizabeth and John handled the news of her cancer. How did that response change as her disease progressed?

4. What emotional process did Erin and Sam go through as they yearned for a child, and then experienced a failed adoption?

5. Have you ever adopted or do you know someone who has? Why is it wonderful that certain women and girls put their babies up for adoption?

6. Describe the blessing of an adopted child. What are some of the issues that can make adoption both a source of joy and sorrow?

7. How did God lead Erin and Sam through the process of loss and unknown circumstances? What specifically did they do or decide to do that brought them peace and miraculous changes in their situation?

8. John Baxter has been strong through most of the Redemption series. Explain why he was afraid in *Reunion*.

9. Have you or has someone you know ever grown fearful after being strong, after having an unshakable faith? How did this person deal with the fear?

10. How did John Baxter deal with his fear? How did his emotions and attitude change as Elizabeth's disease progressed?

11. Elizabeth prayed for a miracle healing; instead God gave her a series of other miracles. Explain these.

12. Describe what you think a miracle is. Do miracles still happen today? Explain.

13. Tell about a miracle that happened in your life. Did you recognize it as a miracle at the time?

14. Ashley has loved Landon Blake for years, but things between them never seemed to work out until *Reunion*. Describe the highs and lows of their relationship.

15. Have you ever experienced a relationship or a situation where the process of growing closer and more serious took far longer than you expected? Tell about that time, and how God led you through it.

16. Dayne Matthews has everything the world tells us is important: good looks, fame, and fortune. Why wasn't Dayne happy?

17. Is there someone in your life who is feeling empty about life? Why do you think they feel this way? What can you do to help that person know God's truth better?

18. Have you or has someone you know lost a parent recently? Describe the feelings you or that person went through during the process and afterwards. What hope does God give us in this situation?

19. Describe a favorite moment from a family reunion. If you can't tell about one, maybe it's time to get out the calendar and plan one.

20. What are the greatest lessons you learned from *Reunion*? Explain what Elizabeth meant in her letter when she said that redemption was their family's theme.

Three great series
One amazing drama

From the start of the Redemption series, *New York Times* best-selling author Karen Kingsbury captured readers' hearts. The gripping Baxter Family Drama, which has sold nearly 4 million copies, begins with *Redemption*, continues through the Firstborn series, and reaches a dramatic conclusion in the Sunrise series. Pick up the next book today to discover why so many have fallen in love with the Baxters.

Available now in bookstores and online.

Other Life-Changing Fiction by

KAREN KINGSBURY

To see what readers are saying about Karen Kingsbury's fiction, go to www.KarenKingsbury.com and click the guest-book link.

REDEMPTION SERIES
Redemption
Remember
Return
Rejoice
Reunion

FIRSTBORN SERIES
Fame
Forgiven
Found
Family
Forever

SUNRISE SERIES
Sunrise
Summer
Someday
Sunset

RED GLOVE SERIES
Gideon's Gift
Maggie's Miracle
Sarah's Song
Hannah's Hope

SEPTEMBER 11 SERIES
One Tuesday Morning
Beyond Tuesday Morning
Every Now and Then

CP0038

FOREVER FAITHFUL SERIES
Waiting for Morning
A Moment of Weakness
Halfway to Forever

WOMEN OF FAITH FICTION SERIES
A Time to Dance
A Time to Embrace

LOST LOVE SERIES
Even Now
Ever After

CODY GUNNER SERIES
A Thousand Tomorrows
Just Beyond the Clouds

STAND-ALONE TITLES
Oceans Apart
Where Yesterday Lives
When Joy Came to Stay
On Every Side
Divine
Like Dandelion Dust
Between Sundays

CHILDREN'S TITLES
Let Me Hold You Longer
Let's Go on a Mommy Date
We Believe in Christmas

MIRACLE COLLECTIONS
A Treasury of Christmas Miracles
A Treasury of Miracles for Women
A Treasury of Miracles for Teens
A Treasury of Miracles for Friends
A Treasury of Adoption Miracles

GIFT BOOKS
Stay Close Little Girl
Be Safe Little Boy
Forever Young: Ten Gifts of Faith for the Graduate

www.KarenKingsbury.com

CP0038

LOOK FOR THESE ADDITIONAL RELATIONSHIP RESOURCES WHEREVER FINE BOOKS ARE SOLD:

THE DNA OF RELATIONSHIPS
by Dr. Gary Smalley

Have you ever felt as if you're repeating the same mistakes in your relationships? Dr. Gary Smalley tells you the whys and hows of relationships.

YOUR RELATIONSHIP WITH GOD
by Dr. Gary Smalley

In this book, Gary reveals how the stresses and busyness of life distracted him from his relationship with God. Through a series of difficult and life-threatening circumstances, God got Gary's attention, and now he enjoys a vital and refreshing relationship with God. In this book, Gary gives you six daily habits God taught him during these trials in order to stay grounded and rejuvenated.

HEALTHY WEIGHT LOSS
by Dr. Gary Smalley

Weight and relationships are intricately intertwined. How we eat affects our relationships, and how we relate to our loved ones affects how we eat. Often weight-loss diets ignore the key relational dynamic that helps keep people motivated to practice healthy eating habits. In this book, you'll learn how to lose weight in a holistic way.

MEN'S RELATIONAL TOOLBOX
by Dr. Gary Smalley, Dr. Greg Smalley, and Michael Smalley

Men understand the world in a unique way—and they approach relationships in a special way as well. This book is designed to help guys figure out the nuts and bolts of satisfying relationships—both at work and at home.

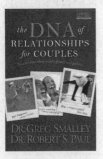

THE DNA OF RELATIONSHIPS FOR COUPLES
by Dr. Greg Smalley and Dr. Robert Paul

Through the stories of four fictionalized couples, Greg Smalley and Robert Paul help readers understand how to work at correcting dangerous relationship habits. The lives of the couples depicted in the book illustrate how to break the fear dance, create safety in a relationship, listen to each other's emotions, and much more. This book is a unique relationship book that uses stories to demonstrate what real relationship change looks like.

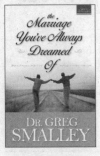

THE MARRIAGE YOU'VE ALWAYS DREAMED OF
by Dr. Greg Smalley

Discover what the marriage you've always dreamed of looks like. Find out how to transform marriage problems into opportunities to love each other—how to look for treasures in the trials. Discover how to experience God's best for your marriage.

DON'T DATE NAKED
by Michael and Amy Smalley

Straight talk to single guys and girls on what healthy relationships look like.

Oct. - 2011